Ryan's Journey
Book One: Boyhood

- JOHN BARNES -

An environmentally friendly book printed and bound in England by
www.printondemand-worldwide.com

Mixed Sources
Product group from well-managed
forests, and other controlled sources
FSC   www.fsc.org Cert no. TT-COC-002641
© 1996 Forest Stewardship Council

PEFC Certified
This product is
from sustainably
managed forests
and controlled
sources
PEFC   www.pefc.org
PEFC/16-33-418

This book is made entirely of chain-of-custody materials

http://www.fast-print.net/bookshop

RYAN'S JOURNEY: BOOK ONE: BOYHOOD
Copyright © John Barnes 2015

A catalogue record for this book is available from the British Library

ISBN 978-178456-257-1

First Published 2015 by
Fast-Print Publishing of Peterborough, England.

Acknowledgements.

There are many people to thank. First, a big thank you to the staff of the MA Creative Writing Course at Nottingham Trent University, notably principal David Belbin, tutors Georgina Lock and Graham Joyce. You guys gave me encouragement, teaching me that in addition to natural talent, writing is a craft that can be learned and improved upon. You helped me to avoid some of the more glaring errors writers make. As probably the oldest student ever to attend the Course, I now fully appreciate that that no-one is ever too old to learn new skills! (I particularly appreciated your encouragement, Helen.)

Thanks to all those who have helped with editing, proof reading especially Shelia Taylor, also David Rayment from the Erewash Writers' Group and for the friendship and encouragement of all fellow writers from that group.

Thanks to Jim and Kath Willis who gave me their time revealing useful and interesting information about the life the Catholic Church in England between the two world wars.

Bibliography

As well as information gleaned from the Web, two books helped me in research for the period: *That Neutral Island* by Clair Wills. First Published by Faber and Faber 2007: a history of Ireland during the Second World War. The events of Bloody Sunday, 1972: Lord Widgery's report published by The Stationery Office, 2001. Also. Scorer, Richard, *Betrayed* (Biteback Publishing, 2014) Grayson, Jane, *Goodbye Pink Room, Rose's story* (Lion Books, 2014)

And finally, thanks for the great fellowship and friendship of my fellow believers at my local Anglican churches of Breaston and Draycott, Derbyshire.

John S Barnes.

John S Barnes was born in Ipswich, Suffolk in 1930. Leaving school at seventeen, he was employed at the Borough Treasurers' Office. At eighteen he was conscripted into the Army, and billeted in Germany. After demobilisation he worked as a negotiator in an Estate Agents in Croydon, Surrey. He was called to the ministry of the Church of England, studied Theology at Queen's College, Birmingham, and was ordained priest in 1962, retiring in 1996. At the age of 78 he was accepted on the Master of Arts Creative Writing Course at Nottingham Trent University gaining a merit. The three books are the result of four years work. John is married to Enid, has three grown-up children, Claire, Robert and Ruth and lives in Breaston, Derbyshire.

Author's Note

With all of us childhood memories are never entirely forgotten I was nine years old when the Second World War broke out and though seventy five years ago memories of that time are vivid.

The three books, are entirely works of fiction and the work has taken me four years to complete. Each book is a separate story, complete from the other two. It is not a series. The central character, Ryan Brannigan is portrayed as a boy in Book One, a youth in Book Two and an adult in Book Three.

As a victim myself \I wanted to portray the confusion, shame and sense of worthlessness abuse brings.

Forgiveness is so prized by Nadina, but at times I wonder are there crimes so monstrous that they are impossible to forgive? Imaginatively, I identified with Ryan who goes alongside his vulnerable eleven year old friend, revealing first alarm, compassion, and the desire for revenge. I wanted to identify with the experience of all victims of abuse in their distress. So the work is dedicated to the countless Nadinas (and Nathans) who suffered in silence and never achieved justice they deserved.

John S Barnes. Winter 2015

e-mail: johnsbarnes10@btinternet.com
website: johnsbarnes-writer.co.uk

Chapter One

"You devil, you!"

From the depths of the armchair, Fergus stretched out his arm to the table. Enveloped in blue cigarette smoke, his fingers searched for their target. Finding it, his hand shaped slowly into a fist then banged down on the flat top of the wireless set.

"Jaysus! By all the saints – to hell with this damned thing!"

His fist struck a second blow, this time making not only the instrument jump but the littered kitchen table on which it stood, sending an assortment of items clattering to the floor.

"Devil!" The voice from the chair shouted again: poor reception was the cause. The wireless was a cheap purchase from the junk shop, the least presentable along the shabby row at the top of the road.

Gathering closer, the family strained to listen to the nervous, high-pitched tone of the speaker that faltered and threatened to fade away altogether. It was a momentous announcement. They had missed Sunday Mass to hear it. And like millions of others glued to their sets that Sunday morning, Fergus guessed what was coming. "Jaysus! Get the hell on with it, you stupid idiot."

Surprisingly perhaps, after the second strike with his big fist, the voice of Neville Chamberlain rallied, battling static interference to deliver his message to the citizens of the United Kingdom and the subject peoples of the Empire that he had failed in his mission. With a final clearing of the throat, the thin quavering voice ended with the doom laden words: "I have to tell you now, this nation is at war with Germany."

"Oh, what an utter fool! Sure, the idiot, the total idiot. Now he's put us all at risk." Fergus struggled out of his chair to his feet, wincing as he leaned on his cane and turned off the wireless. With a groan, he waved the stub of his cigarette as if appealing for someone to retrieve it.

This was a signal for Ryan to spring to attention from his accustomed place on the floor by his father's feet. He rushed forward with the treacle tin lid that served as an ash tray, presenting it with both hands like the offertory plate at Mass. Fergus acknowledged his response with a nod, squashed the butt down firmly, twisting it several times. He again waved his thin, nicotine-stained fingers around seeking further assistance and once more, ever anxious to meet the needs of this man he so feared, loved and admired, the boy went to the large dresser against the far wall and opened the top drawer. He took out a packet of ten Woodbines from a carton of two hundred, checking first for cigarette cards, then with a sigh of disappointment lifted the flap, allowing one cigarette to protrude. He hurried back with the packet. Fergus took the solitary cigarette, this time acknowledging the boy with a smile of appreciation.

Ryan, through long-established practice, searched among the jungle of bits and pieces on the kitchen table and grabbed the lighter. His da drew hungrily on the flame. As usual, the effect was the same: friction on the lungs caused the pale face to change from an unhealthy grey to a deep shade of pink, which turned red then, finally, purple. As the smoker became overwhelmed in a paroxysm of coughing, a vein in the middle of the forehead began to throb like an unreliable rear light on a bicycle.

"Bastard!" Spluttering, Fergus thumped himself vigorously on the chest, watched by the two women in the room, Marie, his wife, and Kathie, his daughter. Ryan, again vigilant, positioned himself behind the chair and banged his da on the back with his small fist. Obligingly, his father bent forward.

Ryan knew his father's moods could veer from tenderness and humour one moment to an overflowing rage the next, but could not be sure whether the cause of his da's anger was the poor state of the wireless – a bad purchase – or the declaration of war by the Prime Minister of their new homeland. As his father sank wearily back in his chair, Ryan concluded that it was probably the latter: in some way Mr Chamberlain had let his da down, but he wasn't sure why.

He wished again that he was English. The kids at school told him that the Irish were ignorant peasants from a primitive land across the sea. They reminded him of England's enemy, the IRA, who murdered people. Soon after he started at Kelliwell Road Catholic, Kenny Evett had called him a 'Fenian bastard'. He had asked his da what it meant and Fergus had hauled him off the floor, pulled him against his chest, ruffled his hair and grinned through nicotine-stained teeth, but said nothing.

Ryan soon became aware that the way he spoke at school, seeming to turn everything into a question, was a cause of ridicule. He had tried hard to speak like his new classmates, practising before the bathroom mirror with a marble in his mouth pretending it was a plum, but it made no difference. After almost a year in his new homeland, his distinctive brogue had not changed. They continued to mock, pointing their fingers at him. It made him nervous, the reason for his stutter. He decided that the best recourse was to play the fool and he was soon in trouble.

Now, bending to pick up the things that had fallen to the floor and place them back on the kitchen table, Ryan could see that clever Kathie was about to speak and he would be upstaged. He jumped to his feet again to stand by his da's side and nudged him.

"Who's the idiot, Da? Is it him, that Chamber person? Like you said he went over to have a pow-wow with Hitler and Hitler give him a piece of white paper? Was it a promise that old Hitler wouldn't attack Poland? Hitler signed the paper but then he ...what's the word – renag...ated?"

"Reneged," Kathie interrupted as he knew she would.

"Yes, yes, I know, I know."

Show-off, thought Ryan, with her long nose and professor glasses with the little wire frames to make herself look clever when she don't need no glasses at all is what. He wanted to be first to get his da's attention and sometimes he got words mixed up. He felt his face redden, his ears go hot. Lately, he had taken the big dictionary, the Oxford, upstairs to keep it safe and secret under his bed. Every time he heard a big new word, spoken by his sister; tubby little Miss Ashby or that fatty in the class who sat among the cleverest in the back row - the religious fanatic Naddy Brown - he would look it up and add it to the list in his exercise book, which he kept with the dictionary. Tonight, he would add 'reneged' under the one above it: that strange word, 'Fenian,' He hated that word. Kenny Evett, with his big sweaty face, taller than Miss Ashby, the tallest boy at school always trying to show him up. Ryan had turned the pages, thin as lavatory paper, until he found the word. It had told him that the Fenians were Irish rebels who fought against the English hundreds of years back. He did not understand any more than that and his da did not seem to want to tell him. The more words he knew, the cleverer he would become, and no one would guess how he had got such amazing knowledge. He would own a string of words that would spill off his tongue, stretch like the line of washing his mam hung out in the backyard to dry on a Monday morning.

"That's right, reneged. You're angry, Da, aren't you? Chamberpot has let us down; let England down."

"Mother, go and make a pot of tea," said his da.

Watching his father stretch out in his chair, still in his Sunday best suit, the black pin-stripe worn at the Mass and funerals, hands hanging out from the cuffs of his shirt, Ryan looked up at the fresh clouds of smoke. They rose to the ceiling, adding further brown stains to the cream paint and changing the colour to a dirty yellow. His mam hurried out to the scullery.

Ryan spoke softly into his da's ear. "Would you like a game of table tennis, Da? Take your mind off things, eh?"

Whenever they played, Ryan would always let his father win the first game because he knew he was at a disadvantage, him not being able to move fast with the bad leg, sometimes grasping the thigh when the pain like the hot needles got him, and being short of breath having to stop to take great gasps of air. With a cigarette in his mouth, the sparks blowing across the table, his da would brush away the smoke with a wave of his hand, peering over the net so he could see his opponent.

The second game Ryan would always win, but pretend it was a struggle. The third he would also win but only just, with even greater difficulty. He knew his da was a poor loser and it could put him into a bad mood for a whole day if he lost badly.

"I'll go set it up shall I?" Ryan said, his hand on the door handle as he looked over his shoulder to see if there was any sign of interest. The response from the chair was not encouraging.

"Maybe in a bit, but will you not calm down? You surely tire me out with your rushing all over the damned place. Stay still, son, for the good Lord's sake."

Smirking at her brother, Kathie asked, "Would you think it likely, Daddy, that me and Ryan will be evacuated?"

"Could be, Pet. But a bit too early to say yet, I'm thinking."

Ryan seized his chance. A silence for him to fill. "There's some at our school that's already going. Would Kathie and me go to Canada on the big liner? That's where some of the kids are going, Da."

His father struggled to his feet waving his leg from left to right; the wounded one that always gave him gyp. He seemed worse these times, when the autumn damp had come and the darker evenings spelled the end of summer. Ryan recalled the Bible stories Father O'Donnell told in school assembly and at the homily at Mass, about how Jesus healed people from everything. How wonderful it would be if *he* could do that, he thought. Then he would believe all the twaddle Naddy Brown, with her creepy big brown Jesus' eyes, believed. First, he would heal his da. Then he would heal the tubby girl with the ruined face who followed him around everywhere.

His father sighed. "The place you'll be likely to go is an early grave if you go on and on with your never ending talk about this evacuation. By all the saints and the holy Virgin Mary, could you not just learn to shut up for once?"

The door from the scullery opened and Kathie took the tray from her mother. Ryan frowned and eyed his mum, small and scared-looking, clad in a long blue apron dotted with big yellow sunflowers, her hair under a net with things like clothes pegs poking through. She waited at the door like a servant.

"Shall I put a little drop of whisky in it, Fergus?"

"Jaysus, woman, at this time of the day? Use your loaf."

The others watched as the head of the household stood, took his cup and poured the tea into his saucer. He blew on it before pouring it back. Placing one hand on the arm of his chair, he sank his long lean body cautiously down, while Kathie filled the cups for the others and added milk.

Suddenly, the door bell rang. There was an urgency about it that demanded immediate attention. Kathie thrust her cup and saucer back on the table and ran from the room.

Shrieks of laughter, then footsteps clattering up the bare stairs. Ryan knew what would happen next. They would go to Kathie's bedroom, she and black-eyed Daphne, the one with the hair stretched so tight over the scalp you could see the pink skin showing, and a fringe that reached down to her eyebrows: a black beetle that ought to be squashed.

He knew where the other was, the tubby one with that long length of hair hanging like a curtain to hide the horrible flesh: the red and blackberry splodge of a map, jagged along the edges like a splash of wine thrown in temper at her cheek. Reddish purple, the mix you get when you put ice cream on your blackberries. The other side of the face white like snow.

His father continued to puff noisily on his cigarette, now wet at the end. Fresh clouds of blue smoke hung motionless above. Against the wall opposite the grime-smudged window a weak sun struggled to cleave a path through the smoke. Ryan watched its progress as it crept up the sideboard and above it, lighting up the photos of the famous heroes of the Cause. A single naked bulb in the ceiling flickered weakly.

"Will we win, Da? The French have a bigger army, but the Germans have the roads, the *autobahns* they got built where their tanks can roll fast, and loads and loads of soldiers moving fast too – that's the infantry. I heard them say it on the News. Shall I get the table ready for the game now? Or don't you feel like playing, Da?"

His father continued to sit in silence, filling his mouth with smoke then exhaling through thick lips. Ryan admired the rings expertly shaped, heard the clattering sound of dishes coming from the scullery, the giggling upstairs.

He took the overflowing ashtray, poured the contents into the coke hod. He left his da; walked reluctantly along the gloomy hallway and stopped outside a room at the front of the house. Inside were the items of furniture bequeathed by Great Aunt Mary to her favourite niece, his mam. Hanging over the fireplace a painting of a rustic scene from somewhere in the South of the old country. Along the mantelpiece, a stuffed owl with a missing eye that stared out like a sentry through a smudged glass dome. Faded photographs from long ago found a place there, curled at the corners like sandwiches left too long in the sun: husbands and wives with their children staring ahead with fixed expressions. A three-piece suite, the stuffing peeping out of an arm, springs protruding through the seat of the other armchair. A cocoa-coloured carpet, grey-streaked where his da had aimed for the hearth, missed, then rubbed the spilt ash in with his shoe.

Ryan opened the door cautiously.

The girl looked up from the settee and smiled. Her hair was light brown. It stretched down over one eye like a pirate's patch, covering the whole of the right cheek as if hiding some secret, half-covering her mouth and ending at her shoulder. The other side was of normal length. She was well-developed, a somewhat overweight girl of almost eleven years, with an intelligent but sad expression and a worried frown that looked as if it might soon become a permanent feature. The uncovered eye watched him warily.

"How are you, Ryan? A long time since I saw you."

"Friday."

"But you wouldn't speak to me, would you?"

Her voice was muffled because of the curtain of hair. From the half-mouth the smile hovered then disappeared.

"You was with that Dickerson foul-face, nattering like always," Ryan mumbled, looking down at his shoes. He folded his arms like a teacher, glaring at her.

She took out her hankie from under the sleeve of her beige cardigan and dabbed at the unhidden eye. "I don't like Pat much. She's al-right in small doses, I suppose... but she's a dirty girl." She looked up at him as if wondering how he would respond.

"That's not real dirty, not changing her knickers like. You should get friendly with June Greengage, or Nitty Richards. Protect you from the rest, they would." Her apologetic voice always irritated him. With her hands on her lap twisting her handkerchief round and round, he knew the tears would come, first like a trickle from a tap then running stronger. Always crying Naddy Brown was, or else about to.

He knew the ways acne-face Dickerson was dirty. It was not body stink, though the girl rarely washed, but dirty goings-on. Everyone knew that Kenny Evett went with the Dickerson girl into secret places like the big store cupboard, or behind the big oak tree dug in concrete at the far end of the playground. Ryan had spotted him fondling her at break or in the lunch hour, hands running up and down her legs, and her squealing. Pathetic, it was.

As for June Greengage, small and thin like himself, painting her lips with red crayon. Know-all Kenny, biting into his jam sandwich one break-time, had said of her, "Tart, she are. Like her mum. Goes for 'em up Naughton Road. Old before her time, that one. My mum knows Lil Greengage. Says she's in the Horse and Hounds, evenings. Pick-up joint. 'Lavatory Lil' they call her. Don't charge more'n a shilling. That June hangs around outside drinking ginger beer most nights," Kenny had added, spitting on the asphalt and aiming for daft Foureyes who was passing at the time.

June and her friend Julie always shrank back against the big fire guard when Miss Ashby's podgy hands seized the bell for break. Then him and his mates, Kenny Evett and Foureyes Johnson, thrust their way past like a rugby scrum, enjoying the sound of screaming girls and laughing at their fear. Blind and batty Foureyes with the dribble and the bottle glasses, traces of white pant sticking through the hole in his trousers showing his bum. Him with the big turnip-shaped head, thick as treacle.

Ryan hoped his game would be rugby. Already in his mind, he was there on the field at the big Southgate Grammar, where if you played football you were a cissy: a game reserved for

Naughton Road Secondary - the end place for Foureyes, who could scarcely write his own name.

Suddenly Nadina's voice broke through Ryan's contemplation.

"Kiss me." She pushed the thick curtain aside to expose the ruined flesh. "Go on, Ryan," she whispered.

He shook his head, horrified, dismayed at the threatened intimacy, frightened that it might be known that he had kissed the 'Leper Girl.' He turned his back, moved over to the window, peering out to take an interest in a passing car, pretending he had seen a dog or cat sniffing around the neglected front garden.

"You're afraid, aren't you" said the voice from the settee. "Because you're scared. Ryan, it's not catching. Honest."

He knew she had paid Foureyes a threepenny bit to kiss the rotten skin. He hated them both for it. Foureyes would do anything to get a girl to like him, even freaky Naddy Brown. He would never let her get *him,* not in a hundred years, he wouldn't. Ryan strode from the window and leaned over her. He could smell the shampoo of her hair. He screwed up his eyes, counted to ten and let his lips brush hers, lingering for a hundredth of a second.

"There. And that's all you're getting, so you are."

The hair flopped back into place like someone had flicked a switch. Nadina looked up with a beaming half-smile. "There's a war. Did you listen?"

"Me da knows it's Chamber Pot's fault."

Further conversation was interrupted by the clatter of footsteps on the stairs. Big Daphne Brown with her black shiny top of hair, pushed by him and stood over the smaller girl. She jerked her thumb towards the front door. "Right. Come on then, ugly."

There followed goodbye hugs between Daphne and Kathie while Nadina looked on. She gave a half-smile to Ryan, who nodded curtly. He left the room to set up the table tennis on the dining room table. That done, he poked his head round the kitchen door. "I'm ready, Da, if you like, you know, table tennis."

With a sigh, Fergus stumbled to his feet, shook the bad leg to get the circulation moving, then followed his son into the dining room. Ryan took his bat and got into position. It was usual to give his father a few words of instruction: how to make his forehand a priority, to warn him of the folly of using his backhand, reminding him that it was always his weakest stroke and likely to remain so.

"Now Da," he said, as Fergus looked on, leaning against his end of the table, "rule number one: always look for an opening. Look for my weakness. Like yours, it'll be my backhand. Once you get an opening, then smash the ball home with your forehand. I think you're improving. One day, you might even be as good as me." He smiled, but with a certain deference, not wanting to appear superior.

Throughout the three games Ryan would constantly tell his da that he was getting better, adding, "We should play more often, Da."

Frequently, in the midst of these earnest instructions, his father would wander back to his chair in the kitchen. There he would lower himself into his seat, stretch out his skinny legs in the brown corduroys smudged with black streaks from frequent contact with the coke hod, then his head would drop forward on his chest. His outsize hands would rest on his crotch and a gentle sound of snoring would begin, gradually increasing in volume. On these occasions, Ryan would follow his father to the kitchen, remove the smouldering cigarette from between his da's finger and thumb and stab it out in the makeshift ashtray. Then he would immerse himself in the exploits of his comic heroes from the '*Dandy*' and the '*Beano*.' When he judged the time was right he would go into the scullery to make them both a cup of tea, returning to nudge the sleeping giant and cautiously enquire, "Tea, Da? After you've had your drink, is it al-right if we play some more?"

Fergus would stretch, yawn, scratch his head, and Ryan, turning his attention to the corpse-like leg where the blood flow was sluggish, would start the massage using both hands, working his way up from the ankle to the thigh. That would earn him a smile of approval as he stopped to hand Fergus his cup.

Today, however, his da played all three games, winning the first and losing the next two as usual.

That night Ryan was too frightened to sleep much. The knowledge that he had kissed the 'Leper Girl' was scary, but an even bigger fear kept him awake. When would it come? The shriek of the siren, which his da had told him would sound like a cat having an operation without anaesthetic; bombs falling from the sky like hailstones the size of boulders. England, his new country, at war.

Chapter Two

At last he roused himself, falling out of bed, sheets smelling of his sweat, a churning in his stomach as if a crowd of rats were chewing on his innards. Kissing her on the lips was bad enough, but at least he hadn't pressed them on her blancmange. Thank God, he had not! Nor would he ever. But ten to one her only friend in the whole world, the Dickerson streak, with the mouldy stench of unwashed clothes and armpits, would find out and pass it round the class of jeering girls, especially Nitty Richards and that skinny Greengage girl with roots like burnt toast.

Downstairs, Ryan kissed his mam fondly, clinging to her for an extraordinarily lengthy two minutes, his lips pressing her pale cheeks still wet from her head-and-shoulders early morning wash, her stringy hair dripping, tendrils like corkscrews sticking out beneath the towel covering her head. He knew it might be the last kiss he would ever give and he wanted it for her, not the creepy Jesus kid, Naddy Brown.

Flustered, she shooed him away with a tight smile.

He sped along the Harefield Road, his head down, not even stopping to tie a shoe lace, nor to examine an empty fag packet floating in the gutter after the recent rainfall. Nor did he stop to rap on the window of old Mrs Jackson's pie shop to warn her that the flies - which with her dim eyes she thought were currents - were moving, spurred into fresh activity by the sunshine filtering through the grime-stained window. He usually took note of the number of pies left from the previous week and was always sad to see so few were sold. But not today.

Today, he hurried past. For any second the drone of enemy aircraft would be overhead, filling the sky with black shapes, like the crows squawking on the shabby trees that lined his route. Any time now there would be the shriek of the siren warning everyone to take cover. He knew the bombs would turn everyone into strawberry jam squashed into the pavement. He remembered his da's advice: *"If the Jerry bombers come, fall on your face, son. Cover your head with your arms and hope for the good Lord's sake that it's not you this time."*

He crossed the coastal road and started along Kelliwell Road for the final half mile before the welcome sight of the big iron gates, with their smell of old paint and rust, and though his lungs were bursting, he still would not look up.

At last he was safe, pushing his way through the children greeting each other after the weekend. War-talk was on everyone's lips even the young ones. Ryan breathed a quick prayer of gratitude to the God he no longer believed in.

He looked ahead. Beneath the big oak at the far end of the playground there they were: two girls, bent heads talking and giggling underneath the tent-like covering of Naddy Brown's hair. If he caught her boasting to acne-face Dickerson that he'd kissed the India, he would grab hold of the long softness and shake it till it came loose. And with the other hand he would smack the good side of her fat stupid dial fifty times, so he would.

Assembly time. The children formed up in their long rows in the big hall with the huge windows, where the sun shone with full force in summer and where the wind rattled in winter and the snow piled in drifts. On the stage, the Headmistress raised herself to her full height, her silver hair spun round and round like the whirl of ice cream on a cornet that added an extra two inches onto her six feet two, and glared at the two hundred plus children arrayed below her. The floor on which they sat, legs crossed and arms folded, was built from wooden blocks, some missing, others so loose your feet got caught. In the front row, amidst the infants, sat the big troublemakers from Class Six, notably Irish and Kenny Evett, along with the educationally impossible Richard Johnson and a scattering of others. Miss Millison disbelieved strongly in the maxim that children should be seen and not heard. On the contrary, she told her staff, they needed to both see and hear – especially Ryan Brannigan. Her gaze skimmed the front row and she sighed. Two more years before she could escape to a Suffolk village for a comfortable retirement, and meantime she clamoured for a troublemaking-free zone.

Eight other teachers placed themselves around her like a protective guard of honour. The ninth, Thelma Ashby, her pint-sized deputy, about half her height and three times her weight, shuffled forward nervously to stand by her side. Assemblies always began in the same way.

"Good morning, children," said the Head with a clenched fist of a smile.

"Good morning, everybody," they chanted. "Hail Mary, full of Grace, the Lord is with you. Blessed art thou among women, and Blessed is the fruit of your womb, Jesus. Holy Mary, Mother of God, pray for us sinners, now and at the hour of our death. Amen." Then, together, as soldiers on parade, they made the sign of the cross.

Ryan wanted to show that he wasn't really bothered what anyone thought. He guessed the outrage would soon spread throughout the school if hadn't already. *Did you hear, now? Ryan Brannigan, the Irish kid kissed it!* He knew there was only one source for the lies. Dickerson, who sniffed gossip and tossed it around like a dog discovering an old bone buried in a garden.

A chance to boost his reputation came as they chanted the Lord's Prayer: always repeated three times at Millie's insistence to improve diction. When, in that falsetto voice cracking with emotion, she called out after the third attempt, "Amen," and her long pink tongue probed for the two wobbly front teeth to push them back into place, Ryan seized his chance. Looking at Kenny along his row, he whispered. "Our ladies. Get it? Our ladies!" Kenny, frowned, puzzling it out, then rewarded him with a grin of appreciation.

Smiles and giggles broke out like the ripple of a fast-moving stream. Ryan reckoned they were not clever enough to have thought of it themselves. Next to him, Foureyes' forehead creased like a bloodhound's, his spittle oozing through the gaps in his teeth as he looked from Ryan to Kenny and back again trying to get the joke, ever fearful of being left out. Ryan noticed his bewilderment. "Look, Rich," he whispered, "let me explain it, like. Amen is like *our* men. So I say the opposite, 'Our Ladies', see?'" But the boy's blank expression showed he had not understood.

Ryan's good feeling vanished as he felt the collar of his maroon jersey jerked upward and he was dragged and pushed across the floor, out of the hall and along the corridor to the council-green painted room with the aspidistra in the corner, dusted daily, from where Miss Millison ruled her kingdom. From the stage, Miss Ashby gave an order for the teachers to accompany their charges to the classrooms.

The towering figure in the grey-pleated skirt bent her willowy frame. Ryan's mouth twisted in dismay.

"I really don't understand you, Brannigan. A good average intelligence, yet always having a desperate need for attention, longing it seems to hear the sound of applause. A joker in the pack. Are you aiming for a stage career? A boy unable to sit still for more than a few minutes at a time needs to be disciplined. The Scholarship will soon be upon us. Oh, I dread it for you. Dread it."

"I'm frightened, Miss. I admit it. The war, you know."

"Don't you believe in your new country, Irish? Its cause? Its righteousness? That we will fight this dreadful Nazi war machine and overcome this evil man, Hitler? We have nothing to fear. God is on our side."

"Yes, I do believe, Miss, for my da came to England. He couldn't get work," Ryan gabbled, "he was wounded, see Miss, in the Great War, Battle of the Somme, year of our Lord, Nineteen hundred sixteen. I know he would join the army again if he could, Miss Millison. But he's always in pain from his wound an' all, Miss."

He looked up at her, seeing her proud and majestic in the Nazi uniform with the brooch shining at her neck like a silver swastika; saw her squirrel-like eyes narrow, her old-paper skin creased and cracked.

"Let me ask you, Irish, do you believe in our Saviour?"

"Indeed I do, Miss Millison. Oh, yes, I do that."

He lied.

Each Sunday Ryan attended Mass at his parish church. Few observers could fail to notice his customary dull expression throughout the whole of the service. He might occasionally glance at the solitary plaster figure splashed with red paint, fixed with large nails to the polished wood of a cross on the altar, then look hurriedly away. The defeated Saviour always made him feel uncomfortable. To escape the sad gaze from the crucified figure, surrounded by twelve spluttering candles taller than himself, Ryan would glance around at the many little statues where people placed their candles when they entered the church, crossing themselves, murmuring speedy prayers before finding their places on the hard oak pews.

She believed it all, did Naddy Brown. Foureyes too, but he was dim enough to believe anything, the blind batty with the beer glass specs and spit dripping down his jersey all the time. Religion, Ryan decided, was all make-believe. For what was the use of a Jesus who healed the sick back then, but could do nothing now? If Naddy Brown's rotten flesh could be made Persil-white, same as the other side, then he would have faith and even train as a server if he could overcome the stink of incense clouds that lingered for hundreds of years, like tobacco clouds back home. If his da could be freed from the stiffness of his leg, wounded fighting for England, and the ice cold of it all and the pain that shoots up like a million hot needles, then he would believe. *"And yes, while you're about it, Lord Jesus, if you're up there and not too busy, get me through the great Scholarship. Amen and amen and amen again, twenty times twenty hundred, as many as you like, Lord."*

Beneath the Head's impatient gaze, Ryan stared at the floor. The fear of the Scholarship became more terrible day by day. A year and a half yet, but a black cloud on the horizon moving stealthily closer. When it was over and he had passed, it would be heaven. But failure meant hell: the hell of Naughton road Secondary where they tortured you from your first day. But an even greater hell would be the Saint Joseph's Catholic, where the monks dressed in long black dresses and flayed the skin off your back with the cat o' nine tails.

He shuffled his feet, noticing the lace still undone. It was wise to agree with whatever Millie said. The big white handbag tight in her hand swung like the pendulum of the grandfather clock in the Miss Appletons' lounge – the two sisters who lived next door at number one hundred and five. Ryan flinched, eyeing the bag: a heavy weapon crammed with papers, books, keys, make-up, and other stuff she carried everywhere. The sound of a pistol shot when it landed on some poor kid's head knocking it six inches sideways. Once, when Foureyes was the target, his glasses had flown to the ground. Fool that he was he went on smiling, not knowing what he had done wrong, holding his head and shaking it to one side like a dog coming out of a river, before slinking away. Kenny had been impressed. "See, he's so thick, Rye, he don't feel no pain." They had watched their friend shuffling along in the playground at break. Foureyes had denied Kenny's observations, telling them all morning that his head felt like a block of wood. "Always does, that'n," Kenny had said.

Ryan licked his lips, waited for the bag to fall.

"Well, dismiss, Brannigan," said the Head. "Go and learn some control over your tongue. Otherwise, I might be forced to pluck it out."

"Yes Miss, Thank you, Miss," Ryan said, touching his forelock like a peasant carrying peat to the Master's lodge back home.

Time came for the mid-morning break. The asphalt floor of the playground was surrounded on three sides by green-painted railings, the paint fading and peeling like strips of loose skin. Everywhere, noisy children from five to eleven years armed with skipping ropes or playing tag rushed hither and thither. Others in groups of three, four, or five, were chattering, giggling. Elsewhere, in ones and twos, heads inches apart, confidential matters were shared.

Ryan looked around. He had been kicking a ball back and forth to Foureyes, and looking out for the enemy: the Dickerson girl with her pitted skin loaded with pimples, puss oozing from recent pickings. Suddenly, noise from an excited throng came from the far end of the ground. Children from all six classes were rushing there.

Ryan picked up the ball, tucked it under his arm and beckoned Foureyes to follow. The sounds of shouting grew louder, a crescendo of taunts so loud they echoed round the school building.

"Leper! Leper! Leper! Leper! Leper!"

It was happening again. At the foot of the big oak tree that marked the boundary from a farmer's field sat Nadina Brown, her shoulders shaking, wailing like a distressed cat shut out at night from a warm kitchen. Ryan stood watching. He turned his head to see Foureyes running back inside, then reappearing with the stout red jumper shape of Miss Ashby trotting beside him. Ryan moved away to the gate to continue the game. Kenny who'd been messing with Pat in the storeroom, came out to join him.

"What is it, Rye?" When Ryan didn't answer, Kenny said, "Okay, who's in goal, then. My turn, ain't it, boy?"

"Cowards! You despicable, horrible cowards. How dare you! Catholic children? Our Blessed Lord would disown you. I will report you to Miss Millison and Father O'Donnell." Little Miss Ashby turned on her heel, marched back inside, her black curls tossing in the breeze, her bosoms shaking in frustration and despair.

Ryan ignored the shrillness of Miss Ashby's voice so he could concentrate on his shot.

On his way home that afternoon, bouncing his ball on the pavement, he noticed Nadina a few paces ahead of him. Her head was down. Reckon she's still crying, he thought. He stopped, picked up the ball, practised his heading. The ball drifted into the road. He fetched it, then tucked the ball under his arm to catch up with her. He was getting closer, but he stopped, began to dawdle. Funny the way they call out "Leper." Lepers are always white.

Suddenly, he recalled the story Father O'Donnell had told them at Mass and then at assembly, about Peter, the great apostle who let Jesus down. "Peter, the bad lad," he'd said. "Well, you know he was more concerned about warming his backside by the fire in the courtyard rather than helping Jesus out when he was arrested, was he not? The Lord had warned him that he would deny Him. Yes, he said, the cock will crow and you'll deny me. So, when the servant girl said to Peter, 'Oh, I've seen you with Jesus, you're one of his disciples, Peter shook his head. 'I don't know who you're talking about,' he said. Then, boys and girls, the cock crowed. The Lord turned to look at Peter in the courtyard, such a look it was, and Peter...

oh, oh, never forget this, boys and girls. Peter, who had boasted that he would always stand up for His Lord, would never ever let him down, who would be willing to die for his Master, denied he ever knew Him! And later, later, the crowd yelled for His death. 'Crucify Him! Crucify Him', they shouted. Then the Lord was led away to be crucified."

Coming to the end of his story the children saw the priest take a hankie out of the big pocket of his long black dress. His shoulders shaking as he wiped his eyes. That prat Foureyes had laughed, but he, Ryan got the message. And he imagined he was there. He was Peter, more interested in keeping the coldness of the night at bay and not caring what happened to his mate, his friend, Jesus. Father O'Donnell carried on crying as he repeated several times, "And Peter wept. Oh, how he wept!"

I was in the playground and I could have stopped them. Gone in with my fists not waiting for Ashby to sort it out. He had hung back like the great apostle. Like he was Peter warming his backside and not standing up for Jesus who was being led away to be crucified. He had seen and heard the yelling, the jeering, fingers pointing.

Ryan started to run to reach her, but her bus went past. Too late. Still, don't she deserve all she got, stupid Naddy Brown? Sure thinks herself better than the rest of us, tossing her big hair around, shooting up her hand, always answering the questions before anyone else has half a chance. He practised heading his ball again.

Chapter Three

He found his da in the greenhouse leaning on his cane, moving tortuously, hovering over wooden boxes of minute cabbage plants, a cigarette between his lips.

"Hello, Da. I'm home. Shall I get you tea? It's cold for you out here. You know the story from the Bible that Father O' Donnell told us? He told it at the Good Friday Mass but we heard it again at Assembly, so we did."

"Aye. The Father tells them well. Which one?" Fergus continued to lift the tiny plants with his trowel. Gingerly, he spread them on a sheet of newspaper ready for planting in the black earth. He took no notice of his son's eager face as he added a fresh scorch mark to those already criss-crossed on the long table where the boxes lay.

"Yes, Da, he was telling us, remember? At Mass, yeah? See, I remember that story. About the way Peter let Jesus down. And Father O'Donnell, he was going on telling us the way the great apostle got himself damned because he was warming his backside by the fire in the courtyard and the Saviour was being led away to be crucified and that. And Jesus had warned him it was going to happen. And he give him that look, you know. I reckon it was the kind of look Mrs Chamber Pot give Mr when he come back from Munich with the bit of white paper you was telling me and Kathie about. It would be kind of… 'How could you let Great Britain down, you idiot. What good is a pow-wow with Adolf?' He renegated,…renaged, Da. He went on to attack Poland!" Ryan grinned at his father, proud of his understanding, sure that other kids, even that big show off Kenny Evett, wouldn't have known.

His da moved back and forth examining the frail plants, holding the box to the light, pausing to light a fresh Woodbine.

"Yeah, I remember you was telling me and Kathie," Ryan continued. "So Peter let Jesus down like old Chamber Pot let our country down. And Jesus give him a look like he was saying, 'You've done the dirty on me, so you have.' And then it went cock-a-doodle-do a couple of times." Ryan clapped his hands, grinning again.

Fergus shook his head, a grim smile hovering on his lips continuing to attend to his plants.

Ryan's voice dropped. "There was a-bullying going on. And I wanted to stop it, but I never. Today it was."

The trowel was still. "What are you saying, son?"

"It was at break. They was all round her. Naddy Brown, her that comes with the black-eyed beetle, Kathie's mate, the one with the horrible blotch, map of India like on her dial, and they was calling out, 'Leper, leper, leper, leper, leper,' Going on and on. Not stopping.... Well, Miss Ashby she come running, so she did, Da. Then they stopped."

His da dug into the tray of plants with the trowel. "So why didn't *you* tell them to stop?"

"Because... because... I don't know, Da. I don't know."

His father sighed, turned his attention to a fresh box of plants.

Ryan walked away. At the door of the greenhouse he called over his shoulder. "Shall I make you tea then?"

"Aye, you can that. And Ryan?"

Ryan stopped still, looked back.

"When someone's in trouble it's your solemn duty to help them. She's a sweet child and deserves pity, for the good Lord's sake, does she not?"

His da took the cup of tea without smiling. In the small square of lawn Ryan practised shooting goal. He remembered that his mam wanted him to go to the shops. He tucked his ball under his arm. In the kitchen his mam smiled as he came through the door. "On your way now, darling. I need bread. Make sure they don't palm you off with the two-day old. Pinch it first."

"Al-right, Mam."

She was still in her dressing gown, the belt missing. The shapeless breasts under her nightdress so different from the suet puddings of Miss Ashby. He reckoned the little teacher and his mam were around the same age, but a different shape: one tubby like a packet of lard, the other as skinny as a streak of bacon. He could smell the bath salts and the carbolic soap. He heard the big kitchen clock on the mantelpiece ticking. He looked up. Almost half-past five. He'd have to be quick before they closed. It would be dark soon.

His mam took the purse from her handbag from the muddle on the kitchen table, counting out the coins like treasure. "Nine pence; a sixpence and a three-penny bit. One large white, one small brown, and I need the change." She winked at Ryan. "And Ryan, you know your da gets mad if you pick at it. I will too. Pinch it to check but don't pick at it."

She hurried back to the scullery. He guessed she'd be putting a towel round her hair like the turbans they wore in Arab countries. She had a great love of keeping clean, had his mam. Bathed twice a day if they could eke out the coke ration. He would hear the swishing of the water, know she'd be there for hours, forgetting all about the time. In Belfast they'd had no bathroom but that didn't stop her. She bathed in the scullery, locked the door to keep it private, the big tin dragged out from under the kitchen table when it was bath-time. Each of them had special times on a Saturday. He remembered when he and Kathie were dumped in together. Now all the family enjoyed the luxury of a bathroom and there was no more popular place for his mam to go.

"Ryan, don't forget your gas mask, darling."

He followed her into the scullery, took down the small cardboard box hanging by its string from the nail on the scullery door. It was awkward to carry, bouncing against his hip, and though it was only about a hundred and fifty yards or so to the shops, he would start out with it on one side and then half-way, swap it over to the other.

Marie watched him hurry out the door, heard his footsteps running down the concrete passage. She thought how Fergus spoiled Kathie and was so hard on Ryan. She'd often told him so but it didn't seem to make a difference. She sighed as she went into the scullery to see what she could invent for supper.

People were on their way home from work, mothers hurrying from the shops pulling their children with them, for any day the Germans would come and the sky would blacken with enemy planes. Ryan didn't stop running until he had got to the bread shop.

'Hatchet-face', the red-nosed assistant at the bakery, was getting ready to close. She had begun to take the unsold bread and cakes away from the shelves. Ready, he thought, to be brought out for sale the next day. I want fresh, he reminded himself, recalling his mam's warning. He waited, spinning the coins on the counter.

Always a cold, he thought, seeing the drip from her nose landing onto her cream overall and the sodden handkerchief protruding from the top pocket. On the otherwise empty shelf behind her remained four large white loaves, two small white, one small brown and a half-dozen brown rolls. He wouldn't mind betting they were last week's. He pointed.

"Fresh?"

"Of course." She sniffed and a fresh dew drop formed then disappeared. That severe look she always gave him. Not even the faintest glimmer of a smile on the thin line of her lips. He felt her hatred. Because he was Irish. The English hated the Irish, his da constantly reminded him: "And as far as I'm concerned the feeling is mutual," he would add. Ryan found it hard to understand why Da should hate the Brits so much, a soldier, wounded at the Battle of the Somme fighting for the Empire. But he didn't ask. Past experience told him he'd have to hear again and again how the English had treated the Irish over the centuries. It would go on for hours and his da would get into one of his rages, which bored and frightened him at the same time.

Sure, if I was making a film I would have Hatchet-face as a top Nazi, assistant to Miss Millison. Here it comes, the usual wrinkling of her nose like there's a horrible stink under it and then a sniff and you see a dollop of puke disappear back up her snitch. Those black evil eyes, mouth always turned down like a horseshoe the wrong way. Funny the way her face grows longer every time. Soon she'll have no chin.

She turned to look behind her to see which loaves he was pointing at. "Small brown, large white?"

"Yeah."

"Don't they teach you manners at your school?" she said, reaching for the loaves.

Ryan thought he would try out his British accent. "Of course. As a matter of fact, I'm known as the most politest boy in the whole school."

She gave him a strange look and handed the bread across the counter.

He picked up both loaves, pinching the sides, seeing how deep his fingers would sink.

"You'll buy them anyway now, you will," she snapped.

"Is it today's? Not yesterday's or the day before, or last month's?"

"Haven't I just said? All our bread is fresh. Fresh every day."

He changed his box with the gas mask over to his other hip, put the change in his pocket and started for the door. Nadina was there. She stood and stared. Ryan dodged round her.

She shouted, "Wait! Ryan!"

A dozen paces he stopped. "I couldn't have stopped them, Naddy. There was too many of 'em. All of them others. Anyways, Foureyes got Ashby for you."

There was no time to say more, for suddenly the air was filled with the ugly wail that his da had warned him about: a cat in agony: an operation without gas. Ryan shuddered, stood still, frozen with fear. The siren's mournful sound echoed along the narrow passages between the houses, shrieked above the rooftops. He joined the stampede: screaming children clasping their mothers' hands; men, white-faced, cycling past; an old lady dropped her shopping. Ryan stopped, picked up a couple of oranges, put them in her shopping bag, then ran on. His gas mask jogged against his hip, the string bit into his shoulder. He stopped. Behind him, the sound of footsteps grew louder.

Maybe it was the memory of the playground incident, his da's disapproval, or the slurred whisky voice of Father O' Donnell addressing them at Assembly telling them that Catholic children should always be kind to others and animals. Or perhaps it was Miss Ashby, or the memory of the cowardly apostle turning his back on the Lord. Whatever the reason, he shouted at Naddy, "Put your mask on!" Quickly, he tore her box open and then his own. Now, both taking deep breaths, they ran side by side as fast as a four minute mile. They had covered half-way to his house when, suddenly, a different tone, not up and down the scale this one, but all on one note, the sound that people always welcomed with smiles of relief and prayers of gratitude: the 'All-clear.'

Everyone's pace had slowed now, people smiled at each other. "False alarm, you kids," said a man passing by on his bike.

Panting, they reached the passageway that separated his house from the Miss Appletons.' which his mam called a 'little palace', the two old retired teachers. 'Busybodies,' she said they were.

Two pairs of feet clattered up the concrete passage, passed the over-full dustbin, through the tall gate into the back yard. A few steps more and they were inside, panting with fear. Ryan noticed that in all the excitement, he'd clawed great chunks out of both loaves, stuffing them into his mouth.

In his chair his father, pouring whisky into his tea, looked up and murmured, "For the Lord's sake, what the hell were you in such a hurry for? Didn't I tell you that if your number's on it, that's it? Where's your trust, son?" Then his da raised his cup and gave them his big grin.

Seeing his da's smile, Ryan knew all was well again. He handed the bread over to his mam with the change and whispered his regret for his attack on the loaves. And though his mam frowned as she put the change carefully back into her purse, she made no further comment. Neither did his da.

Chapter Four

Throughout that first bitter winter, the coldest in Europe for a hundred years, Ryan and his family expected that the raids would begin, but nothing happened. In time, folk began to call it 'the phoney war.'

That day at school he felt Nadina was raiding *him*, feeling her one-eyed gaze from the back row, like a bright searchlight, then trying to waylay him at break. He did not want to be seen with her. Nor with any of them. So when Miss Ashby grasped the big bell in her podgy hands to give the final clang of the day, he lingered. He needed the toilet, which gave him an excuse.

Thinking he was the last to leave, he strolled towards the gate bouncing his football. Swinging on the gate, gypsy ringlets like strings of black liquorish, was Greengage, the hair thinning at the scalp, the roots sooty.

Not blonde today he mused.

The gate squeaked as she rode back and forth. Climbed down as he approached, sauntering up to him, swinging her hips, crimson lips pouting. He picked up his ball, tucked it under his arm.

"What you want? Think I want any of you?" he asked. "You girls! No damned use in a man's world. No good for fighting, see? You stay at home you lot, knit and that for the troops. Any case I got my own friends. And none of them are girls!" He let the ball drop at his feet and began to show his prowess at dribbling. Julie Richards now joined her friend, climbing on the gate. Both girls shrieked with laughter at some comment Julie made.

He was in a rage. His new resolution to be kind to Nadina and all girls because of their weakness, useless for nothing except bed and babies, was forgotten. The girls watched in silence as he took a long run, kicked the ball at them as hard as he could. They ducked.

Nudging and giggling, they watched him go out into the road, retrieving the ball and tucking it back under his arm. He turned to give them a rude sign, which produced more laughter. Then came his boxer's walk, shoulders rolling from side to side, then sudden shadow-boxing, then small skips as if in the ring.

Nitty-picker Julie called after him, "Ryan, we know you like the leper girl."

He froze, then hurried on ahead.

"Yeah," shouted the Greengage girl, "kissed her, didn't you? Ugh!" She hoiked up, then spat.

Shame and embarrassment rose hot in him. Now they rushed past to join a cluster of girls ahead. "Bitches!" he called in his fury. And again, more laughter, others joining in.

As he drew closer to home, he saw the familiar sight: three bicycles bunched against the railings. *She'd* be here again. He marched through the back door, ignoring his da's greeting from the depths of the chair, striding along the dark hall to thrust open the door to the front room.

"What you doing? Why're you here?"

Nadina was sipping lemonade through a straw, peering up at him with her half face. She'll be in black-out all her life, he thought, even when the war's over and everywhere is going to be lit up, half of her will stay in the dark.

"Ryan, among all the others, we were the only ones wearing our gas masks," Nadina laughed.

"So what?" He knew she was hoping he would sit down next to her.

"You let them get at me," she said, pouting in a silly way, so different from Greengage with that gash of crimson, as if someone had run a knife along her mouth. For Naddy Brown's lips were full, pink and soft. He couldn't help staring at them. They were kissable lips, like the film star Patricia Roc's. He had once got a grown-up to smuggle him into the pictures to see her. Patricia Roc and Margaret Lockwood, two of his favourites, along with Deanna Durbin.

She began to whimper. He reminded himself how pathetic she was, silly one minute, crying like a baby the next. Yet despite his scorn he moved forward until he stood a yard away.

"For God's sake, Naddy, what the hell's wrong with you? You've got to stick up for yourself, girl. You're expecting me to be like a bloody bodyguard. I'm not. I can't be."

"You let them get at me, " she said again. This time there was no pout. She took a handkerchief from the sleeve of her cardigan and dabbed at her eyes that were full then patted the settee next to her, but he shook his head. He spoke as softly as he dared.

"Look, don't get so scared, Naddy. Show them. Not your fault you got a horrible mark. Yeah? Was you branded with a hot iron or something? Any case, not your fault, kiddo. Told you before. You're crippled, yeah? Well, so what? Any case they got it wrong. Lepers are white, sure they are. He pointed a dirty finger nail at the uncovered cheek. "White one side and the other's sort of purplish, like blackcurrant jam and strawberry all mixed up together. Sure it's horrible sight it is, but, see... not your fault."

A wail greeted this deliberation. He saw the tears drip down the unhidden cheek, shoulders beginning to shake. She glared at him. "It's my birthmark, stupid!"

Suddenly, he reached forward and grabbed a bunch of her hair in his fist. "You was telling Dickerson, weren't you? Told her I kissed your splodge? Didn't you?" Ignoring her yell, he yanked the hair to one side. The blemish so ugly that he shivered.

In classroom discussions he had said he always thought it looked like India, though Kenny said Africa, pointing out in his atlas the various countries that made up that great Continent. Most of the class argued that it was more India, though Julie said she thought it was Australia. Pete Steggles said it was more like the Sahara, putting his atlas on top of Kenny's, who pushed it off his desk and onto the floor, claiming that if it was desert it would be all sort of yellowy. Foureyes had said he didn't mind kissing it again, though he'd be charging sixpence next time. With an astonishing display of intelligence, incredible in one so dim, he had dribbled out one word that stunned them all into silence: 'inflation.'

Ryan let the curtain fall back into place. "Stop being ashamed of it.''

"Well *you* are, aren't you?"

His rage caused him to sweat. He shook his fist in her face. "Not me that got to wear me hair long, like you don't want no one to see your splodge. So, yeah? It's disgusting, but all of them know, so why go on hiding it? You let 'em all see it and they won't bother you no more, 'cause them'd get bored, see?"

He folded his arms, his expression softening, wanting to be kind. "Okay, Naddy, so we've all got wrong things. Like Kenny Evett. You seen his feet? Huge they are; gigantic, giant's feet. You seen 'em, Naddy? You must've. And his great elephant's ears to go with them, and him being eleven in three month's time and bigger than fatso Ashby. He'll be a giant when he's grown up. He'll have to live in a special-sized house. And old Foureyes, daft as a brush, dribbling all the time, snot all over his jumper, dirty little devil. Without them thick glasses he can't see nothing. And Tojo with them big teeth and slitty eyes, can't close his stupid mouth his teeth are so big. He can't help it, being foreign. He's going to be deformed all his life and when he's grown up he'll look more than ever like a Jap, see? He's never going to look British. They'll pass him on the street. Won't speak to him. A Jap? Yellow peril, me da calls them. Quick, cross the road, the beggar's coming our way. You've got something. I have an' all. I talk funny I do. I dunno, you girls got no guts. Oh, poor me. Poor little Naddy Brown, poor ickle diddums." At the end of his tirade he glared at her.

"Kiss it then." She swept back the thick covering, held up her cheek to him.

Ryan stepped back almost tripping over. "No. No, I won't. I won't. No."

"If you'd kiss it just once Ryan, it would make so much difference to me. All the difference in the world, it would. More than you ever realise."

"No, I won't."

"I'll promise to be your friend, forever and ever, for all eternity. Cross my heart and hope to die."

He hesitated for a full minute, looking down at her inviting smile, seeing the full film star lips. He recalled standing on the top diving board and waiting ages. Then, his heart thumping, he'd tiptoe forward. On the very edge he would stand shivering, before finding the courage. Now, he lowered his face, let his lips touch her mark for the briefest of seconds. The curtain fell back into place and the half a smile seemed to light up the rest of her face. It made him feel strangely happy, like scoring a goal past Bunny Harris, the best footballer in the school. Like wrestling Kenny, who was at least a head taller and a load lot heavier and hurling him to the ground. Like a rare spot of praise from Miss Ashby, like everyone roaring with laugher at one of his jokes.

Such a sunbeam he'd never seen on the soft moon-shaped face before. He grinned sheepishly down at her, but just as quickly frowned. "Naddy, don't you ever, ever tell. Promise? Not that foul-faced Dickerson streak of piddle. No-one. You promise me, Naddy, you hear me now?"

"I promise you, I won't," she said, solemnly making a sign of the cross over her lips and heart.

He could deal with June Greengage.. And Nitty Julie, scratching her scalp. He would be tough and harsh, like Charles Laughton as Captain Bligh in *Mutiny on the Bounty*. But to Naddy Brown from now on he'd be different, quite different altogether he would. For now, for the first time, he felt genuine pity.

Chapter Five

Over breakfast, Ryan, eating his porridge, called out the headlines from the newspaper propped up against the teapot.

"First man killed, Da. Right up North, the Orkney Islands."

"Bastards," muttered his father, stirring sugar into his tea.

"The Russians have won the Finns."

"Beaten them," corrected Kathie, crunching on toast, looking over her brother's shoulder.

Ryan ignoring the interruption, continued reading, "Denmark and Norway been invaded."

Like everyone else, they knew the so-called 'phoney war' was over. After the hard winter, spring had turned to summer and now autumn brought the bombers not only to London but to the towns and cities of England. The Brannigan family huddled in the little cupboard under the stairs as the bombs rained as thick as hail in a storm and the houses rocked under the blasts. Ryan thought that any night could be his last. The walls would fall on him, squashing him flat. He would be buried under a pile of bricks just as he'd seen on the newsreels at the Pictures: firemen fighting huge blazes, buildings crumbling like matchwood. People burnt to cinders, lives snuffed out. He, Ryan Brannigan, would be forgotten, the boy from Belfast who wanted to be as English as the English. During the raids he forgot: school; Millie Millison, top Nazi with the loose gnashers; footie with blind Foureyes and Kenny who with them big feet give him an advantage. But not forget Naddy Brown now he'd kissed her splodge.

Of course, *she* had a posh shelter outside in her big garden: an Anderson, her dad could buy one, seeing he had an important job, a public health inspector, sniffing out filth from restaurants and hotel kitchens, warning them he'd close them down any time now. She'd told Ryan he enjoyed threatening people.

He liked Mrs Brown with her jumbo arms and wobbly bum, but not Mr Brown. He hated the sight of those fish eyes, like on the slab at the fishmongers; the twisted little mouth, the jerky way he talked and the tiny shark's teeth. Old Croc-face Brown. He hated him. So did Naddy, which is why she always came to his house. He liked Mrs B's cooking though.

He looked at Kathie reading under the bicycle lamp held by his mam. Clever-clogs at thirteen still reading Enid Blyton? Just shows she don't know much, he sneered. Would Da get us evacuated? The house shuddered under the blasts and he sent up a hurried prayer to the God higher than anything in the sky except maybe Mars and meteorites, that he would get evacuated. Canada was the place Going such a long way was scary but surely it meant missing the Scholarship. Yet he was in two minds. Part of him wanted to stay in England. And though he hated to think it, if he left would he not miss *her*.

He got to his feet. His da didn't scare at all, standing on the doorstep watching the sky, ready to blow his whistle for the firemen and the air-raid wardens to come running if a bomb hit a house close by, or if he saw flames over the roof tops in Ratby Road.

"Nothing can stop you getting a bomb up your bum," Ryan had told Foureyes on the way home from school. "Sure, you and Naddy Brown going on about prayer protecting you is daft, kiddo." And he had placed an arm round the skinny shoulders, the big turnip head wobbling, "See, Rich, there's no point getting scared. Told you before, didn't I? If your time is up, that's it. Nowt you can do."

Foureyes wrinkled his nose, swallowed saliva, shook his head.

"Don't understand, do you?" Ryan asked.

"Nah," the boy had said.

Yet, despite this advice given with such strong conviction, when a bomb shrieked down and he thought the end had come, Ryan yelled out with Kathie, "Oh, God, no, no, please!" Then breathed a sigh of relief, his mam and Kathie crossing themselves. Someone else's turn, he thought.

The sounds of fire engines, whistles, falling debris had stopped and Ryan went to the front door. He stood by his da's side, took the cane off him and was given a welcome smile.

The powerful lights from the searchlights penetrated the clouded sky, wandered around seeking out the enemy raiders as if ready to squash an insect. They heard the distinctive throb of the Dornier bombers' engines. Suddenly, his da shouted, "Would you be looking at that?"

An enemy plane caught in a searchlight twisted and turned like a moth trapped under a light. Black smoke poured from a wing while puffs of smoke from the guns blasted the air around it. Ryan could see the pilot, struggling to open the canopy. Were there going to be parachutes? He thought of the crew landing in his back garden. What weapons did they have in the shed? A fork? Spade? Or what about the hoe with its sharp edge? They would hold them prisoner until the Home Guard or the police came. His picture would be in the newspapers and he'd be interviewed on the wireless. England's hero. He began to clap, whistle and cheer like a spectator at a football match.

The blow from the big fist knocked his head sideways. He fell to the floor, struggled to get up, beginning to sob. In the glow from the cigarette he stared into his father's face.

"You little devil, so you are! Would you delight at others' misfortune? Have you no idea what those fellas are going through? For the good Lord's sake will you not just show some compassion?"

Crestfallen, he watched as his da looked up at the burning plane, solemnly made the sign of the cross and prayed, "Holy Mary, Mother of God, pray for us sinners now and at the hour of our death."

Ryan answered through his tears: "Amen and Amen... Da."

The whining of the plane got louder, the searchlight joined by others holding it captive. Flames now spread to the fuselage. The pilot had the canopy open, dense smoke stopped the onlookers from seeing more. "Wonder where it'll crash," said his da. Ryan hoped it wouldn't be the Rec where he played football with Kenny and Foureyes.

"Oh, the poor fellas!" His da made a further sign, this time his head low against his chest. "Come on, son," he said with a deep sigh. "Let's get back inside, shall we?"

Ryan handed him his cane. Back in the makeshift shelter, his father laid his long body carefully by his son. In the dull light cast by the bicycle lamp held by his mam, Ryan saw a smile on the nicotine-stained teeth. He grinned back, reassured that all could be well again. "I'm sorry, Da, you know." His da nodded.

Now all seemed quiet at last. He listened to his father breathing, interrupted by occasional coughing. At any moment the All-clear would sound. Before he climbed back into bed he'd take his dictionary and exercise book. 'Compassion' struck him as an important word. A big new word, his da's word should go to the top of his list. He mumbled it several times under his breath, savouring the sound of it. He'd write in red ink, use the fountain pen his da and mam gave him for Christmas. The other words on the list he'd write in blue.

At last the ugly sound of the All-clear shrieked its welcome and the family trudged back upstairs.

"*Compassion,*" he read out, swiftly flicking the pages of his dictionary. "*Pity: inclining one to be helpful or merciful.*"

Fresh doubt came again to the surface. "Whose side was his da on, ours or theirs" A question that would not go away.

Next morning the hammering on the back door announced the arrival of Foureyes. He stood in his once-brown jersey, stains of soup, grease from the Chippy and the remains of a heavy cold giving it extra covering. He was cramming the remains of a bacon sandwich into his wide mouth. Fresh saliva trickled through the gaps in his teeth. Ryan noticed that he never seemed able to eat his food without losing half of it, spending a lot of time searching for lost pieces. When he found some residue, a piece of rind perhaps, an odd cornflake, jam from a past sandwich, he'd pop the leftovers into his mouth with a grin of triumph.

Bacon fat ran down his chin. He told Ryan excitedly, "We ain't got school today, Rye. Me mum told me. Why I'm here." Yesterday's dollop of jam on his forefinger plopped into his mouth "Sure, but it's early, Rich? See, half eight," Ryan pointed to his watch. "Sure, I haven't had my breakfast yet, have I?. Hey, you see the Jerry plane caught in the searchlights? Where did it land, Rich? On the Rec? My God, there was all this smoke and the flames. Me da and I watched it all. There was no parachutes, though. Rich, concentrate, will you? Where did it land?"

"I never see nothing, Rye."

"Nothing? My God, Rich, you're not only blind you must be deaf an' all, as well as daft as a loony. Da and me, we stood on our front doorstep and there it was, large as life. I was thinking we'd have to take the Jerry pilot and the crew prisoners!"

"So where would you keep them, Rye?" asked Foureyes. Behind his thick spectacles, he was wiping bacon fat from his chin with his sleeve.

"Keep the Jerries?"

"Yeah."

"I'd lock 'em in the outside lav where the spiders and beetles live."

Both thought this hilarious. For nearly a whole minute they chortled with delight until, as suddenly as it began, the joke ended. Ryan left Foureyes searching for more food particles while he went to dress.

A few minutes later, carrying his bowl and spooning porridge into his mouth, he followed Foureyes through his back gate and down the concrete passage. Kenny was waiting on the pavement. "You saw it, didn't you, Kenny?"

"Saw what, boy?"

"The Jerry plane that got shot down." Ryan put his dish on the ground. "Eeeeeeeeeee!" He stretched out his arms, ran round in little circles, then clutched at his stomach. "Oh, my God, my God, they got me." He staggered back, doubling up in pretend pain.

Foureyes laughed and clapped, his glasses slipping down his greasy nose. Kenny scowled. "Them Nazis! Yeah, I seen it. Glad they got 'em. Me dad at Dunkirk, he was, holding them buggers back. Prisoner now, and me mum dunno where." He pulled back his fist, "Where's your dad, Rich, you daft sod?"

As the fist landed Foureyes shuddered, blinking back tears as he clutched a reddened ear. Kenny said, "No, you never know where that dad of your'n is, do you? Left your mum again, has he? On the run from the Boys in Blue, is he?"

Ryan wasn't taking much notice. He was thinking about his da being sorry for the Jerry air crew. Under his breath he said his new word as Kenny gave Rich another blow, this time to the chest. The boy staggered back against Ryan, glasses flying off his face. Ryan cupped his hands and caught them, handed them back, then stepped up to Kenny, pushed him back against the railings, "We're mates, aren't we? You, me, and Rich here. We should be patriots, yeah? Stick together against the Hun." He went over to Foureyes, who was rubbing his ear. Placing a protective arm around the smaller boy's shoulders he glared at Kenny. "You're always going on about your da, so you are, as if he was the only soldier at Dunkirk. Well, mine done his lot already, if you want to know. Battle of the Somme. Year of Our Lord nineteen hundred sixteen. He got a bullet in his thigh. If he could join the army again, he would. And Rich here, not his fault his da's on the run from the police—"

"Huh, traitors you Irish. They're going to inter you lot me mum says. Damned Irish. Bastard Fenians. They're going to ship you off to Wales somewhere."

Now it was Foureyes' turn to be peacemaker. He stood between the two. "We shouldn't fall out, we shouldn't. Rye's right. Hey, come on, let's go look for shrapnel."

He ran ahead, beckoning them to follow. As a final show of contempt Kenny spat, narrowly missing Ryan's discarded breakfast. Ryan had no idea what 'inter' meant, but he wasn't going to ask big-head Kenny. He hated the way he kept calling him a Fenian. Still, he'd bet he didn't know what it meant.

They walked along three abreast, hands in their pockets, telling Kenny where they'd keep Jerry prisoners if they ever captured any. Kenny didn't think it funny. He was in a sour mood. Ryan reached up to pat his back. Kenny seemed to brighten then, telling them about a recent visit to the Pictures with his mum. "I seen this film. God, you should see what them Gestapo do to the prisoners. They pull their finger nails off. We should do the same. Toenails an' all."

Foureyes winced. No wonder he hates violence, everyone hitting him, the poor little devil, thought Ryan. He said his special word again. This time out loud: "Compassion!" The others stopped and stared. Kenny, his mouth open, Foureyes wrinkling his nose, pinching it, then giving a loud sniff.

Ahead of them others, mostly boys, were taking advantage of the unexpected escape from school to gather souvenirs. Down the main coastal road that led to the docks where the anti-aircraft guns were positioned, evidence from the raids was all around them.

More slates missing than remained; some roofs with gaping holes exposing joists blackened and splintered; the frames of windows, all glass smashed; garden fences and hedges uprooted and piled high by the force of the blasts.

Roaming into the gardens they gazed in awe at chimney pots lying on lawns like discarded garden gnomes. Astonished, they looked up to see beds and wardrobes flung haphazardly about, sheets and blankets strewn carelessly on the floor, here and there drenched in blood.

Foureyes pointed up to a bathroom where a washbasin lay smashed on the floor and water gushing from a tap. A bath dangled precariously ready to fall down on them. They hurried past well-to-do homes with brickwork scorched black, gaping holes in garden walls as if a giant had furiously shoved his fist through.

They came upon police tape, warning them to KEEP OUT. Here, air raid wardens working with firemen brought out bodies on stretchers, covered by blankets.

"Dead, all of 'em," whispered Kenny. "I'd kill them Nazis if they ain't dead already. Yeah, and why didn't you see owt, you daft twerp?" Kenny gave Rich a sharp slap on the back of his head.

Ryan elbowed the big boy to one side. "For God's sake, Kenny, cut it out will you? Where's your compassion?"

More bodies appeared.

In one front garden, at the bottom of a huge crater lay a leg covered by a bloodstained stocking. "Where's the rest of her?"

Ryan wondered, turning to Foureyes, who was bringing up his bacon sandwich in the gutter, sick as a dog. Through a front door, strangely still intact, firemen brought a woman out on a stretcher, her face like marble. Under the blanket, Ryan thought he could make out a space where the leg had been. That woman's time has come, he thought, never mind the posh place. Money don't stop it if your number's up. He nudged Foureyes, who was bent double clutching his stomach. "See, don't matter how rich you are, me da says if a bomb's got your name on it, nothing will stop it."

The other two wandered ahead without responding. Ryan ran past, then turned to them, to hold up his hand like a policeman directing traffic, "Listen, you two. Sure, it's all a matter of luck, see? Fate, is what it's called. If your name's written on a bomb that's it. You've had your chips."

Foureyes wrinkled his nose, pinched it and sniffed, the skin on his forehead criss-crossed like a tangle of wires. "Rye, how come a bomb's got my name on it?"

Kenny sneered, but Ryan thinking compassionately, pulled Rich to him, squeezed the skinny shoulders. "Poor ignorant little fella, so you are. Just a saying, see?"

They stopped next outside a garden where people with bare hands were hurling bricks and timber onto a growing pile. Among them, his cassock sprinkled with plaster and grime, stood their parish priest, Father O'Donnell, a black smudge down one cheek.

He strolled over to them, taking a cigarette out of a silver case from the pocket of his big dress, lighting it from a gold lighter. Rich, Ryan thought. Just like the priests across the Water, taking in the peasants to believe their twaddle so they can get their big collections.

"Well lads, it's going to take more than a few bombs to conquer the indomitable spirit of our people, don't you think so now?"

The three boys nodded solemnly. "Yes, Father."

Ryan stepped forward, touching his forelock. "Excuse me, Father, but where did the Jerry plane land that got shot down last night?"

Father O'Donnell screwed up his eyes, "Ah, Ryan Brannigan, every teacher's nightmare. Well, by the mercies of providence, lad, it didn't land on the houses. Crashed in Farmer Sutcliffe's field, close, but not too close to the church, thanks be to God." He laughed, looking up at the sky, and made the sign of the cross. "Well, I must get back to my labours." He crossed himself reverently. Kenny and Foureyes followed suit. Ryan kept his hands in his pockets.

"Was them, the Jerry crew, all killed?" asked Ryan.

"I don't doubt it, lad. Ah, those Nazi thugs. Good riddance to bad rubbish, eh?" Father O'Donnell picked up a blackened piece of timber, tossed it on the growing pile then rubbed his hands together. "Goodbye, lads," he called as they turned away.

They walked along in silence, taking in more and more the sights of destruction. The Jerry air crew all dead? So why be sorry, Ryan thought, weren't they the enemy? Dropping their bombs on us? Killing us? He thought of the one-legged woman on the stretcher, the other leg left behind at the bottom of the hole, stocking covered in blood. Kenny's voice, loud in his ear, said. "Them lot in the plane, eh? Father's right. Good riddance to bad rubbish. I'm going to be a pilot and kill them Nazis when I grow up. Bomb their damned country to smithereens. That's what they're doing to us. So don't you talk about compassion, boy. It's an eye for an eye, tooth for a tooth. What they done to us, we should do to them, eh Rich?"

"Suppose."

"What do you mean, suppose, you dense sod?"

Foureyes moved hurriedly behind Ryan for protection and the blow from the big lad's fist failed to connect.

It's compassion that counts, Ryan thought, the memory still vivid of the enemy bomber belching out flames and smoke, the crew trying to escape as the plane twisted and turned to break away from the fierce beam of the searchlights that held it captive.

Soon they were clambering into what had once been people's homes, only the walls remaining. Further debate ended as they chose various treasures, shrapnel in varying sizes in an orgy of collecting. They compared their finds, tucking them under their jerseys before setting off home.

Next day's *Evening Star* centre pages showed the effects of the raids. Photographs of flattened streets as if an earthquake had struck, and listed below the names of almost five hundred citizens who had died. One large photograph showed air raid wardens and firemen in front of a pile of rubble and in their midst a grinning Father O'Donnell, a brick in each hand. The black smudge as if he hadn't had time to wash, the grey crinkly hair dishevelled and dusty. The caption over the picture said, 'HERO PRIEST.'

Fergus, sitting in his chair by the boiler, the smell of cooking from the open scullery door wafting through, was reading the reports. Ryan leaned over his shoulder. He read out loud the Editor's comments: *"A priest toils alongside our tireless rescue workers amidst the rubble, showing the spirit of Great Britain, that unconquerable spirit of our brave citizens that will never be defeated. Thanks be to God for priests like Father Seamus O'Donnell."*

Ryan looked up from the newspaper, "We saw him, me and Kenny and Rich. He says the Jerry plane landed in a farmer's field, Mr Sutcliffe's it was, near the church. And the whole lot of them, all the crew killed, gone for good, so they were... he said." His voice trailed away as he noticed the anger in his father's eyes.

"Aye," Fergus said, drawing on his cigarette. "And did the good Father express any condolences toward the families of the crew who were only doing their duty as they saw it?"

"No. No, he never, Da. He said good riddance to bad rubbish."

A spiral of smoke drifted slowly towards the ceiling. Fergus turned the page. They looked at a photo of a British pilot, swathed in bandages sitting up in a hospital bed.

"Another hero," said Fergus. "One of ours though this time, eh?"

The heading said, *'MORE HOPE FOR RECOVERY: SKIN-GRAFT SKILLS IMPROVING.'*

Ryan frowned, "D'ya think Nadina Brown's skin could be cured? Like it's all sort of purple and red. Like you get from the juice of blackberries. It's real sad for her. The kids at school take the Mick the whole time, so they do."

His da sighed. "A long time yet, son. There's a lot more to be learned about the skin-grafting." Fergus stretched. His hand reached out and ruffled his son's blond hair.

Ryan smiled. He went over to the sideboard where a half-opened packet of cigarettes waited. He took one out, returned to his father, took the lighter from the table. There was the usual burst of coughing and gasping for breath, the red vein in the middle of the forehead throbbing. Ryan patted his father's back softly, gradually increasing the pressure. Little by little the coughing slowed and finally stopped.

"Thank you, son."

Ryan watched admiringly as rings formed. "You know something, Da? I'm glad I'm British. It's funny but since we come over here and then the war got started I'm feeling like I'm more and more British. I'm beginning to like it here now, Da."

Fergus burst into a fresh bout of coughing. Without warning his hand slapped Ryan's smiling face. "You turncoat! You're not British. You're Irish. Don't you ever forget your roots! Don't you ever deny the suffering of your people." And as he'd done so many times, he twisted round in his chair, pointed with a shaking finger at the collage above the sideboard. "Patriots! They're the true patriots. Every single one of them: Patrick Pearse, James Connelly, Eamonn De Valera...." He continued fervently to reel off the names, sixteen in all, then solemnly made the sign of the cross over each one.

Ryan rubbed his sore cheek, blinking back tears. Fergus sighed, placed a gentle hand on his son's shoulder and said, "Never turn against your own people, son. You be patriotic, oh aye, but an Irish patriot."

Patriot? Another new word? That night before he got into bed he took out his dictionary from its usual place. 'Patriot', he read, 'One who defends or is zealous for his country's prosperity, freedom or rights.' A fresh list, but again ensuring that 'Compassion' was well at the top, yet once more finding it difficult to sleep wondering which side of the war his da was on.

Chapter Six

At Nadina's request, Miss Ashby had set her homework. "I'm looking at the Plantagenets," she told Ryan, offering a cucumber sandwich from her lunch box.

"Who's them?"

"Oh, it's a bit complicated. Apparently some sort of family linked to King Henry II, but I'm not quite sure as yet. History's a fascinating subject I always think. I can't get enough of it."

"Yeah, whatever. Listen, Naddy, you want to stop answering all the questions like your hand shooting up all the time, that's what gets them, see? You give a big toss of your hair and us getting that know-all look of yours. Sure, you're worse than fat slug Matthews. It gives them the excuse see, to push you about, take the Mick. You ask for it. Yes, Naddy, you do. I can't stand up for you no more when you do that." He bit into his sandwich, his eyes focussing on Mrs Brown's jam sponge.

"Julie's been a lot kinder to me lately. Did you speak to her?"

He shrugged his shoulders, boxer style, not answering.

"Anyway, I want to learn. And they're so unintelligent they don't care... well it's up to them if they end up at that House of Horrors along Naughton Road. I've got a new word for you: 'Condescension.' That's what they're like. So condescending. It'll probably take the Scholarship to shake them to the core. It'll be their hour of Judgement, Ryan."

"You what?"

Walking back into the classroom, he puzzled it out, remembered a favourite saying of his mam's: 'The pot calling the kettle black'.

Later, homeward bound, past the parade of shops at the top of his road, pausing to give a fond smile to Mrs Jackson keeping close watch over her pies. Ahead, he saw a parked car. Was it outside his house? Closer he saw it was a Morris Eight, the kind that Millie Millison drove. What's she doing here? His pulse jumped. Relief came like a shower of rain in a summer drought, for now, ten yards away, he could see it was far too filthy to be hers.

Visitors? We never have visitors. He walked round the car, examined it, running his finger along the dusty hood, writing his name there. Who's come? The last visitor was Mr Pinkerton who had fitted them with their gas masks. That was ages back before Chamber Pot's speech on the wireless, well before the bombers came, and the back seat piled high with little cardboard boxes. So it wouldn't be him. "Tell me, how does that feel?" Mr Pinkerton had asked, his pointy nose dripping like a tap with a worn washer. "Breathe in, son, now breathe out."

"I can't breathe," he'd shouted. And they were all laughing at him through the cellophane stuff that was like a pilot's goggles. Da was laughing, waving to him, and even Mam was giggling. And Kathie, taking her mask off, grinning through her crooked teeth and saying, "Looks like you've got a dud'n there, little brother. You'll be gassed! I know it. Sure as eggs is eggs, you'll be coughin' up the blood and your lungs'll be all shrivelled up and be no use to you any more." Mr Pinkerton went back to his car to get a replacement.

Now Ryan crept like an Injun across the threadbare lawn. He hoisted himself up, clinging to the window sill. Through the grime-stained panes he could make out two strange men with his da. He dropped down, jumped over two dusty lupines in the weed-choked flower bed and ran along the concrete passage, loud enough to sound like a platoon of soldiers. He thrust open the back door, "Mam, who the devil are they?"

And Marie Brannigan, unusually smart at four in the afternoon, excitement shining out of the deep blue of her eyes, grabbed his cheeks, kissing each one.

"Who are they, Mam? Tell me."

In three strides he opened the pantry door, carried out the Hovis Brown, cut himself a doorstep on the draining board, spread on the dripping.

"Who?"

"Don't you go into the front room, will you?" Still a broad smile, but the voice was sharp, urgent.

"Who is it, Mam?" His mouth full, spitting out crumbs like a shower of rain. His mam stared out of the scullery window, a far away look in her eyes.

"Good lord, your da hasn't seen Danny O'Brien in years. Not since...."

"Not since when, Mam?"

She busied herself cleaning out the teapot, grim faced. Ryan knew there were secrets that he and Kathie were not allowed to know. Hush-hush stuff that went way back to when his mam and his da were young, back in the old country. They'd be home from the Infants class, him and Kathie, sitting with their milk and biscuits, the parlour filled with strangers singing their songs from long ago, a strange flag pinned to the wall above the fireplace. He knew that the creased and faded photos of the sixteen heroes were from those days and special to his da. Back in Belfast, he'd stand alongside his da, reach up to grasp his hand, then still and silent, then make the special sign of the cross, a far-off look in his eyes.

A bit of dripping fell on Ryan's chin. He stretched a finger, popped the blob back into his mouth and said, "Come on, Mam, who's this Danny O'Brien?"

She frowned and waved her arms, her face darken, a sudden change of mood like a sudden squall of rain. "Nothing to do with you. Nothing, I say. Get youse upstairs. Outside, if you like. Take your football. Don't ask no more questions, eh? Sure they'll be off in a moment."

She closed the scullery door behind her. He had reached the top stair but curiosity was too strong; one foot on one stair, the other moving to the stair below. Quickly he reached the hall, placed his ear to the door. He knew a little Gaelic, could distinguish the strange, foreign-like inflection. One voice was like a growl from a dog. Another voice, softer, laughing.

"You'll remember him, Fergus, won't you? Oh well, Martyn, you're far too young to remember Patrick Pearse – in the flesh, I hasten to add. For we surely know him in spirit. And don't forget James Connelly—"

"Oh, the wicked devils, Danny," Ryan heard his da say. "Did they have to shoot a wounded man, strap him to a chair? Not one ounce of compassion, so there wasn't. Not an ounce. Would we ever have behaved like that?"

"Aye," came the man with the growl, this time speaking English. "Yesterday's martyrs. Did you ever read Pearse's speeches, Mr Brannigan?"

"Surely to goodness I have, Martyn. Read them all. I can get hold of them whenever, you know."

The angry voice dropped and Ryan, straining to hear, caught only snatches of speech: "The glory days... good... over. Gone forever.... Not the past.... No use," the man named Martyn growled, then coughed. A dog with a cough, smiled Ryan, his ear pressed so close to the door that it felt sore.

"Good English ciggies, Fergus," Danny said, laughing again. "I guess your brother's been interred along with the rest then?"

"Aye, they're trying to tame the hotheads."

The dog growled again, his voice punctuated by a fresh bout of coughing. Cough worse than Da's, Ryan thought. "Pearse was a romantic, an impractical idealist, we must have a clear strategy."

"I strongly dispute that, Martyn," Danny said. "We mustn't forget that whatever else Pearse was the inspiration for the Movement, and a quarter of a century later he's still our leader. A truly inspirational man. Spiritual. Don't forget that. Through men like Pearse we keep the Succession alive. To be sure you'll agree with me, Fergus?"

Ryan couldn't hear his dad's answer.

"Al-right, I'll give you that," said Martyn. "But the struggle goes on and you should know, Mr Brannigan, it has to, even after Coventry—"

"Sure it was madness to bomb the mainland!" his da shouted. "For the good Lord's sake, this is not the time. We were fortunate the Brits didn't invade. They still could, given half a chance."

Again the doggy growl, "England's enemy is Ireland's friend."

"Come on Martyn, Fergus is right. The true old hands are cautions, and right to be so. De Valera is a cunning old owl. Inch by inch he's making the Brits see sense. The alternative is too terrible to contemplate. It'll put the clock back a hundred years, so it will. Now, come on, Fergus. God knows you've earned your reward. Sure, you'll be up there with James and Michael Collins and the rest of the saints." Again, the soft chuckle.

The voices got louder, then silence. It was Martyn's growl that Ryan heard through the coughing: "Rifles, ammo, light-machine guns. For God's sake, you've a good-sized house here, Mr Brannigan. A loft maybe?"

Ryan heard his da exclaim: "Is that what you came all this way for, Danny? Sure, I've done my bit, and a bullet to show for it. Want to see it my young friend? I'll pray for the Cause from my armchair. Sure, Pearse wouldn't wish for more than that, would he?"

Ryan heard Danny's friendly chuckle just as the blow came. It was light on the back of his head, more a finger than a fist, since in one hand his mam gripped a tray on which stood a teapot, milk, sugar, cups and saucers. Shocked, he fell against the door. His weight pushing it open.

"For the good Lord's sake, woman, I told you to keep him out!" his father exclaimed.

Stepping into the middle of the room, Ryan looked around. "Who's in here?"

The air was gunpowder blue from all the cigarette smoke. He rubbed his eyes then covered his nose to stop himself from sneezing as he looked from one to the other. A man, younger than his da, scruffy, with dirty fingernails and long brown hair down the back of his neck tied with a blue ribbon, who scowled at him and growled something unintelligible. The other looked older even than his da: almost bald with a fringe of white hair around his head like a monk. In his hands he held a hat, his fingers moving along the rim then back again. He smiled at Ryan, who smiled back imagining how his grandpa might have looked if he had known him: friendly, harmless.

"Da. What's happening?"

Fist bunched, his father rushed to him, "Get out of it, you. Get upstairs. I'll talk to you later."

Ducking to avoid the blow he ran. Up the stairs and into his bedroom. He stood at the open door, heard the goodbyes, the front door slamming and the Morris engine being cranked up, then chugging to life.

He moved along the landing and heard his mam and his da arguing in the kitchen, his mam's voice raised, "Sure is it his fault that he puts two and two together? He was going to find out sooner or later with all your talk."

"Get me a whisky, Marie, please."

Ryan tiptoed to the top of the stairs and what he now heard shocked him so much he was forced to cling to the banister. "Get it yourself. I'm tired of being your skivvy."

"*What*?" he heard his da's voice ring out.

"You heard," his mam said. "And another thing. Are you not constantly favouring Kathie over him? For heaven's sake, Fergus, will you go easy with your fists now? You'll drive the boy away from you forever the way you're carrying on."

His da must have heard the creak of a board, for he appeared at the foot of the stairs and called up, "Come on down, son. Your mam and I want to talk to you."

Cautiously, Ryan came, step by step. On the bottom stair his da glaring and Ryan glaring back.

Together his parents ushered him into the front room, normally reserved for Christmas and funerals and rare visitors like today, though Nadina was allowed. They sat side by side on the broken settee looking up at him. His da said, "Sit down, son."

"I'll stand."

Expecting the fierceness of his dad's rage, like the winds that blew with such force along the coast a dozen miles distant near knocking you over, and the crash of waves on to the beach, untamed, uncontrolled, the spray stinging your face, soaking the skin. Yet as happened so often before, it was happening now; the fiery mood changed as if it had never been and the voice became the caress of a gentle breeze.

"Please, son. Please. Sit yourself down."

But the defiance continued.

"No, I want to stand."

Fergus took out a packet of Woodbines from his pocket. His fingers trembled as he took one out. Marie was the first to speak.

"Things that happened years back, Ryan. Your father and I—"

He didn't let her finish. "Is it that you're going to store weapons in the loft? To kill British people like the Jerry pilots dropping their bombs? *'Only doing their duty.'* That's what you said.

His father laughed.

"What's funny? I don't find it's funny! Whose side are you on? You always said you was at the Somme. But you was never in the British army. You lied to me and Kathie. And I get called a Fenian bastard by big Kenny!"

It was all too much. He began to shout, then to weep.

His mam and Da, both looked at each other. His da seemed nervous, lost for words but it was his mam who spoke again. "We're on the side of justice, Ryan."

"Aye, son, for Ireland," said his da, stoutly. "For the rights of our people, for freedom from the British yoke. The Cause is just. But there'll be no weaponry here, son, no weapons, you can be sure." His da got up from his chair, the cigarette smouldering in the hearth where he tossed it. Covering the distance in three strides he reached out to ruffle his son's hair.

"Ryan, son, I never said I was at the Somme."

Ryan jerked his head away. "You did, you did, you did! What I tell them at school. You lied... lied to me and you lied to Kathie. I tell them you was a hero, wounded so's you couldn't fight no more."

Fergus reached out to pull Ryan towards him, but Ryan pushed his father's hand away. "You betrayed me. You let me think that..." Hot tears flowed.

"Listen son, all I'm guilty of is that I let you go on thinking it. I never said it."

"You did. You did!"

Fergus had no answer to give. He bowed his head and mumbled, "Ryan, I'm sorry."

But Ryan, who would forgive all the harshness, the fists to his head, the cursing, shouting, would not - or could not - forgive his father that. Spinning round, he rushed for the door, shouting, "I'll never ever forgive you!"

Upstairs, he stretched out on his bed, the anger making him hot. Then, taking up his exercise book, he read through his list, underlining the top word, 'Compassion' three times. From tomorrow he'd be different. Compassion didn't mean being weak, but strong. He would leave the silly baby talk behind, like the religion he'd jettisoned, the fat Father spouting at them in Sunday Mass, all the gobbledygook religious loonies like Naddy and dimwit Foureyes spouting Him, dribbling his way into heaven, the prat.

He would try and blot out the day of the visit, but he knew it could never be forgotten, fixed forever like the strong oak tree in the playground, cemented there for all time.

Tossing and turning that night he remembered the excitement of getting off the boat. Coming to the big house, walking the wide streets with the trees each side, breathing the fresh air of the old town, so different from the stench of the crowded tenements in Belfast.

His dad had him believe he'd been fighting for the Brits. As good as told him. Should never have believed him, should he? The way he was always going on about Ireland, ranting on about the past history, the famines and that, talking about the great Cause, raising his glass to the long line of the creased old snapshots on the kitchen wall, making the sign of the cross over each one. Dad's heroes, sixteen of them, and every one of them Irish. He should have known. Dad taking him to the Orange Day parades. Him and Kathie standing at the side of the road with loads of others to jeer at the men in their bowler hats and umbrellas like rifles marching down the Bogside. Then, home from school, strangers crowding the floor in the parlour, singing the old songs in the Gaelic, the Tricolour on the wall above the mantelpiece.

The realisation hit Ryan like a punch in the gut. The date of the Battle of the Somme was 1916 and the Dublin Rising the same date. Brain-box Nadina had told him that. Told him too that her parents believed his dad was IRA. And he was! He was!

From under the bed he snatched up the dictionary, flicked open the pages. 'Betrayal', he read: *to be disloyal, to lead astray, reveal treacherously, or involuntarily.'*

True it was. And that was him – his da who betrayed him. He punched the pillow with both fists for several minutes and wept afresh.

Chapter Seven

The war dragged on, and a new year followed the old. Nineteen forty became nineteen forty one. A momentous year, Scholarship Year. No Assembly passed without Millie warning of the dire consequences for those who failed: the living nightmare of Naughton Road Secondary.

In addition to the mental requirements came the spiritual demands. Of equal significance, she said, announcing her plans for the top class at the start of summer term. They were to prepare for the essential occasion of Confirmation, the privilege of all true adherents of the Catholic faith. Every Friday afternoon for the next eight weeks, she and Miss Ashby would accompany them to the church for their instruction.

The pale, freckled skin that stretched over high cheekbones changed to sunset red as she warned that eternal hell fire awaited all unbelievers and Protestants. Warming to her theme, she added that along the wide road to destruction paraded adherents of the Salvation Army with their appallingly bad manners, undignified shouting and banging of tambourines. Also barred from the Pearly Gates would be adherents of certain sects; theological oddities like the Jehovah's Witnesses, whose dowdy womenfolk dressed from head to toe in shapeless dresses that had been out of fashion as long as fifty years ago with the Victorians. Others to be denied entrance would be those known as the 'Exclusive Brethren', whose strange practice excluded everyone from attending their services apart from themselves. These peculiar people, she told her bored and restless listeners, herded together in windowless barns the size of aircraft hangers.

Less than halfway through this tirade, Ryan switched off. Struggling with a freaky name and talking strange was enough. If he had to be something, he would stay Catholic. Didn't matter anyways. Soon he would escape to Southgate Grammar, where your religion was only a couple of hours' instruction a week and a morning Assembly, where the master in charge rattled off prayers the speed of a bullet – or so he'd heard.

Ryan had not one ounce of interest in a load of religious weirdoes. If talking about them made Millie even more grumpy than ever, it just showed religion don't make you happy. Anyways, he'd never swallow the mumbo jumbo of the so-called 'True Faith', with the fat Father bellyaching at them from the pulpit at Mass each Lord's Day, pointing his sausage, hairy finger at them in Assembly, warning them they were going to be consumed by flames alongside atheists, mockers and something called what? Oh, yeah, non-conformists. The Bible stories that were interesting enough to kept him awake, seemed to have dried up of late.

The thirty-four eleven-year-olds lined the pavement outside the school gates. Miss Millison at the head, umbrella tight under the arm like a sergeant major's baton, shepherded the unruly flock along the length of the Kelliwell Road, Miss Ashby in the rear struggling on her little fat legs to keep up.

When they came to the main coastal road, any danger from traffic was averted by the Head, who marched to the centre, preventing any vehicle from continuing its journey by holding up a white-gloved hand with all the confidence of a traffic policeman, while the children scampered across.

The column would continue for roughly another three hundred yards, until the fifth turn on the left, the Conway Road. After a further one hundred and fifty yards, past houses and a couple of shops, the straggling procession reached the heavy oak doors of the church whereupon Miss Millison cried out, "Halt!" After a further command in her sergeant major's voice, the children shuffled their way into the dingy interior.

Here, the smell of incense, which hung in low clouds, together with the climbing green mould on a far wall where the sun never reached and where plaster flaked and fell to the floor. Ryan held back as long as he could, but finally reached bursting point. The sneeze was like the shout of a man who'd just been shot, echoed and re-echoing. His classmates, herded into the two front pews doubled up with laughter. More and more sneezes exploded, followed by a succession of burps. The children began to count: "Four; five; six; seven; eight; nine... They had to stop at fourteen, their laughter leaving them breathless.

Miss Millison glared, waving her brolly in agitation. "Silence!" Ryan looked up. He half expected the ancient rafters to split and splinter and the little figures of the saints placed at strategic intervals around the building to cry out, "Sssh! You mustn't shout. This is special. This is a church. We're always quiet in here." He decided there was no sense in bringing on further bouts of indigestion, aware that if he held back it could take the rest of the day to recover, ending up with severe stomach cramp. So ignoring the consternation of the Head, he continued. After the eighteenth sneeze, his eyes watering, gasping for breath, he finally came to a standstill. The children began to clap.

"Be quiet all of you," the Head exclaimed. "Ryan Brannigan. For heaven's sake have you now finished at last? I think you'd better stay outside if you can't control yourself." She seemed astounded that he should cause such a disturbance, perhaps forgetting that her scream for silence had been far louder.

"I'm okay now, Miss, thank you. It's the stink of that incense stuff and the damp and that. That's the reason why I can never be a server, Miss."

This explanation caused further merriment.

As the children began to quieten, an air of exhilaration grew. Heads were turned in the direction of the vestry anticipating Father O'Donnell's entrance as if it were the arrival of a famous film star. For, since the dreadful bombing of England's towns and cities the year before, the fearlessness of the parish priest of Holy Innocents' had become widely known, not only among his parishioners, but in the town itself and other towns and cities. Ever since the photographs in the 'Star' showing him standing shoulder-to-shoulder with the police and air raid wardens amidst the devastation, a brick in each hand, stories of his heroism – albeit with some exaggeration - had spread: how he risked his life many times rescuing bomb victims in the middle of air raids, dragging them out of the rubble, visiting the injured in hospital, administering the Last Rites to the dying. He had achieved almost canonical status, revered as a man of God who cared for all, Catholic or not; a man of the people, constantly in the public eye, his actions and opinions frequently printed in the local paper and sometimes even in the national dailies. Despite his Irish nationality, or rather because of it, Father O'Donnell was seen as a true patriot for Great Britain, two union Jacks in the pulpit displaying his allegiance.

The atmosphere that afternoon was in sharp contrast to past times when he had addressed them at assemblies, the visits causing no particular interest.

Now, a shifting in their seats, the craning of necks heralded the priest's arrival as the vestry door squeaked open.

Kenny, actually began to cheer until the Head gave one of her frighteners: a curl of the lip and a wrinkle of her long nose as if detecting a bad odour, the handbag's leisurely pace speeding up. Foureyes blinked nervously behind his big glasses.

Ryan's knew his da disliked Father O'Donnell. Apparently the priest was not prepared to consider a single German, man, woman or child, worthy of one ounce of compassion. A recent edition of the local paper had revealed a scowling priest holding up a tin marked 'Rat Poison' and a finger pointing to the label. Underneath, the quotation: 'Send this to the lot of them. Every single one!'

In the correspondence columns the following day, a reader had taken issue with this aggressive posturing, pleading for fairness. It was important, this reader claimed, to distinguish the Nazi from the ordinary German. But in reply, Father O'Donnell had demonstrated his uncompromising attitude. An column entitled, 'LILY-LIVERED COWARDS,' he stated caustically: 'Believe you me, the only worthwhile German is a dead German!' They were all Nazis, he claimed. No distinction should be made between civilians and combatants. They were all against England, they were all the enemy; all part of the vast German war machine and not one of them deserved mercy. Though he came from the South of Ireland, he made it clear to the congregation of Holy Innocents' that he had no time for the neutral position taken by the Taoiseach, Eamon De Valera.

"By Jaysus!" Fergus had exclaimed when Ryan read the offensive column out loud that morning at breakfast. His father's clenched fist had banged down on the breakfast table with such force that Ryan's cereal bowl had jumped two inches.. "Are not the German people worthy of some at least of the good Lord's care? Whether they approve or not of that strutting little twerp with the 'tache, for the good Lord's sake, son, what choice do they have?"

Now at last their hero stood among them, iron-grey hair neatly trimmed, his cassock unusually clean, he strode purposefully up to the lectern.

"Good afternoon, Father," said Miss Millison, who moved into the aisle to give a little curtsey.

"Good afternoon."

On cue, the boys and girls chanted their welcome to the patriot and virulent anti-Hun. "Good afternoon Father."

Miss Millison drew herself up to her full height and strode purposefully to stand by the priest. Turning to him she lowered her head several inches in deference to his fame. "I'm sure we would all like to congratulate you, Father O'Donnell. It seems entirely appropriate that here, in this holy place, we should express our thanks for your terrific sacrifice among the victims of all the dreadful bombing we have endured and continue to do so. Also our admiration for the way you speak out so strongly against this terrible evil of Nazism. I am sure – and I can speak for everyone present – that we are so grateful for the stand you are taking and we are all so appreciative that we have you, not only as our parish priest but as a true patriot. On behalf of the school, all the children from all the classes, and on behalf of the community, indeed of our country of Great Britain, may I say a profound thank you?"

This wasn't the first time Millie had praised up the fatso, remembered Ryan. Why, every time he puffs up on to the stage at assemblies, she cringes like a whipped dog. Extra grovelling today. Maybe because it's in the church? He glanced at Kenny's shining eyes, his mouth open in wonder. *Stupid prat.* In the silence that followed the Head's flattering speech, the priest merely nodded. "Right," he said. He gave the impression of modest heroism.

"Would anyone like to ask a question, or make any comment about Father's war-work?" asked Miss Millison, clasping both hands to her flat chest, beaming down at the young catechumens.

Ryan was ready. But someone was faster. He looked along his row. It was Philip Matthews, teacher's pet, top, apart from Cynthia Peal and Nadina Brown, in every subject. A boy whose brains seems to spill out of his huge forehead, yet physically grotesque. Both Kenny and Ryan hit him as often as they could. Only Foureyes took more punishment. At P.E Ryan had to turn away, so appalled at the sight of the fat, wobbly stomach, the belly button almost covered by folds of flesh, a shaking mound of jelly each step. Far more revolting even than the Jap, Tojo, who was actually a Chinese from Hong Kong called Clive, though they all preferred to think of him as Japanese, with his huge teeth and tiny eyes sunk in folds of loose skin.

Matthews was useless at footie, and every game you could think of. The great slug moved slowly, unable to run more than a few yards without getting out of puff and ponging of sweat. Ryan was amazed that the teachers should make a fuss of such a monstrous mountain of flesh, treating him like royalty. He nudged Kenny. No words were needed. It was the accustomed signal. They would waylay the fat boy either on the way home or tomorrow at break.

"Yes. Philip?" asked Miss Millison, eager to hear the boy's words of wisdom.

In his whining treble, Philip said, "As you are aware, Father, my Auntie Freda was one of the victims in the raids last autumn. After many a long month, she is now out of hospital, praise the good Lord, having suffered a broken pelvis, two broken ribs, lacerations to the face and a broken leg. But thankfully, she is on her way to full recovery, thanks to your concern, prayers, and your frequent visitations. Our mighty God is bringing down the Nazi bombers like the one brought down in farmer Sutcliffe's field and surely by Divine Providence missed where we are sitting now. It is your prayers, Father O'Donnell, and the prayers everywhere of Holy Church that will grant this great land of ours eventual victory."

Philip Matthews turned to look about him as if to challenge anyone to disagree. "But also," he continued, "would you ask in prayer, Father, that all of us who are Catholics will have the protection of our Blessed Lord, the Holy Virgin, and all the saints, so that we may be spared in the event of future raids. Thank you, Father."

He sat down. A whispered conversation began between Father O'Donnell and Miss Millison. The priest cleared his throat: "Yes, thank you, Philip. As many of you are aware, Philip is my head server. Always punctual. Always regular at his post. If we are to defeat the Nazis, we need boys and girls of like-minded calibre. You are our future for the well-being of this great country."

"Thank you, Father," murmured Miss Millison, giving another of her curtseys.

She'll be kissing the ring on his hairy finger next, thought Ryan. Or maybe falling flat on her face like they tell you the nuns do, licking the shite off his boots. Sure, there he goes, going to stick out his finger so she can kiss his ring. He's expecting her to go down on her knees to him.

But the priest merely glanced at his watch. Ryan knew it was his one chance before the great admirer would say that they were ready for their instruction. He jumped to his feet, dropping his Catechism booklet in his anxiety. He thrust his chin forward in the way he'd seen his hero Mr Churchill do in the Pathé Newsreels at the pictures, hoping he wouldn't stutter. The children stared and whispered, 'It's the Irish kid.' Thirty two heads turned to look, eyes bright with interest, wondering what he would come up with. Foureyes grinned up at him, his nostrils bubbling, spittle running down his jersey. He held the soiled apparel to his eyes for a close inspection as if it was the result of some important laboratory experiment. Ryan grimaced.

"Yes, Brannigan?" said Miss Millison, not bothering to hide her irritation.

He took a deep breath before it all came out in a rush, "Me dad says that if a bomb's got your name on it, prayer don't stop it. I got a question for you, Father. Real important it is. Are you going to say a prayer for the poor devils in the Jerry plane that got shot down over our parish and died? Isn't it what's called compassion, Father?"

The mottled face of the priest darkened slightly. He frowned then glanced at Miss Millison as if appealing for her support against this unrighteous pupil who seemed to doubt his wisdom and that of his favourite server. He noticed the signs of the boy's agitation: the thin line of the lips twisting and turning, bold green eyes under the mop of blond hair that never seemed to lie flat. A troubled child from a troubled home. The father a fairly recent arrival from the slums of Belfast, with a timid little mouse of a wife who rarely presented herself at Mass. Possibly, perish the thought, the man could well be a member of the murderous IRA!

Ryan saw the Head cross herself and look at the fat Father. His heart continued to jump. But he had done it. He had asked his question. The class wondered and waited. Their hero priest stared at the floor. The Head, her voice aghast, broke the silence.

"How dare you question the integrity of your priest, Ryan Brannigan. I do apologise, Father."

"It's quite al-right, Headmistress," Father O'Donnell replied with a smile. "The lad has asked a question. So I will answer. So now lad, sit down, will you, please. I'm going to answer you, for it is a reasonable question that you've asked." Leaning forward, he said amicably enough, in fact teasingly, "I think I know your father. It's Fergus Brannigan, isn't it?"

Sinking low in the pew, Ryan nodded.

"I'm acquainted with his views and he knows mine. He's a neutral." The smile vanished and the voice increased in volume. "I ask you, boys and girls, how can anyone be a neutral in a war like this? Now, look here, we are fighting a vicious, ruthless enemy. A foe who will give no quarter. Do you think that these enemy pilots in their great war machines would go to your rescue when your houses are aflame and your lives are in danger? Do you?"

He paused and the children looked at their Headmistress, saw her shake her head. Many now copied her as the priest continued.

"No, their very purpose is to wound, maim, and kill! Have they shown any mercy to women and children as they fly their huge machines over our homes? Oh, no, no, no, no. Dear me, no. Not one bit. They fly high above us," he pointed dramatically above his head, "and like the cowards they are, they pour down death and destruction. You, who are innocent children. You, who have done no one any harm whatsoever. Ryan here thinks we should show compassion. Did they show any to us?" His voice became indignant. "Think they'll pray for Philip's auntie who lay with her broken body in the hospital, wondering if she would live or die? Well, do you?"

The wide-eyed children looked from their priest to the Head and back again to Father O'Donnell who began to pace up and down like a circus lion. "Children of the Faith," he said, using his pleading voice now, the pulpit voice, soft and earnest, his hands outstretched. "We are a Christian country. We are not pagans like the Nazi flyers. We have been given the protection of the Almighty One if we will but ask for it. Philip is right. Thank you, Philip," he glanced at his server. "We are on the side of right, we are the righteous ones. Compassion? Oh yes, a wonderful word; a glorious sentiment, to be granted to those when they are safe behind bars or deep in a hole in the ground!" He chuckled. The Head beamed. Ryan noticed that Miss Ashby stared ahead expressionless. The priest said, "We will adhere to Philip's request and pray now for God's continued protection."

Ryan, his hands in his pockets, pushed his feet forward to kick Matthew's fat bottom spilling over the pew in front.

"We will even pray," the priest's voice now changed to a stern, authoritative note, "for those who do not believe in the opportunity we have for that protection, or do not even desire it. Bow your heads, boys and girls. I don't want to see any eye open nor any head not bowed low."

The words rolled off his tongue with ease. He prayed for victory against the Nazi invaders, against every enemy soldier, sailor and airman of the Reich. He cursed them with holy curses. Even Ryan, fearing the rage of Miss Millison, joined in, bending his head with the others, the furrows on his brow deepening.

After the Amen, he gave Foureyes a heavy punch on the arm for staring at him with open-mouthed admiration.

The priest glanced at his watch. "Now Headmistress, time is passing. We must begin our instruction."

Ryan's breath came in short gasps. He gripped his Catechism booklet and lurched to his feet. His voice was barely above a whisper, struggling to stop the twisting of his mouth making the words jerky and incoherent. Fear showed on his neck, crept up his face and ears, ending as deep crimson. "He says... Jesus says, you've got to pray for your enemies, like. It's compassion, Father O'Donnell, sir."

The immediate response was a yell from Miss Millison, "Sit down, Brannigan!"

He sensed the danger; the threatening tone, glaring eyes, loose rabbit teeth bared like a snarling wolf's, the swing of the handbag gathering speed. Yet he felt a warm glow of satisfaction. He sat down, grinning round at everyone. The priest, hands clasped to his stomach, eyes closed, made no response.

The Catechism class over, they were dismissed to make their own way home. Ryan rushed away, not waiting for anyone. "Shouldn't hate, shouldn't hate, shouldn't hate," he gasped with every stride. He reached the end of the Conway Road to bend double, hands gripping his ankles, face red and sweaty, drinking in air. He looked behind, seeing them trailing in the distance. None of them had the guts. Not one of them. Sure, Millie could do her worst, did he care? Not one bit, he didn't.

Now running off again, the pace lessening, and the mantra changing. His favourite word: "Compassion, compassion, compassion." Reaching the school gates, deciding to wait for Naddy. Some of them passed him, staring. Shocked, then looked away. From one or two a rude sign.

Here she comes. On her own, thank God. He wasn't ready for a mouthful from acne-girl Dickerson. Nadina smiled, pushing the hair a little to one side, to give her mouth freedom to speak.

"Gosh, you were in a hurry. I did think you were rather rude to Father, you know."

"Did you now?"

"You look ever so hot."

"You should try running. Might lose some of your fat."

She waved to Julie Richards across the road, who turned her head away.

"Thought you said she'd been more friendly to you?"

"Mmm," said Naddy. "Perhaps I've upset her in some way."

"Yeah, for God's sake, someone's only got to stop to crack a joke with you and say something friendly like and you start gabbling away, like you're so damned scared they're going to run off and leave you for evermore."

"I try so hard, Ryan. I've even spoken to the Greengage girl. Oh, I can't win. Even Pat seems to be avoiding me now. I know he's your friend but I loathe that Evett. Such a lout. So crude. It's disgusting what they get up to. I've tried to tell her."

"Sure, you think you're so much better than anyone! Me, I'd have a bath every time I breathe the same air as her."

She turned her head away to stare after Julie. "I thought you did have a point Those airmen have families back in Germany just like ours do. And of course, compassion is paramount in Jesus' teaching. But Father is right. To deliberately target civilians, what they are doing, is absolutely wrong. It's evil, Ryan. *They're* not interested in compassion. Not in the least."

"Nor is fat-gut Father."

"I know you get a lot of laughs. The big dare aren't you? That horrible Johnson boy, another of your friends. If he carried a handkerchief I might spare him a glance. However, there is one thing I do respect him for, he has a very high regard for Father and he is interested in the soul. Philip too, of course. Not many others. Not Pat, though she has other qualities."

"The angels will need to fumigate her at the Gates."

"Oh, very funny."

"I'm going. Going to have a bath. If me mam is out of it."

"Your mother's really sweet to me. She does bathe a lot though, doesn't she? Surely she can't get that dirty."

"Dunno."

She turned her cheek to him, the hair pulled back, an invitation for a kiss. The longest he'd ever lingered had been five seconds. Dare he? He searched the road. Front of them, behind and over the other side. Then, judging that no one would see, greatly daring, he tongued it. He was relieved to find it didn't taste funny.

Chapter Eight

Monday, a day for choosing monitors. "These positions will teach you responsibility," declared Miss Millison.

In the classroom, Miss Ashby elaborated. "Whoever is chosen as a monitor must be kind, helpful and encouraging to others." Her feet apart, coal-black hair parted in the middle revealing a noticeably white line, she licked her lips; a nervous habit, they'd noticed, as her gaze roamed around the classroom. "Now obviously there's more to it than that. The main task is to help me keep order. I need a boy or girl who is capable of controlling the unruly element, maintaining discipline. I suppose you would say that monitors are the teacher's back-up: my lieutenants: reliable, conscientious, protective towards the weak and vulnerable and tough on the bullies. Are you that person?" she asked, a crimson fingernail pointing along the rows, resting on Philip Matthews' bulging face for a full two seconds before moving on. "Right, any questions so far?" The children looked back at her, puzzled. "After break we will elect two monitors, one chosen by your good selves; the other will be my choice."

Ryan nudged Kenny. His resolve to be compassionate did not extend to the fat boy. Though Ryan was scornful of the whole business, he rather fancied being chosen. Of course, he would refuse – a matter of principle – but to win the vote would be a good boost. He would feel more one of them and perhaps they'd forget, at least for a while, that he was the Irish primitive from the peat bogs, or the Fenian bastard, as Kenny loved to call him.

At the stampede to collect their milk from the two crates positioned by the fire guard half-way down the room, Ryan managed to give the portly boy a quick slap to the head before dodging in front of Kenny. He reached for his bottle, stuck his finger in the top, licked the cream. Wonder if I might get a few votes. Not from her, he thought, seeing the thin girl picking the inflamed spots that littered her cheeks.

For Pat, Ryan Brannigan was a complete nonentity. Watching the milk slide up her straw, she sidled up to him, tapping his shin with the toe of her plimsoll. "Your lot come from across the sea," she announced. "Primitive, you Irish, living in huts, working the land, digging up peat and stuff. And what's more you can't speak the King's English, not proper like us. You don't know how, do you? Anyway, I don't like foreigners, especially Irish. Monitor? Huh, you? Never vote for you in a million years, I wouldn't." She sucked on her straw and the remains gurgled unpleasantly.

Greengage's attitude was directly the opposite. Moving in close she gave him a look of undisguised affection and said, "You, know, Ryan, with them green eyes and biggish clumps of hair like wheat ready for harvest, you look sort of wild-like, real passionate." Her tongue travelled slowly across her top lip, like her Hollywood heroines she'd seen at the cinema. "Yeah, ever so romantic," she added. "I'm yours anytime, lover-boy, you know that." She ran her hand up his arm and squeezed before turning swiftly away, the movement lifting her skirts to reveal a torn stocking with a hole the size of a half-crown near the top of a skinny thigh.

Standing on the bench, Kenny, overhearing the comment, looked down and burped. "Be careful, Rye. You could easily pick it up. She'll have caught it from her mum, won't she? Likely infectious, handed down in the breast from the nipple. Clap or the Pox, one of the two, most likely both. Eleven years old. My God, well, you can see how she'll end up. My advice to you, keep away!"

"She should be locked up," Foureyes said earnestly. He threw his straw away, stuck his finger round the rim of his bottle before lifting it to his mouth, then sticking his tongue down the neck as far as it would go. "And be made to repent of her evil, otherwise she'll go to hell." He wiped his mouth in the usual way, running the sleeve of his jersey along it, adding to the mucky layer.

His two friends stared at each other, shocked at this extraordinary display of biblical insight. Showing off? They were not sure if he had committed the unforgivable sin, but it was best not to give him the benefit of the doubt. While Ryan kept a look out for Miss Ashby, Kenny jumped down to administer punishment, slapping Foureyes' head ten times each side. Ryan, remembering compassion, held on to the victim's glasses.

The end of break and the boys and girls trooped back to their desks. In anticipation they looked up at Miss Ashby. She announced with a smile of pleasure, that after careful deliberation and prayer she had made her choice of monitor. "For my preference I have chosen a boy I know will strongly support me and make an excellent monitor, and that is of course, Philip Matthews." Loud boos easily drowned out a few feeble cheers. She wrote his name in capitals on the blackboard. He waddled out to the front where she shook his hand. More boos followed.

Now it was time for the class vote. The children chatted excitedly as their teacher handed out slips of paper. Sitting on either side of Ryan, Kenny and Foureyes smiled, the latter's intrusion into religious pronouncements evidently forgotten. He whispered, "How d'you spell 'Brannigan', Kenny?"

"Please, I am unable to spell his surname, Miss Ashby," called out Tojo, grinning hugely pointing his pencil in Ryan's direction.

"For heaven's sake, just write 'Ryan'. Everybody knows who *he* is."

The class tittered. Miss Ashby snatched a piece of chalk and in fury wrote 'Brannigan' in small letters in a far corner of the board. Then, her ample bosoms resting on the desk, sharp fingernails flipped through two piles of voting slips in front of her. She looked up. "Julie Richards and Ryan Brannigan have tied with seventeen votes each." Her tongue accelerated along the thin line of her top lip. The pupils cheered, banging the lids of their desks in delight. Ryan felt a surge of pleasure.

With her strong sense of fair play the little teacher announced that there would need to be another vote. Foureyes was jubilant. He climbed on to his desk, waving his arms as if conducting an orchestra, and shouted, "Ryan for this monitor bit, Ryan for monitor."

To much laughter, the candidate stuck his pencil through the hole in Foureyes' trousers. "Ouch," the boy said, rubbing his backside.

Miss Ashby glared. "Sit down, Richard!"

Once again, the voting slips were handed out, gathered up to be counted.

Ryan suspected that Nadina had voted for him: the unhidden eye winked, the half-mouth shaped into a smile. Miss Ashby announced the result in a dead pan voice, double chin wobbling in agitation. "Ryan Brannigan, eighteen votes. Julie Richards, sixteen."

There was loud cheering from most of the boys, Nadina and June Greengage notably among the girls.

"Don't want the job, Miss," said Ryan.

The applause ended as suddenly as it had begun. They all looked from Ryan to Miss Ashby and back again. Everyone knew that Ryan Brannigan would be her very last choice, possibly even practically illiterate, filthy Foureyes would have been preferable. Ryan Brannigan spelt chaos and disorder. Discipline would be impossible to impose. They all knew, the teacher included, that those who chose Ryan did so for a laugh. And some who chose Julie had done so because they thought that monitoring would tame the Irish kid. There was one question, however, that had not been asked. How could Ryan partner Philip Matthews? The two boys loathed each other. They were opposites in every way.

"You'll have to take it," said Miss Ashby, miserably. Her bosoms strained in the red jumper, breath coming in short bursts as she swept back the tangle of unkempt hair and looked down at the floor in despair. "There's nothing else for it. They've voted for you." Toying with a piece of chalk she flopped down behind her desk with a sense of abandonment.

"Well, look here, Miss," said Ryan, "see here, I don't want to be the monitor person. I'm not qualified."

"By a very narrow majority they seem to want you, qualified or not, whatever that might mean."

"Yeah, Rye. You do the monitor stuff!" shouted Foureyes.

"Oh, shut up, all of you," said the teacher, covering her face with her hands.

Ryan, red-faced, abandoning any tendencies towards compassion, got to his feet and vigorously punched Foureyes' head, first on one side, then on the other. Tears began to trickle behind the boy's glasses. He tried to ward off the blows but without much success. Many climbed on to their desks to take up Foureyes' chant like spectators at a football match. Miss Ashby grabbed the big bell. Subdued at last, the children were given sums for the rest of the afternoon as punishment for their unruly behaviour.

Ryan trudged home dragging his feet. He reached the top of his road, passed the row of broken-down shops, counting the apple pies on the glass dish in Mrs Jackson's window. Nine. The same number as last week. He waved cheerily and was rewarded with a sad smile. Must be hard sitting there all day with so customers. He felt better for thinking kind thoughts. *Compassion*, that was it. That was what mattered. He had lost his temper with Foureyes and was genuinely sorry. As he approached his house he saw that the bikes were in the usual place. He opened the back door, went over to greet his da, deep in his chair, long legs propped over the arm. He noticed the seat was sinking closer and closer to the ground.

"Jaysus, Ryan, Holy Mary and the Blessed Joseph, why are you so late? That lovely wee girl has been waiting for you. So patent, that she is. Do you not realise that? Sure, it's bad manners of you. You should think yourself lucky that a lovely young girl should take an interest in a lad like you." His dad started to laugh, "Look at the state of you. For the good Lord's sake, why don't you smarten yourself up and put a comb through your hair?" The laughter ended in a fit of coughing.

Ryan patted his father's back, softly at first then vigorously with a clenched fist. After loud protests the coughing died. He wandered into the front room. Nadina sat in her usual place with a glass of lemonade and a biscuit.

"Hello, Ryan. I think you were wise to decline the position," she giggled, "though I did vote for you. I don't really think you're best suited for it." She giggled again.

"So?"

"Your father said I could wait for you. What have you been doing all this time?"

"Will you stop looking at me? I don't mind being your mate, but that's all. You're like a leech, hanging on to me. That big eye's like an octopus' rolling round and round. Don't keep staring, yeah? Where's that big black beetle?" He went to the bottom of the stairs and yelled. "Daphne Brown! Time for you to go. And take your ugly bitch of a sister with you!"

Kathie leaned over the banisters. "Don't you talk to my friend like that. I'll box your ears for you, you ignorant little pig, so help me."

"I'm still going to pray for you, Ryan," said a small voice from the settee. "That you'll learn to show more compassion."

"Terrific!" He ran to the two arm chairs, grabbed the cushions, backed away and hurled them from the window. She giggled and ducked, finally hiding behind the settee, covering her face with her hands. He had two cushions left. He leaned over to bring them down on her head as hard as he could.

The door opened and Daphne came into the room followed by Kathie. "Right then, come on ugly, it's time for us to make a move anyway."

"Goodbye, Ryan," Nadina called with a wave, making her way to the front door.

Ryan, red-faced, sat on the stairs. He was angry: angry with his father, angry at being forced to be a monitor, angry with one-eyed Naddy Brown. He would kill Matthews. That would be his first monitoring task. Get rid of vermin, the fat slug eating and eating, bulging out of his trousers. He'd kick his backside for him. Kenny would pull his arms out of their sockets.

Kathie dragged Ryan back into the room, yelling and clouting him with her fists. "How dare you! Who do you think you are, talking to Daphne like that?"

He sat on the settee, and burst into a wail of grief. Kathie sat next to him.

"I don't know what's wrong with you and I really don't care. You've not said a civil word to anyone for the last fortnight. Anyway, don't you yell at my friends like that ever again, you hear?"

She got up, hesitated, her hand on the door knob. "Ryan, look, I wish I was back home too, but there's no way that's going to happen. This is here and that was there. Al-right, there's the bombing, but think of what we've got now. Our own bedrooms, indoor toilet, space to move around in. Remember what it was like? The stink of the place, all of us squashed up together, rows and rows of those little places like what? Rabbit hutches, packed together like sardines. And Daddy, and Mam, wasn't at all nice for them too, eh?"

He sniffed, took the hankie she held out to him, blew his nose, let the soiled rag drop to the floor. Tentatively, she placed her hand on his shoulder. He stood up, his fists clenched.

"It's not that. Think I want to go back? I hate the Irish. I hate my stupid name and them taking the Mick all the time. And there's Kenny. He keeps calling me names. Fenian bastard, he says. It's al-right for you. You don't mind. I believe in the Crown and the great Empire, all red in the atlas. *Great* Britain. The twenty-fourth of this month is Empire Day. I'm going to hang the Union Jack from my bedroom window. And I don't care what *he* thinks. I want to be British. Not like the damned IRA murdering innocent civilians, killing British soldiers. Only doing their duty – that's what he says about the Jerries."

"That was a long time ago, Rye. Before you and I were even born."

"Sure, it don't make no difference. And that fat Father, I hate him. And don't say it's wrong to hate a priest, 'cause I don't care. He hates all Germans. He was glad them aircrew all died. He's no right to hate. He's a priest. Not right for a priest to hate. Anyway, I don't like church and I don't like fat people, like Father O'Donnell, and that pig-boy monitor with me."

Kathie placed her arm round his shoulders. "Look, Daphne's my closest friend, you know. I know she's loud, and there's that big laugh of hers, gets on my nerves sometimes, but you could at least try to be civil. Show more tolerance, will you? And what have you got against that poor wee girl, huh? She's branded for life with that birthmark. People make fun of her. Daphne says she feels guilty sometimes because her mam and dad make such a fuss of *her* and take no notice of Nadina. It must be awful for her, and you don't seem to care one jot, so you don't. You've got a good friend in Nadina. A girl with a brilliant brain, Ryan. Kathie sighed. "And she really likes you. Al-right, so she's a bit of a drip, but do you have to be so rude?... Oh, what is wrong with you, Ryan? Tell me."

He shook his head, tucked his feet under him. "Nothing. Don't know. I don't know. Nothing." He looked at her. "They made me class monitor."

"Really?" She began to laugh.

"That's right, go on, take the Mick like everyone else. Sure, they only did it for a laugh. That idiot, that Rich Johnson.." He jumped up from the settee, stomped upstairs to his bedroom, put on his gloves and attacked the mattress hanging on the door - and for a good five minutes beat Matthews to a pulp.

Later that evening, taking the big dictionary from under his bed he flicked the pages. He found the T's and read the meaning slowly: *Tolerance: to allow a person to exist without molestation; to endure with forbearance.* The trouble with looking up big words is that they use other big words. But tolerance, like compassion, had a good feel about it. His list was growing.

It seemed that Nadina had taken him at his word, for at school next day she almost ignored him. She had palled up with Dickerson again. He saw they were everywhere together, two ugly ducklings. One with the spotty skin of acne-grief, holes like craters, old clothes you got at jumble sales that stank of big-body odours like armpits, and unwashed clothes and there was Naddy with the branded face. Compassion? Tolerance? Well, he'd try!

The weeks went by and the two girls with their opposite shapes were seen to spend more and more their time together: at break and on the journey home, hand in hand, like lost babes in the woods. Watching them at break, Kenny had important information for Ryan. "See, Fenian," he said, "I read it in last Sunday's *News of the World*. Some women don't go for men at all. They like women best. Reckon Pat likes both. She's what they call a bisexual. Can't say it bothers me much."

Ryan screwed his nose, sniffed, "Wrong, that is." Julie and June in particular agreed with him and said it was disgusting.

After the final bell proclaimed the end of another school day, Miss Ashby called Philip and Ryan back. They stood before her, a gap of three feet between them. "Philip, you know how I feel about bullying, don't you?"

"Yes, Miss Ashby."

"In your capacity as monitor I chose you because I anticipated the highest standards."

"Of course, Miss Ashby. I'm afraid however, that I don't quite see to whom you are referring. What exactly the problem might be?"

"You surprise me. I would have expected you, Philip, particularly, to be more aware of what has been happening. And Ryan?"

She leaned forward. Ryan was conscious of the jumper, the way it proclaimed its assets so immodestly. He wondered if in his new capacity as monitor he should offer some advice. Should he advise her that those bosoms were a constant source of wonder to the boys, yet so embarrassing that you nearly fell over when you got close to them.

"Ryan, pay attention."

"What Miss?"

"I want both of you to have an attitude of protection towards the vulnerable."

"Ryan?"

"See here, Miss. Why's my name's so titchy and him's got capitals, and you've got me right down the bottom corner of the board, so I don't matter the same. Not fair, that isn't."

Miss Ashby sighed. With his unruly hair that seemed permanently to miss contact with a brush and comb, and the wide green, handsome but troubled eyes, and his habit of going into a dream-world, she wondered what problems this boy was carrying. "I know that basically you are a rebel, Ryan, but it seems to Miss Millison and myself that your problem is that you have no real idea what to rebel about. Is that not so?"

"Don't know what you mean. Never wanted the stupid monitor job in the first place, did I?"

Philip stared ahead, a neatly scrubbed boy with a fat healthy glow, seemingly indifferent to the inferior specimen next to him, small and wiry, wrinkling his nose at Philip as if he was giving off a bad odour.

"It's time for you both to exercise compassion. Now look after those two –you know to whom I am referring. Take some responsibility for their welfare, will you, please? They have been causing unpleasant comment, and though it's not so bad now as it was it could easily start again and I don't want to see it happening. Right?" Miss Ashby sighed again, exasperated, as Ryan and Philip walked away in different directions.

Eventually, most of the class ignored the two girls and the crude gestures and cruel sniggers ended.

I will resign at half-term, thought Ryan, 'and that will be that. Nit-Picker Julie can do it. All the way home he whistled, trying to keep his spirits up, the dreadful thoughts of his da pretending to be at the Somme fighting for the British when all the time he'd been IRA As soon as he was old enough he'd sign on. He kicked the ball to Foureyes on the other side of the road, who kicked it back and called out, "You're happy. I like it when you're happy. You make a great monitor thing, you do."

At the sight of that stupid toothy grin and the dribbling tap of a mouth, Ryan would normally have crossed over and belted him a few times, but he was going to go in for compassion big time, tolerance too, and see if it made any difference. So all he said was, "You should go to the optician's, Rich. Have an eye test, get yourself some new glasses so you don't have to spill your food down yourself all the time. Maybe be better at footie if you did an' all." So saying, he hurried home. As usual she was there, waiting.

"Are you a Lezzie?" was his first question as he brought lemonade and biscuits, placing two cushions between himself and Naddy, moving to the far end of the settee.

"What?"

"Bisexual. Kenny thinks Pat is, so maybe you're the same, the way you've gone all lovey-dovey, fondling each other, like holding hands and that." He crouched low peering over the makeshift barrier of wall.

"No, I am not."

"Being monitor, well until half-term, I need respectability in the class. I'm supposed to protect you, but Miss thinks we, fatso Matthews and me, should put a stop to it."

She looked at him wondering if he was joking. Clearly deciding that he wasn't, she said, "Ryan, can you please close the subject? I can assure you that though I like Pat there's nothing like that between us. It's rather horrible of you to make such insinuations."

He chewed on his biscuits, frowning in thought, and said, "You can be what you like."

"Thank you, Ryan. Here's a few words to add to your vocabulary: 'prejudice', 'bigotry' and 'chauvinism'. Enough to be going on with for now."

Chapter Nine

Nadina did find Pat a little too affectionate at times, the way she linked her arm in hers and sometimes squeezing her hand. Other times even wanting to kiss her. Altogether a bit too clingy, to say the least. And though she was desperate for a friend and at times delighted in Pat, Naddy often felt uncomfortable. She didn't care either for the way the tall girl took charge of her, bossed her about, constantly telling her she was getting too religious.

However, all things considered, the one outstanding quality in Pat's favour was her sympathy. Not once did she refer to the birthmark, and when Nadina wept over it, Pat put a long arm round her shoulders and pulled her to her like a big sister. So unlike Daphne. Sadly, often Pat seemed to blow hot then cold. Nadina suspected that the horrible Evett boy had something to do with it. Jealousy, she supposed, though Pat assured her that he didn't mind as long as she didn't leave him out in the cold too long, then slapping Naddy's arm and roaring with unseemly laughter that always made her wince, she added, "If you get my meaning, girl."

She valued the way Pat treated her as if she was a normal person, and not some religious crank. The only one at the school, apart from Thelma Ashby of course. But she was a teacher and that was different.

Pat was the only other person besides Ryan who was allowed into the sanctuary of her bedroom. Here, like a bank's vault with its security codes and impregnable walls, secure as a prison cell from unwelcome visitors, Nadina felt protected. Recently she'd insisted that her father install yet another lock, a mortise this time, to ensure extra protection. No one was allowed to enter without permission, certainly not her mother with her prying eyes rifling through her diaries, nor Daphne with her sneers, and definitely not her father. She could hardly bear to look at him with his cold fish eyes, clipped speech and the jerky movements of his head like a bird hunting for a worm.

Away from the harshness and coldness of an uncaring world, with its cruelties and crudities, she was able to think her private thoughts, plan her future, but always with the help of Jesus, her greatest friend, so real, so loving, so caring, and always so close.

Opposites attract each other, she had read somewhere. Pat was tall and skinny as she was plump and small, so different in so many ways: different shape, different background, different intelligence. Yes – and different morals. But there was one thing beyond anything else they had in common: both were disliked by the rest of the class. She had tried to influence Pat, but she hadn't had much success, any more than with Ryan. For one thing, Pat still didn't go to Mass with any regularity.

One serious defect that contributed to the girl's unpopularity was blatantly obvious to Nadina. And despite Julie Richards wandering around the playground with a clothes peg on the end of her nose, the hint was ignored or failed to impress sufficiently. So in prayer, Nadina asked her Lord for instruction. The answer came clearly: 'subtlety'. And so, after their time together one tea-time, as Pat was leaving, Nadina took a bar of the specially perfumed soap her parents had brought back from their holiday in France before the war. "Smell it, Pat. Isn't it lovely, don't you think?" Yet, though her friend took the soap gratefully, shoving the bar into her raincoat pocket, her unpleasant body odour continued. Yet for all her faults, and in particular her irreligious outlook, Pat was always a good listener. When Nadina tried to explain how she felt about the blemish, her friend listened carefully, nodding and making soothing noises.

One time, she whispered to Pat about her monthly cycle and the shock of the first time. Pat was early too so it was reassuring. They were able to commiserate with each other. "What about your mum?" Pat asked. "Don't she help you like?" Telling her mother hadn't helped at all, Nadina said. She had been ridiculously embarrassed about it, as if it was something dirty. "That's potty. Only natural, that," said Pat, screwing up her nose. Both girls agreed that it was messy and inconvenient, but normal. And then Pat giggled as she told Nadina that Kenny went all funny about it.

Nadina felt duty bound to warn her. "Pat, my belief is that sex is a very special thing, sacred even, and shouldn't be messed about with. It's the teaching of Holy Church. Sex is God's gift to bring children into the world, to bring them up in the Faith, to dedicate them to the Lord. Don't you realise that?" she asked, immediately regretting her reprimand when Pat reacted angrily.

"God's sake, girl! Much as I like you, you're getting far too religious, you are, and it's not just me what thinks it. Everyone says so. There's not one that don't. I mean, my God, fancy you thinking you're going to get off with Ryan Brannigan, a real heathen, him!"

Wishing she had not confided her liking for Ryan, Nadina blushed.

Quietening down, Pat told her that when she grew up, she'd want lots of babies.

"Not with Kenny, surely?"

Pat shrieked with laughter. "What him? Not likely," nudging Nadina as they sat side by side on the edge of the bed. Then she said, frowning, "You don't half take yourself seriously, girl. Him and me, how can you think that? We're only kids, aren't we?"

Letting down her guard as the atmosphere relaxed, Nadina told her friend about her parents, how she couldn't talk to them, especially her father. She acknowledged, her head bent, that she hated them, well not hated exactly, that was very wrong, but disliked them intensely. She'd love to have a mum with whom she could share things, chat anytime, day or night, talk about things that mattered, "Like you and your mum, Pat," she said, thinking they were more like sisters than mother and daughter. Nadina gave a big sigh. "My parents are always spying on me, you know? That's why I have all the locks put on the door. I carry the keys with me in my satchel."

Pat's mum was a bit of a rough diamond. Nadina tried not to be put off by the bad language, which made her wince every time she heard it, but Mrs Dickerson was full of fun and so often brought a smile to Nadina's face, so that when she was at Pat's place she lost some of her self-consciousness. The

Dickersons' home was dirty and messy; everything higgledy-piggledy. It was even worse than the Brannigan's, which was saying something. Still, cleanliness wasn't everything as she often told her over-hygienic conscious mother. Mr and Mrs Dickerson (*'Call us Rog and Val for God's sake! We don't stand on ceremony here, Nadina, don't you worry about that.)* never put on airs and graces, never behaved as if they were superior to everyone else. Pat's home was a proper home, not all showy where you felt unable to relax. Pat could have the wireless on as loud as she liked and they could all have a good laugh.

"Are my breasts too big do you think?" she asked Pat one tea-time. "They flop all over the place when I run. I hate PE with the boys staring at them."

"A nice size," Pat said. "Not as big as Miss Ashby's but getting that way."

"Oh, Pat, you don't think so, do you?"

Then Pat guffawed, and slapped her arm in the usual way. Nadina smiled as friends should and tried not to mind. Again, Pat told her to stop taking herself so seriously. "You're... what's it called? Sensitive, that's it. Extra sensitive. I know it's a lot to do with the way them kids bully you. Yeah, really horrible to you, but you should try ignoring them. Always worry about what people think, you do. Me, I couldn't give a monkey's." To illustrate her independent attitude, she tossed her short ginger hair from side to side and folded her arms.

"Did you like the soap I gave you?" Nadina asked, but Pat ignored the question as if she hadn't heard and went on to say, "You're scared of your own shadow, you are."

Nadina told her she that she was hoping for a place at the Convent School of the Holy Name. What would clinch it would be a recommendation from their priest, from Father O'Donnell. You had to have a letter. You wouldn't stand a chance without it, she said.

"Religion is the most important thing in my life, Pat."

For some reason the remark made Pat particularly incensed. She left her half-eaten biscuit, quickly swallowed her glass of lemonade and strode to the door, telling Nadina she was a stuck-up pious prig, full of herself, and worse than anything else, a religious nutter.

They had fallen out for quite a time after that. In fact it was well over a month before Pat came to her house again, and so Nadina, perplexed, now renewed her concern for Ryan, turning up frequently at one hundred and three, Harefield Road.

Chapter Ten

May 24th: From his bottom drawer Ryan took out the tattered Union Jack he'd bargained from the junk shop owner at the top of the road and smuggled home, tucked under his jersey. He'd spotted it wrapped round an old cello two years earlier when he and Kathie went with their father to buy the wireless.

There wasn't much of a breeze. Hanging the flag from his bedroom window it flapped listlessly against the wall as if lacking enthusiasm. Outside, he looked up from the half dozen square yards of patchy lawn and solemnly saluted. He knew the retired schoolteachers next door would be pleased, and the people whose garden backed onto theirs, they too would see the sign of the glorious Empire, and blind Miss Hollis on the other side, someone would tell her. Didn't matter what Kathie said either.

Didn't care if *he* saw it. He was IRA, plotted murder, killed people. He could never ever trust him again.

The sight of the flag had embittered Fergus for the rest of the day. When he told Ryan to take it down, he refused. "It's the 24th May, Dad. Empire Day, in case you didn't know."

As the bombing became less frequent, so press interest in Father O' Donnell's vituperative attacks against Germany and all things German began to tail off. However, he was not to be silenced. The pulpit at Sunday Mass still provided a launch pad for his abusive oratory.

Fergus, an expression of disgust on his craggy features, watched from his usual place in the church. How could a priest be so contemptuous of a whole nation? And be so love-struck with the Brits?

The division was clear, the priest avowed. It was a case of good versus evil. "We, the English, are on the side of righteousness: we, the Catholic Church of England, provide the spiritual foundation for the nation, while the Germans - and let's be frank about this: every individual German from the cradle to the grave is an avowed enemy of our country - a people who deserve nothing but utter contempt." He then repeated a favoured slogan from his exalted position, fifteen feet above contradiction, agitatedly waving his arms, saying more than once during the course of a lengthy homily, "The only good German is a dead German," requesting the congregation to join with him.

At first the congregation hesitated, but holding Father O'Donnell in such high esteem, they soon responded, the mantra ending with a burst of applause, hesitant at first, before gathering momentum. It was all Fergus could do to stop himself from walking out. The man is a traitor of the worse kind, he thought, indifferent to the suffering of his people: a turncoat on the side of the occupier.

Ryan shuffled along the pew until half obscured by a stone pillar. As was his custom, he drifted off into a semi-comatose state, occasionally seeking distractions: a new word he had heard related by Nadina, rehearsing its meaning. He might pull faces at the righteous Philip, resplendent in his red robes as he bowed low before the fat Father, prancing about with his usual air of self-importance. Mostly, Ryan stared ahead, imagining he was elsewhere. Scurrying back to his place after receiving the Sacrament, his thighs in his short trousers sticky against the pew, impure thoughts of the Greengage girl would trouble him. But also, throughout the length of the liturgy, Ryan was aware of Naddy Brown, seated behind Greengage, with her mad parents, the one shiny blue eye casting hopeful glances in his direction.

The Mass ended, Fergus filed out surrounded by the usual cluster of O'Donnell admirers. He tried to avoid the outstretched hand. "Brannigan, a moment of your time, please, if you will."

Fergus stopped. Hostility arose like a fire in his belly. He longed for a cigarette to calm him. Ignoring the priest, he hurried towards the door.

"Brannigan," the priest called.

He turned round and swallowed. "You wish to speak with me, Father?"

"Indeed, I do. Now, is that lad of yours serious about Confirmation? It's important that I should know."

"As far as I can tell, he is that, Father."

The fat cheeks of the priest reddened. He took two steps forward to ensure that the conversation was not overheard. "It's obvious that he shows little interest. This morning I see him in his customary place hiding behind a pillar as if hiding from the Truth. Brannigan, please understand. Your son needs to hear the Church's teaching so he can obey it. In short, he needs to be more attentive. At Catechism he is ill-disciplined, restless, irreverent, rebellious and sets a very poor example to the rest of the children. Please understand it is your responsibility as his father to take him in hand. You received my letter I take it?"

Fergus had tossed the complaining missive, countersigned by the Head, into the coke hod for burning. His reply was indistinct, but the barely visible shrug of the shoulders was not missed by his son watching from the door. Now, aware that he was the subject of discussion, Ryan hid behind a grave stone. Fergus, swearing softly, limped up to him. Ryan held the cane while his father lit a cigarette. He drew hungrily on it, then said, "So, I take it your body's here but your soul is anywhere and everywhere else, that it?" Fergus sighed. "The Father thinks you care damn-all about getting Confirmed. Is that right now?"

The response was a slow shrug of his shoulders. "Don't know. No idea. Can't say I'm that bothered, no."

His father took the cane off him and the two began the walk home. Deep in thought, Fergus said, "Look, son. These priests, they have the power, influence, understand me? You leave school, you try for a job. You need references. A priest is respected by the bosses, they take his word. So... you get on the right side of them." He looked at the boy by his side. "You get yourself Confirmed, and maybe a priest can give you good references. Understand?"

Ryan nodded. "Kathie says we're here and this is our country now. I don't want to go back home, not anymore. It's why I hung the flag up, to remind me where I belong. And I'm sorry if you didn't like it... Dad, I'm not a Brit-lover and I don't hate the Germans, I'm on the side of compassion."

Fergus frowned, saw Ryan looking up at him, nervous, as though unsure what the response might be. "You've got to play your cards correctly now, son, stop upsetting him. You've got to think about your future."

The two continued to walk in silence, each with his own thoughts.

Chapter Eleven

Two significant events were about to occur, Miss Ashby told Class Six. So important they would change their lives forever: one concerned the mind, the other the soul.

Philip Matthews, who had made himself a cardboard badge clearly displaying the word 'Monitor', written in gold lettering and attached by safety pin to a colourful purple pullover, was asked, "Is one more important than the other?"

At the little teacher's invitation, he waddled without hesitation out to the front to reply, beaming with pleasure. "Well, Miss Ashby, I would say that our Confirmation concerns the immortal soul, the Scholarship is about the mind. But I would say that both are of equal importance."

"Well put. Thank you, Philip. You may return to your seat."

Kenny and Ryan linked ankles. Tojo, sitting behind, leaned forward, arms outstretched, and with great presence of mind managed to catch the fat boy as he fell.

Friday came round again and Miss Ashby, now at the head of the straggling column, Miss Millison otherwise occupied, led them along the usual route and into the gloomy church. The huge barn of the place, the wooden rafters, the drifting clouds of incense, the dim lighting, inevitably gave a feeling of remoteness, spookiness, even. "Yeah, like it's being haunted," said Foureyes. A thump in the back was the immediate response from Ryan.

"Churches don't get haunted, you dope," Ryan told him scornfully. Kenny's long arm reached past to add a slap to the small boy's head.

Thirty-four pairs of feet echoed on the stone floor as they made their way to the front pews. They stared at the vestry door waiting for Father O'Donnell to make his entrance. Ahead, a narrow staircase going round and round like a corkscrew reminded Ryan of a lighthouse. This was where Father O'Donnell puffed his way up to deliver the homily. Still further back, the altar with its twelve tall candles to remind them of the Lord's twelve brave and faithful apostles. The spitting flames were the 'Light of Judgement,' the priest frequently declared at Catechism class, "These flames are the holy fire that will burn to cinders the darkness of your black souls."

In the centre, the Saviour looked reproachfully at them. "He is the One, more special than anyone who's ever lived. "He," thundered the priest at the Catechumens, pointing at the dejected figure "will constantly remind you how small and insignificant you are."

They stared back, eyes widening in fear.

Waiting, they continued to gaze about them, noticing the plaster statues of Peter, John, Mary the Virgin, Mary Magdalene and other followers of the Lord positioned around the church on window sills, little nooks in the walls and on small tables covered in clean white cloths.

At last the vestry door squeaked open and the portly figure of Father O' Donnell appeared. All talking stopped as if a wand had been waved. He plodded towards them, his eyes focussed on Ryan, who was recovering from his usual sneezing fit. The explosions, at first loud enough to burst ear drums, slowly petered out like the fizz from a damp firework. The priest waited expectantly for his greeting.

"Good afternoon, Father," said Miss Ashby, standing amongst the girls. No bigger than any of them, apart from the size of her boobs, thought Ryan, though Naddy Brown's might even be bigger, kind of deformed, them are, he thought.

On cue the pupils stumbled to their feet, some dropping their Catechism booklets in their nervousness. "Good afternoon, Father," they all said, chirping like canaries.

"Good afternoon," he replied. He belched, putting his hand to his mouth, explaining by way of apology that it had been the strawberry flan that Mrs Henderson, his housekeeper, had cooked for his midday meal. "Has a habit of repeating on me," he said with a faint suspicion of a smile. He made slow circular motions with his hand over the bulge of his stomach that listed over his belt like a ship listing badly, about to sink. The smile hovering on the corner of his lips now broadened out. There was a noticeably relaxed atmosphere, unusual as the Father rarely showed any sign of humour. "Very delicious, my housekeeper's cooking," he said. The children looked at Miss Ashby, to gauge how they should respond. She gave a grim smile. A few of the children tittered.

That afternoon, he said, he would explain the significance of the Mass, stress the importance of the Sacrament of Holy Confirmation, and say something also about the significance of the priesthood. In order that they should have the assurance of heaven, be confirmed in their faith, there was need for a thorough preparation. The means of preparation, he told them, was Sacramental Confession. "Think of me, if you like, as God's surgeon. I will be conducting a delicate operation on your eternal souls, cutting out all that is hindering your progress towards eternity."

Open-mouthed they stared back, a frown on every brow.

He strolled between the two rows each side of the aisle brandishing his podgy finger in their faces like a sword. They followed its progress wondering where it might settle, concluding that Ryan Brannigan would likely find himself the final target.

He would invite them, the priest said, to share any doubts or misgivings they might have during the operation. "The thing to remember," he said, "is that things can sometimes go wrong. An operation can be a botched job. We want you to come through successfully into good health. That is what Our dear Lord requires. Therefore, He wants absolute honesty, not covering anything up, not holding anything back however disgraceful and offensive. You can be absolutely straight with me. I shall not flinch from the task. Think of the surgeon's knife making a deep incision cutting out all foreign matter. So is the sword of the Spirit that I shall wield. Write down all your filth on a piece of paper. Rehearse what you are going to say.

Bring your paper with you."

The sword of Damocles hovered over Ryan Brannigan and remained poised motionless like an angel of death.

Ryan toyed with his penknife in his pocket. One thrust and the knife would penetrate the big belly right to the hilt. He'd let it stay in and the blade would go rusty. He's fat and ugly and eats of the fat of the land while the peasants starve. Bet *you* never know what it's like to go hungry, thought Ryan. His father never tired of telling them of the terrible potato blight that swept Ireland in the last hundred years when thousands of the peasants starved to death. "I was a young lad then, but I'll never forget," he would say. "Sure, the only food we ate was potato." At the dinner table he would fork two or three and hold them out as a visual aid. "And even when the spuds got bad, we still had to eat them. Was there anything else to fill our bellies?" Ryan and Kathie would shake their heads. "Your grand-daddy dropped dead where he fell, tilling the good earth. Now, on the outside these tatties, they looked al-right, but inside, inside, you see, they were rotten. Potato famine, 1845 to 1848. Don't you ever forget those dates, Ryan, nor you, Kathie. They're part of Ireland's long heartbreaking history, so they are. The English occupiers did that. Did they show compassion? Mercy?" Again brother and sister would solemnly shake their heads. The oration would end with the waiting potatoes speedily disappearing down their father's throat.

The Catechesis continued, the priest moving back and forth along the rows, sometimes raising his voice, but more often lowering it, placing two fingers to his lips and speaking in little more than a whisper. He wanted, he said that afternoon, to emphasise the holy calling of the priest. "This is a teaching I have not given before. The priest's calling is a particularly taxing vocation," he continued, still maintaining a low voice, but adopting a slightly menacing tone, "particularly when I am trying to teach undisciplined children of the Kelliwell Road Catholic Elementary who will not pay attention!"

To Ryan the priest's voice was the sound of a soft and gentle lullaby and he was back in Ireland in his crib. His eyes glazed over, unaware that he was one of the causes of the priest's difficulties, oblivious to the raised eyebrows and the frown on the heavy features.

Glaring at the somnolent offender, Father O'Donnell asked him to repeat the last sentence. Interested, the children waited, their heads turning, wondering what the outcome of this latest altercation might be.

Ryan shook his head. "Can't remember, Father. I'm truly sorry, sir, I am that."

"A candidate who cannot keep awake shows little readiness for the Sacrament of Holy Confirmation, Miss Ashby," the priest turned to her. She stretched her plump arm round behind Foureyes' shoulders and with her fist gave the reluctant candidate a smart crack to the side of his head.

"Well?"

"What... Father?"

"Do you think you are a suitable candidate?"

Ryan shook his head.

"What does that mean? Stand up boy when I speak to you!"

Ryan moved fast. Rubbing the side of his head, he blinked, grasping Foureyes' shoulder to stop himself falling. "See Father, being Confirmed and all that, I'm not sure." He cleared his throat, "Like you was telling my dad. Last Sunday at Mass it were, you said I weren't ready." Ryan drew in his breath. Then, blurted out, this time daring to look the priest in the eye, "Because to be honest with you, Father, I don't know what I believe no more." A buzz of excitement swept over the children.

"Sit down. Listen, boys and girls. I've told his father that he is a disruptive influence and a fool. Ryan Brannigan would know the truth of the Faith if he said his prayers, which I doubt he does, made a regular monthly Confession, which I know he does not, and when attending Mass paid attention instead of slinking behind a pillar where he thinks no one can see him. So, boys and girls, if he doesn't believe, there is only one person to blame, and who is that?"

Some of the class wondered if they should respond at that point, but there was no time to consider, for the priest shouted at Ryan, "Get out of my sight. Go to the wall!"

Father O'Donnell now smiled reassuringly at the long lines of children crammed into the pews, their shoulders and knees touching. They smiled to each other, listening to the echo of Ryan's footsteps as he strolled over to the west wall, adopting his boxer's walk, rolling his shoulders like a sailor on the deck of a ship in a storm. Behind him, the tone of the priest's voice was friendly and confidential as if addressing a conference of clergy. "We mustn't take that boy too seriously, must we? He is one of you, yet at the same time he's not one of you at all, because he does not listen to the teachings of Holy Church."

Ryan, isolated like a condemned prisoner waiting to be executed, hopped from one foot to the other and tried not to fall over while the priest continued his lecture on the meaning of the Mass and its significance, the services they were expected to attend and all the Holy days of Obligation. During Lent they were expected to obey a rule of fasting.

After their indoctrination there was relief that school was over for another week. With the weekend ahead the children poured out of church onto the pavement. Some walked, others ran. They giggled at the jokes they told, while a few, isolated and subdued, walked alone, heads bowed.

Looking behind him as he left the building, Ryan noticed Miss Ashby in conversation with Father O'Donnell. Me as usual, he thought, pausing to tie a shoelace. Maybe they'll not want me on Fridays no more. He noticed the eye rolling in his direction, with one half-mouth covered, the other half smiling.

Chapter Twelve

Nadina always enjoyed the Catechism instruction, admiring Father's ability to communicate the teaching of Holy Church. If she ever became a teacher – a Convent school of course – she would owe so much to him: his patience, skill, and of course his dramatic gifts that helped to implant the Truth, though she doubted if any but a small minority really grasped what he was talking about.

That Friday she had been particularly annoyed. Ryan's rudeness was becoming far too frequent. Such a show-off. An attention seeker of the worst kind, as Thelma Ashby had said. True. Though he could be very funny. She had laughed along with the rest at some of his antics: those awful sneezing fits immediately he came into church, and some of his remarks were quite hilarious. But the way he argued and contradicted Father, showing not one iota of respect, was breathtaking in its audacity. Secretly though, she could not but admire his fearlessness. The memory of him clutching his Catechism booklet, red in the face and pulling his ridiculous faces at the rest of the class brought a rare smile.

Now she clutched the tear-drenched pillow and sank further down into her bed, trying desperately to forget.

Towards the end of the session, she had become aware than she was feeling more and more uncomfortable. What an idiot! Always take precautions, she had told herself - and promptly forgotten. Why, oh why hadn't she dealt with it in the lunch hour, the ideal opportunity?

When everyone else was hurrying home, she had stayed sitting in the pew. Ryan, the very last to leave, gave her one of his funny looks, banging the door behind him quite unnecessarily. Attention seeking again. That was always Father's job, closing the door, locking it carefully, putting the key back in its place on a ledge on the window sill behind near the altar.

Assuring herself that everyone in Class Six had indeed left, Nadina had raised a tremulous hand to attract her teacher's attention. Thelma, dear Thelma Ashby, with the eager smile just for her, hurried over, perhaps imagining that as so often in the past, she had lingered behind to question something the priest had taught for further enlightenment. Now Father was distracted, picking up some of the booklets that her classmates had carelessly dropped, gave her the opportunity. Red-faced with embarrassment, Nadina had whispered her predicament to the concerned teacher.

Thelma had told her not to worry about it. She would ask Father O'Donnell and was sure everything would be fine. Nadina could use his bathroom and Father would probably be able to run her home afterwards, she'd said. Looking up, Nadina had seen the two adults talking, glancing in her direction. She'd bowed her head, covering her face, a deepening crimson, with her hands.

"Come with me, child," he had said, smiling at her in a kindly way. So she'd followed him back to his house. So massive with its tall chimneys and the slate roof that seemed to stretch for miles. She had only seen the presbytery from the outside before. There must be loads of rooms. No wonder his housekeeper always looked so miserable with so many to clean.

Still smiling, Father O'Donnell had opened his front door. She wished he'd smile more often at the class, then reminded herself that priests needed always to be serious. Opposite, a little in front of her, was a big winding staircase.

"Right then, Nadina," he had said. "At the top, right along the landing and it's the last door facing you at the very end."

"I'm so sorry, Father. Thank you." And she had run up the highly polished staircase, not daring to stop, barely noticing the large oil paintings of important looking dignitaries, bishops and cardinals adorning the walls. "No hurry, Nadina," she heard him call. "Take your time, dear."

She mustn't be long, dared not linger. She had hurried along the wide landing, beautifully carpeted, counting the doors. At least seven! Then facing her as Father had said, right at the far end, the bathroom, his bathroom. At last!

Now, the memories so vivid, Nadina turned over for the hundredth time. The sweat-soaked sheets smelt so disgusting. She leaned across to the bedside table, switched on the light, glanced at her mantelpiece. Two o'clock. Groaning, she tried to shut out the voice that pounded her brain, telling it to stop, "Not my fault, not mine, never, never." But the accusation continued.

"Please, please...." She twisted and turned, sobbing in the silence.

Turning on her back, she gazed up at the ceiling. White, pure, virginal. The bedroom walls were white too, the faintest pink from a rose-petal pattern just below the surface made for a pleasing softness against the room's pristine cleanliness. She turned her bedside light off then immediately on again, got out of bed, stumbled to the landing and groped her way to the toilet, hoping she would not be heard as she retched over the bowl. Back into bed, she tugged the sheets tightly round her for protection. She sat up. The thumping of her heart was so loud she was sure Daphne would hear from her bedroom opposite. Nadina covered her face with her hands. If only she could block it all out, bury it like a body in Holy Innocents' churchyard.

"Oh, dear Lord and Saviour, help me!" She reached for the glass on her bedside table. Her hand shook and the water spilled onto the floor. She saw the calendar pinned to her door. There it was, *her* day. She had ringed it in red ink. The most special day of her life: Holy Confirmation! A day seeing to be of greater significance than her own birthday.

Ruined, like a blot of ink on a clean page. The thought brought fresh tears.

The candidates had been told they should choose a favourite saint they could identify with, and she'd chosen Mary.

"No. I've always fancied her," Pat had said.

How could *she* be Mary the Virgin? Nadina had thought. It was absurd, an insult, the disgusting way she carried on with that Evett boy. But Pat had gone into a sulk and they had fallen out yet again, so to keep Pat's friendship, a compromise had been reached: they would both choose the Blessed Virgin.

But that was all before....

She lay down again, her face in the pillow, fists clenching and unclenching. Then over on to her back, tears spilling down her cheeks, recalling in its horrific detail, trying to purge her soul from the guilt, though again she told the voice in her head, 'No! It wasn't my fault. Not my fault. Never!'

Yet again she saw herself opening Father's bathroom door, stepping up to the toilet, admiring the mammoth-sized bath with its gold taps, well, probably gold-plated, but still very nice. Ahead of her, a huge wash basin, again with bright gold taps. Yes, everything big scale, and though her own house was a good size, the presbytery completely dwarfed it.

She had washed carefully then dried herself as best she could with toilet paper, not daring to use Father O'Donnell's big white towels hanging on the rail. Fancy having to go to a priest's house to use his toilet, she thought. She pulled the chain, adjusting her underwear. Then, holding carefully onto the banisters, she walked downstairs.

He was waiting, smiling up at her, "All done?" And she had replied, conscious that she was blushing, "I'm sorry. Thank you, Father."

"Think nothing of it," was all he had said. Nothing more, and she had walked past him to the door, for the big car was there parked in the drive and she had wanted to get home, to put all the embarrassment behind her. She had waited at the door, reached up for the latch. He had not moved. She had looked over her shoulder. He was still there, smiling at her. She had reached up again, but the latch was too stiff. "Father," she had said, "I'd like to get home, please." She had heard his footsteps coming up behind her, and then....

She had stopped quite still, unable to believe it. It was just a light touch, so light she had scarcely felt it, but she knew. Her fingers shook as she pulled the door open. And this time, there was no mistaking his touch on her bottom. Twice. She whirled round, astonished. He pushed the door shut with his foot. Then, stupidly, absurdly, she had blurted out, her face flushed, "I am in the manner with women."

"What on earth... ?"

She had stood still, her mouth open, unable to speak. He frowned, then his shoulders began to shake and he held his head back and laughed. Laughed so much, he started to cough.

Now on his knees, his face level with hers, he had whispered, "What a little gem you are, Nadina Brown." He cleared his throat, heaved himself up and said in a normal voice, "Would you like a cup of tea?"

She stared, then gave a brief smile. Why did she smile? What had made her smile? He put his two hands on her shoulders. She remembered thinking how large they were. She tried hard not to flinch, or wriggle, just stood so still and silent as if turned to stone. "Come along, dear," he had said, "let's ask the good Mrs Henderson to make us a pot, shall we?"

Trance-like, she had followed him along the hallway, detached as if it was not happening to her but to someone else. He had stopped outside a door. Opposite were concrete steps that looked as though they led to a cellar or basement. She should have said there and then, "No, thank you, Father, I need to get home now," but she didn't.

He called out, "Mrs Henderson, Mrs Henderson!" Then, opening the door of the room for her, he clattered down the concrete steps still calling for the housekeeper. Over his shoulder, he said, "Make yourself at home, Nadina, dear."

She listened to his footsteps, while she took stock of her surroundings. Like all the rooms in this house, big, very big. Each of the walls lined with bookshelves from floor to ceiling. She walked over to the big desk by the large window that looked out into the back garden. An expensive looking rug, a Persian, in the centre of the room. On the desk a lot of books and papers scattered untidily. This is his study, she thought. She wandered up and down past the hundreds and hundreds of volumes. Most looked very old, but others much newer. For the next five minutes she was distracted, taking in the sights and smells. She never realised books could smell so wonderful, sniffing the leather-bound tomes, running her fingers over the titles, marvelling at their age and value. Must be wonderful to have a room like this. Her father's study was so tiny. She crossed over to the stone fireplace. Here, on the mantelpiece, a photograph of a younger Father O'Donnell along with three other priests, all smiling and happy. Next to it, a more recent picture of him with a bishop, outside Holy Innocents' church. Other photographs of rural scenes, probably taken back in Ireland, she thought. Then a long photograph of lots and lots of young priests, some seated, others standing outside a huge old building that looked like a college. She tried to spot which one was Father O'Donnell.

She jumped as the door swung open. He was carrying a tray loaded with two cups and saucers, plates, milk in a jug, sugar, teapot and a delicious looking sponge cake. He placed it on top of his desk, hurriedly clearing a space and gestured towards the large settee in front of the hearth. She sat down. Astonished more than scared she watched as he knelt in front of her again, this time placing his hands on her knees. Now she was too frightened to speak, simply stared back. Reaching up one hand, he swept her hair back then placed his lips on the mark. They felt sticky. She shivered. "Father, I've got to go," she stammered, finding her voice at last, starting to get up. "Mother's expecting me."

He gave no answer, pushed her down. Still holding back her hair, the palm of his other hand ran up and down the blemish again and again. "Ah, what a treasure, what a little treasure you are," he said, then suddenly he pressed his lips on hers.

Her eyes filled up, tears slowly drifting down her cheeks.

Holding on to each knee again, he propelled himself up, smiling down at her. "I can't help noticing you, Nadina, dear. Always so prompt in answering questions whenever I ask them. So attentive at Mass. Always a pleasure to see *you*. Mark my words you'll go far. Indeed, a very long way."

He moved over to his desk, picked up a spoon and began to stir the tea. "Time for refreshment, I do declare. Shall I be mother?" He turned round to grin. By return she gave a faltering smile.

While he cut the sponge cake, putting a large piece on each of the plates, for something to say, she asked, her voice shaking, "Have you read all those books?"

He laughed. "Well, some but certainly not all. Not all by any means."

He handed her a cup and plate. She had to use both hands, tea was spilling into the saucer. He took the plate off her, placed it on a small table by the settee. Then he heaved his bulk down beside her and smiling to himself, sipped his tea while she tried to drink hers.

"Well, you know, Nadina, there aren't many perks in this job, but I suppose there are some. He leaned back, turned his face toward her. "After all, there's you. And you know, you are not only exceptionally intelligent, but so lovely, Nadina." His big moon-shaped face closed in on hers as he whispered, "Never be ashamed of it, Nadina. God will bless you through it." He took a large bite of his sponge.

"How?" She was angry. Furious that a stranger, for indeed he was a stranger, a totally different Father O'Donnell from the one she had known, should kiss the mark without permission. Then, aware of her rage, in a softer voice she repeated her question, "How, Father?"

He sighed. "All suffering has a potentially redemptive quality about it."

She looked at him sharply. "What's that supposed to mean?"

He coughed, slurped his tea, just like Fergus Brannigan did when she went to Ryan's house, but unlike Ryan's father, who was a big joker, never took her suffering lightly. "You are truly a lovely child."

"No, I'm not," she said crossly, taking her plate, crumbling the sponge as she tried to eat, spilling most of it down her dress. "I don't feel lovely. I don't ever. And I want to go home."

"So you shall, so you shall." His voice a little more than a whisper, his rheumy blue eyes inches away gazing into hers, he said, "Never fear, God will bless others through your birthmark, Nadina, dear. You must learn to embrace it."

She stood up then, slammed her cup and saucer down on the little table and cried out, hands over her face, sobbing. She looked down at her cup, tea had slopped into her saucer and on to the table. "Please, Father. I need to go home. Now."

He stood, pulling her to him, his lips on hers, while his other hand began to loosen the bow at the back of her dress. Terrified, she screamed, "Stop! Stop, Father. Father, please. Where's Mrs Henderson?"

"Out of the way, God bless the old hag. At the shops. Oh, you're so lovely. So lovely."

She fell backwards on to the settee. Felt his sour breath on her face. A huge face, red, coarse, covering hers. She pushed him back, freeing her lips. But his face closed in again. The big bulbous nose with the thin blue veins of the broken capillaries like little tributaries of a river, pressed into her face. His fingers were moving fast, the bow came undone. She stood up, trembling, her dress on the floor at her feet. He pushed her down on the settee, his body across hers, he was gasping, his fat fingers fumbling with her knickers. She cried out in terror and pain.

Eventually, Father O'Donnell lurched to his feet, breathing heavily. Adjusting his cassock, he looked down at her cringing on the floor. "Little bitch," he murmured. He hurried back to his desk, picked up his glasses and sat behind it. He motioned to a chair opposite his. "Come over and sit by me. I have something very advantageous to say to you."

Pulling up her knickers and scrambling into her dress she clutched herself, sat as directed, shaking with fear and pain, face awash with tears. Now his whole manner changed. The voice was the church voice, the preaching voice, the Catechism voice, as if the last few minutes had never taken place.

"Now, Nadina," he said, looking sternly at her over his glasses. "Your parents have recognised your very understandable desire to attend Holy Name Convent School. It's going to be a very tough assignment for you. You do realise that? You will need to attain the very highest marks in the Scholarship examination. That's the first requirement. The second will be the interview with Mother Clare, the Mother Superior and Headmistress. The third necessity will be even more vital. This will be my personal recommendation. Now, Nadina, I can promise you that I'm going to give you all the support you'll need. As I've said, when I come to your Assembly, and more recently to give Catechism instruction, I notice that you show an unusual depth of spiritual perception. I've spoken to the Head about it and she agrees with me that this facility is extremely rare is someone so young." He smiled as she shook her head. "Oh yes, indeed. Whose hand is it that shoots up every time to answer my questions with such alertness? And very serious questions, they are too. Usually it's your hand, possibly Philip's, Cynthia Peal's perhaps, but rarely anyone else's. Now, I understand your aptitude for serious work - in all subjects, according to Miss Millison. As far as the Faith is concerned you reveal a strong desire to know more. Now, Nadina," he stood up, pushing his chair to one side, "what I propose is this. I'm going to suggest to your parents that I give you extra tuition to prepare you for your future. Your parents' agreement is necessary of course. But how say you?" He leaned forward and smiled.

She lifted up a tear stained face, shaking her head. After a moment she mumbled, "I don't know. I don't know. I want to...go home."

"Nadina, you will no doubt achieve a very good result for the Scholarship, but Mother Clare is not only looking for brain power, if you'll forgive me for expressing it rather crudely, but for depth of spiritual awareness. Oh, it's a truly a wonderful opportunity, Nadina. You will go far, not only in the secular sphere, for you are doubtless university material, but in the religious life. Do you know what that might mean?"

She looked down, twisting her handkerchief, and whispered, "I don't know."

"Nadina, dear. I'm sure the convent school will give you that very important first chance for your future, whatever path you may choose."

She sighed deeply, shuddered and taking her hankie, blew her nose, wiped her eyes, cleared her throat and repeated, "I want... want... want... to go home."

"Well, it will be the best support I can give you. Do you know Cynthia Peal's sister?"

She shook her head, then nodded.

"A bright girl, though not of course in the same category as yourself. I wrote Margaret a personal letter of recommendation for her to hand to Mother Clare at her interview." He paused. "Now, you've yet to give me your answer, haven't you?"

She clutched her stomach, her voice a little clearer. "I want... want... to go home."

"Well, of course. But don't leave it too long. Time is of the essence here. Come on then. Off we go. I'll run you home as I promised Miss Ashby."

She ran down the hall in front of him. Silently he reached over her head, opened the front door, then led the way down the three steps to his car. She tried to get into the back, but he motioned her to sit next to him in the front. "Comfortable, isn't it? A Rover. I bought it from an old priest. Now in purgatory." He crossed himself then switched on the engine and in silence drove the three odd miles to her house. She was breathing quickly, bent double, clutching herself, then staring out of the window to hide her tears. She always felt uncomfortable with silences. It was the same at home with *him*, gobbling his dinner, chatting away to Daphne, ignoring her, starchy and aloof. Mother bustling about with her fake cheeriness.

Ten minutes later, Father O'Donnell had pulled up at the bottom of her drive, reached across, opened the door, letting his hand fall on her knee as he did so. "God bless you, Nadina," he said. "I shall be praying that you won't neglect this opportunity."

She shook her head and was about to step out of the car when he said. "I'm sorry. I never meant to hurt you, Nadina, but you struggled so much." Then in a harsh voice, he added, "I'd advise you to keep the little matter to yourself. Will you do that?"

In silence she got out of the car, stumbled up the gravel drive. He called out after her as she ran. "And say a prayer for your old priest, will you, dear?"

Chapter Thirteen

The early sun peeped through the gap in the curtains to form flitting shadows on the bedroom wall. Birds calling and the distant sound of a car engine being cranked up filtered into Nadina's consciousness. She blinked, rubbed her sore eyes and glanced at the clock. Seven-thirty.

"Come on, Nadina!" That silly voice calling up from the foot of the stairs made her grit her teeth. She tumbled to the floor, crawled like a centenarian - and an unfit one at that - towards her wardrobe where the bloodied underwear lay in a discarded, disgusting heap. She sat before her dressing table, every muscle and sinew aching, and touched the hideous deformity that he had caressed and kissed with his sticky lips and stinking breath. Despite her abhorrence, the memory of the touch lingered; the soft tones of his voice soothed. Suddenly, hatred rose from the pit of her stomach. She heaved, stomach churning, swallowed and hurried to the toilet.

Returning to her room she took the cup of tea her mother had brought her and mumbled her thanks. Her mother's weight sagged the bed like a sinking ship in a storm. "I suggest you come straight home from school. You look dreadful. Oh, if only I could understand you, Nadina. You just don't communicate. Look at Daphne, chirping on about everything: Captain of the Junior Netball team; in her House swimming team; good-natured, really fun to be with. And you? You're like a stranger. No, don't turn your head away when I'm talking to you, please. Your silences are not only rude, they're so unnatural. In fact, your father says they are disruptive. You don't talk, you don't communicate. In a world of your own, aren't you? Some sort of fantasy world of your own making. Oh, dear God." Her mother bent over to offer a rare kiss. Nadina jerked her head. The sloppy lips plunged into the pillow.

Her mother flounced away and Nadina staggered into the bathroom, filled the basin to the brim and plunged her face into the cold water. Back in her bedroom dressing was painful and slow, every item of clothing tender to the skin.

At breakfast she sat sullenly, refused her Kellogs, forked her egg and bacon around the plate then rushed away from the table, stumbled up the stairs and into the toilet. She pulled the chain, pulled it again, and yet again. Not a trace must be left. She knelt staring into the bowl, the rush of water carrying away her defilement, flushing it a thousand miles away into the bowels of the earth where it would be buried, forgotten.

Daphne banged on the door. "Hurry up, Naddykins, I want to go in there."

She pulled the chain for the sixth time, wiped her mouth on a towel, then dashed to the bathroom to clean her teeth. Everything must be normal; nothing suspicious to reveal the horrible secret. From her sister, she heard, "God. At long last. Thanks, Dreamland."

Her mother stood at the back door. A fat sentry, jumbo arms folded. "Nadina, you're looking dreadful. Look at her, Arnold." But her father at the kitchen table merely grunted, strands of Shredded Wheat filling the gaps of his teeth.

"You've been crying so much, your eyes are all red and small and swollen," her mother said. "Your father and I are ready to hear whatever problems you may be having. At any time, Nadina. Goodness, you only have to say. Oh, you can't go to school in this state, Nadina, you really can't. You've hardly eaten a thing. Here, take this."

Nadina snatched her lunch box. "I'm al-right, if you'd just stop fussing. Can father put a mortise on my door, please."

"What, yet another lock? For heaven's sake!" came the surly reply from the table. "Would she like a ball and chain to go with it?"

Her mother, face red and flustered, said, "Nadina, you'll be the death of me, you really will. I don't know what it is. You've so much to be grateful for. Your brains, your b—"

Nadina did not hear the rest. For a millionth of a second, the curl of her lip and she was gone, down the drive, her satchel under her arm, her gas mask in its box hanging from her shoulder. She closed her ears to her mother's agitated cry, "Come straight home! You must have an early night."

Whisk her off to see a psychiatrist. Sitting on the stairs she had overheard them, late at night, the lounge door left carelessly ajar. Men in white suits to take her away. That's what they wanted.

Who to tell? Pat? And Pat would tell her parents, lapsed Catholics, but they'd know what to do, who to see. She and Pat had secrets, girl secrets whispered over the lemonade, with the wireless turned up loud to drown out the nervousness, for you never knew with secrets. But this was a secret unlike any other. Loathsome, filthy, terrible, bloodied. She curled her nose in disgust. Pat had no real love for the Church, didn't like Father O'Donnell, and Pat would believe her. Nadina remembered her saying, "Any bloke, whoever he was, would do it given half a chance. Dirty devils them are, the whole lot of 'em, Naddy."

Pat, then? No. no. Ridiculous to tell Pat. Pat loved gossip. She would shout it out in no time to that disgusting Evett, with his big nose sniffing out the dirt, and then it would be all round the school, all over town. Everywhere. His mum, the big lady with a cackle. She'd seen her with her cronies gathered round her stall at the market roaring her stupid head off.

She should go to the police. Yes. Of course, the police. What he'd done – they'd done – no, what *he'd* done to her! It was a crime, illegal, against the law. Thelma? Of course, Thelma. Tell her after Assembly. Her friend, her only friend. She would be on her side, she felt sure of that. And Thelma would go to the police with her. Yes. They'd go to the police together. No, but wait! Thelma would first consult the Head. Millie would never believe her and would speak to her parents. And they must never know. Oh, no, not Thelma. Yet the police must be told, no matter what anyone would think. She would go to the police – on her own, if no one else – and there was no one else. Then she thought of Ryan.... There was one other person she might tell: Mr Brannigan. She had overheard Ryan telling the Evett boy, "My dad says that priest is a traitor because he's got a Union Jack in the pulpit, see? He's not for Ireland, that's what me dad says."

She crossed the main road, forgetting to look. A van driver tooted her. A fresh outpouring of grief overwhelmed her as the full implications of what had happened sank home. Because of his filthy fornication, a deadly sin, a mortal sin, he had taken something from her that she would never have back: *no longer a virgin.*

On and off throughout the day, Thelma Ashby's kind eyes sought her out, for not once did she raise her hand at question time. Through most of the lessons she stared dreamily out of the window, unable to concentrate, holding back her tears.

"Nadina?"

"Pardon, Miss Ashby?" Looking up from her history text book about the Norman Conquest she gave the teacher a wobbly smile.

"I'd like to see you at Break, please."

While the others rushed to the milk crate, jamming their straws through the bottle tops, Nadina walked submissively to the desk. The little teacher placed a plump arm round her waist and smiled.

"You're very quiet this morning, mute, in fact. You know far more than Julie about the great battles of the period, a bit of an expert on 1066 and all that follows. The Battle of Hastings had profound implications for us as a nation. Suppose Harold had won? I liked the title to that essay you gave me. So why have you gone brain-dead for the day? Not once have you made any attempt to join in the discussion. "Oh, Nadina, what is it, dear?"

For the tears were falling and she wanted to tell, let it all come, sob and sob into that comfortable bosom. Blowing her nose, her lip trembling, she said, "If someone did something terribly wrong to you, and you did nothing about it, would you... would you... forgive... that p...p... person?" she mumbled.

"It depends what it was, I suppose." Thelma stared hard, a frown creasing her powdered forehead. "Is there something you want to talk to me about, Nadina?"

"Doesn't matter, Miss," was all she said as she walked back to her desk. For the rest of the day she made a valiant effort to participate.

Home from school, the moment she walked into the kitchen her mother placed a glass of milk and a biscuit before her and announced excitedly, "We have a visitor this evening: Father O'Donnell. He wants to talk to us about your future. He sounded very pleased about you on the phone. Isn't that nice? Nadina?"

But she gulped her milk, crumbled her biscuit and rushed upstairs. She took the keys out of her satchel, unlocked the door, found the key for the new mortise on her mantelpiece, lay down on her bed and burst into a fresh torrent of weeping.

It was his understanding, Father O'Donnell told Nadina's parents, that their younger daughter was far more advanced spiritually than any pupils to whom he had ever given Catechism instruction. "And that is a very big thing for me to say. For it includes not only the whole five years I've been your priest here at Holy Innocents', but other parishes where I've served Our Lord as well."

He smiled at Nadina as she watched him, positioning herself in a corner close to the door to be as far away from him as possible. He would help her, he said, munching his fruit cake and seated in his best cassock on the expensively upholstered armchair, to bring out that particular sensitivity, which was a great gift from God. "But with a new confidence, overcoming a particular timidity. Now that does concern me," he told her parents, waving an arm in her direction. "I believe, you see, that young Nadina over there could well be called along a particular path to holiness." There was the possibility, he explained, stirring his tea, indeed a distinct probability even with a girl of such tender years – and he reminded his listeners of Saint Therese of Lisieux, who after all was only fifteen when she entered the Carmelite nunnery – that the Blessed Lord might well be calling her. "And a rare calling it is too – to be a religious."

"You mean like a nun?" Louise Brown's fat jowls shook. She grinned at her daughter, "Well, what about that, Nadina?"

Guessing her mother's thoughts, Nadina stared at her with fresh loathing. Her daughter in the nuns' habit! What a wonderful reflection of a caring mother. How impressed all her friends and relatives were going to be – and not forgetting the congregation.

Father O'Donnell continued to smile. He would be helping her to realise such an honour, he said. For this purpose he would be willing to grant extra tuition in addition to the Catechism instruction. And this would not of necessity end with her Confirmation, but could continue well into the future.

Arnold, who up until now had stayed silent, apart from anxious stares at his daughter, and now apparently feeling that some contribution would be appropriate, said, "Yes, Father, I'm sure she will make herself available at your convenience. When do you suggest?"

The priest beamed at the figure crouched low in the corner. "A Friday would fit in conveniently for me. Nadina could stay on for an hour or so after all the others have departed? We could make a start next Friday if you wish. That is, of course, if Nadina is also agreeable," he said looking at the parents.

He consumed the remainder of the generous portion of cake, placed an empty cup and saucer back on the table in front of him and smiled at each in turn.

Nadina stared back. Interpreting her hesitation as failure to recognise the generosity of their priest, her mother exclaimed, "How wonderful! You ought to be grateful, Nadina. How good of Father, don't you think so, Arnold?" Without waiting for her husband's assent, she continued, "Yes, of course, she will come. Won't you, Nadina?"

There was an imperceptible movement from the girl. Her eyelids closed, she swayed a little from side to side as if meditating.

"She's in one of her awkward moods, I'm afraid, Father," said her mother. "When she's like this, you don't get a peep out of her."

Arnold, briskly stirring his tea, said testily, "Nadina! Wake up, will you? Try to show just a little appreciation. Thank Father O'Donnell in a proper fashion if you please."

She looked at her mother, then her father. Then, pausing between each word, she said in a shaky voice, "Yes...I will...come."

And so it was decided. From then on, every Friday, she'd wait behind for a further hour's instruction.

On Monday, she was going to tell, but instead she told Miss Ashby. "I'm going to have special instruction after Catechism. Father O'Donnell thinks I am worthy, more worthy he says, than anyone else."

Thelma Ashby looked up from a pile of exercise books. . "Oh, well Nadina; that sounds interesting. I'm glad you seem a little brighter."

"I shall definitely be going to the Convent School of the Holy Name where Margaret Peal, went."

Miss Ashby looked at her with her kind, tired eyes, "That's splendid news, Nadina. I'm very glad for you." She turned back to her marking.

The following Thursday evening, waiting for sleep to come, her mind in turmoil, Nadina rehearsed the reasons for accepting. Yes, wasn't there a need to know more? There *were* difficulties, many questions she wanted to raise, like how the ordinary food of bread and wine became the holiness of Christ Himself? How could it be Holy food, the Body and Blood of the Saviour? It was awesome this doctrine of the Transubstantiation. Only we Catholics have it right, Father O'Donnell had insisted. He'd tried to explain at Catechism class, but she was still mystified. Yes, and there were lots of other teachings that confused her. You could never stop learning. And by the time she got to the Convent School, she could be ahead of her new classmates. And then there was the possibility of her becoming a nun. A nun? Poverty, chastity and obedience? Failed before she would even start! Ridiculous. Spoilt goods like her bloodied knickers.

So she had agreed, hadn't she? Not because of any pressure from *them*, the hypocrites, but because she knew that spiritual awareness of the soul went hand in hand with the mind. Mind and soul together, two sides to the same coin. She thought she would ask to borrow some of the priest's important looking books. She was well aware of her physical limitations: the port wine stain, the dumpy figure, but there was one thing she had and no one else in class came anywhere near it, and that was spiritual perception. He had been right about her. Even Philip

Matthews and pretty Cynthia Peal, and one or two others, had never shown such a depth of holiness; that longing more than she. That's what he'd said and he was right.

And then there was that precious letter of recommendation. She had to have that. The thought of going to Southgate with Daphne filled her with horror. She would never go there. Of course, there was the interview with Mother Clare, and passing the Scholarship with high enough marks, but then she would be there! 'The Convent School of the Holy Name.' *Her* ambition, *her* choice, not theirs. All they wanted for her was to push her off to Southgate Grammar so the wonderful Daphne could take her in hand. She'd kill herself first.

There was, of course, the other thing, the wicked sex thing. That will never happen again. She'd threaten him with the police. Once she'd got the recommendation – no, as soon as she'd settled in to her new school, the very first day of her first term – she'd tell Fergus Brannigan and they'd report that disgusting priest to the Church authorities – Mr Brannigan would know who to write to – and to the police. She could go to Mass in the school chapel! She need never see him again after that.

On Friday, before the class left for the church, Miss Ashby announced that Nadina Brown would be staying behind after Catechism. She had been singled out for extra tuition by Father O'Donnell. "Why? Yes, you may well ask," said the little teacher, gripping the sides of her desk and standing on tiptoe, a favourite stance when making announcements. "Father O'Donnell thinks that Nadina Brown is a particularly worthy candidate for Confirmation and has a thirst for spiritual knowledge unknown by the rest of you, with one or two exceptions, perhaps. No doubt," continued the teacher, her chin wobbling belligerently, "through her commitment to her Catholic faith as well as to her school, she's putting the rest of you to shame. I wonder, Ryan, if that might apply in any respect to you?"

"Me?" He shook his head, grinning round the classroom, opened his mouth about to say something.

Miss Ashby reacted predictably, "Drawing attention to yourself again, I see. Just shut up, will you?"

Head swivelled, Ryan's included, to stare at her along the back row. Nadina guessed what they were thinking: something else that marked her out, besides her ugly face. She could see Ryan whispering to Kenny, loud enough for her and the rest of the class to hear.

"That one's real mad religious, so she is. Fanatic."

It was a new word he had recently added to his rapidly lengthening list.

Chapter Fourteen

The cavern-like interior, a ceiling that seemed to stretch to the sky, rock-sturdy pillars and drifting clouds of incense, forever reminded Nadina of her unimportance. A lesson in humility, she had always felt about the church. But since that day of unbelievable terror, she felt a nothingness; a numbness, dwarfing her into complete insignificance; a nonentity. She wondered again how she could have been such a fool. But there was no going back.

Friday, everyone gone. She was seated in her usual place, half way down the church, waiting.

The sound of footsteps and she looked up. Thelma tripping along on her size two's, the smell of Woolworth's perfume making Nadina cough.

"Just wanted to see if you're al-right. Oh, Nadina, dear, you're trembling. Are you cold?"

"No, I'm fine, thank you," she said smiling.

"Well, see you on Monday." The little teacher hesitated, "Nadina, if there is anything, anything at all, troubling you, you will tell me won't you. Yes?"

'Now!'

But she hesitated two seconds too long and the sound of the heels clicking on the concrete floor receded. The heavy door squeaked in protest and Thelma had left.

Nadina glanced at her watch. One thing she knew. She would not go back to the place of horror. And she would either walk home, however long it took, or catch the trolley bus.

She was still kneeling when the pew creaked. Immediately a hand went to her knee. With eyes closed, she thrust it away as she would an insect. She got to her feet, brought the prepared list from a pocket in her dress, her hand trembling, and without preamble said, "How can Christ be present at the Mass? I mean in the bread and the wine? It is something that has always puzzled me, Father O'Donnell. You tried to explain, but I'm sill unsure."

He coughed, stretched out his legs. She could smell the drink on his breath. His voice thick from the catarrh.

"Ah, well now. First of all, get rid of literalism. It's natural but it's surely impossible to proceed in that vein. In other words, you must not think of the teaching, little Nadina, in that way at all. Otherwise it would be impossible for Christ's Body and Blood to be on the altars in all the churches all over the world at the same time, would it not? 'Tis a miracle, then; a mystery, and many of the doctrines stretch our minds to the limit and we can go no further, but that doesn't mean they're not true. Truth, deep truth can only be grasped by the searching of the soul. And you, my child, how can you possibly puzzle it out? Your brain would burst. Sure it's going to give you a pain in the mind. Do you not see that?"

He chuckled, she wasn't sure why. It sounded as though he was laughing at her, belittling her. She sat down again, upright, her body taut. He leaned towards her, smiling through brown-stained teeth, his hand drifting back to her knee.

Nadina made a show of consulting her list, holding on with both hands, the paper rustling. "I have this question then for you, Father. Why was I born deformed? Is that a mystery as well for me to search out with my soul? I know a lot of people who are sick. Mrs Forrester in the front pew in her wheelchair. You take her the sacrament because she can't climb the sanctuary steps. What about her? Al-right, then, you get... well, you get some people who never have anything wrong with them. They live a long life. They're always healthy. Others die young. People... children, all diseased. Would you agree that it's all unfair of God. Isn't it?" She twisted her neck to stare at him, thrusting the list back in her pocket. So, do you answer that in the same way?"

He looked troubled, sighed. "Suffering – well we can't understand it, Nadina. Suffering remains a mystery. It always will be – to all of us. But you see, it's what is on the inside, not the outside that matters. Your beauty, for example is hidden, but those who can see below the surface know it's there." He chuckled. "Nadina, now please don't object. Your quiet disposition, your serenity moves me."

"Take your hand away!"

He did so, reluctantly. Let it drop from her knee. She stared ahead at the figure on the altar. "Father, I have felt so close to Our Lord. But sometimes more than at other times. Why is that? I believe He understands. Ryan Brannigan says that if Jesus was real he'd heal me, he'd be able to answer my prayer about this. She pointed to her cheek. "This!"

He sighed, shook his head sorrowfully. "It's hard for you not to be angry."

"I pray every night, Father O'Donnell, that the dear Lord will heal me, but nothing ever happens."

"And do you, my child, pray for your old priest now?"

"Why are priests more important than other people? Cardinal Synolsky, the Polish Cardinal calls on the world's Catholics to pray for him. Why? Why don't we pray for Mrs Forrester in her wheelchair?"

"Because from the Cardinals the Pope is chosen. They are separated, called apart."

"Answer me this question, then. Why do some people believe and not others? You take Ryan Brannigan. His parents, well his father then, is regular at Mass, just as mine are. Yet, he does not believe. I know his father worries about the state of his soul."

The priest's voice had an edge to it. "Don't be taken in by that lad's filthy atheism. He has a choice, and for now he's taken a wrong choice. You know I could get him transferred to a State school, even at this late stage, if I chose to. You know that?"

"Yes, of course. Do you think Ryan Brannigan and others like him will go to hell, then? The torment of the damned. And what of unbelievers? Miss Millison says only Catholics will get to heaven. So what of criminals – al-right I know that's another question, Father, but I was reading an article in the Sunday paper – *The Times* it was – it asked: 'Why are there bad people? Where does badness come from? How can you be born bad?' It was a debate between two people. One said it was due to upbringing, suggesting that maybe they had no example, or worse, a bad example set them by their parents. So, Father, what example do you think my parents have set me? Their faith is skin deep. No, I don't expect you to believe that, Father, but it's true. And what of the Germans? You tell us they're all wicked. How can we be certain that it's only we Catholics who can be sure of heaven? Sometimes I think there are a lot of good and kind people up there who never once went to Mass. Mrs Brannigan, now, she's always kind to me. She strikes me as a really good person. And she doesn't come, well only Christmas times, maybe Easter. Are you saying they're all going to end up in hell? I find that hard to believe. God forbid! I object to it, Father O'Donnell."

Her words tumbled out, barely pausing for breath, her voice shaking. She watched his hand. At the moment it rested with the other in his lap.

The priest stretched, yawned, then sighed. He was in his old cassock, it smelt like him: old and mildewy. There were holes in the armpits where the stitching had come undone. He sighed once more, chewing his lip, a frown on his lined face.

There was silence.

"Father?"

"Well, Nadina, dear, you have a lot of very deep questions and they are going to take a long time to answer. Just let me say for now..." he paused to lick his lips, removed a piece of cigarette paper that had stuck there. "First, I can tell you that if you love Christ, don't neglect your Confession and the Mass, keep yourself holy, put your faith into action, which is to be kind to others, especially the lonely and the suffering, you can be assured of heaven. That is the teaching of the Catholic Faith."

As his voice droned on, Nadina thought of Ryan. Suppose Father O'Donnell carried out his threat and made Ryan leave? So, what of it? He would be at Southgate soon anyway, and she at the Convent. Once he went to Grammar – that is if he passed, and there was some doubt that he would – he would probably stop going to Mass altogether and that would be that.

Another question. *The* question. Would the priest keep his promise to her? She sat down, stared at him, her voice level.

"I hope to go to the Convent of the Holy Name, Father. And having your recommendation, Father, I know I have a good chance. I wish Ryan and I could be friends. Will you pray for his soul, Father?"

"Ah well, little one. You know you're a bit young to be sweet on the boys, are you not?"

"No. I don't think so. It's only one boy, anyway. And we're just good friends."

Father O'Donnell chuckled. She thought rapidly of another question, fumbling in her pocket. His hand was back on her knee, moving under her skirt. It could happen again. But it mustn't. *Couldn't.* Her heart pounded.

She pushed his hand away, feeling her eyelids prickle. "Friends shouldn't do that to each other, especially priests," she said. She wanted to warn him then and there that she would go to the police. But the moment passed.

"My next question is... why do Protestants take no notice of the Pope? I mean, they don't acknowledge him at all, do they? We Catholics see him as the true leader, descendant from Saint Peter and down through the whole history of the Church. I'd like to borrow some books please. About what you said at Catechism we Catholics believe... called the Apostolic Succession?"

"That's correct. Sure, it's the ignorance of these people. They are not the true Church. There is only one Church, the Holy Catholic Church.

Her breath was coming in short gasps. She jumped up from her seat, one hand clutching the back of the pew in front. "Can I be a server, Father?"

He laughed, then smiled up at her, "Oh, Nadina, Nadina. You know very well girls are not permitted."

"My mother says that women are the equal of men and now the women are working on the land, in the factories, doing exactly the same work, they should get the same pay. It's going to be different – a lot different when the war's over, she says.

Anyway, I don't see why girls shouldn't be servers. At that Protestant church, erm... I can't think what it's called, the one down the bottom of the road here. Methodist, I think. Yes, that's it, Methodist. They have a woman in charge. She's called a Deacon."

Father O'Donnell looked irritated. Nadina consulted her list.

"Sure, it's their ignorance," he said. "Holy Church is Christ in the world and Our Blessed Lord chose only men to be his disciples, his priests, not women. Now then, time is passing. What do you say to a little prayer together, eh?"

He reached up, his hand hovering around her waist.

"Please, Father."

"What is it, little one?" he whispered.

She shook her head, blinking back her tears.

"We'll have our prayer now, shall we?" he said again.

She stared down at him. "Is that all you're teaching me for tonight?" Her tone was angry, but she didn't care.

His hand fell back into his lap. He sighed and glanced at his watch, "I'm sorry, Nadina, dear. Unfortunately I have another appointment. I have to administer the Last Rites. A parishioner has asked for me. Her husband is dying at the hospital. Cancer." He sighed again. He seemed to be full of sighs. "A very good example, Nadina, of the undeserved suffering you were talking about. A faithful soul, regular at Mass."

She sank back onto the pew, in silence considered her thoughtlessness. "I'm sorry,

Father, for him and his wife. Thank you, Father. Will you please pray that I may make a good confession, Father."

The line of his thin lips tightened. He looked at her, his hand once more descending to her knee. "That, child, is your responsibility and yours alone. You should know that."

Again, she was about to demand that he stop, warn him of the consequences, but she could see he was getting angry. So she hesitated, and instead asked, "Father will you pray for me that this horrible birthmark will go, and pray that I may obtain a place at the Convent of the Holy Name through your recommendation, that I will pass the Scholarship well enough to be accepted, and have a successful interview with Mother Clare?"

"Yes, of course." He eased his bulk out of the pew and in silence took Nadina's hand to lead her down the aisle, their footsteps echoing on the stone floor. At the Communion rail in front of the altar, he stopped. "Now just kneel by me," he said. The tone of his voice had softened.

Nadina loved to hear him pray so fluently, so effortlessly at the end of the Catechism. He prayed for John Williams with the cancer, whom he was going to visit, and Heather Williams, his wife with her fear and dread. For all the parishioners; for the suffering of British and Allied prisoners of war; for a child who had been killed in a recent air raid; for victory over a ruthless, evil enemy.

"Amen," Nadina said clearly and loudly, screwing up her eyes, yearning for the healing she was so desperate to receive. She felt the priest's hand on her shoulder; his arm slipped a little, until it was round her waist. She stiffened, but his hand stayed there as he prayed that she would grow in Grace, be a faithful soldier of Christ, then the healing she longed for, to which she listened intently. "Heavenly Father, you know, this sweet child is worried about so many things, O Lord. So I ask, O Heavenly Father, that if it should please Thee, that Thou will in Thy good time, according to Thy gracious purpose, grant her request and take away this blemish."

Rising from their knees, priest and penitent stood together facing the suffering Saviour. Then, with the back of his hand Father O'Donnell swept back her hair and before she could object, kissed her cheek, his lips lingering there a brief moment then, as suddenly as he'd begun, he stopped. Her hair fell back into place. His voice became strict again. The Catechism voice, the school Assembly voice, the voice from the pulpit.

"Right, I think I'm going to be very, very pleased with you, Nadina, as is Our Lord. Your questions have depth. You think carefully. But you should not make a worry of questions that have no satisfying answer. We must accept by Faith what cannot be answered rationally."

Taking her hand, he walked with her to the big West door. "Now, Nadina, I want you to appreciate your beauty," he said.

Nadina blushed, looked at the floor and shook her head vigorously.

The priest laughed, playful again. "Oh, Nadina, dear, I can't convince you, can I? Your beauty is there, child. Below the surface." He chuckled, then winked. Once more, the voice changed. Thoughtful, serious. "You see, Nadina, I have never yet met a child with such a deep spiritual yearning and a naturally enquiring mind. An eleven-year-old for goodness sake, with such deep interest and concern about spiritual matters." He paused, the tip of his thumb under his top lip. "Now I'm not sure I should be saying this, so keep it under wraps, won't you, but I was talking to the Head about you and she said... what was it? I don't get much out of Miss Millison, but when I do it's always something very revealing regarding her pupils. But about you she did say, and I'm remembering her exact words now, 'Sometimes I feel I am no longer talking to a child but an adult. A child with an adult mind.' And that funny little fat one, your class teacher, she joined in, agreeing. Now you know that our Miss Millison doesn't pay compliments easily. So you see you are so unusual, and you have no idea

how wonderful it is for me. You have brought special joy into your old priest's life.

"Thank you, Father," she said, and with a final, solemn hand shake she pulled her fingers from his sweaty clasp and left the building, breathing in the fresh, incense-free air. The early summer sun was low in the sky. She loved the sun, warming the mark through the veil of her hair.

Getting off the trolley bus at Gregory Avenue, she walked the fifty yards into Mercia Close and skipped up the drive. Her mother came to the door. "You haven't been long," she said in a reproachful voice.

"Father O'Donnell had to leave early to visit a dying man," Nadina told her.

"What a splendid priest we have, Nadina. So good of him to offer you this extra time with all he has to do. I do hope you are showing your appreciation."

"He knows I'm more spiritual than the others. All the others he's ever had for the Confirmation training. He said talking to me is like talking to an adult. That's what he said. Miss Millison told him."

Her mother frowned as she took Nadina's gas mask to hang on the hall stand. "I see. Well adults usually converse, Nadina, not withdraw into themselves."

"Going to my room," she said.

Her mother called out to her as she climbed the staircase. "Do put your dirty clothes in the laundry basket, Nadina. I keep telling you."

Nadina froze. With a shock she realised she'd left the bloodstained underwear in her wardrobe. She waited in horror, but her mother said no more.

Getting out of bed next morning she hurried to look in the mirror on her dressing table. Was she imagining it? Was the mark a little less vivid? On Monday she'd seek out Pat. She wouldn't say, just see if she'd noticed. She knelt by her bed and said a prayer for Father O'Donnell again, as he'd asked her to. She tried to think kindly of him, blotting out the memory, but without success, the words sticking in her throat.

The weekend passed uneventfully. In the playground before Assembly, Nadina looked around. "Seen Pat, Julie?"

Julie Richards, chatting to Cynthia, nodded, grinning.

Interpreting the grin, Nadina supposed Pat was with the Evett boy again. She didn't like him, never would. He was crude, a loud mouth, irreligious and irregular at Mass and was a bad influence on Ryan; a bully, pushing younger kids about. Unless he pulls his socks up he'll end up at that awful Naughton Road. And that goes for Ryan too. She wanted to believe what Father had said, that most of them who went there were bound for hell, yet despite his certainties, she felt uncomfortable.

In Assembly, assured of her superiority over the others, she looked up at Miss Ashby, lovely, kind Thelma Ashby, standing on the stage by the Head, and was rewarded with a smile. Two spiritual beings together. Al-right, so she was alone again, Pat dumping her and off doing dirty stuff with Evett. But soon she would be away from them all, at the school where she truly belonged with new friends, friends who loved the Saviour, who never mocked the Faith. Nadina touched her cheek with the tips of her fingers and remembered Father kissing it, and there, standing in the row with all the others in the big hall as they waited for Miss Millison to begin, she was aware of a little shiver of pleasure. It was like the touch of Jesus on the lepers in Galilee, a holy kiss. Suddenly, she remembered the horror of that first Friday and was ashamed. She tried desperately to push it out of her mind but it wouldn't go away.

The weeks went by. Nadina became accustomed to the sudden changes of Father O'Donnell's moods: silliness, then suddenly stern; kind, then angry. Sometimes her questions were met with long moody silences. At other times he would be talkative, explaining, gesticulating. And not once did he touch her. Gradually, she began to relax in his company, though the memory lingered, raw and festering like an open wound. Yet, as each Friday approached she began, at first reluctantly and then positively, to look forward to the extra tuition.

Chapter Fifteen

At the end of a particularly thought provoking question and answer session, Father O'Donnell asked, "How would you like to come to the presbytery for a special meal? A really lovely tea. All the good food in the world comes from Ireland. Did you not know that? What do you say? You see, I have my good family across the Water. No rationing over there! Not yet, anyway, though it is possible that we shall see it before long. So, how about it, Nadina? Just the two of us? How will that be? Would you like that?"

She didn't answer, stared ahead. "I was reading about Saint Therese of Lisieux in that book of the Saints you lent me."

"Ah, yes a remarkable young lady. And no reason to suppose you wouldn't be following in her footsteps."

Yes, she thought, except that *she* had taken a vow of chastity and kept it. "I have a question for you, Father. You tell me that suffering is redemptive. Is my guilty conscience that keeps me awake at night serving any useful purpose?"

He shifted in the pew, looked uncomfortable, his gaze dropped to the floor. "Our Lord was very easy with the whores. It was the spiritual sins he concentrated on: pride; imagined superiority over others." He pursed his lips, paused, added, "Sometimes, Nadina, I think you feel very superior."

"No I don't!"

"Yes, I think so. You have so much to give, Nadina. You don't need to boost yourself up over others."

"Like who, for example?"

"Your sister, Daphne; your mother and father; the other boys and girls in your class."

"What? With this?" She turned her head, swept back her hair exposing the discolouration, jabbed it with her finger.

Suddenly changing the subject, he said, "Now how about Saturday week, then, for our little tea party? Best not tell your mother so she doesn't feed you first, eh?" He smiled.

Indifferently, she asked, "What time then, Father?"

"Our tea? Oh, I'm so looking forward to that. Well, look, dear, let's make it five o'clock. Will that suit? It's the one day in the week I usually take a bit of time off, unless I'm hearing confessions. You'll no doubt find me in the garden. So, instead of coming to the church, Nadina, go straight to the presbytery, to the back door."

"Thank you, Father."

After their prayer he strolled back with her from the Communion rail. At the door, she picked up her gas mask and walked briskly out. "Not long now, Nadina," he called after her. "Five weeks and then the great day."

Once outside she hurried along the Conway Road to catch the bus – and laughed out loud. To the presbytery? To be on her own in that big house? Alone with him? Never! Not even the miserable Mrs Henderson hovering about in the basement would make a scrap of difference. She laughed again. What would be a good excuse? Stomach cramp. Nothing easier.

All the way home she went over the prayer he had said again for her healing. Priests were always special with special powers. Her skin would be pure and white, like marble, like the big statue of the Madonna by the altar.

The following Friday, after another restless night, Nadina was relieved when once again the priest made no attempt to touch her. Lately, some of the muscle spasms she had been experiencing had begun to lessen, especially round her shoulders, and the constant need to be sick and then nothing coming up had subsided. The sun's rays beamed through the stained glass giving everywhere a holy glow. He answered her questions thoughtfully and thoroughly. Some of the books he had lent her, she returned.

Afterwards, as she stood at the great west door, he lifted the veil of hair from her cheek. "Yes, I do think there has been some improvement, small but significant. You must keep persisting, Nadina, and please don't forget to pray for me," he smiled.

"Father, can I truly believe the Lord is healing me? Yes? Thank you for your prayers, Father. Goodnight, Father."

While she put the string of her gas mask over her shoulder, he said, "I can well imagine that you won't ever have experienced a meal like the one that our good Mrs Henderson is preparing."

As she hurried out of the church, he sounded cross, calling after her. "I'm expecting you here five o'clock sharp. Don't be late, will you?"

When she awoke the next morning, Nadina felt dreadful. Though her stomach no longer lurched like a turbulent sea, there was a constant dull ache followed by a sharp pain whenever she tried to eat. Was she getting an ulcer?

She recalled with horror the stench of his breath, his body across hers, the pain of it all, and immediately tried to suppress the memory. She stood before the mirror naked, examined the mark, running her fingers down it. *Was* it less vivid? Now, she was not so sure, despite his confident words.

Pat was right. At this rate her breasts would soon be as big as her teacher's and though she loved and admired Thelma Ashby, she didn't want to look like her. Glancing over her shoulder as she walked away from the mirror, Nadina saw how her backside rolled from side to side. "Not a pretty sight," she said to herself, "in fact overweight and ugly, whatever *he* says." And the blotch? She turned back to face the front. There it was, vivid and raw as ever, blackcurrant juice and raspberry jam, just as Ryan said. She flopped down full length on the bed. How could she expect the Holy Virgin to heal her when she had been impure? The priest telling her that spiritual sins were more horrible. than physical ones? He was bound to say that. She recalled him shifting his feet, unable to look at her. So does he feel guilty too? He *is* guilty.

With an effort she pushed herself up, slowly started to dress. What could she do? She would telephone. That would be it. Cramp, she'd explain. And that would be completely genuine. No, better still, why not cycle there, start off about four fifteen, shove a note through his door? She was all ready to come, she'd say, had got on her bike and started out in good time when a spasm of pain was so bad it had made her cry out and she was actually sick in the road. Then she'd say how sorry she was with all the trouble Mrs Henderson must have gone to. She would end the note by saying that she was looking forward to the next Friday's instruction and how helpful it had been, and that she was sure she would be better by then.

As she put on her favourite frock, the yellow one with the bow at the back that she'd had for her birthday, Nadina made up her mind. She would write the note of apology and do it after breakfast. Out of the way, and out of her mind. Yes, but it would be best not to take it round until almost five. Why not? Simply because any time before, he would be ringing up and asking how she was and her mother would tell her to stop making a fuss about a little discomfort from a simple thing like a period and then she'd have to go.

She was still undecided. The last three sessions had been so different. He was like a priest and yet also a friend. And one thing was very clear: she must do nothing, nothing whatsoever to spoil her chances of getting his precious letter of recommendation. But if he did try anything, anything at all, even kissing her mark, she would warn him, then immediately run to the front door and go home. What sort of warning it would be she wasn't sure. But he had to know that she would not allow it under any circumstances. It was terrible, shameful, disgusting, what he'd done. The touching, even, running his hand down her cheek and kissing her there, and then on the lips! But she hadn't stopped him. She could have walked away; could have run for the door. Why hadn't she? He'd attacked her, lain with her?

Nadina shuddered, trying again to push it to the back of her mind. But who could she have told? Anyone. She should have told someone at the very beginning, that first Friday. Yet, what was the point? Who would ever believe her? And wasn't she as much to blame? She had allowed her body to be violated. Try as she might to stop her tears, they began again.

She thought of Thelma Ashby. She had a feeling that Thelma didn't like Father O'Donnell very much. When Ryan was cheeky, even rude to him, you could tell she was on Ryan's side. At times Nadina had caught her smiling, even trying not to laugh, and nodding when Ryan talked about compassion, though when Thelma became aware that she and Pat were looking at her, she had put on a stern face. She'd had to thump Ryan that time, of course. Had to get cross with him and then lost her temper. After all she was the teacher and had to be strict. Nadina smiled. I wish I could have a smile like Thelma's, she thought, so warm and kind. It must be wonderful to be so happy.

There had been other times, like yesterday, even though he'd been like a proper priest, she could have walked out and never gone back and that is what she should have done, for the Blessed Virgin was surely prompting her, all the time. And all the time she hadn't. And why? Why had she stayed? Was it because when he kissed her disfigurement she had felt a thrill, a kind of warmth?

She remembered how she had told Pat off when *she* tried to make excuses. "You are as much to blame as Kenny," she'd said. "More, because... because men and boys can't control themselves." Pat had laughed at that, told her she was becoming an old maid, then swore, blasphemed in fact, used the Holy name of Christ.

Grimacing, Nadina thought, how can *I* ever be an example to Pat? How can I become more humble, grow in Grace, like the great saint Therese. I must ask for guidance. Father O'Donnell had told her she thought herself superior. Was she? Pat thought so, and Ryan certainly did. Ryan. It was such a long time since she last went to Harefield Road. Does he miss me? She doubted it.

At breakfast, she told her mother that Father O'Donnell had invited her to tea. She knew he had told her not to, but she didn't see why not. She was pleased to see the look on her mother's face. "Why, how lovely for you, Nadina! What have you done to deserve that, I wonder?" Nadina did not answer. Ate her breakfast in silence. She could tell that the fat frump was jealous.

The day went by slowly, most of it spent reading her *Girls Own* Annual or listening to the wireless. She prayed, read her Bible, though she knew Catholics should not read the Bible on their own – something else to ask him about. She took out her little notebook, began a fresh list for the following Friday.

After lunch she told herself, "Come on, you lazy thing, write that note now." She knew she'd been putting it off. Procrastination, it was called. A new word to tell Ryan: to delay doing something you were meant to do.

She went up to her bedroom, took out her best notepaper from the drawer in her desk and began to compose a regretful letter. Soon the floor was littered with rejected sheets. What could be easier? A few lines to explain that she had severe stomach cramp; she was all prepared to come. She was very, very sorry, asking him to thank Mrs Henderson for all the preparation she'd made. *'Thank you, Father, for yesterdays' teaching. I did enjoy it. The way you put it over. Better than Miss Millison. Sometimes she confuses me when she talks to us in Assembly.'* No, better not bring in Millie. He wouldn't like that. She screwed it up, tossed it into the already full waste paper basket; took a fresh sheet.

Finding the right words was so difficult. She was probably trying far too hard. She set about the task quickly and efficiently. Suddenly, with a shock, she noticed the time.

"Nadina?"

Once again, her mother meddling as she always did, standing in the usual position at the bottom of the stairs, one foot on the first step ready to come up. "Are you getting yourself ready? Coming up to four o'clock. You're going to be late unless you leave now. I'll ask Daddy to run you over."

Always interfering, butting in when she wasn't wanted, taking over her life whenever she chose and leaving out the most important things, like finding out about skin grafts for instance. Why on earth did I tell her about the invitation in the first place? She knew why: they'd never been invited for tea. She was special. She was Father's favourite out of the whole school, more important than her parents. Maybe that's what he meant by thinking herself superior over others. An important lesson to learn. Saint Therese would help her. She vowed to pray to her.

Now there came an urgent knock on her bedroom door. "Nadina, it's too late for you to get the trolley bus and Daddy's going out. You'll need your bike. Daddy's taken the trouble to put the chain back on for you. He can't take you in the car now, so it's no good expecting him to."

"Don't want him to."

"Oh, be late then!"

Hearing her mother's exaggerated sigh as she waddled off down the stairs, Nadina battled with her anger. After a moment, she calmly tore her last effort into shreds, watching them flutter down like so much confetti. All in her best handwriting, of course, and the best attempt so far. Now it was all too late! Gathering up the balls of screwed up paper from around the floor and jamming them into the overflowing waste paper basket lest her interfering mother should read them, she ran to the door, unlocked it and pocketing the keys, ran down the stairs.

When she reached the top of Mercia Close, Nadina stopped, hesitated, started again.

She stopped when she reached the main coastal road. Set off again; stopped when she reached the turning into Conway Road. She saw from her watch that it was five minutes to five. She tried out a little test. She told herself that when she reached the fifth lamppost, about thirty yards ahead, if she still didn't feel it was right, she would not go, but would cycle around for an hour or so. Never mind about an apology and never mind what that mother of hers might say - and never mind what *he* might think.

She reached the lamppost, yet still was uncertain. She knew it was no good. She leaned over the handlebars. Father O'Donnell would ask her parents all sorts of questions at Mass. Why hadn't she come? It was very upsetting, discourteous, rude even. He'd say to her parents, "I don't find Nadina at all reliable." So why hadn't she come, he'd ask. And her mother would shake her head and say that she'd set out al-right. Then she'd turn to her and ask what on earth she thought she was doing? And Father O'Donnell would say that Mrs Henderson having gone to so much trouble, Nadina was very inconsiderate. And then her mother would ask her again what on earth she thought she was doing letting Father down like that, and her father would shake his head at her in that despairing way he had, agreeing with all that was said, and would ask where on earth did she get to, if she hadn't gone to the presbytery?

But none of it mattered. She wouldn't go. She *couldn't*. Nadina turned her bike round and started back, pedalling furiously. She reached the coastal road again, slammed on her brakes. The recommendation! Father O'Donnell might even tell her that he was unable to recommend her because she was proving untruthful. A liar.

Now a revised plan began to take shape. She would stay long enough to eat her tea as quickly as possible, then explain that she was about to be sick and must go home. She was very sorry, but it couldn't be helped. "It was a lovely tea, Father O'Donnell, and so kind of Mrs Henderson," she imagined herself saying. "Please thank her for me. But I have to go now, I feel awful. I hope to be at Mass as usual on Sunday, of course. Please forgive me."

The more she thought about it, the more convinced that this was the way out and was surprised she hadn't thought of it before. Back she pedalled. She reached the church, proud and distinct, dwarfing the houses round about, and next to it, the big house where he'd be waiting. The tinny bell from the Protestant church chimed five times. She realised with relief that her watch was fast. Shoving her bike up against the railings, Nadina ran quickly up the steps to the front door to bang the knocker. It was too late to go to the garden to look for him.

The door opened as though he'd been there listening for her. She stared. He was wearing a thick woollen jumper, shirt and trousers, like everyone wore on their Saturdays off from work. The big mottled face broke into a grin. "Don't look so surprised, Nadina. Saturday. My day off. I told you. You've no objection, I take it?"

"No, it was just... unusual, Father, to see you... like..."

"You're all out of breath." He flung the door open, reached out with his hand to pull her in. "Come in, come in, my dear Nadina. Let's see now. Have you padlocked your cycle? No? Well go and do it, please."

Obediently, she ran down the steps, her fingers trembling as she turned the key of the lock. He waited for her at the door.

"Good. Now, let's have your coat, shall we? How quiet it is - just a bit of a wind. So different from this time last year when our pilots cleared the skies of the Hun, eh? Well, you can't tell with English weather, can you? Now in Ireland, in the South, well you get the mist you know, early in the morning, and then, oh dear, can it rain? My goodness, it can rain for days on end. Where's your gas mask? Left it at home? Naughty girl."

He chuckled, his tummy jiggling underneath the big fisherman's jersey as he hung her coat on the hall stand amidst a jumble of other outdoor wear. He placed an arm round her shoulders. She stiffened, wanting to shake it off, but she didn't, telling herself it didn't necessarily mean anything. After all, her father, who showed her no affection whatsoever, sometimes put a hand on her arm or even around her shoulders. Nevertheless she felt she should give some kind of warning and give it now.

"I very nearly didn't come...."

His reply was stern, the smile slipped to be replaced by a sulky look, the frown between the thick eyebrows, mouth down at the corners. "Oh well, I would have been very disappointed, Nadina because..." Suddenly his voice brightened, "Well, anyway, you're here! Now come along, come along, let me show you," and he waddled along beside her, out of breath, his short legs taking little steps. She tried not to laugh because it was like having a poodle on a lead. He stopped outside a door close to the study, thrust it open. "Now what do you think of that? Oh, do tell me you're glad you've come!"

She took in a breath, then exhaled, amazed. "Golly!" was all she could say. On a long table in the centre of the room were plates piled with food of every variety: sandwiches, jelly, trifles, sponges, iced buns, currant buns and a delicious looking fruitcake. She was genuinely shocked. "But how do you do it, Father? I mean, with the rationing?"

They stood together, framed in the doorway. "Well, I live quite simply and save up my coupons for occasions like this: welcoming a dear sweet girl like Nadina Brown to tea. But much is due to our fearsome Mrs Henderson. Now, come along. First things first."

She followed him to the table, he turned to her. "Nadina, dear, where would you like to sit? Shall we put you at the head of the table here, or halfway down, or right down the far end?"

"I don't mind."

"Well, how about..." he put his thumb under his front teeth as if it was a difficult decision. "Suppose I sit here," he patted the back of a chair, "at the head of this lovely long table. Refectory table, it's called. Did you know that?" He continued without waiting for her answer. "Now, there's that peculiar English expression again – what is it? Oh, I know, 'I'll be mother." He giggled appreciatively at his own joke. "And so you, my dear Nadina, where would you like to sit? Oh, shall we say, halfway down?" The words tumbled out excitedly; he was like a kid, a big kid, she thought, and despite her fear she couldn't help smiling. He could be really funny.

"Now, Nadina, just go to the top of the basement steps will you and call out, 'We're ready, Mrs Henderson!' And she should," he put his finger to the side of his nose and winked, "come running."

He rubbed his hands together, patted his tummy. "Oh, how wonderful! This is just mouth-watering, isn't it?"

She was frightened again. The silly voice. He was like that when he started, his hands, the kissing. It was so unlike last evening when he'd been so different, so proper. It was like he was two people. Thank goodness Mrs Henderson is here, she thought. Mrs Henderson with the moustache that made her look like a man. *Oh, thank you, Jesus!*

Nadina walked to the top of the basement steps, calling out as she'd been instructed. Then she returned and took her place at the table, her hands in her lap, a smile of contentment lifting her lips as she surveyed all the food in front of her, wondering where to make a start. She determined, though, that as soon as the meal was over, she'd make her excuse and go.

Mrs Henderson appeared carrying a large teapot, milk and sugar, cups and saucers on a tray. She even gave Nadina a passing smirk as she set the contents of the tray in front of Father O'Donnell then quietly withdrew.

Both priest and parishioner were now seated. He bowed his head and reeled off a Latin Grace. When he had finished, for something to say, Nadina, accepting a paste sandwich from the plate held out to her, asked why Mrs Henderson always looked so miserable. "Something bad must have happened to her, Father, because... well, she never looks happy."

"Oh, it's her husband. Poor Jack Henderson is in such poor health. It's not easy having a husband at home all day unable to work."

Nadina decided that she'd think kind thoughts of Father's housekeeper and pray for her and her sick husband.

The meal continued, the priest pouring the tea, handing her a cup, urging her on to taste every sandwich and sample every kind of fare on the table. Eventually, Nadina had to stop. "I'm full, Father," she said, embarrassed, putting her hand to her mouth to stop herself burping.

"Mrs H has excelled herself don't you think?" he asked, pouring her another cup of tea. "Now, take your tea and let's sit together over on the sofa. You'll find it very comfortable. I'm going to fetch my pipe. Filthy habit I suppose. So I do hope you don't mind."

Now!

But the words wouldn't come. Instead, she shook her head, smiling, but moving to the farthest end of the comfortable sofa as he left the room. He returned a few minutes later wreathed in smoke. It wasn't a bad smell, she decided. In fact, quite nice; sort of comforting. She sipped her tea slowly then let her head rest on the back of the sofa. With all the stress leading up to the visit and all the food she had consumed, Nadina was scared that she might drop off to sleep. He sat next to her, puffing away at his pipe. Near, but not near enough to touch her. Though sleepy, she remained alert. At the first sign, she would make a run for it, not before giving him a warning.

"You know, Nadina, you probably think that I have so many friends, so many people to talk to, but I haven't. None at all. In fact, dear, you are the only person of any age group that I really feel comfortable with. I am on duty the whole time. Do you understand what I'm saying to you?"

Flushing, she licked a crumb from her lip. "How do you mean, Father?"

"Well, you see, a priest has to be prepared for a lonely life." He placed his pipe in an ash tray on the floor, stretched out his short legs and leaned back so his head was level with hers. Turning his eyes to her, he said, "Nadina, dear, I'd like you to think, bearing in mind of course that you are a parishioner and I am the priest, that we could be good friends."

"I know what loneliness is," she said, staring ahead.

He adjusted his position, shifting a little closer. "I am surprised to hear you say that, Nadina. A young girl with the whole of her life in front of her. Why should you be lonely?"

"In every way, I'm lonely. I've always been lonely, Father."

Then she talked, but the whole time watching carefully. To her relief he didn't move any closer. It was so wonderful to be able to talk to a grown up, and especially a priest. He was the first and only adult she had ever confided in, apart of course from Miss Ashby and then it was mostly about the Church, about belief. Not about her home, not about the horrible blotch, nor about the bully of a sister, or her stupid parents. And though she longed to talk about it to Thelma and thought she'd understand, she held back. For the others would find out, be jealous and bully her even more.

The words stumbled out, stopping, then starting, stopping again: about Daphne, about home, her father, school, everything. "You tell me I feel superior. But I don't, Father. Not at all. I feel the opposite. Daphne is smart and popular with everyone and good at games. Captain of the netball team. She swims as well. We all had to go and watch her at the swimming gala at school. She can swim the crawl. She wins races. Not as clever as me, though you wouldn't think so the way mother praises her up. She's always favouring her above me. Mother's the one who's proud. I don't like that sister of mine. I know I should, but I don't. I've tried to. I'm always trying to, honestly." She moved her head off the back of the settee to face him, "But I can't. I know it's wrong."

Then she leaned back, continued in the same vein, losing all sense of time, her voice threatening to break, eyes smarting as resentment poured out of her. She told him how her parents were always comparing her with Daphne. "You don't know them. They put on a front for you. I feel... Oh, I feel... I'm second best. I'll never be good enough, however hard I try." The tears started then. "I can't get on with them – my father, especially. He's not interested in me. Not like a normal father. He doesn't even look at me when he talks. He's not interested in me. Always busy at work, work, work, work!" Important. Chief Air Raid Warden. He loves to find people who break the law, so he can tell them off." She paused, her voice edged with sarcasm, "Oh, he's always got time for Daphne, of course. Oh, yes, always time for *her*."

Then of course there was the blemish. It was like a curse, she told him, like Cain who was marked for life. "He was a fugitive, wasn't he Father? Like me? Not belonging anywhere. Why, Father? Why? And I believed your prayers would be answered."

She even felt she could speak of Ryan. "I like him because he's like me. That's what he said. He said, 'you don't fit in, that's why.' He says I've got to stand up to them. Do you know what I mean, Father?"

He puffed away on his pipe in silence, here and there, nodding gravely. The more she talked, the easier she found it. He asked questions, giving her time to answer.

Both looked towards the door as a feathered hat appeared around it, the gloomy face of the housekeeper underneath. "I'll say goodnight, Father. Be here an hour earlier tomorrow to clear away."

"Ah, thank you, Mrs Henderson."

"Thank you," murmured Nadina.

Mrs Henderson's leaving!

The sudden realisation made Nadina's heart thump, her eyes widened, mouth opened in shock. She had not noticed the time. Minutes had become hours racing by. She saw it was nearly a quarter-to-ten. She hated cycling in the black-out. The lights on her bike had to be covered in tissue paper and she never felt safe. She jumped up from the sofa. "Goodness, I'll have to go."

"Don't leave just yet. "Please, Nadina, sit down again. Please." His voice was pleading; a little boy's voice. She stood, her eyes filling up, legs carrying her forward towards the door.

"Sit down, please," he said, patting the sofa, his voice stern. She had reached the door, then turned back. This time she sat perched on the arm, every so often turning to look at the clock. She was sure that she would not make the same mistake as other times, knowing that immediately he tried to kiss her, or fondle her, put a hand on her knee or stroke her blemish, she would run. This time she was ready.

But he made no move towards her and the danger seemed to pass, so Nadina slid down on to the seat and leaned her head back, hid a yawn, her eyelids pricking. And it was her turn now to listen. She forced herself to stay awake as he talked about his upbringing, his childhood in Dublin; about growing up and realising his vocation. He spoke about the parishes he had served in and again mentioned his loneliness.

"I understand loneliness," she said again. And then she felt a thrill, an excitement. Here was somebody who was like her. It was silly, she knew. But here was a man, a grown up, a priest who understood her. Friends? He said we could be friends.

"You see, people think with all the parishioners making a big fuss of you, you could never be lonely. But priests are. It's a lonely life, Nadina." He reached over, his hand finding her knee.

Now!

She stood up. He stood up as well. She started to back away towards the door as he came towards her. He held his hands out to her, the palms upwards, as if appealing to her, his eyes twinkling mischievously, "I hope you'll come again, dear little Nadina? Yes? Yes?"

She ran towards the front door struggling desperately with the catch – wondering in terror if he had locked it. She heard him call out, "Friends. All I want is for us to be friends!"

Then he was behind her, reaching up, opening the door for her. Breathless, she pushed through the gap. "Good night, Father," she called out as she half fell down the steps, struggling to keep her balance. At the foot of the steps she looked up, some of the original message she had rehearsed coming to her lips. "It's been a lovely tea. Thank you, Father. Please thank Mrs Henderson for me. She must have gone to a great deal of trouble." Looking up at him silhouetted against the dim glow of the hall light, she swallowed, added, "I shall want your recommendation letter. You won't forget, will you, Father?"

He made no reply. Fumbling with the lock on her bike in the dark, she knew he waited there, watching her.

She pedalled as fast as she could. The road was clear, few people were about. Lonely? How can a priest ever be lonely? If she had his task she'd be so busy telling people about Christ and the Holy Virgin, she'd never have time to be lonely. Yet, she would let him be her friend... *after* she'd got the recommendation! And then? She knew now. She'd go straight to Miss Ashby, and together they would go to the police. She was sure that Thelma would believe her.

For the whole period of instruction the next Friday, Father O'Donnell's behaviour was perfectly correct. He made no attempt to molest her. He taught her a great deal: about the need for daily meditation, the duties of a priest, the structure of the Church, the Calendar for festival times and special seasons of the Church Year. Nadina learned about the lives of other famous saints. He had such a knowledge. She came home with the basket on her bicycle full of more books. As long as she never went to the presbytery again, she felt sure she'd be safe.

Chapter Sixteen

Kathie squinted round the cornflakes packet at her brother, trying to catch his attention as he dug his knife into the bottom of the marmalade jar. "Any idea what's up with Nadina?" she asked.

Ryan, absorbed, shook his head. He had far more important matters on his mind than the whereabouts of the one-eyed freak. "Search me," he said, scraping out the residue on to his toast. Today was the worst day of his life: the Scholarship. He'd woken up with his stomach spinning like a top.

"Rye, her mum's going spare. Nobody knows what's the matter and Daphne says she's getting the blame. So, little brother, it's up to you, seeing you're *her monitor.*"

"Nothing to do with me. I'm chucking it in anyways."

Short-sighted, Kathie peered over her spectacles, raising her voice. "Doesn't anyone at your piddling little school know? What about that pongy acne-ridden child, Dickerson?" She stood to pour the tea.

"Sure, her and that Dickerson kid don't have nothing to do with the rest of us." He bit into his toast, held up his cup. "Kenny and Dickerson back together full time; Pimple-face and Naddy fall out, back together, then hate each other's guts. Can't keep up with it, I can't. It's like you girls do. Up and down all the time, like yo-yos. She tells him loads. Nattering away all the time, she is. Beetle-brow should speak to Acne-crater."

Kathie sighed. "Maybe that fat mum of hers should go and see your cranky Head. See if she knows anything."

Miss Millison had other things on her mind than the strange behaviour of one of her pupils. Today was Scholarship day. The children's success or otherwise was a reflection on her ability as their headmistress to impart education to reluctant charges, though even so, she thought grimly, eyeing the lines of nervous faces assembled beneath her steely gaze, no one, not even her could make silk purses from sows' ears.

Approaching retirement within two years, her policy was to keep parents well away from school premises. As she always made clear when confronting a mother with a prospective pupil, her job was to *educate*, not to become involved with domestic issues outside school. "That is *your* job," she would announce, agitatedly pushing her top teeth back in place and leaning across her desk, her disagreeable expression barely a foot away from the face of the frightened parent. This draconian policy allowed her to run her school largely free from parental interference.

With easy access to the jangle of keys in her great white handbag, Miss Millison was thoroughly in control not only over pupils and staff and but fretful and belligerent parents. Whenever she became aware that one was on the way up to the school to confront her, she would retreat to the security of her office and place a notice, DO NOT DISTURB, on the door. There was an overriding motive for this policy. Quite simply, she did not like children very much - apart from a few favourites, Nadina Brown, being one.

Ryan was well aware that Naddy was absent. A couple of weeks now. Before, she'd seemed okay, still a fanatic, but more cheerful about it. Not that he was bothered. What irked him was the sad spaniel's eye, that weepy Jesus look, and the constant promises to pray for his soul. Then again, if Miss Ashby expected him to be a kind of baby-minder, she'd got the wrong person. They should give it to nit-picker Julie. Of course, big-head Matthews with his baby dimple cheeks and double chin loved the job. Not Ryan Brannigan. Half-term he'd throw the towel in. Definite. What with the Scholarship hovering over him for weeks now like a black cloud filling his bedroom at night and still being there in the morning, it would be one thing less to cope with.

Feigning indifference, at break he asked if they knew what was up with Dream Girl. The clearest explanation came from Pat. "Monthly stuff, I reckon. You wouldn't know nothing about that, Irish. So don't pry."

"Thanks for nothing, Face-ache," he said kicking the football to Kenny.

"That kid Nadina's in dream land, most of the time," Ryan told him. "God, Religion, Church, is what's wrong with her. It can get you into a kind of trance, so you don't know where you are going or what the hell you're doing."

Kenny shrugged his shoulders, heading the ball back. The stupidity of Naddy Brown was of no concern to him. "Boy, you keep going on and on about that fat bum. You want to make your mind up, you do. Dump her or love her. You're getting on my tits, you are, going on and on and on." Kenny, who always showed annoyance when Ryan brought up big subjects like Faith and Church, yelled, "Any way, don't be disrespectful to the Lord, you Fenian bastard," and with his left foot aimed a return shot at Ryan's head.

Ryan laughed and ducked easily. The way old Kenny goes all hoity-toity over religion, he thought. He gets the idea that not to believe in God is like not being a proper Brit, and if you went to Mass main times, like Easter and Christmas, you proved you were a good Catholic. Canoodling with Pat in the store cupboard or behind the oak was all that mattered to the big oaf.

From headers they dribbled the ball, the big boy pushing others away who wanted to join in. Kenny got flustered because his outsize feet in the big boots could never match Ryan's nifty footwork.

Too late for Assembly, Nadina took her usual place on the back row, reacting to his stare with a scowl. She was bound to be back today, he thought, sticking his tongue out. Her, of course, but no one else, apart from Matthews, Cyn Peal, and one or two others, could be certain of getting through. And there would be at least half a dozen who would crash at the first hurdle: the Intelligence Test.

Their teacher sped along the rows, slamming down on each desk examination papers she took from a fat brown envelope. As she reached Ryan, elbow resting on his desk, chin cupped in his hand, staring mournfully ahead, she gave him a shove. His elbow dropped. He looked up in shock. She gave him a grim smile as she moved on.

Ryan stared at Foureyes. Mouth open, blowing bubbles, spit dribbling through the gaps in his teeth, down his chin and on to his filthy jersey. "No point you taking the Test at all, you moron." He liked the sound of that word, the latest on his list. "Hey, moron," he repeated, thumping his arm.

The boy swivelled his head round to face Ryan. "Hurt, that did. What did you say, Rye? "

"You should clear off home, kiddo, that's what. 'Cause this is an Intelligence Test and you got no intelligence. Might as well go now, you daft prat."

Foureyes wrinkled his nose, sniffed, ran the sleeve of his jersey along the slime and looked around him, wondering if he should take his friend's advice. But at that moment, Miss Ashby approached.

After two hours of answering puzzles, general knowledge questions, and simple arithmetic, the papers were collected and the candidates sat with their arms folded as instructed. Ryan turned to the back row, stared at Naddy. What's up with her? The one eye widened and rolled about, pink and sore, and the top of her nose was sunset red. Probably the only time she was really happy was when old Foureyes put his spit on her. A three-penny bit for a kiss? Ridiculous. Not even worth a farthing. Can't be the test, though; that wouldn't make her cry. She should walk through it blind, being the brightest that ever sat there for the last hundred years, a walking encyclopaedia, knowing as many or even more words than fatso Ashby. So what the hell's the matter with the stupid kid?

"What's up, Naddy? he called out.

Her only response was to stare out of the window.

"Silence!" thundered the teacher.

Lunch time and Ryan blinked in the strong sunshine. One part of the big ordeal over he sought out Naddy, his gaze lighting on her, silent and alone by the oak tree. He turned to Kenny. "It's what I told you. Look at her," he pointed. "Not even your pimply-dial Pat bothering with her. She's in a trance. Religion's what's got her. Religion always does that to you."

"Yeah," Kenny narrowed his eyes. 'Given it a great deal of thought, I have."

Inwardly Ryan groaned, recognising the signs. Know-all was about to instruct a lesser mortal, trying to show intelligence.

"Al-right, you Fenian bastard, I know. The opium of the people. Bloke called Karl Marx." Kenny sucked slowly, contemplating the journey of the milk up his straw before swirling it round in his mouth and swallowing. "Yeah, been giving the subject a great deal of thought, I have, as a matter of fact. Yeah, clocked up a lot of time in the British Museum, did Marx. Big black-bearded beggar. Had a number of mates. Engels, was one. Freddy Engels. After Marx, Lenin come along, that's how you get your Communism." He paused from dispensing wisdom, sucked, the milk bottle emptying with a satisfying gurgle.

"October Revolution, 1917," he continued. "Date that changed history. Them Bolsheviks shot the Czar, the lot of 'em, their Royals. Stood 'em up against a wall. Those Commies, tough as old boots. Good that they're on our side. They'll show them Nazis no mercy. Hitler should have learned from Napoleon. You wait 'til winter strikes."

Ryan watched him take his straw, flick it in the face of a girl from Class Five. He swirled the residue of milk around, held the bottle to his lips, gasped and burped. Ryan knew the jumble of facts all came from the same source: the *News of the World*. Stuff Kenny liked to trot out when the mood took him, trying to prove they were intellectual equals.

All around them the conversation centred on the recent exam. Ryan avoided post-mortems. They always made him nervous. He strolled over to where Naddy stood, the roll of his shoulders maximising his muscles. "You al-right?" he asked.

"Why should you care?"

"I don't."

He moved away. A ball headed by Foureyes landed at his feet. He picked it up, put it under his arm, called out over his shoulder, "*I'm* not bothered, am I? Your mam's worried about you, is all."

He bounced the ball up and down, practised his heading to impress her and anyone else who might be looking on.

"Think I don't know that?"

Ryan shrugged. Miserable twit. Fat freak. He dribbled the ball away. Then, without a warning, he turned to kick it as hard as he could, aiming for her head. She ducked just in time. The ball banged against the tree, bounced back towards him. He picked it up, smiled at her. "Bet you didn't know that was coming, did you?"

Foureyes wandered over to join him. Pat, pimples bleeding from a recent picking, appeared. In a show of loyalty she stood next to Nadina.

"Get lost, Brannigan. You don't care about no one except yourself, you don't."

"Get lost yourself, Foul-face."

Several more insults were traded. Then the bell sounded. Miss Ashby, at the door, called out, "Back, back, back inside, all of you. At once!"

The children trudged in obediently, sat at their desks, their arms folded, waiting.

"Be absolutely quiet," said the little teacher. "These are examination conditions, which once again means silence and absolutely no talking, particularly remembering *your* disposition, Ryan, disrupting proceedings whenever there's an opportunity. I shall be watching you like the proverbial hawk. And stop punching others."

"Don't you worry yourself, Miss, me being a monitor like. Good as gold, me." He grinned round at the rest of the class.

His remark made for some relaxation in the nerve-racked atmosphere, until Miss Ashby curbed their amusement with a shout of disapproval, the red blancmange of her bosoms wobbling agitatedly, her arms waving. "Silence!" she called out. She took out the envelope from her desk, white this time, and waved it at them.

"This second part of the examination determines your knowledge of the English language and proficiency in Mathematics."

The two monitors refilled the inkwells, Ryan deliberately spilling some on Foureyes' already ink-stained fingers. Miss Ashby handed out the papers.

Ryan scratched his head, chewed the end of his pen until the taste made him want to gag. He began to count the number of ticks the big clock on the wall in front of him made every ten minutes. Suddenly he realised that time never stayed still and bent industriously to his paper.

"Finish now!" Miss Ashby shouted, clanging the bell. She went from desk to desk, snatching up the papers. When she reached Ryan's, she glanced at it, shook her head.

"What's wrong, Miss?" he asked, his mouth twitching.

"What's right you mean, don't you?"

For the last hour of the afternoon, Miss Ashby relaxed. They were allowed to talk quietly or play board games. Ryan stared at Nadina, with growing curiosity. "If she blubbers much more, that big eye that's never still will run out of tears, dry up forever and she'll go blind," he said to Kenny.

"Good!"

Miss Ashby rang the final bell of the day. The children from all six classes streamed out of the classrooms, merging together at the school gates, the smaller ones squealing in protest as big Kenny's hands moved from left to right, pushing and shoving. Ryan, Foureyes, and others from the top class were close behind.

Everyone was anxious to get home, knowing that at any moment there could be the wail of the siren and the enemy planes like giant buzzards would unleash death and destruction. The memory of air raids and the horror they brought was still vivid. The threat was always there.

Along the Kelliwell Road, the three friends stopped. Kenny looked up at the sky. It was almost clear, though in the distance clouds were moving slowly.

"My mum says there's going to be bombing tonight. You got a shelter yet?"

Foureyes shook his head. Ryan too, but more vigorously. Ever since Arthur Evett had been taken prisoner, Mrs Evett always looked on the black side. "You suppose a shelter's going to stop you getting done, if your number's up?"

"God protects you," said Foureyes gravely, drawing in saliva.

"You moron! Think like that, and you're a goner! I don't believe in God. It's to keep the Church in the money. Fate is what happens. You either got a chance to go on living or you go six feet under."

"The Church is a holy place and the priests guide you," the boy intoned solemnly. His theological input was cut short by Ryan landing a punch to his gut. Winded by the force of the blow, Foureyes nevertheless continued doggedly.

"And... the... Lord... looks... after you. God, I feel sick now." He straightened up.

"Listen, Dumbo," Ryan continued, "You either get a bomb up your bum or you don't. It's all fate. You can't stop fate. I tell you, whatever that fat Father spouts on about it makes no damn difference at all. Stupid prayer don't stop it."

"It'll give you bad luck if you go on about priests like that," said Foureyes. He pulled his jersey up, revealing a red mark on pale flesh. Rubbing his stomach, he tried hard to stop the tears drifting down his cheeks, failed; they mixed with mucus leaving a snail's trail. Ryan hit him again. The place his father had always aimed for, the side of the head.

"Brannigan!" Suddenly Miss Ashby's voice boomed out. She was behind the smaller children, jumping up to see over their heads.

It was time for Ryan to make amends. He realised he'd been hard on his friend and despite his vow to pack in the monitor's job, he valued Miss Ashby's opinion of him. Foureyes was thick as treacle, yet he deserved some explanation. He put his arm round the smaller boy's shoulder and spoke in his ear slowly and deliberately. "Look Rich, there's a lot of lies about God and stuff. It's done by the Church and the priests to keep us down, like they did in the potato famine last century in Ireland. Me dad knows all about it. The priests dress up, and get the money off us. Then they have their big meals while the peasants starve. Me granddaddy dropped dead in the field he was ploughing. You read up on the history of Ireland – if you can read, of course – then you'll know about it."

The lecture ended with a shove, but carefully this time. It was more like a barge, followed by a grin of friendship. Ryan was tempted to give him a head lock but he resisted, still thinking of his key word, compassion.

Foureyes looked grateful and asked, "Don't you pray no more, Rye?"

"Hell, no!"

The boy's voice trembled a little. Behind the pebble spectacles his eyes widened. "Don't you believe in nothing?"

"Damn all."

"Ryan!" Miss Ashby yelled again, now only yards behind him.

"Better see what little fatso wants. See you tomorrow, unless you get your daft self buried alive." Ryan turned away and followed the diminutive teacher back into the classroom.

Nadina was waiting by the teacher's desk. Miss Ashby curled an arm round the girl's waist. Nadina looked up reproachfully as Ryan appeared, the one eye covered by the curtain of hair. The other, wet and rimmed with red as if someone had painted a circle round it.

"Nadina's very upset about something. And she won't tell me, I'm afraid. Nadina, will you be able to tell your monitor?"

She shook her head. Miss Ashby's eyes narrowed. "Ryan, have you been saying nasty things about her, poking fun at her with the others? Has he, Nadina, dear? Has he been taunting you - he and those other two incompetents?"

Once again, Nadina shook her head, the corner of the lip that was visible curled unsteadily.

"Can I go now, Miss?" Ryan asked.

"Have you no concern? Can't you see the girl is upset? For goodness sake! I thought you and she were supposed to be friends. Aren't you any more?"

Ryan shrugged his shoulders. "What's happened to you and Pat then, Naddy?"

She looked away, said nothing.

Miss Ashby pursed her lips, "Ryan, I want you to walk home with Nadina." He began to protest, shaking his head from side to side and muttering under his breath. "Yes," she continued. "Show some compassion. You seem very keen on the idea, the way you stressed its importance to Father O'Donnell. I should like to see you put it into action. And whatever it is that's come between you two, you are to sort it out. You have a responsibility as her monitor."

Ryan huffed a loud sigh. He rolled his shoulders exaggeratedly, as if about to come out of his corner of the ring for a big fight. "The responsibility is getting too much for me, Miss. Sure, I've got to pack in this monitor job."

"While you have been chosen by your fellow pupils as their monitor, though goodness knows why, you have that responsibility whether you like it or not. So sort it out."

"Miss Ashby? Why is it always my fault? Whenever she gets all upset, I gets the blame. I done nothing, Naddy, have I? It's nothing to do with me, Miss. Surely to goodness it isn't."

Nadina lowered her head and her lank hair began to shift a little way over her left eye too. The teacher sighed. "I really think I'll have to speak to Miss Millison about you, Nadina. And, yes, we'll have to have your parents up at the school. I'm afraid there's nothing else for it. Your father's note just saying you haven't been well is not sufficient. You are obviously deeply unhappy about something. As your teacher I have a duty to be concerned for your welfare. It is affecting your whole outlook, as well as the atmosphere in the entire classroom. You've missed lessons for a whole fortnight, and most of the time, until comparatively recently, you have shown deep distress."

Miss Ashby paused, "Oh dear. Have you a handkerchief, Ryan? No, I imagine you haven't." She searched in her handbag, "Seems I've left my spares at home. Right; off you go the pair of you. And Nadina, my door is always open for you. I can't say more than that, can I? Whatever it is that's troubling you...yes?"

Wet-faced, Nadina managed a weak, tearful smile.

Looking with impatience at the reluctant monitor, Miss Ashby reiterated, "Ryan, you are to look after her. It is your monitor's duty."

Chapter Seventeen

Ryan trudged ahead, aware that Naddy was at least five to ten paces behind and the distance increasing. Now and then he would turn round, an expression of disgust on his thin face, running a hand through his thatch of straw-coloured hair in exasperation, watching her drag her feet, her head low. He had forgotten their friendship, her visits more welcome than not, showing her his list and her adding fresh words, letting him savour the sounds like tasting ice cream. Compassion was on hold.

He looked for any debris drifting in the six-inch depth of brackish water in the gutter, spotted an empty Players cigarette packet. He picked it up, turned to run at her, threw it, aiming for her legs. It missed, though she gave no sign that she had seen it. He moved on, looked up. Kenny's mam was wrong about it being a clear night. The light clouds that gathered had grown black and menacing. A clap of thunder startled him and a fine spray flew in their faces. "I'm supposed to see you home, aren't I?" he shouted. "We're going to get soaked, so come on!"

Her hair hung down like a tattered mat. He became aware that she was crying softly. He whirled round. "Oh, come on, Naddy!" He went to her, seized her arm. She shrugged him off. Again, he moved ahead, then waited, his back against a garden wall.

"I wish I was dead," she said.

He frowned. "Naddy, you're a complete wet weekend, so you are. You get sorry for yourself all the time. Look, haven't I said we've all got something that's not right. Never will be. Look at me, I talk funny because of where I come from and they all take the Mick, don't they? Well, let 'em, I say. I can't help the way I am. I've tried and it don't make no difference. And if I gets sorry for myself, sure the worse it gets. I get me words all mixed up. Stutter I do. You've heard me. Hey, ever notice Kenny's feet? Like an elephant's they are."

She gave a slight nod.

"You noticed them, have you? Seen his ears? Like an African elephant's - stick out, they do. I've said all this before, but you don't take no damned notice. Look at Rich. You try to explain everything to him and even then he don't understand. Sure, he's daft and he dribbles, got no control over his spit. He should be in a zoo. Hardly spell his own stupid name, but can't help it, can he?"

This time she shook her head.

Ryan sighed, then went up to her, flipped his hands under her hair to lift it and was pleased to see a fleeting smile. "You look at your mate Dickerson's face. God, what a mess, all pimply and bloody where she picks 'em. See, you got to realise. None of us can help it, Naddy. None of us. Well Dickerson could, of course. Could get herself cleaned up, like change her knickers, wash under her armpits. God, she stinks. How can Kenny go near her? Never washes at all, I reckon. And there's you. So okay, you can't help it; massive great blotch of purple and red. India, *I* think. They say Africa. Same difference. All down the side of your fat dial. God's sake! Get over it, girl!"

A wail greeted this well-meant advice. "It's... it's not that. Not..." Naddy's voice sank to a whisper and died.

"Well, what then? Think I want to be a stupid monitor? But if I am, God help me, I'll knock it out of you if I have to, you great fat religious freak, so you are."

Miserably, she shook her head. Ryan, without a coat, pulled up the collar of his jersey to his chin. The blackness of the clouds had moved directly above them and the fine spray was blowing faster. Any moment it'd be proper rain, he thought.

Nadina had dropped back again. She is trudging along like an old peasant woman with her shoulders all bent, like she's loaded down with a sack of coal on her back, he thought. He'd seen the coal man coming to their house, his shoulders permanently bent. That's what she's got already. Fat freak. He softened his voice, remembering compassion, "Please, Naddy, it's going to piss down any minute. Don't be such an old lady. You're like them peasants with bent backs you get in Ireland, carrying peat and stuff for miles."

He picked up speed, turning round every few yards to urge her on. Now the rain came, accompanied by claps of thunder and from the blackened sky jagged forks of streak lightening, lighting their way. He spotted an empty lemonade bottle in the gutter. He kicked it as hard as he could in her direction. Water splashed his socks, wetting his trousers. Nadina gave a fresh howl, a cry of such despair that he stopped still. His stomach churned. Then another, the sound muffled by the length of hair that blew into her mouth. She was a stupid kid of a girl with that Empire map on her cheek, and why should he care? He'd pack in the monitoring tomorrow, see if he didn't. But despite himself, her sobs disturbed him. He whirled round again then ran up to her, his fists clenched. But suddenly, mindful of the need to be compassionate, he put his arm round her shoulders and squeezed, pulling her to him, the softness of his voice in her ear, "Oh, what the hell's wrong with you, Naddy? Sure, you've got to move, kiddo, or we'll both bloody drown at this rate. Come *on*! For God's sake girl!"

This time she yelled back. "It's wrong to blaspheme! You shouldn't use God's name as a swear word."

"Oh, shut up."

Along the grass verges, like the tentacles of an octopus, the branches of the trees reached out, smacking their faces, clinging to their clothes. Ryan increased his pace, shouting at the storm, angry at a God he didn't believe in. He couldn't stand misery people; people like Nadina Brown with her sad, soulful spaniel's eye and that creepy Jesus look she gave everyone, like she was so much better than everyone else in the world. "Why do you let that leper slag follow you about, boy?" Kenny would ask, and he'd respond to Kenny's question with his boxer's shrug: shoulders shifting, hands open, palms upwards. It was becoming quite a common response to questions when he wasn't sure what answer to give. If he did know, yet for some reason was reluctant to say, he would go into Quasimodo stance, an exaggerated form of his boxer's pose. The Quasimodo had the right shoulder hunched, left elbow stuck out at an angle, back bent low. It gave an impression of mystery, he thought. Most of the time, however, he felt James Cagney to be sufficient, even though traces of the Irish accent came through the American twang. "Search me, my friend," he'd say. "No idea why the dame has this kinda fixation. Guess the dumb broad can't help herself."

"Suppose you ran out of chalk and got no blackboard, you could use her face if you was teaching geography," Kenny would guffaw and Ryan would smile, though he never liked the way Kenny spoke about her. Kenny had less respect for girls than he had for the junk on his mum's stall - apart from Dickerson.

Now, Ryan's feet squelched, shoes falling to pieces, the glue his dad had used to try to weather proof no use. He stopped again, lifted each foot in turn to see holes the size of pennies. Beneath his sodden jersey his vest was sticking to his skin. He turned up his saturated face, red and raw from the biting wind, shook his fist at the sky and yelled. "Make her normal. Me, an' all, O Lord!"

By then, Nadina had caught up with him. The wildness of her hair was driven by the wind then flattened down by the rain. Ryan shoved his fingers thorough it, making a path, dividing it to right and left. He imagined he was Moses, parting the Red Sea. He laid his hand on her head. It felt good to hear her giggle for the first time since they had set out. He shouted up at the sky. "Jesus, if you're that real, do it. Take it away from her, Lord." In case the Lord needed more explicit instructions, he added, "That black currant jam splodge, that's what I'm on about, goes all the way down the right side of her dial, like it's spilt there. And while you're doing that, make me speak proper like the Brits, will you, please? And, get me through the Scholarship so I gets to Grammar – that is, Southgate Grammar School for Boys, please Lord."

Then, to Nadina's open-mouthed astonishment, he knelt on the pavement for at least two whole minutes, the palms of his hands open in petition, before grabbing the belt of Nadina's raincoat with both hands to haul himself up.

He laughed aloud and Nadina giggled again, spitting out her hair where it tangled and found its way into her mouth. Ryan began to feel a little of what he thought she must be feeling, stuck with the wine stain like it was spilt from a glass; like someone had got drunk and barged into her. You couldn't say it was the same as having a funny voice or Kenny's big feet and jug ears, or even Foureyes with only half a brain, or Tojo with his slitty eyes.

Looking at her standing there in the pouring rain, Ryan thought that as well as asking the Lord to do away with her splodge, he should ask Him for a double dose of compassion because she was fixed firm into a straitjacket, stuck with a belief in dreamland.

As cloudburst followed cloudburst, making conversation difficult, he cupped his hands together and shouted in her ear. "See, Naddy, if He was up there, wouldn't he come down and do it like it says He done in the Scriptures? But He don't. All He does is send us rain." And Ryan held his head back and laughed and laughed like she had never heard him laugh before. Then he shook his head, as if bemused by the frailty of the Almighty.

"You shouldn't mock our Blessed Saviour," said Nadina, her grin disappearing.

"Oh, come on. You're like the peasant women all over Ireland. They believe everything they're told. It's like old wives' tales. He tucked his arm into hers. Bent his shoulders and spoke in a quavering voice. "We're like an old married couple, you and me, like we're a hundred years old."

For a time they trudged along in silence.

"You know Pat," said Nadina at length.

"What, you mean that sour-faced slag with the acne? Smelly skin all sort of yellowy? Never hardly washes? Strange that old Kenny goes with her. Shows him her drawers, she does. Same every day. Mauve and big they are."

"Well she's not my friend anymore."

Ryan shrugged, showed no particular interest. Her and Pat fell out as often as they washed their hair, which was maybe once a week like his sister, except, of course, ugly mug Dickerson who only washed hers every other year. He and Kenny had their bust-ups: he remembered one a month back when he and Kenny really hated each other, not speaking for days on end, but it did not happen often, only now and again.

Raising his voice above the noise of the rain, Ryan explained this to her as an example of the superiority of the male gender, but there was no response. Just a flick of her shoulders. Ryan tried to move her on faster, trying out his James Cagney. "Come on, you dumb broad, I'm soaked, ain't I?" Then, speaking in his normal voice, "Hey, Naddy, think there'll be a cup of tea for me when we get there. I'm dying for it."

A crackle of thunder like gunfire echoed around them, then a jagged flame of lightening lit up the sky for miles and he had a job to hear her next words, but when he caught on he stepped back a pace, eyes opening wide in alarm before his heartbeat slowed again.

"I'm much, much worse than Pat," she had said. "I'm more dirty. I hate myself. I'm going to kill myself."

Ryan hesitated, shouted in her ear, "Stop talking like a loony for God's sake, girl." He pulled her on and they walked arm in arm, quickening their pace. At last the rain had begun to slow to a fine drizzle. Feeling wet, cold and miserable, Ryan broke away and again began to pull ahead, walking six, then twelve paces ahead. At least Naddy had stopped crying. He'd done that, he told himself. Showed her she'd got to be more like him; got to show everyone she's not got to be scared. He turned round to face her and began to walk backwards, picking up speed. "Like I told you, you've got to stop getting so scared. You're kind of terrified of your own shadow, you are. Stop thinking they're all talking about you."

"How? And you, you doing nothing to stop them. I haven't forgotten, Ryan. But I've forgiven you."

Indignant, he spun away from her. "Oh, marvellous! You've forgiven me. See if I care. Anyway, they got it all wrong. You should know that. Lepers are white. You're a big mix-up, kind of like Liquorice All sorts." His thoughts raced on: "No, more like trifle. Yeah, that's it. Trifle. Never thought of trifle before." He turned back to her again and licked his lips, "I love trifle, I do."

Her angry expression vanished and for the first time since they had set off, she laughed aloud; not just a giggle but a real, proper laugh. I done that, he thought. My compassion done it.

When they reached the corner of Mercia Close, they ran all the way to number 16, clambering up the drive. He hung back while Nadina pushed her finger urgently at the button several times.

The door swung open. "Goodness, just look at you!"

Mrs Brown threw an extra-large towel over Nadina's head and started to rub vigorously. Both mother and daughter stumbled inside, Nadina struggling to free herself from her mother's exertions. Ryan was about to follow when Mrs Brown saw the puddle of water spreading like a small lake at his feet.

"No! No! Ryan, back, back, back. Not on my floor, dear. Stay outside. Nadina, continue to rub as hard as you can. No, Ryan, stay there, dear. Yes, outside. Off my step. Your feet firmly on the gravel until I get a towel for you. Otherwise you'll ruin my nice carpet." She laughed good-humouredly. "Just wait two seconds, dear."

Ryan looked down, saw the puddle spreading. Then, another towel the same colour and size, landed on his head like a parachute. "A nice bowl of thick vegetable soup is what I have in mind for you two," said Mrs Brown.

His head and shoulders now cloaked by the towel, Ryan imagined he was Lawrence of Arabia. Then, standing together, both children continued to dry their hair while Mrs Brown could be heard clattering about in the kitchen.

"Don't tell my parents, will you? Promise you won't," Nadina whispered.

"What?"

"Don't tell them what I told you!"

Ryan's one thought was of pouring hot soup down his throat and filling his empty belly. In any case he couldn't remember what she was supposed to have said or what sort of secret it was: "Think I should take my shoes and socks off?" he asked.

"I don't care. Yes, I think you should, I suppose. Whatever you like. Just don't tell my parents."

He frowned, began to remember, grinned, "You're not dirty like Pat-"

"Ryan... please!"

"Her tits are as flat as pancakes." He began to giggle as he took off his shoes. He peeled each sock off and a little water spilled out on to the parquet flooring. He dried each toe thoroughly with a corner of the towel. Then he dried the rest of his feet, leaving his shoes and socks in a corner of the vestibule.

Now in the warm, he was looking forward to Mrs Brown's cooking, which he had sampled before. Nadina was frowning at him.

"Sssh," she said, "remember?"

In the silence he stared back at her. "Whatever it is, Naddy, like Miss Ashby says, you can tell *her*. If I had a secret I would tell her. Whatever secret, however big it was."

She didn't answer. Just looked at him. He wandered ahead, sniffing the air. "Lovely, lovely. Come on, Naddy, I'm desperate. She's a great cook, your mam. "

"I can't tell anyone, Ryan," she whispered fiercely. But he had hurried ahead, disregarding her cries, conscious only of his empty tummy. In the kitchen Mrs Brown beamed at him, a big saucepan in both hands. Ryan liked coming to Mercia Close as long as he didn't have to meet Mr Brown. Everything was so nice and posh. It was old, but unlike his house it was always so clean and new looking, the windows were always shiny and there was never any stink of whisky or the fag smoke that caught in your throat. Everything was different. It would be like this in Rita Hayworth's home, or Veronica Lake's place over in Hollywood, he supposed. He had been in the Browns' kitchen before. And even here, where you'd expect to find things in a bit of a muddle, everything was in place: the cups high on a shelf above his head, all the handles pointing in the same direction. Plates piled up together according to their size: small plates in the front, then medium plates, the biggest ones stacked behind them.

"The boy's literally got his tongue hanging out!" Mrs Brown laughed. It was a deep and throaty sound, very different from his mam's high cackle. She heaved the saucepan over to the table. "Here we are, children. Vegetable soup."

"Just vegetables?" Ryan asked, sniffing the appetising smell.

"Oh, Ryan, you can still make a good soup just from vegetables, you know, though I've added a little cube of oxo." She grinned at him. He thought her nice and friendly with her big smile, wobbly cheeks, fat arms and bosoms like cushions. Steam rose from the two bowls in front of them. Ryan tucked his serviette carefully into his jersey before plunging in his spoon. Mrs Brown moved a chair up to the table to join them. "Actually Ryan, I'm glad you're here at this time."

Nadina, next to him, kicked his calf, directed an angry stare from the unhidden left eye. "Nothing to do with him," she mumbled, a brown stain like a pencil moustache spreading over her top lip.

Mrs Brown banged her fist on the table. Startled, Ryan spilt a little soup down his jersey. "It's just got to stop, Nadina! Your father and I are no longer prepared to watch you get so dreadfully upset." She turned an anxious face toward her guest. "Ryan, she just won't stop crying. You must have noticed, surely?"

Ryan's gaze was on his soup. Ignoring another nudge, harder this time, he blinked rapidly, unsure what to say. He looked up to see Nadina's big pink spaniel's eye still focussed on him. He let each spoonful stay in his mouth for a second or two, swirling it round before letting it make its way down his gullet, savouring the taste as well as giving him time to answer. It seemed Mrs Brown had added some sort of spice. Mr Brown probably pinched some from a kitchen somewhere – one of them Italian places he inspected.

"Ryan?"

"Sure, this is a most wonderful soup that you have here Mrs Brown. Terrific." He realised he could not delay a response any longer, but it was taking him time to remember what the question was. He looked from one to the other. Then it came to him. "Yeah, you do seem a bit upset, Naddy," he said, his mouth opening and closing rapidly, the sound of the spoon against his teeth. He turned his head to look at her, frowning in concentration. "Yeah, I've noticed, Naddy. Something on your mind, is it? Can't be the Scholarship. I bet you done really well." He looked across at Mrs Brown. "Nadina's cleverer than

me. Sure, a lot cleverer. Cleverer than anyone in the school."
He gave his best smile to his hostess, "Oh, you're a great cook,
Mrs Brown, so you are. Could you spare a little more, please?"

She got up from the table, moved to the draining board. He
watched the saucepan as it came over held firmly by her large
hands, fresh soup filling his dish. Meanwhile Nadina had slunk
low in her chair. Mrs Brown bent over Ryan to look into his
face. "So, is she like this at school then? Utterly miserable all
the time?"

How should he answer now? There was no need, for at that
moment Nadina jumped up, knocking her chair over, threw her
serviette down on the table, moved to the door and shouted,
"Mother, it's got nothing to do with him! Nothing!"

Both Mrs Brown and Ryan winced as she slammed the door
behind her.

"Can I have a bit of bread with it, Mrs Brown, please?"

"White or brown?"

"Oh as it comes, Mrs Brown, I don't mind," he smiled.

Silently she moved her big frame over to the draining board,
opened a drawer and reached for a bread knife. She cut a large
crust from a brown loaf, reached up for a plate on the shelf
above, then brought it over to him. To his alarm, she sat down
next to him, in Nadina's chair.

Ryan glanced at her, his spoon stopping mid-way to his
mouth. Was she going to cry? She had that look that women
have. He had seen Miss Ashby when things got too much for
her, and his mam. They chew their bottom lip, he had noticed,
then it wobbles like a fish ready to take the bait, then there is
a trickle, and they dab at their eyes with their handkerchief,
but they can't hold it back because it's like a dam that's burst
and a great waterfall pours down their cheeks, and then it
takes ages for them to stop.

Runs in the family he thought. And just as he'd seen his dad
do when his mam got upset, Ryan stretched out his hand and
patted the plump arm resting next to his. "Please now, don't
you fret, Mrs Brown. I'm sure that by all the saints and the
Blessed Virgin and Our Lord Himself things are going to work

out for you. Surely they will. I'm really hungry, Mrs Brown... please?"

He watched as she moved once more to the draining board. "Just the scrapings left now, I'm afraid, Ryan."

He was pleased to see that apart from a few more sniffs there were no further signs of upset, which was unusual. It must be his compassion. He was in a cheeky mood. "Come on there, then. Please, yes! More, missus. Give us all you've got there." He grinned at her, "I'll come again sometime. Sure I will."

She smiled briefly then left him. He heard her footsteps on the stairs. Gone to sort that freak daughter out, he thought. He let the spoon drop with a clatter in his empty dish, then hurrying over to the draining board he bent over the big saucepan, scooping from the sides and the bottom with the wooden spoon, then with his fingers, thrusting them into his mouth. When there was no more to be had, he sat down to wait, conscious of his clothes, warmer now but clammy against his skin, his bare toes curling on the cold lino.

His mind was on the Scholarship, thinking he could have scraped through. He had a good chance, but it was going to be close. If his father had any ideas of sending him to Saint Joseph's Catholic, being taught by the monks with their long black dresses who enjoyed beating the living daylights out of you, he would refuse. But far worse, he reminded himself, would be Naughton Road, the school for stupids. Thicko Foureyes would have no chance. They'd stamp on his glasses; that'd be the first thing, then put his head down the lav and pull the chain, then he'd get the railings. He'd heard they'd had to call the Fire Brigade sometimes. Foureyes' head being so big they'd have a job to pull it through.

If I *have* to go there, I'll scarper, he thought. Lie about my age and join the army and fight the Jerries. Or, run away to sea. Be a cabin boy. Might join the French Foreign Legion.

He cocked his head on one side. No sound from upstairs. He wondered about getting the recipe for the soup then jollying his mam along to make it. No meat, so you wouldn't need coupons. One day, when he'd got his own place, he'd have an allotment, make gallons of the stuff. He leaned back in his chair and burped.

The door opened. Mrs Brown quietly closed it, shaking her head. She sat down next to him in the vacant chair and sighed. "Honestly, Ryan, I don't know what we're going to do with her. Do you?"

Ryan felt the pressure of her heavy hand on his shoulder. He felt guilty, though he'd no idea why he should. He shifted in his chair, making a slight Cagney move of his shoulders was gratified to feel her hand slip away. Then, again as he'd seen his dad do when his mam got upset, he placed his small hand on hers and squeezed.

"Try not to worry, Mrs Brown. Think positive, my dad always tells my mam. He has a saying, it's, erm... what it is now? Ah, yes, *'There are worse things at sea.'* Have you ever heard of that saying, Mrs Brown?"

"You're a very sweet boy, Ryan. Tell me honestly. You're a boy with a good head on his shoulders... oh, dear, oh dear —"

His heart thudded. Here were the warning signs again, worse this time: chewing her bottom lip the way cows do, sort of in a circle. In fact, she did look like a cow with those big eyes rolling this way and that. Now the trembling came, bottom lip quivering and the tears starting to trickle down the big cheeks. She looked at him appealingly. To his dismay she got out of her chair to move behind him, placing her hands on his shoulders.

"Mr Brown and I – by the way, Mr Brown will run you home in the car –always think that you are a considerate, kindly little chappie, with a wisdom well beyond your years. Nadina always speaks affectionately of you – when she does speak, that is."

"Mrs Brown," he said, giving a Quasimodo-like roll of his shoulders, desperate to change the subject. "Is there a recipe for the soup I can take home for me mam, do you think?"

The hands lifted; Mrs Brown returned to her place opposite. She sighed, turned her big cow's eyes upon him. "Like all boys you only think of your stomach, don't you? Well, you can stop right now and think about Nadina. Ryan, answer me this. Can you recall anything, anything at all, any incidents between

Nadina and some other girl or boy? Think, carefully. Oh, of course, I know Mr Brown and I should be prepared to go along and see that awful woman, Millison, but she always seems to me to be, oh, I don't know, so much on the defensive, you know? Always protecting her reputation; scurrying about with her jailer keys in that enormous handbag. Oh, what's the use? I can't expect you to understand."

Ryan scraped his spoon round his dish, swallowed the few remaining drops. He cleared his throat, the words tripping out fast, frightened that the big woman might make a move again. "Naddy, I mean, N...N... Nadina's well-liked by all the teachers, especially Miss Ashby, and well... Miss Millison, who I know is kind of fierce. Me and Kenny – that is Kenny Evett - think that her teeth bother her. They're loose, see? Probably in pain with them. But I've noticed they sort of hit it off, Millie and Nadina. Sorry, I mean Miss Millison. Proud of her, I reckon. They both are. That is, Miss Ashby and her. Not like me. I don't get on too well with them, none of the teachers, really. Millie... sorry, I mean Miss Millison, doesn't like me. Me dad says it's because I'm Irish. But Miss Ashby, she and Naddy are kind of close, like friends. I tell your daughter, Mrs Brown, that if *I* had any problems I'd see Miss Ashby. I'd tell her everything, I would. You should speak to the Head Teacher, Mrs Brown, you and Mr Brown, but also have a word with Miss Ashby – she's Naddy's... erm, Nadina's class teacher. A very kind lady, Miss Ashby; I'm only a monitor myself, and I've got to give it up half-term. The responsibility's getting too much for me really." Face red, he ran out of breath.

Louise Brown reached over and absent-mindedly crumbled a piece of bread left on Ryan's plate. "Thank you, Ryan. That's very interesting. So you don't think either Miss Millison or Miss Ashby have been telling her off about her work? Despite being a clever girl, she's an awful day-dreamer."

Ryan, busily scraping his spoon round an empty plate felt her head move closer to his. She spoke slowly and deliberately. "Ryan, my daughter is a very sensitive child, very much so. Very spiritual, you see. Too spiritual, my husband and I think. Would you agree with that?"

Suddenly, he was jubilant. He could respond to Mrs Brown without a moment's hesitancy. That was it! He'd known all along the root of Naddy's problem. Ryan looked up from his plate, answered as he knew he could, with the utmost sincerity, smilingly, shaking his head from side to side, bemused by the weird naivety of Naddy Brown and all the other weak-kneed fools taken in by the priests.

"Definitely, Mrs Brown, definitely. Now, religion is okay for some," he said, screwing up his eyes with the look of a philosopher puzzling out the maze of ideas known to mankind then, recalling the snatch of facts trotted out by Kenny, gleaned from the *News of the World,* and continued, "But as Karl Marx said, Mrs Brown, the man that wrote *Das Kapital* – you know, in the British Museum – religion is the opium of the people. See, it can get like a drug, like opium, get you into a kind of dream world, Mrs Brown, so it can." He looked across at her with a triumphant smile.

Mrs Brown's frown showed she was a little doubtful, but at the same time seemed impressed. "Thank you, Ryan," she said. Her frown deepened, "You've met Daphne. Chalk and Cheese, Ryan, wouldn't you agree? Nadina takes life so very seriously, so unlike our happy-go-lucky Daphne. Now, no doubt you know of this extra tuition that Father is giving her." She hesitated, "Do you think that is a good idea?"

Ryan felt he shouldn't say more. He felt he was being dragged into a swamp. It was pressure. The kind his dad put on him when he talked about the cruel English and the way they killed all the peasants in the years of the great famine, and the Orange men in their bowlers and umbrellas from the North in the marching season, how they put the Catholics down all the time. Then there was the pressure Father O'Donnell put upon him to be a proper Catholic, believing when he couldn't, and the pressure Naddy Brown was always putting on him, telling him she was praying night and day for his soul. It was all a swirl going round and round in his head. He wrinkled his nose, pinched it where mucus had collected, and sniffed. He wanted to get home. He was feeling uncomfortable in his half-dry clothes and his bare feet were getting cold, and all the questions coming so fast, unsure now where it was all leading.

He cleared his throat. Playing safe, he said, "Honest, Mrs Brown, Naddy's real good in class. Clever, she is. In the back row among the clever ones. In fact the cleverest, I reckon."

Teacher's pet, he wanted to say; tell her how it got on his nerves the way her hand would always shoot up and answer every question, tossing that long wave of hair in that show-off way like she was better than the rest of them, and that could be very boring. But what he said instead was the kind of thing Miss Millison would say, clearing his throat, he announced, "Nadina is a very bright, very clever girl, Mrs Brown. She is the school's most brilliant pupil. I know your daughter does you proud, so she does."

The smile was the warmest and friendliest he could summon. He wanted to show compassion, feeling sorry for the big woman having a dreamland for a daughter. Now to his disgust she got up, her chair scraping the floor as she pushed it back, moving round the table until she stood next to him. He looked down at his plate not daring to move. She leaned forward to place her cheek next to his. There was a horrible wetness. It was a moment of the closest intimacy, more chummy than his own mother had ever been even at her most affectionate. He shuddered. He rolled his shoulders the way James Cagney did under stress. Thank God, her fat cheek went away, but the wet residue began to itch. He rubbed his cheek with the sleeve of his jersey and jumped to his feet. His chair fell; he picked it up, mumbling a stuttered apology. "Excuse me, Mrs Brown. I must go immediate like, me d...d... dad w...w....will be w....w... worried, you know?"

He clean forgot about the soup recipe as he ran down the hall to find his socks and shoes. He looked up, wrinkling his nose at her in fear as she stood over him. He had a job to tie his laces, aware of her drying her eyes on the corner of her pinafore. She spoke as if reading from a prepared script.

"You're a very, very good friend to Nadina, Ryan. I like you. Nadina likes you. Try to keep a look out for her, will you? And as I say, if you *can* find out what might be eating away at her – and there definitely is something, Mr Brown and I are sure of that – we will both be eternally grateful to you. Just let us know, please. But I shall go up to school. I think I shall dare to face the awesome Miss Millison, though it will take a lot of courage, as you can imagine." She gave Ryan a slow wink and giggled. "Oh, I can see you're anxious to leave, bless you. Make sure you get out of those damp clothes as soon as you get home, won't you, dear?"

He struggled to his feet, and nodded. He was shivering on the doorstep when Arnold Brown appeared, grim-faced, from his study. Nadina's father looked at Ryan, mouth tight with disapproval. "Right, young man." He took his gas mask off the peg on the hall stand. "Where's yours, lad?"

"At home."

"Not a good idea that. As a Warden, Chief for this area I might add, it's my solemn duty to remind you that you could be fined. Carry your gas mask at all times, boy. It's still possible that the enemy will use gas. After all, they used it in the last war. Right, car's in the garage. Wait at the bottom of the drive, if you please, and open the gate for me. Thank you."

Ryan watched Mr Brown walk briskly down the drive to the garage at the side of the house. Thinking that Mrs Brown, still standing at the open front door, might be about to love him again, he was ready to move quickly down the drive. But she moved in front of him. "Thank you, Ryan," she said solemnly, grasping his hands in hers. "You have been a great help to us."

Pulling them free, he shot off down the drive, pulled open the big white gate. As the Humber drew up, Ryan opened the door to climb in. He was about to take his place when Mr Brown took out a white handkerchief from his breast pocket and handed it to him. Ryan opened it up and examined it: Persil white.

The driver pointed irritably to the seat. "Put it there, boy. Put it there." Ryan realised its purpose. He spread it out like a road map then sat down.

"Well, the rain seems to have eased off," Arnold Brown said in his clipped manner as he turned the ignition key. In silence Ryan stared ahead. He wondered if the dampness from his trousers would penetrate through the handkerchief to the expensive leather upholstery. "Are you going to get called up, Mr Brown, sir?"

Mr Brown did not reply.

Ryan continued. "Jus… jus… just wondering if you're going to be called up to fight the Hun, you know?"

"I take it that you will not have heard of Reserved Occupations? And I *am* approaching my fiftieth birthday."

"Oh. Jus… jus… just asking. Except my dad would go if he could. I know he would, but he was wounded at the battle of the Somme, you know, year of Our Lord, nineteen hundred sixteen."

"Sure about that, are you?" was the response.

There was a long silence as the car sped along, eventually arriving at the Naughton Road before turning off into Harefield. Ryan felt he deserved a better response to such an important issue as his dad's war service. It no longer mattered that it wasn't true. It was important that no one should know he was IRA, especially with Kenny calling him a 'Fenian bastard'. He waited. When nothing more was forthcoming, Ryan was ready with another question.

"Was *you* ever a soldier, Mr Brown?"

The car stopped outside number 103. Mr Brown turned to him, "Now," he said, "I will ask *you* a question by return. What is the matter with my daughter?" He turned off the engine, pulled on the handbrake.

Ryan blinked back tears, opened the door, jumped out. "Your missus goes on and on asking me. You ask me. Teachers go on as if I done something. How the hell should I know? Why does everybody keep asking me what's the matter with your bloody loony daughter? Why can't you just all leave me alone!"

Mr Brown's eyes opened wide, he swallowed and the Adam's apple jerked upwards as fast as cannon ball shot from gun. "How dare you use your filthy language in front of me! I suppose that's what they allow these days in school. Disgusting little animals. And another thing," he leaned across the seat, stuck his head out of the door, his long face inches from Ryan's, his eyes widening ever further, voice trembling with rage, "and I want a straight answer from you, this time." His face as white as the handkerchief – though now slightly grubby from contact with Ryan's trousers - he said, "Have you been having sexual relations with my daughter? Just answer, will you. Yes or no?"

Startled, Ryan's mouth dropped open. "P... p... p... p... pardon?" He took a step backwards.

"We're talking about sexual intercourse, young man; an assault on an innocent young girl." Then, with one gloved hand gripping the steering wheel, he shook the other in Ryan's face, barely an inch from his nose. "You may not have been aware in your animal lust that my daughter is a virgin – or was! She is also a minor!"

Mr Brown slammed the car door and with a squeal of tyres and cloud of exhaust, sped away.

In shock, Ryan, tears starting to his eyes, ran up the concrete passage and through the back door. And into his father's arms.

Chapter Eighteen

"**B**y all the saints and the Holy Virgin! Just look at the lad, Marie. You're soaked, boy. Wet through to your skin! Where the hell have you been? Get out of those wet clothes at once!"

Ryan moved fast, but before he got as far as the stairs, a big hand clasped his collar to haul him back. Now the hard tone changed to an unusual softness. "Just answer my question, son. Where have you been?"

"They made me. Miss Ashby did. That Naddy Brown, she got all upset. I had to take her home."

"What, in all that rain? Sure, they had no business. You're drenched."

"Dad, I never wanted the job, but they voted for me. Monitor. Mr bloody Brown-"

From the scullery door, arms folded came a voice, "Don't you ever swear in this house!"

Mr... B... B... Brown, he hates me, Mam! Always got it in for me, Mam. He's thinking that I'd d... d... done it to her. But I never done nothing!" His voice dropped like a stone down a bottomless well. "So help me, God, I done nothing, nothing." He choked on his tears, letting out a wail as loud as an air raid siren.

Shocked, his father reined him in like a runaway horse, hugged him to himself. Ryan buried his face deep in the ancient cardigan with the accumulated smells of whisky and fags, shuddering and crying so much he felt he would never stop.

"Hey, come now. What's with you? Mother, make the lad a cup of Bovril, will you?" Then, in a voice that was even softer still, hardly beyond a whisper, "Now, you tell me son, what's that ignorant fool of a man been accusing you of?"

Head bent, chin against his chest, Ryan spluttered out the words, a hand over his mouth, scared of what might come out,

- 163 -

"L... l... l... like I done it to her," he stuttered incoherently. "The sex thing. I never, Da, I never did." In his distress he'd forgotten the vow he'd made that he would never call his father 'Da' the way he once loved to do. "Real mad he is, Da. Like he hates me and I done nothing, so I haven't."

"Take it slow, now. For the good Lord's sake, will you please take your time, but come on, tell me."

Marie scuttled into the scullery as fast as a mouse. She put the kettle on the gas ring, called out through the open door. "For God's sake, Fergus, don't force it out of him. The boy's still in shock. Can you not see that?"

She returned swiftly, fell on her knees before him, kind eyes meeting his. "What is it, darling? What in the name of the good Lord have they done to you, sweetheart?"

"Ah, they've been accusing him of something, that they have," Fergus said. "Get the Bovril down you, son. Then upstairs and change out of those wet clothes. How did the exams go?"

"Good. Yeah, I think."

His mam got up from her knees, disappeared back into the scullery, returning in a moment with his Bovril. Steam from the mug rose, mingling with smoke from his father's cigarette. Gratefully, he drank. His parents watched in silence while he downed it.

Running upstairs to change, Ryan slid the damp clothes off his body, letting them collapse to the floor. Later he'd take them down and his mam would put them in the big concrete wash tub in the draining board, light the little fire underneath, take the great wooden spoon and push the clothes under. With her other hand, she'd pour in the Persil. He'd seen her do this more times than he could count, but he always liked to watch.

Naked, he went to the bathroom, grabbed a towel, rubbed himself down, then back to his bedroom, pulling out the top drawer to take out vest and pants. He held them to his face; felt the warmth of them, clean and pure. Then over to his wardrobe to find a shirt and trousers and set them out neatly on his bed.

Someone done it to her, then. Why did Nazi Brown think it could be him? Clenching his fists, still in his underwear, Ryan reached for his boxing gloves, sank his fists into the makeshift punch bag hanging on the door time and time again, until his muscles ached, his breath coming in great gasps of rage. At length he sank exhausted to the floor.

The door opened. Fergus, a smouldering cigarette dangling at the corner of his mouth, picked him up and gently sat him on the side of the bed. Between fresh tears, Ryan said, "I don't like him, Dad. Not that Mr Brown. Yeah, Mrs Brown, she's okay, you know. She asks me what I think is wrong with Naddy and I tell her." He looked up at his father, "She got too religious. Like opium I tell her mam. That's why I don't want to go to Saint Joe's, you know. I know you got it in mind for me, but no, Dad. I'm sorry. I get scared I'm going to get like her, too religious like. Ah, Mrs Brown, Dad, she's great with the soup. I was wanting the recipe." He turned up his tear-stained face. "Know what? Eleven, she is, but she looks like...like fourteen. Little, you know... but... erm, big?" He looked at his father, suddenly shy, then shaking his head vehemently, said, "See, I'm sacred I'm going to get like her if I go to Saint Joseph's. Mrs Brown, like I said, Dad, she's great with the soup. I was wanting the recipe, but then forgot. First thing I do tomorrow is give up the monitor job. Because, Dad, I'm not right for it. Not right, I'm not, not right...." The unceasing flow of words subsided to a whisper. He rubbed his sore eyes with his gloved fists, his shoulders heaving wearily as he sank again to the floor, like a boxer who's thrown in the towel before the end of the match.

"Look, son, you're getting yourself in a state, so you are. Do you not see that?" Fergus nipped the nub of his cigarette between thumb and forefinger. Sparks blew and scattered, some carried by the draught and a few landed at their feet. He smothered them casually with his shoe, went over to open the window. "Devious, they are, the Brits. You can't trust them. You never could. Sure, you never will."

"What's a Reserved Occupation?"

Fergus did not answer, but continued to lean out of the open window.

"He thinks it's me, that I'm to blame, Dad. She's always crying and that in class, then staying off school. I done nothing, nothing. Honest to God. I hate him. Hate old crocodile face. Sure I'll never go to her house no more."

Turning towards him, patting his pockets for another cigarette, his dad said, "Then to be sure you've not got nothing to worry about. The innocent man remains innocent until proven guilty. Come on, downstairs, now. We'll have a game. Just like old times, eh? You and me. Shove ha'penny or table tennis – what's it to be then, son, eh?"

Ryan shook his head, "No, if you don't mind."

Table tennis required too much from him. He couldn't cope with his father's bad temper when he lost points; not today; not after having had a gloved fist shoved under his nose and been yelled at. And he always lost badly at shove ha'penny, the size of his father's thumb making for distinct advantage.

His father untied the boxing gloves and took them off, then gently squeezed Ryan's hands. "Look, son, if you're in the clear, and for the good Lord's sake you surely are, you've got nothing to worry about. Sure to God those toffee-nosed Browns got no business to talk to you like that."

Slowly, Ryan dressed while his da looked out of the window, then the two of them went down the narrow staircase, his father leading the way.

"Why should they say it's me? What's the m... m... m... matter with them?"

At the foot of the stairs, Fergus placed a thick-veined hand on his son's shoulder. Then, taking out a large, none too clean handkerchief from his trouser pocket, he wiped his son's tears, the other hand resting on his cane. "Sure, you've got nothing to be scared of. Just tell the truth. So, shall us play a game then?"

"No. Sorry, and that, Dad. I can't. Not for now. No."

In the kitchen he made himself a doorstep jam sandwich. Despite the soup that gurgled in his innards, he was still hungry. He sat down at the table. Across by the boiler, his father settled deep in his chair and the sounds of Irish Folk songs came distantly from the wireless. Ryan bit deeply. A drop of jam on his chin felt like blood. His tongue flicked out like a lizard's and scooped it back into his mouth. Naddy. Thank God he'd never touched her, not properly. Tried to feel her boobs once. He remembered the sponginess, like the dumplings his mam made for the rabbit stew. Naddy's heavy punch had taken him by surprise, sent him sprawling, hitting his head on the branch of the beech tree. She had rushed up to him, hauled him to his feet, laughed – both of them laughing. Just one other time there'd been: the time he'd rubbed himself up against her. She'd struck his face then; slapped him hard both sides. There was no laughter that time.

He took another bite of his sandwich.

Then the thought struck him and he gasped: *Was she going to have a baby?* When a woman gets pregnant there's a big bulge in her belly. But she'd got nothing there except her usual fattiness, had she? What was it old Kenny had been telling him and Foureyes about? Something like a 'phantom pregnancy'? Ryan ran his tongue round the sides of his sandwich as a precaution before taking another bite. What was it he'd said?

"You take a girl frightened of not been able to have a kid. She thinks about it, dreams of it, longs for it. So she wakes up pregnant." Old Kenny, smiling at them, thinking he's an expert, the prat. He don't read nothing except that crap newspaper. Never opened a dictionary in his life, so he hasn't. Then he goes on talking about some kid on one of the roads off Kelliwell, only a bit older than Naddy, twelve or thirteen, who was what they call, 'expecting.' He got that off Foureyes. That stupid prat, no-brain Foureyes Johnson, talking like a priest.

"I reckon, Ryan, if you was in big, big trouble you'd turn to God for help, you would. You'd cry out 'Help, help!'"

As if he was as dim-witted himself, as if he needed a demonstration, Foureyes fell down on his knees on the pavement outside the school gates, eyes closed, hands clasped together like he was praying. Then after giving a huge sniff, calling out "Help me, O God. Help me!"

Not wanting his friend's specs to break, Ryan had closed them in his fist before walloping him with the other hand. He smiled at the memory: old Foureyes begging him to stop.

"Ever heard of a hymen?" Kenny again, grinning with his big teeth in his sweaty face, the show-off. "When you do it, the hymen cracks and you get blood, see? It's bright red, redder than Greengage's lips, like gut blood. That's how you know a girl's got herself in trouble."

Ryan didn't believe half these stories. Any case, Naddy wouldn't want a kid. It all made it clearer than ever, more urgent. He'd resign tomorrow, first thing. Stupid monitor job. Let nit-picker Julie do it.

The sandwich consumed, it was not surprising that Ryan was dropping off to sleep, with all he'd gone through. But suddenly he jerked awake. A spasm of coughing came from across the dimly lit kitchen. He rubbed the sleep from his eyes, strolled over to where his dad was bent double, the red vein in the forehead blinking like a dodgy rear bicycle light with a loose connection.

Ryan leaned over the back of the chair and patted his dad's back. Softly at first with the palm of his hand, then a little harder. When the coughing continued, he curled his fingers into a fist and imagining his dad's back was Arnold Brown's face, gave it full force.

"Ouch. For the Lord's sake, son, ease off if you will now!"

But there was a good result. The coughing came to an abrupt end and all was quiet, except for the Irish singers warbling their timeless tunes. His dad turned his head and smiled.

"Just rub my leg a bit now, son, if you will."

Ryan knelt. Starting with the ankle he worked his way up the troublesome left leg and then when he got to the thigh he kneaded the thin flesh gently.

Fergus cleared his throat. It was time to put things right. An opportunity should not be missed. "Son, things have not been right between us. And I'm sorry that I let you go on thinking... you know."

"It's al-right." Ryan went on kneading. "Maybe she wanted to tell me and she couldn't," he said absently.

Tell you what?" Kathie asked, at that moment coming into the room.

"Someone done it to her, like. Got her pregnant."

"Who, Nadina?" Kathie laughed. "She's not pregnant! Whatever gave you that idea? Girls of eleven don't have babies, you idiot. Daphne says some of the big boys from Naughton Road stop her on the street and tease her about her birthmark, poking it, making nasty remarks. That's what's been upsetting her, Daph tells me. Wants to blame my little brother. Sure she's a wet week and no mistake."

"I never tease her! And it's more than teasing, I know it is. Got to be."

Chapter Nineteen

After a long restless night, his leg paining him, Fergus awoke early next morning with a deep sense of grievance; a mood that lasted all day and well into the evening.

What right, he thought, have those high and mighty Browns to accuse his own son of something he plainly could not have done? Why should such a man, a so-called pillar of the Church, get away with accusing his own flesh and blood? What sort of a man was he? Who the hell did he think he was, frightening the very life out of my son?

What could he do? He should speak to the priest, but could he? A collaborator of the worst kind. Having a Union Jack in the pulpit? A man not from the North where many of the priests backed the Cause; good men of God giving succour, men true to Ireland's goals. But this one, a turncoat! In fury, Fergus stubbed out his cigarette half-smoked, added a heaped spoonful of sugar to his tea, churned his spoon round, slopping tea into the saucer. This priest, not just indifferent to the struggle: far worse – on the side of the enemy! Always praising the Brits from his pulpit without a hint of denial and full of hatred against the German people and nation. If he had any appreciation of Ireland's rightful and true destiny, he would have shown it by now. Not a bit. None whatsoever. This priest has become so much of a Brit that he is one! There he is, playing to the crowd, the high and mighty stuffed shirts crowding in on the Lord's Day, the likes of Arnold Brown.

Fergus was convinced that his hero, De Valera, had taken the right course in the *Dáil*: the recovery of the land, a Free State, the fulfilment of the dream would come. "But all in the good Lord's time," he murmured. "Let there be justice, Lord, for them," he prayed, standing in front of the collage. "Justice for all. All of you who fought, suffered and died for the Cause."

He limped back to his chair, stretched out his long legs, called out for Marie. "Where are you? Get me a whisky, will you, please?"

The war had changed everything. An unnecessary war declared by that spineless Chamberlain, refusing Hitler's offer of a pact. And hard as it was to believe, men from the South volunteering to fight for the enemy in their thousands. So, it was better than a life of idleness and hunger, for the Brit army fed their men well, but what then? They were betrayers of Ireland's destiny. But can you blame them for taking the opportunity? He sighed thinking of his old friends, rounded up and interred, even his own brother, Liam. Yet, may God be praised, despite the deprivation of their liberty, they had not renounced and never would. And wasn't Partition an act of violence? Accept the situation for the time being, that was good diplomacy. Thanks be to God for Eamonn. Fergus reached for the teapot, turned his head.

The door from the scullery opened and she appeared, pushed past him in her dressing gown, bent low to floor level to reach inside the cupboard where the whisky was kept. She left the bottle by his feet and closed the door into the hall.

"Thanks, love," he called. Her footsteps were on the stairs. Soon there'd be a rush of water filling the bath. With a sigh, he filled the half empty cup. He swirled the contents round, then raised it in salute to his heroes.

Sure, though, he shouldn't think too harshly of the priest. Father O'Donnell had personally shown him great kindness when he was a stranger in a strange land, heading for the church with his young family, comforted by the warm greeting from him at the door at the end of the Mass.

Fergus was all for directness and he could deal with this priest man to man. Father O'Donnell was surely a man who called a spade a spade; direct, forceful. Ah well, the boy must come to the Faith in his own time. He would not pressure him. That did no good. But he hoped at least he'd make it to Confirmation. He would wait until half-term. Get the whole thing sorted out. Priests were given wisdom from above. Ah well, he'd always been taught that. But there should be an apology though, to put the matter right, he would surely insist on that. For hadn't a terrible injustice been done?

He swirled the golden liquid at the bottom of the glass, thinking of home across the Water, the memories that never left: the stench of smoke, the shouting, the cries of the wounded, his own screams, running down Sackville Street for his life.

He flung the butt of his cigarette into the coke hod, drained the contents of his glass and smiled grimly at the memory of the letter. He knew the Father didn't like Ryan, which was not surprising. How could he be friendly to the boy when the lad gave him so much aggravation? Brit-lover that he was, he would talk to him anyway. Glancing at the clock on the mantelpiece, he yawned again: always tired, the wound rarely giving him a night's refreshing sleep. Now the evenings were lighter, he would go to the greenhouse before the darkness came. Now, what of the wee girl? Surely to goodness wasn't she the example of holy piety that Ryan needed? He had watched her at Mass. Oh, to be scarred like that! And trying so hard to hide it! The ways of the good Lord are sure past finding out. He stumbled to his feet, stretched, reached for his cane.

After supper, Marie in her dressing gown, towel shaped into a turban over her damp hair came down the stairs, went to the scullery and emerged, sewing basket under her arm. They sat opposite each other, a couple of yards distant in the little smoke-filled room. Fergus recalled the young wife who had once been so pretty, even beautiful, watching her tired eyes as she took out wool and needle and began to darn the grey socks that he recognised as Ryan's.

"Sure, he's upstairs making a terrible noise, Fergus. Do you not hear him? Kathie's been shouting at him," she said.

"Aye, I know. Taking it out on Arnold Brown again. Punching him into the ground." he chuckled.

"What will you do?"

"Go and see the priest."

"Be careful of your temper now."

"Brit-lover." He spoke contemptuously, putting a fresh cigarette between his lips. "He's not for Ireland, but as far as the priests go he could be worse."

"As far as the priests go," she repeated dully, jabbing her needle.

He smoked in silence, flicked ash in the direction of the coke hod and missed.

"Are you taking the lad with you?" she asked, unperturbed.

"Of course."

"He should have more respect."

"I know, my lovely, I know. But maybe he'll see a good side to Father O'Donnell. I hope for the good Lord's sake that he will."

She sighed, "Is there a good side to any of them?"

Fergus, eyeing her mouth set in a despairing thin line, her shoulders permanently drooping and seeing the pain in her eyes, still dull after so long.

Chapter Twenty

Sunday night, thought Ryan, snuggling under the covers. He'd take it easy the first morning of the holiday. Stay cosied up in bed 'til midday or thereabouts and not minding too much the biscuit crumbs that got in his navel and between his toes and crept into the genital area. In the afternoon, they'd meet up: him, Kenny and Rich. Then, maybe, football on the Rec or find an adult willing to smuggle them into the Pictures for an 'A' film, or fish for tiddlers in the canal. It did not matter much because the Scholarship was over. Just the result to come, but he didn't want to think about that, not for now. For now it was half term. And no more stupid monitoring! He was surprised how she had taken it, her eyebrows shaped into question marks as he strolled up to her desk, widening his green eyes like the way of his film hero, James Cagney, rolling his shoulders, his hands on his hips. Most of the class were occupied taking out their history text books, though a few looked up with interest.

"Yes?"

She'd stuck her lipstick on in a rush and it had missed, like raspberry jam oozing out of a sandwich. Pretty disgusting that, getting it all over her teeth. But her sloppy appearance helped to overcome his nervousness. If I ever get a wife, which God forbid I ever will, sure she'll never plaster her gob with all that muck. Stuff gets everywhere. He had noticed it on Mrs Brown's tea cup, on the tea towel in her kitchen. Holy shite!

"I've decided," he said. "Finished with it, Miss, the monitor job, like." He'd stopped short of putting on his James Cagney voice. Just folded his arms and clenched his jaw, like Cagney under pressure.

Miss Ashby had sighed exaggeratedly, the puddings heaving, her tongue running over her teeth, then rubbing them with the corner of her handkerchief. "Well, I suppose it was inevitable sooner or later. But I must say I am very disappointed in you, Ryan. Still, I can't say I ever had much hope for you. To tell you the truth, I am rather relieved." She stretched out her hand to reach the pile of exercise books, work the pupils had done the day before.

He had strolled back, grinning at Kenny, who screwed his nose up at him. Reaching his desk and feeling the teacher's gaze on his back he'd turned to smile at her, copying her raised eyebrows.

Now, between wakefulness and sleep, he pulled the bedclothes over his head, attempting to resuscitate his dream, which had been broken by movements in the house. He screwed his eyes shut, the newscaster's voice drifting back into his head...

'Colonel Ryan Brannigan is a big man, if not the biggest in the whole regiment, bigger even than his sergeant, the huge Evett, fighting against overwhelming odds. The Colonel, almost single-handed, pushed back a whole German division. As everyone knows he is the youngest ever commanding office to receive the Victoria Cross. Here at Buckingham Palace, in the distance through my binoculars, I can see his father in the crowd, cheering him on with fifty thousand, no one hundred thousand others. What an exciting time for Fergus Brannigan. How proud and pleased he must be for his soldier-son!

'Now, His Majesty and Mr Churchill are waiting for him in the grounds, outside the palace. King George the Sixth is pinning the medal on his chest. We must never forget that the Victoria Cross is the highest award for gallantry and is granted to very, very few men. Now Mr Winston Churchill, our splendid Prime Minister, shakes his hand, blowing cigar smoke in his face. The Colonel, who of course does not smoke, coughs politely. Mr Churchill apologises...'

Ryan stirred. The sound of unsteady footsteps making their way up the stairs were very different from the crunch of Colonel Brannigan's boots outside the palace. He sat up yawning and rubbed his eyes. "Dad?"

"Wake up now, son. Get yourself into your Sunday best. We're going to see the priest."

"I don't want to see *him...* why?"

"There's something that surely shouldn't be. We need advice, we need justice and that's why we're going to see Father O'Donnell."

His hand shaking, Ryan took the biscuit and mug of tea held out to him. "Dad, what will he do?"

"For the good Lord's sake, that man abused his position. Nobody, not even the high and mighty Mr Brown is going to accuse you of something you plainly haven't done. So get your tea down you, son, as quick as you can. We'll be seeing the good Father at ten."

A few minutes later, Fergus was knocking on the bathroom door, calling out to his wife, "We're off, Marie, love. Say a prayer for us, because by all the saints in the heavens, we shall need it. Come on, Ryan."

His dad was hardly recognisable. Gone were the brown corduroys smudged with coal dust, the green cardigan devastated by age, moth, ash and whisky stains. In their place the very best of the two best suits, the black pin-stripe, worn only at funerals Christmas and Easter. Ryan felt resentful in *his* new suit. To save money, his dad had made sure it was a size too large and the collar chafed his skin.

At a brisk pace they set off for the bus stop outside Mrs Jackson's Pie shop. Ryan could tell his father was nervous, fingering his collar, tapping the cane against the lamp post, hopping a little.

"Your leg is bothering you, Dad, I'm thinking."

"Aye."

"Why does he live in such a big house all on his own?"

"'Tis always been so. Sure, it's of no consequence. Not what a man owns but what he is that matters. The Browns have a smart house, do they not?"

Ryan shrugged his shoulders. "I know I'm in the right and I don't see why we have to see the priest. He hates me anyways."

"The priests are taught wisdom by the Grace of the Almighty. They are experienced in dealing with the troubles of men. You understand what I'm saying to you now?"

Ryan shrugged his shoulders again, "S'pose so."

Arriving at the presbytery they walked up the overgrown path. His father ahead, clearing his throat, mumbling under his breath as if rehearsing a speech, unbuttoning his collar. He reached for the knocker.

Waiting on the step, his thoughts drifting, Ryan heard a shot from a cannon on the battlefield: *Sergeant Evett and Private Johnson, surrounded by smoke and the stench of gunpowder, stood well back on the advice of their Colonel. He was about to hurl a hand grenade through the front door of Nazi Headquarters. They were there to help the Russian soldiers. The Germans were getting close to Moscow. Dead Germans lay strewn about like the dandelions and daises prodding their way through the gaps in the path. His sergeant was quoting some daft stuff he'd got from the 'News of the World.' He held up a warning hand. His sergeant and Private Johnson saluted respectfully. The three of them gazed at the dead German soldiers. Sergeant Evett started to cheer. One stern look from the Colonel, and his sergeant apologised. "Sorry sir." Colonel Brannigan pointed to his Victoria Cross. "See this, Sergeant. For valour – and compassion. Don't ever forget we must forgive in victory. Have you no compassion, sergeant?"*

A nudge from his father brought Ryan back to reality.

"Fergus Brannigan and his son, Ryan," his dad mumbled. The skinny woman in the apron, glared back at them.

"Yes, Father's expecting you. Follow me." To Ryan, she said, "Make sure you wipe your feet on the mat before you come in."

Following his father, Ryan raised his eyebrows at her, Miss Ashby fashion, and stared about him. The house was huge, dark and gloomy. A wide staircase seemed to go on forever. Oil paintings of miserable looking people: bishops, cardinals, whatever, went all the way up. Just shows religion don't make you happy, thought Ryan. And why come to see *him*? Sure, he'd be on *their* side anyway. Whenever he'd seen the priest at Mass, he was always clucking away to old Brown, his crocodile teeth gleaming, long scaly neck sticking out like a giraffe's, mouth all twisted. And Mrs Brown too, with her wobbly backside and her stupid laugh. Still she makes great soup, he reminded himself charitably.

The two followed the housekeeper along the corridor towards the back of the house. Opposite some concrete steps, which he imagined led down to a dungeon where they tortured people, she stopped at a door and knocked three times.

"He hates me, Dad, that Father does," Ryan whispered.

"Show a bit of respect, will you?" Fergus whispered back. "Maybe he just doesn't like the way you fool around, so I don't blame the man."

There was silence.

Mrs Henderson's bony fingers played with the thick gold band of her wedding ring then knocked again on the well-polished door. At last they were given permission to enter: a gruff voice announced, "Come."

The housekeeper opened the door. Fergus shuffled his feet, fingered his collar and cleared his throat. Ryan, standing next to him, remembered how you had to queue to get in to the Mass back in Ireland. Scared of the priests, all of them. They could cut God off from you if you stayed away. What was the word they used... excommunication? Throw you out of the Mass, they could. Keep you out of heaven. And a whole lot of baloney, sure to God it was. No matter what those fanatics like Naddy Brown said, or that thicko Foureyes thought, *I'll* never be scared of priests. Any case, how could old Foureyes hope to get into heaven with spit and shite all down his jersey?

The tall, ugly woman turned to the visitors, her pinafore as gloomy as her face. It had no flowers on it. Not a bit like the happy one his mam wore with the big yellow sunflowers all over. "Father will see you now," she said, a fleeting smile ending with a grimace as they were ushered ahead of her, like two stray sheep to be shoved into a pen. With something resembling a curtsey, the housekeeper withdrew. Fergus pushed his son in front of him. Seated at his desk, the priest looked at them over his spectacles.

"Well Brannigan, what brings you here?" he said, affably enough, shuffling papers about as he spoke. "From what you said on the telephone it sounds as though it's quite serious. The smile changed to a frown. "I'll remind you that Monday is always a busy day for me. It's the day I minister the Sacrament to the sick in their homes. So be brief if you will."

Standing next to his dad before the priest, Ryan shifted uncomfortably from one foot to the other. He knew the stories his father had told him of peasants standing before the rich landowner, come to collect their wages or to plead not to be evicted from their little strip of land and the tiny hovel they were obliged to call home.

His father cleared his throat for the umpteenth time. "Good of you to see us, Father, and on a busy day for you. See now, Father O'Donnell, I'm not sure how to put this to you, but Ryan here has a big problem. Sure it's ridiculous, but he's been accused of a... well... a sexual attack on a girl from the school. It is Mr Brown who has made the accusation. And it's not right, Father, so it isn't, sir. He could never have done it. Tell him, Ryan, tell the Father."

Ryan felt his dad's eyes turn to him. He shook his head and told of his ordeal, all the time looking down at the floor.

Seamus O'Donnell watched the lips of the urchin before him, twisting this way and that; noticed the way he shuffled his feet and screwed up his eyes, blinking rapidly. A deceitful, dislikeable child, he thought, glancing at his watch. He liked routine and any unexpected disturbance to the order of his day irritated him. Further, he had not been feeling at all well of late. His bowel movements, usually satisfactory, had become loose and irregular. Not for the first time that morning his stomach lurched uncomfortably. He'd always looked forward to his breakfast after the daily Mass, the food served to him by the frostbitten Mrs Henderson, her acerbic manner only reprieved by her excellent cooking. Usually a man with a healthy appetite, he had not been enjoying his food, even being sick at times. Some mornings he had to forgo his egg and rasher of bacon. He hated the powdered egg with its violent yellow texture and was grateful that Jack Henderson, who was now too poorly to eat solids, had sent his ration over with his wife. That morning she had brought a fresh egg for him and served it lightly boiled, the way he liked it. A little runny ochre had trickled down his chin and he was wiping his mouth with a linen serviette when the call from the boy's father had come through.

After learning of the outpourings of rage from Brown, one of his most loyal supporters, he had been half expecting Brannigan to come hot-footing round. The two men thoroughly disliked each other: their families were poles apart in every way imaginable, and he knew he'd have to handle the situation with more than his usual degree of diplomacy. Normally, his practised skills were sufficient to defuse situations when members of the flock had disagreements and harsh words were exchanged. These situations, though thankfully rare, always needed to be nipped in the bud. If they were not, animosity intensified and others could be drawn in and the ensuing conflict could take far longer to resolve.

This particular situation, however, was not quite normal.

As he half-listened to the boy, noticing the way his father nudged him every few seconds to keep him going, he could see that Arnold Brown had behaved with more than his usual lack of restraint. The man was obviously unbalanced, obsessed with sex. Probably a sexual deviant. At least so it seemed, according to that that unstable, giggling wife. Her constant complaints about her husband's excessive sexual demands, pouring out her distress in the Confessional, sobbing through the grill as she told of some secret drawer in a bureau in the man's study where apparently he stored piles of disgusting magazines. Evidently, their daughter had asked him to put an extra lock on her bedroom door and while prowling about in her room had discovered her bloodied underwear hidden in a wardrobe. It was typical of the man that he had rushed to conclusions. From the mother's point of view the problem was confounded by the child's reluctance to talk about her monthly period.

Again he sighed. No doubt the woman gave her husband little satisfaction. He wouldn't be at all surprised if the wretched man wasn't consorting with prostitutes.

As Ryan shuffled in his badly fitting suit, O'Donnell felt his stomach heave again. He winced. As for Brannigan, you could see he was a malingerer, work-shy, a spineless individual. Those shifty eyes and what appeared to be a permanent sneer on those thick lips, and the readiness - even an eagerness - to blaspheme was disgraceful. The man was in all probability a once-active member of the IRA. Even an armchair one could be dangerous. Brown, of course, ever jumping to conclusions, was convinced of the man's Republican sympathies, saying he believed he had a secret armoury at number one hundred and three Harefield Road.

In his own opinion, as he'd told the Browns at Mass, this was very unlikely, and in any case, whatever their suspicions they should keep them strictly to themselves. Pursing his lips, the priest tented his hands and viewed father and son standing before him. He invariably restricted his communication with Brannigan to a curt nod at the door of the church, a brief word of sympathy on occasion for his injured leg. The man deserved no more: he made no effort at all to assimilate with the congregation and only dropped small change into the collection plate. He couldn't be that poor. He would be seen at the Club, sitting alone in a corner with his pint of Guinness or sipping a whisky. The good folk of Holy Innocents' seemed charitably disposed towards him, kind enough to overlook his peculiarities. That insolent son of his was surely following in his father's footsteps.

Throughout the Mass, whenever his gaze strayed down the cavernous building and rested on this loafer and his son, he would turn away to search for more attentive listeners, such as little Nadina or her parents. Brannigan always looked as though he was about to drop off to sleep: eyes half-closed, a bored expression on his craggy features: a poor example to the boy, who could be seen grinning round the church at his friends. An obvious attention seeker. As for the wife, despite his warnings, she hardly presented herself from one year to the next. A frightened looking little thing, as well she might be, living with that lazy tyke of a husband brutalising his family. Kathie he thought rather a plain child, but, unlike her brother, pleasant enough and respectful. He could see that it wouldn't be long before young Ryan would be missing Mass altogether. Now, with his Confirmation approaching, the Catechism tuition gave the boy opportunities to exercise his wit, contradicting his priest to the amusement of the other candidates, challenging his authority and therefore, of course, by implication, the authority of Holy Church. Oh, thought Father O'Donnell, how he'd love to take his belt to that dishevelled, loathsome little horror, whose shock of blond hair looked as though it never saw a comb from one week to the next and was doubtless full of nits.

He'd had discussion about him with that obsequious Headmistress, Millison. Not surprisingly she'd be just as relieved as he when the boy took himself off to the State Grammar. She thought it likely he would scrape through. Apparently, young Brannigan was not unintelligent, but was far too lazy to apply himself.

Father O'Donnell yawned, glanced at his watch again, and broke into the boy's stammer. "So, what did you say was the name of this girl?"

"N... n... n...Nadina Brown, F... F... F... Father O'Donnell."

"Ah, of course. Staunch Catholic family the Browns. Very reliable. Good pair. You know them, Fergus?"

"Would you mind if we sat down, Father? Partook of a little of your hospitality?"

"Yes of course, of course. Indeed. My apologies." He waited while they carried two upright chairs by the window and sat facing him. "Once again, tell me lad," he said. "Let me get this straight. What is it that Mr Brown has accused you of?"

The boy replied, looking first at the floor then up at his father. "D...d... d... doing it with her, F... F... Father."

The priest chuckled. "So, think you're capable of it?"

Colouring to the tips of his ears, his face hot, Ryan wanted to tell the fat Father that his was nearly as big as Evett's, but he kept his mouth firmly shut. Looking up at his dad, Ryan waited for him to speak, could see that he was ready to explode.

"Father O'Donnell, sir, Mr Brown should not be accusing my son. Did he not come into the house crying his eyes out? Terrible upset, he was. And my wife and I were upset to see him so."

The priest looked from one to the other. "Well now, what do you say, Ryan?" It was a soft tone, serious but reassuring: the customary tone in the Confessional when pronouncing forgiveness to the penitent.

"She's l... l... lying. S... s... s... stupid. That's what I say, F... F... Father. 1... n... n... n... never touched her, so help me God." So saying, Ryan thrust out his chin; a fair impression of the great leader, his hero, Winston Churchill, then crossed himself to impress the priest with a sudden display of piety.

O'Donnell pushed his chair back and stood up. "Now, here is my ruling on the matter," he said briskly. "Arnold Brown is a splendid parent. Oh, he maybe a little over-zealous in protecting his child, but as a father yourself, Fergus, you should appreciate that. He's got the wrong end of the stick here, obviously. The child has been missing school and as a parent he's worried, and worried people sometimes overreact."

He smiled and looked from one to the other. "Personally, I don't think Ryan here could in any case ever be guilty of such a thing, could you, lad? As you'll no doubt recall, Fergus, with your own Kathie, girls at a young age are very sensitive. Now, Nadina Brown... well she comes to mind as being of an extremely sensitive disposition. A nervous child, and possibly prone to exaggeration, don't you think?" He winked at Ryan. "You ever kiss the girls, lad? Ah, yes, you don't want to admit it, but you have." He waved a finger. "Nothing to be ashamed of, boy. So, maybe one time you went a little bit further than you should, hmm? Would that be correct? Yes?"

"I never touched her!" Ryan blurted out, looking at his father. "Never done nothing to no girl. I hate girls!"

"Ah," Father O'Donnell nodded, sat down again. Ignoring the outburst, he leaned his bulk across the desk, lowered his voice, "Now, let me surmise what took place, on the evidence. The wee girl is sweet on Ryan here. She's bemoaning the fact that he's not taking any interest in her. And she made certain, erm... exaggerations, distortions to her daddy. Insinuations, you understand. Devious, no doubt, but that's children for you, and just a sign, early hints of adolescence? Don't you think so, Fergus? I've told Arnold Brown to appreciate that and not take it too seriously. As far as I understand it there could be a perfectly natural explanation and that's the one the mother believes. The child is well-developed and had a particularly heavy time of the month. Somehow, the father saw the... erm... the show... erm, of blood and jumped to the wrong conclusions. Arnold Brown is, well, over-protective, as father's can be towards their daughters. To him she is still his little girl. Of course if he has any doubts at all he should have got a medical opinion." He paused and looked at the father and son sitting before him. "I don't need to add anything more to that, do I?"

Ryan, his gaze fixed firmly on the floor, remembered what Kenny had said about what happens when a hymen gets cracked and gut blood pours out. He couldn't follow all that was said, but whatever it was, it weren't nothing to do with him. Anyways it was all horrible and messy. All he wanted was to get home. He rolled his shoulders and raised his eyes to the fat Father, subjecting him to a full Cagney stare.

Father O'Donnell stood up and now launched into his pulpit voice, waving a podgy finger at Fergus. "You parents, now, you have to let your girls grow up. They're a splendid couple, Arnold and Louise Brown, but appear reluctant to let young Nadina go. If they could, it would appear likely that the child would lose some of that extraordinary sensitivity and extreme self-consciousness. Have you noticed her at Mass, Fergus? A rather morbid disposition for a young girl, don't you think? Obsessively so, it seems to me. Mind you this is all very much in confidence. I expect you to respect that."

Ryan's head was aching and he felt dizzy. Whatever else, it was *her* fault, she was a liar, and old Croc-face got taken in. He picked up the word 'insinuation.' He would look it up in his dictionary, add it to his list.

Father O'Donnell, seated again, leant back in his chair and changed tempo, speaking in a relaxed and friendly manner. "Now, Fergus, what I'd like to do is for me to have a little word with your fellow Catholics, Arnold and Louise Brown, and suggest an apology should be forthcoming. And there I think we should let the matter rest." He looked at Ryan, who had lost interest and was gazing up at the ceiling, then at the crowded bookshelves.

The priest raised his voice. "Would you be happy about that, Ryan? And perhaps a little monetary gift to go with it? Pay attention to what I'm saying to you."

At the mention of money, Ryan responded quickly to say that yes, he would be happy about that. "B... b... but she got no r... r... right... t... t... t... to put it on to me. I done nothing!"

The priest glanced at his watch again, openly this time then, his fingers steepled, he continued his summing up, like a judge in a court of law.

"Naturally they're upset about whatever took place – or what didn't take place." He stared at Ryan, who had opened his mouth again to protest. "You're always about to interrupt me while I'm speaking, lad. You're always doing so at Catechism class. I'm telling you not to. As I say, I think it's all been a storm in a teacup. Things got a bit out of hand." The priest leaned further back in his chair. "Children are so different, aren't they, even in the same family? For instance, there's another child in the Brown household, Daphne. Known to your Kathie, I believe. A bit headstrong is that one, so different from her sister. Sure of herself. Fergus, I say this to you again, in confidence mind," he held up a warning finger. "Both Mr and Mrs Brown should let young Nadina stand on her own two feet. I'm giving her extra tuition to establish her stronger in the Faith, and yes, in order that at the same time she might grow a little away from them."

He cleared his throat, looked purposefully at his watch for a full ten seconds. "So now, Ryan, I'm going to suggest to Mr and Mrs Brown that they should make a proper apology and by way of compensation, include a small remuneration.

"That's it, then." Father O'Donnell stood up, shuffling some papers in front of him; a signal that the interview was over. "I'll get Mrs Henderson to see you out," he said, moving to the door.

The priest turned to Ryan. "You're a cheeky young monkey, aren't you, hmm? You need to get a grip on yourself at Catechism and at the Mass, and behave yourself. But I'm convinced you're completely innocent in this other matter, and I shall tell Mr Brown that it is indeed the case."

The bony hand of Mrs Henderson clasped the door handle and thrust the door open as wide as it would go. She wore her usual censorious look.

Fergus shook Father O' Donnell's hand. "Thank you, Father."

"Fine, Fergus, fine. Look, Fergus, I know your circumstances but let me remind you that the Lord loves a cheerful giver. Think about my new Offertory scheme, will you? I don't believe you are a contributor yet. Good day to you both."

Father and son were shepherded through the front door by the housekeeper, her mouth set in a disapproving line. Back in his study, Father O'Donnell opened the bottom drawer of his desk and reached for the whisky bottle.

Tight-lipped, Fergus struggled down the stone steps as fast as he could. Ryan took hold of his cane. "Dad, would you wish to walk through the park now? We could go and get some stale bread from the bread shop, feed the ducks. Would you like that? There's a bench by the pond. You can sit down. He shouldn't have kept us standing. Only, when you asked, he let us sit, didn't he?"

His father didn't answer, but fished in his jacket pocket for his cigarettes, his hand shaking. He brought it out empty. "Jaysus and Holy Mary, where the hell are they?" Ryan reached up to pat his other pocket.

"Here, Dad." He removed the cellophane, pulled open the flap then pushed a cigarette forward, but Fergus' fingers were unable to hold it. Ryan took it from him, on tiptoe stretched up to place it between his father's lips, brought out the lighter. The flame struggled against a soft wind. He flicked it again. This time it took hold.

"Thanks, son." Fergus drew heavily, standing upright, his mouth filled with smoke, then exhaled.

Ryan promised himself that from that day on he'd steer clear of all girls. Girls were liars, girls could never be trusted. He looked at his dad as he stumbled along the uneven pavement. Hurrying alongside, he asked again, "So shall we go then to feed the ducks, Dad? I'm thinking you could do with a rest."

His father coughed and began to choke. Ryan took the cigarette from his fingers, stubbed it out against a garden wall.

"Treating us like idiots, like criminals. Sure, the way he was lording it over us, he was enjoying it. Playing around with us, like a cat with a couple of mice."

Ryan linked his arm in his father's to give support. "You're dead right, Dad. Sure you are. But that Father knows I done nothing to Naddy Brown. He knows I'm innocent. He said so."

Fergus leaned against a fence. His breath came in short bursts. "Jaysus!"

"Dad, there's a bench by the pond. You can sit there. It'll be kinda peaceful for us both, hmm?"

"D'you think those Browns would be left standing in front of him like that? And I'm telling you, he's not getting one penny in his cursed Offertory Scheme. He's a scheming two-faced liar, a Brit-lover."

"Come on, Dad. I think maybe we'd better get back home. I'll make you a cuppa. Nice and strong. Sugar in it and maybe the whisky? Maybe you can beat me at table tennis for once, eh?"

Ryan trotted along beside his father, his several short steps equal to one of his dad's stumbling but lengthy strides. He felt a welling-up of happiness. Though there'd been a whole rigmarole of words he didn't understand, he'd heard enough to know Father O'Donnell knew Naddy was nuts, well and truly barmy. And Crocodile-face was even crazier. But he was sure Mrs Brown knew he hadn't done it. She was al-right, Mrs Brown. Like she knew it was monthly stuff, the blood then was sort of brownish according to what Kenny said. He shuddered at the thought, then began to wonder how much money he'd get. A Fever? Maybe even ten shillings? He linked his arm in his dad's again. "Come on, Dad. Put it behind us, eh? Like you tell Mam I was advising Mrs Brown, like. You got to forget things that go bad on you."

But though he was confused, Ryan knew one thing. He'd not speak to Nadina Brown ever again. Never. Not one word.

Chapter Twenty One

Ryan was willing, even eager, to forgive Mrs Brown. He recalled with pleasure her wonderful soup and the way she welcomed his advice on how to deal with her loony daughter, but it was clear that his father coupled the pair together with Father O'Donnell. The blue smoke from innumerable cigarettes that filled the kitchen like smoke from a battlefield carried venomous words. "These Browns," he said, furiously thrusting the stub of his cigarette on to the makeshift ashtray, "kow-towing to that worthless Father, crowing in his pulpit, flying the ensign of the enemy!"

Ryan's attitude towards Father O'Donnell, however, had revolved one hundred and eighty degrees. He even viewed him with something close to affection, certainly with a new esteem, for the way the priest had promised reimbursement, saw that he had been wronged and was unmistakably on his side. And though disinclined to be Confirmed - in fact as thoroughly dismissive of the whole practice as ever and determined to do everything in his power to avoid it - as a mark of a new respect for the priest, Ryan vowed that he would be on his best behaviour at Catechism class.

That morning, rubbing sleep from his eyes he stumbled down the stairs in his dressing gown, eager to know if the thud on the doormat from the postman contained his cherished reward. He hurried to the kitchen. The shocking sight made him cry out in dismay. A five pound note was being torn up into a thousand pieces, drifting like confetti into the coke hod, ready for the boiler.

"No! No, Dad," he shouted as he saw another fiver about to end up the same way. "Give it here!" Scrambling round the table, knocking chairs over as he went, jumping as high as he could, he managed to snatch the note from his father's fingers.

"Hypocrites!" yelled Fergus.

Clutching the money in his fist, his face streaked with tears, Ryan tried to explain,

"Sure it's the compensation. They know they done wrong, Dad. Father O'Donnell has got them to give it us. If it's ten pounds, then it's five of it is mine – is there more?" He looked around him.

"Jaysus! Do you think I want their damned patronising handouts?"

Ryan peered down into the hod. "Think what you could do with five pounds, Dad. You could almost buy a little car!" He looked around the shabby kitchen, his father's armchair inches off the ground. "At least, you could have a new chair." He held his note high in his fist, "You've burned yours. But this is mine and I'm keeping it."

Still shocked, he carefully folded his note into four, placed it carefully in the pocket of his dressing gown. After breakfast he'd take it to his bedroom and add it to his birthday and Christmas money: a creeping pile of wealth accumulated over the years, secure under his Persil-white underwear stacked neatly in the top drawer of his dresser.

Eyeing his father, he picked up the letter that lay on the table.

Dear Mr Brannigan and son,

Mrs Brown and I would like to apologise. After consulting with Father O'Donnell we realise that we have acted a little hastily. As you are no doubt aware, our younger daughter, Nadina, has been very unhappy of late, even refusing to attend school which is extremely unusual for her as she is a diligent and able scholar. Thanks to Father O'Donnell, acting on his advice, we are willing to rectify our mistakes. Therefore, we trust the enclosed remuneration will assist in restoring our friendship together as fellow Catholics at Holy Innocents' Church.

Kind regards to you both,

Yours sincerely,

Arnold and Louise Brown.

Fergus, calmer now, sat at the table. He lit a cigarette and after the customary explosive coughing fit, leaned back, poured his tea into his saucer in the usual way and continued to complain about the Browns' duplicity.

"Why, by all the churches in our holy land of Ireland, can't you see through them, son? That fool with his high and mighty ways was accusing you of something couldn't possibly have done. Now he realises. Oh to be sure, Father O' Donnell has had a word with his favourite parishioners. They just want to keep us sweet. Know why?" Fergus stretched out his long arm, the cigarette making circular motions adding impetus to his invective.

A sprinkle of ash landed in Ryan's porridge and he carefully negotiated his spoon around it. Thinking of the five pound note safe in his pocket, he concentrated on his breakfast and did not reply, past experience having taught him that the best policy to deal with his father's rages was silence.

"I'll tell you why, shall I? Thinking of their reputation is why, lest it should come out and what the rest of the good English crowd at the Mass would be thinking? The man's a complete joke, so he is. Jaysus, by all that is in the heavens, they make me sick! Oh, I can't stand this any more. I'm off." With that, Fergus poured his tea back into his cup, gulped it down and taking up his cane hobbled towards the back door. On the way, he leaned over his son's shoulder, the cigarette making circular movements. Ryan placed a protective hand over the remains of his breakfast.

"Tis a bribe, son, surely you can see that? Oh, yes! A bribe. And don't you shake your head at me like that, little fool that you are." His dad's voice softened, then thumped the table. "All right then, keep your Judas money!" Fergus stomped away, slamming the back door behind him.

The letter floated to the floor. Ryan picked it up and read it through again then took it to the boiler. He took the lid off. The blast of heat was so strong it hurt his eyes, the fumes making him choke. He dropped the letter in and replaced the lid then peered down into the hod. Tiny pieces from his father's five pound note lay scattered among the coke. He stretched his arm down and picked up every fragment. Could he paste them back together? He stared at the shattered remnants in his hands. Sadly, no, he knew he couldn't. He wept silently at the terrible desecration.

Well, at least he'd saved *his*. He ran upstairs, took the big white note from his pocket, smoothed it out on the surface of the dresser. Holding it up to the light, he admired the crispness of it, putting it to his ear to listen to it crinkle, smelt it and finally, extravagantly, kissed it. He opened the top drawer of his dresser and made a quick count. Twenty-nine pounds and sixteen shillings. A fortune! He placed the new note on top of the others, covering it all carefully with his freshly laundered vest and pants, then sat on his bed, reached down for his exercise book and opened it to the first page. He put another line under his favourite word that topped the list. The best word he'd ever found, a great word, a wonderful word full of meanings: pity, kindness, mercy. He smiled to himself. Blimey, if he got a fiver every time old croc-face accused him of messing up his daughter he'd be worth millions. He even felt a little more kindly towards Nadina.

Stretching out on his bed Ryan remembered squelching through the rain. He was like a big brother and it gave him a good feeling. Round and fat she was, like a big ball of wool that his mam used for knitting. That horrible splash all the way down her dial. Sad for her, wasn't it? He sat up, put the exercise book back in place, went to the bathroom, washed his face slowly and cleaned his teeth. Suddenly, remembering the gloved fist in his face, he hurled his toothbrush into the wash basin. His dad was right: croc-face was the biggest hypocrite in the whole wide world. He never looked at you, just down his nose, like you was an insect. Ryan narrowed his eyes; he would put them all in a film so he would. The top Nazis – Herr Brown, Miss Millison, a top lady Nazi in her grey uniform with a silver swastika like the brooch she wore. Both Fifth Columnists. Spies. Mrs Brown? She was all soft and spongy, always crying, getting upset. He'd make her a posh British housewife, making her super soup for her husband. *She finds secret papers in his pockets, finds out about his spying, so she sprinkles a little arsenic in his soup and he dies screaming in agony.*

Ryan went back into his bedroom, knelt on the floor and opened the exercise book, this time adding the word, 'hypocrite.' He was pleased to see the list getting longer by the day. He took off his dressing gown, hung it on his door and gathered up his clothes. As he pulled out the second drawer down containing his shirts, he glanced across the room. He pulled a book out from the bookshelf, examining the title. '*The strange case of Doctor Jekyll and Mr Hyde,*' a library book that he'd forgotten to take back. He'd seen the film, '*Doctor Jekyll and Mr Hyde.*' and remembered every detail.

It's like everyone has a bit of Hyde in them, he thought, turning the pages, reminding himself of the story. And what's more, you never know when it's going to happen, like a boxer who'd been losing all along when all of a sudden he gives you a knock-out punch in the fifteenth round. His dad tearing up the fiver and burning it. That's Hyde al-right. The badness taking over. Doctor Jekyll is always gentle and kind, like Uncle Joe Stalin puffing away on his pipe in the Kremlin, all nice as pie, like his dad at lot of the time. Then, all of a sudden, something happens and they go as mad as hell.

Closing the book, he went downstairs, feeling new and good, thinking of his treasure safe in the top drawer and determined to be more Jekyllish. Quickly, he dressed. It was time for school.

"Bye, Mam," he called out, hearing the bath filling up.

There was old Rich over the road, mouth open, dribbling as usual, calling to him. "Hey, Rye, you know that Naddy Brown. A sex madman done her, so they reckon." He sniffed, and the contents of one nostril disappeared.

Soft in the head, thought Ryan. Patience was another new word, a Jekyll word he liked. So he stopped himself from smacking Foureyes round the head and all he said was, "Got your ball with you, Rich? C'mon we're gonna be late."

"Underneath me jumper. Here. Look, Rye, I've only got one boob, but it's a big 'un. Hey, if I was to do it to her, I'd have to put a bag over her head, eh, Rye?"

"Shut up, will you!" Forgetting Doctor Jekyll, he crossed the road to land a heavy punch to his friend's belly. Foureyes doubled over. As he gasped for breath, Ryan knew Mr Hyde had come to stay. He ran on ahead and was soon tagging onto the end of the long line filing into Assembly.

"Children! Every eye look at me, nobody talking."

The heavy curtain rustled in protest as the Head pulled it across. Dust drifted to the floor, some of the children coughed. The staff shuffled across the stage to stand protectively round her in the usual semi-circle like a guard of honour. Ryan noted that she was getting more and more Hydeish Not a bit of good her dressing in white, white can never hide Mr Hyde, that harsh trill of the voice like the cry of a rook; the Hyde gleam in her black eyes. Very little Jekyll at all unless she's talking to her favourites, Matthews and Peal and mad Naddy, who's still nowhere about, he thought, looking around. Elbowing Philip in the stomach as he passed, he pushed his way along the row of infants, stamping his feet, mumbling apologies, explaining he was Hyde. He nudged Kenny, "Bet those wobbly teeth fall out, bet you sixpence."

"I said, no talking! Irish again, of course. Bound to be." The Head made a swift adjustment to her teeth with her thumb. "Now, we are over half way through term and soon we will be at the end of the school year and a new direction for the top class on their academic journey. A number of you will pass the Scholarship; certainly a few will achieve considerably strong results." She gave a special sunbeam for her favourites before continuing, "And then there are the other lot." Miss Millison sighed as if giving a last breath of life, shaking her head slowly from side to side like the pendulum of the clock the retired teachers kept in a corner of their front room at number one hundred and five Harefield Road.

Ryan counted: six times the long head moved like a spectator watching Wimbledon. Must have been like Chamberlain's missus when she knew the bit of white paper from Munich was no cop, he thought. "No, no, no. I told you, Neville. Hitler can't be trusted." And Chamber Pot, he says, "He seemed ever so nice, dear."

"Well, I dread to think," said Miss Millison, slow and sad like a very old tortoise.

They gazed up at her in a kind of torpor, two hundred and fifty pairs of eyes, dull and sleepy, back on a Monday morning from half-term's freedom. She raised herself to her full six feet two inches, her front two teeth now completely out of control, the hidden spring that kept them secure having long since lost all influence. A look of panic, and they were levered back into place with a pink tongue.

"Naughton Road Secondary for some," she said. "Oh dear, oh dear. May the dear Lord preserve us."

The children watched her thin chest heave. "Is she going to puke?" Ryan whispered. "Three pence if she does." But as rapidly as it had begun, the bosom settled, the frown almost disappeared, the angry eyes, wide and glaring behind the glasses, softened. A bit of Jekyll after all, he thought.

"Well, you made your choice, didn't you, Class six? You either worked hard and are looking forward to a proper career or else...?" There was another pause, another huge sigh. Yes, a teeny weeny bit of Doctor Jekyll, thought Ryan: a little kind of sad shaking of her head, a few strands from the ice cream cone of her silver pile coming adrift.

"Well, may it please Almighty God to come to your aid. Rest assured I will pray for you. I promise you that. That's all I can say."

As the teachers clapped, Ryan gave Foureyes a swift bang on the back of his head, once again completely forgetting the good doctor. "God help *you*," he whispered, "ignorant toss-pot." Ryan knew it was Hyde, coming out suddenly like you never expected and he knew he was enjoying his sudden arrival, like he enjoyed describing the discolouration to Naddy's cheek, telling her it was India-shaped. Yet where was compassion? Why was it so easy for Hyde to do the dirty on his mind. "Sorry," he whispered, noticing green snot mixed with tears rolling down the poor little devil's cheeks.

At break Ryan tried to explain his theory to Kenny. "See, Hyde's in everyone, deep in your soul or whatever, like he hopes to take you over. That's how it was in the book. Got it out from the library. *The Strange Story of Doctor Jekyll and Mr Hyde*, by Robert Louis Stevenson. See, the doctor, he's all kind, dolling out medicines and that. Then, he has this special brew which he drinks and it takes him over. He becomes evil, real evil. Goes out and murders people. It's happening all the time. Take Miss Ashby. Most of the day, she's okay. Then she goes nasty. Her Hyde-ishness coming out, see? Same with Millie.

Getting more and more Hyde-ish now, I suppose because... I dunno, maybe getting older, getting fed up with us all. Old people can get nasty. Mrs Jackson though, her with the pies, she'd never ever be Hyde. Real lovely she is, like Doctor Jekyll, though she's a woman."

Kenny, looking down from his favourite perch on the bench like it was a pulpit, adding four feet to his superior height, shook his head as if mystified and said, 'What the hell you on about, boy?"

"Just helping you understand goodness and badness, like in everyone."

Later, at afternoon break, Ryan noticed a gathering by the gates. He walked over, Kenny following. As he drew closer he heard the name, 'Dave Berry'. Evidently the police had caught the boy, an ex-pupil from Naughton Road, with Polly Townsend in the toilets on the recreation ground.

"Who you talking about?" Ryan pushed his way to the front.

"My dad always said that some of 'em ask for it," someone said.

Shrill, raucous laughter; Kenny laughing loudest. A discussion followed. They recalled the touch from those restless hands at the pictures. Polly Townsend's hard bumps on her fingers and thumbs as she fiddled with buttons. It was only when the lights went up in the interval that you saw them. "Tell you what them are," said Kenny, fresh from a perusal of the 'News of the World.' "Warts. Infectious, I reckon. You be careful," he said looking at some of the younger pupils. Several nodded, a few shuddered. It was wise to steer clear of old Polly, an ex-pupil from Naughton ten years back "Hey, listen," said Foureyes. "I wouldn't do it with that Naddy Brown if you was to pay me one million pounds. Not even with a big sack over her horrible bonce."

The punch landed on his nose and he keeled over. There was the sound of broken glass, blood on the lenses. More children now gathered, hearing the commotion, girls this time. A makeshift circle formed. Doctor Jekyll had vanished, and Hyde, his blond hair standing up like a dog's hackles, stood spitting and snarling over the prostrate Foureyes. "Don't you ever think what it's like? To be deformed?" he shouted, diving on top of the weeping boy, who covered his face with his arms.

If it hadn't been for Miss Ashby, throwing her stout little self into the midst of them like a rugby player in a scrum, pushing boys to left and right and finally pulling Ryan out of the melee by the collar of his jersey, Foureyes might well have ended up in hospital. She pulled him to his feet and smacked his assailant hard on the head. One boy, Peter Steggles, stepped up and thoughtfully pressed the shattered spectacles into the howling boy's hand.

"Filthy-minded disgusting creatures, all of them. Vermin!" was Miss Millison's verdict when Miss Ashby related the incident. "At least that halfwit, Richard Johnson will soon be gone. Virtually unemployable, of course, that one. As for Irish, thank the dear Lord he'll soon be someone else's responsibility. On that score, I imagine, Father O'Donnell will be as relieved as I shall be, Thelma."

The general conclusion from Class six was that it must be the Irish blood in him that gave Ryan Brannigan such strength, for though he was thin and small, he was a great fighter.

"Truly, his strength is untamed, animal-like," pronounced Peter Steggles solemnly. "Like he's got the strength of ten men."

"Yeah. Primitive-like, from a funny old backward country that's got goblins, leprechauns, elves and fairies and such," said Pat Dickerson knowingly.

"Muscles, them have, an' all though," said Greengage, admiringly at Ryan, tasting the red crayon recently applied to her top lip.

Rumours about Nadina Brown continued to spread rapidly through the school, the girls imagining how she would look with a pillow underneath her skirt, Miss Ashby giving them a good tongue-lashing when she overheard their remarks, warning them of the dangers of gossip, cautioning they should know there was absolutely no truth to the rumours. Despite her warnings they continued to fantasise.

Pat's vindictive nature showed through like the hem of her grimy petticoat. She put it to the rest of the class, "It's all her la-de-da ways, I can't stand, her posh talking and that. I used to like her but she's too full of herself. Thinks she's better than the rest of us. She got religion, see, got it really bad, that one."

For once Ryan was able to agree with the Dickerson streak. Julie Richards though was quick to defend Nadina's reputation. "Well, she changes her underwear and washes her hair, don't she, which you never."

The others wondered how many times a year Julie washed *her* hair. Her habit of scratching 'till her scalp bled surely indicated rare contact with soap and water.

A fierce debate among the girls as to how they would defend themselves if they were ever attacked by someone like Dave Berry or Geoff Bolton. The banter ceased abruptly when Julie Richards, having secured a place on the bench in the absence of Evett who was canoodling with Pat behind the big oak, stood to address them from the makeshift pulpit with the wisdom of Solomon, "First, see, I'd grab his thingy and squeeze, then I'd wind him, punch him really hard in his belly, then I'd go for the eyes. I'm going to grow my nails real long, like about two inches. I'm going to paint 'em bright red, like for blood, and the ends are going to be razor sharp." She lunged forward to demonstrate her fighting skills. The other girls shrieked with laughter. Several applauded.

Ryan, on the outer circle, shook his head sadly. "Hyde has taken that one over. Complete like," he said to Steggles. Then explaining his theory: Hyde and Jekyll each wanting control, mostly Hyde wins.

On the Friday of that week, meandering home from school, passing by the shops and waving his customary greeting to Mrs Jackson presiding over the moving currants, Ryan crossed the coast road and recognised in the distance the familiar chubby shape leaning against his front gate. Any possible influence from kindly Doctor Jekyll was smothered as he drew close.

"Excuse me," he said, "do you mind? I live here, right? I don't know who you are, but this is private property, see?" On the gatepost he traced the one, nought and three with his forefinger. "Yes, that's right, this is my house." He released the catch. "You should be back at school. They know you're not pregnant." He eyed her dress, unusually creased and shabby. "Nothing showing is there? Sure, you're a little liar you are, like always."

Seeing her tear-streaked face and the octopus eye, which seemed redder than ever, moving round like a marble, noting that her hair, once washed and smelling of carbolic, had lost its sheen, the compassionate doctor struggled to make his presence felt, but a Hydeish look of contempt was distorting the doctor's sensitive features.

"Ryan, listen. I... I wanted to write to you, to explain everything. My father is so ignorant. He got it all completely wrong. It's all a dreadful mistake. I'm really, really sorry."

Ryan shrugged his shoulders. "Father O'Donnell got your dad to apologise to me. He's al-right, he is. And he got him to give me money after all the instinuations."

"Don't you mean insinuations?"

"Yeah, al-right, insinuations, girl. Whatever. Always a show-off, aren't you? Always think you know more than anyone else, don't you? He stared at her, started to snarl like Mr Hyde. The result was disappointing.

A thin smile creased her lips, then she giggled, trying hard not to laugh aloud.. "Are you trying to frighten me? If so, you're not succeeding. "Ryan, you look so utterly ridiculous."

"Your dad's a complete loony, so he is. He shook his fist in my face, telling me I done it to you. Sure, he's got every screw missing, more that anyone could ever have. He's a top Nazi. I seen him on the Newsreel at the pictures, so I have."

Then kindly Doctor Jekyll burst through like the sun breaking up a cluster of cloud. "Oh, God, Naddy, will you go and see Miss Ashby. That's what I was telling your mam. I says to her, she should go and see Miss Ashby. If I'd got into big trouble, whatever, I told your mam, *I'd* see Miss Ashby."

Tears trickled down Naddy's face, her shoulders heaving, "It's not *me*. Why do you have to blame *me*?"

He slammed the gate behind him and crossed the patch of lawn. She called out, "Ryan, whatever's happened to Foureyes? He's all bandaged up."

"Because he keeps on and on about it. Spreading rumours about you and that Berry kid from Naughton. That you done it with him, or Geoff Bolton."

"No, no, no! Please, Ryan. Nothing happened. Please, let's be friends. Put it all behind us, can't we?"

For a second he stopped at the edge of the lawn, stared hard at her, hands on his hips, rolling his shoulders then squaring them like James Cagney under stress. For a moment his face softened, his Doctor Jekyll face. She looked like she was more than normal upset. "You gotta see Miss Ashby, Naddy. See if she can sort you out, whatever's wrong." But on the other side of the lawn Hyde was back, grinning like a fiend enjoying her unhappiness. "We're not best friends no more," he shouted, "not now, not ever. Get off following me around like you're always doing. It gets on my tits so it does, you fat freak."

He hurried along the concrete passage, stamping like a platoon of soldiers. Then, changing into Quasimodo mode he turned round. The result was again disappointing. Despite the tears, she was chuckling. He reverted to the rank of Colonel and making binoculars with his hands, surveyed his regiment. He stopped when he saw her dab with her hankie at one rolling tear making its way from the unhidden left eye. He felt glad. He knew he wanted Jekyll; wanted to be the compassionate doctor, but he never came to stay very long. Hyde was taking over more and more. Remembering a line from the film when Hyde said, 'This evil is a fine thing,' he felt ashamed and just a little scared.

Chapter Twenty Two

Disconsolate, Ryan's harsh words ringing in her ears, Nadina drifted along unfamiliar streets, unsure where to go, realising school was finished for another day. Around her a blaze of colour as classrooms emptied and their occupants teemed homewards. Saint Mary's High in dazzling azure blue. Saint Joseph's Catholic Independent, the black pin-stripe and straw boaters with a purple band temporarily abandoned in favour of war time dull grey. Suddenly, the hated crimson of Southgate Girls. She heard the crude shouts and laughter through the narrow opening from the road with its high hedges, untrimmed, untamed like the pupils. She hurried by, fearful that she would encounter Daphne.

The Convent School was some distance away. It would mean catching two buses. Inconvenient but not impossible. Oh, to be with those softly spoken girls with their smart lime green and gold uniforms and their straw boaters with the gold band.

On her way to town one Saturday morning half a dozen of them had boarded her bus. She had taken note of their kind expressions, listened to their earnest conversations. Two of them smiled at her as she alighted. Another time, on the corner of Gregory Avenue, on the way home from school, she had stopped to speak to one, a little older, who had told her all about the school, reinforcing her expectations.

The Convent School of the Holy Name. On recent mornings, sitting at her dressing table, instead of staring at the blemish, desperately hoping that it was fading and inevitably being disappointed, she had questioned her reflection, "Whose name is the school called after? Why Jesus' name! The name above every name. Whose name?" she would ask again, "Why, Jesus' name! The Convent School of the Holy Name!" She loved to savour the delicious flavour of the words, like dipping a stick of liquorice into a bag of sherbet, or the scrumptious taste of ice cream on a scorching summer's day, repeating the name of the school slowly, then suddenly, letting the words trip off her tongue.

Her fingers touched the blemish. She had a sense that once at her new school she would no longer be ashamed of it or embarrassed, for no one would notice it, not even mention it, except possibly to sympathise. There, at her new school she would be able to forget the dreadful past.

What of the two other requirements: passing the Scholarship with sufficiently high marks? Well, she had no qualms about that, noting that she had finished the Maths and English papers well ahead of even Cyn Peal or Philip. Thelma Ashby, collecting the papers, paused at her desk, quickly scanned hers, then gave a wink and her lovely smile. What else? Old Mother Clare with her crinkled skin like a walnut would be an easy interview, she'd heard. Once that was over and she had *his* recommendation in her hand to post, she would tell Miss Ashby, and together they would go to the Police. Just as soon as she had the precious recommendation....

She strolled homewards. As soon as she was through the front door, smelling the polish as her mother furiously cleaned everything in sight, hanging up her gas mask, she said, "Ryan's really fed up with you, you know. I can't blame him the way father went for him. You'd think a Chief Health Inspector would know the facts of life before rushing at things like a bull in a china shop." She stomped upstairs to her bedroom, ignoring the reaction: the sloppy mouth open in surprise, the hostile stare. She took her bunch of keys from the pocket of her dress, pulling the door to, drew the bolts across, then lay on her bed, hands behind her head, staring up at the ceiling.

On the other side of the door the silly voice prattled on. "Open the door, Nadina. We've given you time to adjust. Patience is a virtue, but there is a limit. Just recall for one moment will you that you promised your father and I that you'd be returning to school after half-term. Confirmation in only three weeks away! Do you think you can suddenly reappear at school and expect Father O'Donnell to present you to the Bishop. Whatever next? Anyway, we are completely agreed on one thing, your father and I, despite our many differences. Yes, one thing, Nadina. When the Scholarship results are declared, and which undoubtedly you will have passed..." the voice droned on.

Two Yale locks, the mortise and the drawing back of the bolts took time; it was twenty seconds before Nadina's tearful face looked round the door. "I am not going to Southgate! Never! never, never, never! I'd rather die than go there! I think you and father must have some sort of mental blockage."

Louise sighed, held out a cup of tea and a piece of fruit cake, which Nadina took with a murmured thank you, then said, "I've told both of you millions of times. I am going to the Convent School of the Holy Name where I shall be taught by the nuns. So get used to the idea, get it into your thick heads, will you?"

Louise blanched, her head wobbled as she tried to think of a suitable response.

Eventually, she said rather lamely, "Well, Father thinks it best that you don't. I've spoken to him about it."

"What?" Nadina stood stock still, framed in the doorway, her eyes wide in shock. "What? I can't believe what I'm hearing here."

Attempting to hide her nervousness behind the wobbly smile, Louise said, "Yes, well I have, Nadina, but he's promised to continue to take a special interest in you. Oh, Nadina, think how fortunate you are! Do realise, please, that you can't have everything you want in this world. None of us can. I can't. Nor can Daddy. How many children in the parish do you think are getting all this attention from such an attentive caring priest? You are spoiling your chances, and it is just such a shame."

"Say it again, mother. What did he say about me?"

Now stumbling over her words, Louise replied. "Well, his advice, in a nutshell, Nadina, and I'm putting this to you very bluntly – very down to earth is Father – his advice is that you should try and be a little less religious. Oh, I'm sorry; I can see that hasn't gone down very well. What Father means is that you should take yourself a little less seriously. I must say I never thought I'd ever hear a priest saying something like that. But, Nadina! At such a young age you can go too far. You're barely eleven. Eleven years old—"

"What of it?"

Louise stared at her daughter and hesitated, ready to burst into tears for the umpteenth time that day. A daughter whose behaviour was so unnatural, abnormal, secretive and having to put up with so much belligerence, it was too much to bear. All her careful restraint now suddenly ended like a burst balloon. "For God's sake, child! You mope around in your bedroom with your doors locked as if you're expecting a burglar, your hair covers your mouth; you talk in whispers, if indeed you have the courtesy to talk to us at all, well I can't stand much more of it. I think the world of Father O'Donnell, everyone at the church does. I think he's being very sensible.

"Sensible? Sensible?"

Louise dabbed at her eyes with a corner of her pinafore, "Yes, sensible, Nadina. I'm sorry but you are becoming far too serious. It's morbid and it's got to end. Oh, for heavens' sake, Nadina! When I was your age I was up and about enjoying myself. Look at Daphne..."

"Oh, yes, didn't think it would be long before we'd be coming back to her. Oh, how marvellous! Three cheers for the wonderful Daphne. Every mother's dream! Bring on the wonderful Daphne!"

Louise flinched; she knew she'd said too much, but it was too late to back down now. "Yes, off with her friends, doing her hobbies, taking part in her sports. There are so many interesting things she finds to do. Why can't you be more like her? Oh, al-right, just a little bit, then. And this refusing to go to school, yet again. At this rate, we'll be having the Schools Inspector round!" Louise drew breath, aware that her voice was shaking, conscious that she was losing control. Yet, try as she might she could not stop the big, pearl-shaped tears rolling down the flabby cheeks. "I've spoken to Miss Millison on the telephone, a most disagreeable person, she wouldn't hear of granting me an interview. But I can tell you this, Nadina, she's not at all happy with your attitude and behaviour and I can't say I blame her. What sort of report is she going to give you? Have you thought about that?"

"See if I care. Do what you damned well like!"

Stunned, Louise stepped backwards. A duster tucked in the belt of her dress, like a housemaid from a previous century, stranded on the landing, gasping like a fish without water while her mistress slammed her door, drew back the bolts and once more withdrew inside her fortress.

Tomorrow, his rest day, she'd demand an explanation. She was tempted to give him a warning, but that could wait. Talk of friendship, friends support each other, don't they? Friends don't go behind your back. She hurled the *'Book of Saints'* he had lent her at the door.

Deciding to have a bath, she stripped and donned her white dressing-gown, hugging it to her like a fur coat in a freezing winter. Listening at the door to be sure her mother had gone, she tiptoed to the bathroom. Turning on the taps she watched the steam rise, swirling the water with her hand, making it as hot as she could bear it. She climbed in and lay still and silent, letting the water soak into her, cleansing, purifying, washing away the filth of her polluted soul, blocking out the terror of that last terrible time. As soon as she had the recommendation, she would tell all. She was sure of it.

Back in her bedroom she dressed, turning on the wireless. Choral music from Westminster Abbey. She let the mellow voices of the choir envelop her and thought again of the future, free of everything and everyone – except Thelma of course. Free of Pat, with that foul-mouthed, disgusting Evett and that filthy Johnson tyke grinning at her through his horrible teeth, the memory of his slime trickling down the mark still causing her to shudder. And Ryan? Would she see him again? Despite her misery, she shook her head and smiled, recalling his stupid contortions. Then, all at once serious, realising that she was unworthy to pray for his soul.

Next morning at breakfast Nadina apologised to her mother for swearing. Struggling to eat her toast and marmalade, a lump in her throat like an obstruction, she swallowed a mouthful of tea and got up from the table to announce that she was going to see the priest. Her parents glanced at each other. Suddenly her father, slamming his cup down on his saucer, shouted as the door closed behind her. "Southgate! No ifs, no buts. Southgate."

Louise, buttering her toast and sipping her tea thoughtfully, lips puckered, brow wrinkled, hoping the years would pass and somehow her younger daughter might some day in the future become a reasonably healthy normal human being.

As Nadina cycled down the Conway road, she rehearsed *'Father, did you or did you not agree with my parents that I was getting too religious and for that reason you agreed with them that I should go to Southgate Grammar?'*

Stomach churning, she leaned her bike up against the railings, stepped up to the door and grabbed the knocker. Immediately, the door was yanked open.

"Why, it's Nadina." His hands reached out to hold her. He pulled her over the threshold.

"Please," she said.

He dropped his hands. "How lovely. Do come inside." His smile always seemed so genuine. "To be sure, this is an unexpected pleasure." He closed the heavy door after her.

"I'm sorry, Father, that I didn't make an appointment, but it's not fair of you. Just isn't.—".

Her voice dropped as his countenance changed. He frowned, his mouth down at the corners and his nose wrinkled as if he detected an unpleasant smell. "We need to talk. Come on."

She followed him into the study, but made sure she stood by the door. By his desk he turned to face her. "You haven't been keeping any appointments of late, have you? No sign of you at Catechism class, and therefore not being present for the extra tuition. Miss Millison tells me you have even been absenting yourself from school. Why is that?"

"What did you say to my parents? They said you told them that I was getting too religious? Did you... did you...?" She began to sob, her chest heaving. Gently he tried to lead her to a chair. She thrust his arm away. "No! I won't!"

"And you honestly expect my recommendation? Dear Nadina... tut, tut, tut." The silly voice was back, mocking her, his head shaking in silent laughter. He leaned back in the armchair by the hearth. She felt so small, so insignificant, so... nothing.

"I have to go to the Convent School. I must." She glared across the room. "You promised. When you came to the house, you told my parents I had a... had a... you said something about a brilliant future as a religious. You were full of... of enthusiasm for me, making plans."

"Was I really?" His sarcasm plunged into her like a sword. He patted his cassock pockets, brought out a packet of Players, stood up to light up. "We can of course always reverse that decision. But, my dear Nadina, it's entirely up to you." So saying, he walked across the room to the door where she stood, looked at her gravely. "I shall expect you on Friday for your Confession."

"Yes, I'll be there, Father, but... but... I don't want to... and..." Nadina swallowed, felt a flush flooding up her neck, aware that her face was pink. "And... I will tell on you. I will, Father O'Donnell, if... if...." Her voice trailed away; it was so clumsy, sounded so silly: 'I will tell on you.' Like a child would say. She searched his face for some response, but he stared back, his expression blank.

Chapter Twenty Three

Ryan stirred, shuddered in his sleep. No longer the big burly Colonel Brannigan, shiny black boots crunching the gravel at Buckingham Palace, standing six feet tall before his hero, Mr Churchill, but reduced to the size of a louse from Nit-Julie's hair; a fearful shivering in front of two chattering front teeth the size of tombstones in the huge cavern of Holy Innocents' Church, Miss Millison glaring at him.

When he woke that morning he was relieved to get out of bed.

The Big Day was getting closer. But before the verdicts were passed: either Southgate Boys' or Girls' Grammar; Catholic High, Saint Joe's Independent, the Convent School of the Holy Name, or the inferno of Naughton Road Secondary Modern, there was another ordeal they were to undergo that seemed even more important, the fuss Millie was making of it.

This great event needed thorough preparation, she had announced at Assembly, fingering the silver brooch, the white handbag swinging menacingly at her side. Eyes focussed particularly on the troublesome trio in the front row she said, "Remember! Our Lord forgives every wrong deed, every dirty word and disgraceful thought. Therefore, I say, to each of you make out a list... a thoroughly detailed list of all wrongs. Your disgusting language, your base and filthy thoughts. The good Lord knows. He always knows. Nothing escapes his scrutiny." This was the preparation, she told them, to be undertaken before the great event of Holy Confirmation. "This is the prelude to the Great Day," she paused for effect, the forefinger hovering, ready for action, the handbag accelerating. "Your Holy Confession to be made before Father O'Donnell."

Since his financial restitution, Ryan had stayed silent and even attentive at Catechism class, so much so that his classmates thought he must be ill. Even Father O'Donnell had looked on wonderingly at this sudden change of behaviour.

Ryan cheered himself with the thought that once through the whole bag of tricks, he would be among the heathen lot at Southgate, where he's heard that assemblies lasted all of five minutes. There would be a few announcements; 'Onward Christian Soldiers' warbled off-key, the whole business ending with the Lord's Prayer rushed through at the speed of a meteor.

He didn't see why the priest should enquire into his private life. Ryan tried to explain his views to Kenny as they sat on the bench in the playground, having ousted some girls from Class Four. "It's like this. Why should I tell *him?* And once you've told him things, he'll keep them, like stored away in his brain, and when he gets up there, he'll make sure the angels know all about them, not that I believe in angels, that's just what they tell you." Ryan peeled back a corner of his sandwich his mam had packed in greaseproof paper. To his disappointment, it was spam again and no chutney.

Kenny put on his thinking face: eyes screwed up against the sun, head slightly forward, shoulders hunched, one hand stroking his chin: a philosopher's pose. After a moment's silence, he said, "Why should he specially remember your sins when he's heard thousands telling him stuff for hundreds of years. Don't make no sense that don't, boy." He bit into his apple, pulled a face, chewed for a bit, then spat it out at Foureyes, who happened to be passing.

"So, what *you* going to tell him then?" Ryan asked.

Kenny now climbed up on to the bench to illustrate not only his superior height but his supposed greater intelligence, his big face red and sweaty, "You got no right to ask that. You know nothing about it, you don't. Don't you know that Confession is what's called a Holy Sacrament? It's a private thing between you, Father O'Donnell and the Almighty. You got no idea, you haven't. Ignorant, yeah, that's you," he said, jumping down.

Ryan, having asked a direct question felt it warranted a response. He glared at Kenny and waited.

"Me, you're asking?" Kenny responded at length. "Not much to tell," Looking pensive he squinted up at the sun, folding his arms. "Few things, s'pose, like staying in bed too long Sat'days, not doing the garden when I'm supposed to. You know, cut the lawn, things like that. A lot of piddly little things, boy. Yeah, that'll be my confession." He sat down.

"That all?"

"What else?" The grin on his face widened. Then he looked astonished. "Hey, you're not thinking I'm telling him that stuff are you? No chance I'll tell him that, boy."

"Yeah, those things you get up to with that smelly Dickerson kid."

Kenny's voice softened to a whisper. "Private, that is Rye. Would shock him rigid! He'd remember *that* al-right. Poor old fella, he'd never sleep nights again. Have nightmares he would. Wouldn't be fair on him." Punching Ryan's arm he guffawed.

Just like old Kenny pretending he was a proper Catholic. If a priest sat in his little box like he's on the throne of England, or like God, he shouldn't mind anything you tell him. Shouldn't matter what you come out with. Yeah, but maybe the big know-all is right. The fat Father might get a big shock like an electric current going up his backside. It was worth trying. There was a chance, not much of one, but still a bit of a chance that he might escape the charade altogether.

Later, back in Class, Ryan felt inspired. He would explain it this way. *'I'm much too bad to be Confirmed, Father. See, Father O'Donnell, I'm like an apple. I look good. I'm red and shiny. But when you peel me, you'll see there's loads of bad bits. Bruises, sir. they go right down deep. Even the pips, Father, they should be brown, but they're not, in me they're all white. When I bite into that apple, I have to spit most of it out, sir, because it's so bad. See, Father, that's me. I'm like that bad apple. On the outside I look good but it's not true, because, Father, right to the core I am rotten. So, what I'm trying to explain to you, Father O'Donnell, sir, is that I'm not ready to be Confirmed. I don't think I'll ever be ready. I'm bad, Father. Like a bad apple, sir, so help me God. Amen.'*

As on previous Friday afternoons, the class of eighteen boys and sixteen girls congregated on the pavement outside the school gates. As this was the final preparation before the big day, the Head was to accompany Miss Ashby and, as befitting such an important occasion, Miss Millison had changed her costume. All she needs is a swastika against the black arm to be a proper Nazi, Ryan thought.

With her twirl of silver hair, rising as high as a guardsman's bearskin, umbrella like a sergeant major's baton tucked in place, they were ready to proceed. She darted back to poke a stray boy in the back. "Keep on the pavement, everyone! Do you wish to get run over? Form up in pairs. One girl to one boy." There was a shuffling of feet and considerable chopping and changing. At the rear of the column, one girl walked on her own.

"Are we ready at long last, Miss Ashby?" cried Miss Millison.

Her deputy, straining to look over the heads of her pupils, called out, "Yes, Miss Millison."

"Forward," the head of the column called.

Near the end of the line Pat and Kenny, clutching hands. Following behind with Julie he tried to listen in to their conversation, heard Pat whisper, "Not now. Later."

That would be something extra to add, thought Ryan. Temptations of the flesh crowding in.

'So you see, Father O'Donnell, being bad, I'm led to do bad things, worse things. I know I shouldn't. They are a bad influence, sir. They lead me astray. Like Evett and that filthy, disgusting girl, Dickerson. I tell you, Father, I'm rotten. Sure I am. I'm rotten to the core, so help me God.'

He patted the wad of paper in his back pocket; an exhaustive list of sexual wickedness that had taken him well over three hours to prepare. If what Kenny said *was* true, the priest would know he was far too bad to be Confirmed.

Nadina tapped him on the shoulder. Silence should be the most effective treatment.

Julie Richards turned to give a snappy smile with her buck teeth. "Push off, you. I'm with Irish."

Ignoring her, Naddy said, "Ryan, once I get to my new school, you won't ever need to see me again."

Julie giggled. Ryan stayed silent. He didn't want to look at her. Every time he did, his anger welled up. He knew Hyde was winning, Jekyll was pushed into the corner of the ring with a knock out punch, but he didn't care.

"No more talking," shouted Miss Millison, swinging round and raising her umbrella on high like a sword. "This walk to church should be undertaken in absolute silence. Any boy or girl I catch talking will be severely dealt with." She tucked her umbrella back into place, looked up at the sky and made the sign of the cross as if pleading for help to control her straggling, ill-disciplined pupils.

After the crocodile line had crossed the coastal road, she called a halt, turned to address the pint-sized penitents. "We are on a holy pilgrimage," she shouted. "You are to make a good, thorough Confession. On this coming Sunday, Miss Ashby and I will be present to witness your Confirmation as full members of Christ's Church. What a privilege! What glory! The battle of life to be fought and won."

Ryan found it hard to think of going into battle against something you couldn't see: Lucifer, the Devil, the Evil Being they tell you is slinking about, always watching, listening in to your conversations, ever trying to get one over on you, getting you to do bad things; worming its way into your brain to get you to think disgusting thoughts, worse even than Hyde. A ghostly enemy, all dressed up in black if you ever saw him, like the Father or Millie. He, Ryan Brannigan, would fight the *real* enemy: the Nazi hordes close to Moscow. Winston Churchill, who'd taken over the year before from useless Chamber Pot, had taught them about the real devil, Adolf Hitler. Ryan loved the new Prime Minister. He would fight for him on the beaches and in the fields...'*until that wicked man, Herr Hitler, is defeated*' He practised the great war leader's speeches before the shaving mirror in the bathroom.

The procession of disciples reached the church. The big West doors were open ready to receive them. They trooped inside. Ryan sniffed. As usual, the stench of incense set him off. He made heroic efforts to hold back and for a time he succeeded. But it couldn't last. Sneezes like rifle shots ricocheted round the building.

The Head glared at him, then at his classmates unable to stifle their laughter. She led the girls into the very last pew on the left of the central aisle, while Miss Ashby waddled her way into the pew on the right, shoving the reluctant boys before her. Ryan, still sneezing, finally took his place.

An air of nervous expectancy hung over them like barrage balloons. The vestry door squeaked open and Father O'Donnell appeared. The teachers stood. The pupils needed no reminder to follow their lead.

Father O'Donnell shuffled towards them on his stout legs and stopped a few feet away, watching, then smiled. They smiled back. He was going to conduct a delicate operation, he told them. It was to cleanse their souls from sin. "Think of me as God's surgeon," he said. "I hope each one of you has come prepared for major surgery!"

Just wait until I am on the operating table, Ryan thought.

The priest rubbed his hands in pleasurable anticipation. "Well now, in the future, very, very soon, there will be in this holy place, this Church of Holy Innocents', a very important, *significant* occasion, an occasion that you will recall well in the weeks and years ahead. In fact, you will remember it for the rest of your lives. Now, can some clever person tell me why this afternoon has such significance?"

Ryan looked across the aisle. Cynthia Peal stood up. A small, pinched, waxy face scrubbed clean with carbolic, orange freckles shiny like marbles and a small chest puffed out like a garden sparrow's: Miss Clever-Clogs. Who'd ever want to see *that* face on the pillow first thing in the morning? He shuddered. To look holy she had put on a head scarf to cover the stringy hair that was always pulled back like a clump of corn, fixed together with that same red elastic band. Still, better than Greengage: roots like burnt toast. At least you could tell Cyn Peal was proper blonde.

The girl spoke in her high-pitched voice. "We are here, Father O'Donnell, in the Church of the Holy Innocents', to make a good Confession in preparation for the great occasion, which is the Confirmation service this Lord's Day coming, when we shall take that all-important step of commitment before the Bishop, God's chief representative of the Diocese, and know that we will become adult members of the world-wide Holy Catholic Church."

Ryan guessed she had written it all down, then learned it off by heart.

"Excellent." Father O'Donnell licked his lips appreciatively, clasped his podgy hands over the wide expanse of stomach. "Now," he continued, "what I'm going to do is to move over to the Confessional. You will recall from your Sunday attendance its position – those who are disciplined sufficiently to attend the Mass regularly will know – just to the right of the sanctuary steps. Over there in the far aisle." He turned to point behind him.

Ryan elbowed Foureyes, realising his limited attention span.

"That's where I shall be," the priest continued, "waiting expectantly. Now, I'll have the boys up first. Oh, maybe you think that's not right. Isn't it always ladies first? That's the usual order, isn't it?" He chuckled and the children smiled in response.

Father's in a good mood, Ryan thought. Softening us up, making with the funnies so we'll let our guard down and it'll all come out. He glanced along his row. Yeah, and I bet there's none of you who'll be glad to give him this little lot. He reached down to pat his back pocket containing the seven pages of iniquities in painstaking detail written in his very best handwriting.

The voice continued, the forefinger raised. "But, boys and girls, that's the world. That's the order of things there. Ladies first, gentlemen second." Again he chuckled and the children smiled. Now the words rolled off his tongue steadily like surf on a beach. "But, boys and girls, Holy Church is different. Quite, quite different. Oh, yes, with Christ's Church the man who comes first. Men who have the calling, the power, the authority; men who are called to be priests. What for? Why are they given that authority? Well, to administer the sacraments, to lead the services, to visit the sick, to teach the Faith *and* ...to hear Confessions." The voice now rose dramatically with a note of excitement. "Our Blessed Lord always called *men* to be His disciples! But...," and now came another impressive pause, the children growing anxious as he wandered closer.

Ryan smelt the old familiar cassock smell of sweat and mildew, noticing the cigarette ash deposited like dandruff. The priest stopped in front of Foureyes, whose eyes behind his spectacles magnified in fear. "Now, you boys, who knows? There could very well be one among you, maybe the very least likely who will one day be called by God to be a priest. Could it be possible?" Father O'Donnell frowned, hesitated as if unsure whether to continue, shaking his head as if troubled, "For instance, I mean, hard as it is to believe, young Ryan Brannigan here...." The priest's eyes opened wide as if he had only that moment realised an astonishing possibility, his mouth open in shock. "What? Surely not?" The children began to chuckle, enjoying the surprise entertainment. "I mean, as if such an absurd idea ever would occur to the Almighty to call *him?*" Dramatically he pointed a thick forefinger in Ryan's face.

"Not a chance, Father O'Donnell."

The children burst into laughter, delighted yet astonished at the Irish boy's audacity. It's Ryan, he's back to his usual form. Good that he's given up monitoring. The two teachers stared ahead stoically.

Scrutinised by thirty-three pairs of eyes, Ryan knew the blush had begun. The redness creeping like a rising sun from neck to ears, then over the whole of his face.

Father O'Donnell was about to address the girls to his left when he noticed Foureyes. He reached down to hold up the sleeve of a blue jersey, peering at it closely then letting go, as if fearful of contamination. "Looks like gravy stains, cornflakes embedded there, as well as stuff from your snout. You disgusting little pig. I take it that when the Bishop comes, at least you'll be wearing a suit?"

The priest returned to stand midway between boys and girls, the laughter beginning to subside after a loud reprimand from Miss Millison. "So, to conclude then. Even the very least likely of all could be called to the priesthood, though it is doubtful that this revolting creature will ever make anything of himself."

From the film, Ryan recalled kind Doctor Jekyll in his long white coat in his laboratory surrounded by his test tubes. He thought of Churchill's ally, Joe Stalin, smiling away in the Kremlin, hoping the Allies would soon launch an invasion. Then his favourite word whispered in his brain. He glanced at

Foureyes squirming in his seat, blinking back tears, a fresh block of snot bubbling, ready to drip. He jumped to his feet. At his other side, Kenny clung to his sleeve to pull him back. He glared at him, shook him off. "Sure, you've no right to take the Mick out of him, Father. He can't help it. Like only half a brain, thick an' all, but he's a human being for God's sake, aren't you, Rich?"

Foureyes looked up gratefully.

To everyone's surprise the priest completely ignored the interruption, now adopting a quieter, confidential tone. "Ah, I see one or two of you boys shaking your heads, even grinning in your unbelief. Yes, Our Blessed Lord sometimes calls the least likely of men to be His chosen ones. Think of Judas Iscariot. Yes, Our Lord even chose him, the very least likely of all the twelve. Yet, nevertheless, Judas was called to be a disciple. He had a devil, the Holy Scriptures teach. He was so ashamed of what he'd done to our dear Lord, betraying him, that he went and hanged himself. The man was not fit to live."

The priest turned up the volume. "In the name of our Blessed Lord, I ask you, boys and girls, are you ashamed of what you've done? You should be. You've let Christ, Our Blessed Saviour down. You've crucified him afresh. He died for you. It's as if He needn't have bothered, the way you have behaved. So now, boys and girls, this is the great time for you to put things right with your Saviour. Come to Confession and know the sweet forgiveness of Holy Church because... oh, and let this sink in." The deep sombre tone ended. The children leaned forward for he had begun to whisper, his voice like a soft breeze, barely audible. Placing two fingers to his lips, he spoke one word only: "Listen."

There was silence broken only by Foureyes' snuffles. It was a lull before a storm, for suddenly Father O'Donnell shouted and everyone, even the two teachers, jumped as if struck by an explosion. It was a shout of rage and it seemed to be directed at one boy in particular, though it could have been two or possibly three. The priest pointed an accusing finger and yelled at two boys huddled together: Foureyes, clinging on to Ryan's jersey, a stream of mucus mixed with tears running down both his cheeks, and Ryan staring back with undisguised hostility. The priest yelled, "The world is going to hell because of you!"

Foureyes' glasses slipped down his nose as he began to wail. He thinks it's his fault, the poor little devil, Ryan thought. Remembering his favourite word and imagining kind Doctor Jekyll in his white coat, he placed a comforting arm round his companion's shoulders, pulling him close. The girls huddled together, terrified at this ferocious onslaught. But then, relief swept over them all, for as suddenly as it had begun, the voice returned to a friendly, quiet, relaxed tempo. "Now for the practicalities," the priest said. "I'll have the boys up first. You will come up one by one." He pointed at Foureyes, "Shall we begin with you, my filthy young friend?"

Foureyes looked up at Ryan, mouth open, saliva seeping down his chin. Ryan nodded, giving a reassuring smile.

"Yes, you," continued the priest, raising his voice a little. "You with the thick glasses and the smashed lens, and your disgusting apparel. What's your name, lad? Stand up when I'm speaking to you."

Motionless as if in shock, blinking rapidly, Foureyes looked at Ryan, who stood to say, "Richard Johnson, he's called, Father."

"Right. Now, when Richard comes back, the next one comes up and so on. Then I shall hear the girls. The same procedure. Brannigan, you will come up last of all the boys." The priest, his backside rolling, hurried away to disappear inside the Confessional, closing the door behind him. They all waited. The door opened and Father O'Donnell's head appeared, "Come on then!"

It was time for Miss Millison to assert control. "Absolutely not a word to be spoken while you wait. I demand utter silence. Not even a whisper. Watch those boys, Miss Ashby, especially Irish."

"Yes, yes, Miss Millison," murmured her deputy.

Feeling buoyed up by Ryan's protection, Foureyes imitated Father O'Donnell's walk, his backside rolling like a ship in a storm. It was a fair impersonation, good enough for the boys to smile, while a few of the girls tittered, stuffing handkerchiefs in their mouths, pretending suddenly to develop severe coughs.

No one laughed openly aware that they were all under close surveillance.

One by one the boys, white-faced, hurried to take their place in the Confessional. Kenny came back grinning at Ryan. Then it was Peter Steggle's turn. As the two met in the aisle they raised their arms and touched hands like footballers. Kenny thumped Ryan on the arm as he squeezed past. "That's me done. Piece of cake that was, boy."

The performance continued until there were just two of the boys remaining: Philip Matthews and Ryan Brannigan. When Matthews returned, a fervent smile on his dimpled cheeks, Ryan knew that his moment had come. He was shaking with nerves, yet excited. He walked quickly, opened the little door, sat on the bench and began to speak rapidly through the grille.

"Bless me, Father, for I have sinned. Since my last Confession, erm...erm... erm... Christmas, last Christmas it were, Father, I done these wicked things... Father."

He fumbled about in his back pocket and brought out the sheets. He spread them on the floor at his feet. In the enthusiasm of preparation, he had forgotten to number the pages. He picked them up, shuffling them like a pack of cards hoping to find the original order. Father O'Donnell breathed through the grill. "Get on with it, boy."

"First, Father, I play with myself, you know. Three, maybe four times a day. Sometimes half a dozen times in the night. See, I'm like a bad apple, I am, Father, rotten to the core, Father. I look good on the outside, like rosy and shiny, but I've got badness inside. You take a bite from me and there's all bruises, all the way through. Rotten to the core, I am, Father."

The response was disappointing. Father O'Donnell merely sounded irritable. Through the grill a deep sigh and then, "Don't be ridiculous."

"Can't help it, Father. See, I don't know what Evett said, but I bet he never told you he does dirty things with Pat Dickerson. And if she don't tell you, like she's holding it back, then she'll be lying. And so you see, Father, I find myself thinking about it. It's the temptation, sir."

"Don't try passing the buck."

"Pardon? What's them, Father?"

"Blaming others for your own filthy behaviour. You know perfectly well. Thinking of girls. Lust."

"I get that. Honest, Father, I don't think I'm a very good Catholic, Father. Me dad says it's natural. Kind of developing into a man, doing private stuff. Like I was in the bath and he looked in and... erm... saw my... erm... my w... willie and he says that he sees it's growing al-right, and he says that's good like, he says."

"You disgust me, Brannigan. Say the words on the card, and if you think this is something of a joke, I shall not give you Absolution."

"No joke, Father, being so bad. I haven't finished yet, Father. Fact is, I've only just got started, I have."

Ryan struggled to hold the sheets, his hands shaking. One page, then another dropped to the floor. They were all out of order. He tried to recite from memory. This was much harder than he'd expected. But soon he would be out of the place with its stink of incense and the plaster saints like little solders scattered everywhere, and the Holy Water for Baptism kept in the empty whisky bottle, re-labelled 'Jordan' to impress the young mums when they came for the Christenings, when everyone knew Mrs Henderson filled it from the tap in the vestry.

He still had five pages of sins left. He reshuffled them, hoping he'd not drop them again. "I done a lot of bad things, Father," he said, glancing down at his writing. "I looked up Pat Dickerson's dress when I was fetching the ball, the football, that is, in the playground. The way it was, Kenny kicked it to me and I was trying to save it and missed, so I had to get down and lie on the ground. I've watched Julie Richards in the girls' lav, I mean, lavatories. You're right, Father, sir, I am the most disgusting of everyone, that's for sure. The word I'd use is dep...p...p...praved, sir."

Ryan was sure the priest shuddered. He took the next sheet. In his haste the rest again fluttered to the floor. "I watched erm... I...s...s...s...saw her, that is Dickerson touch up Kenny, sir. Break-time, behind the big oak tree in the playground. At the far end, it is. Later that same day, it was, I asked her if she'd do it to me. I was sorry she said no. I touch myself all the time, except Sunday, the holy day of the week, for the Lord's sake."

There was a snort from behind the grille. "Oh, shut up, Brannigan! You are utterly appalling. I do not wish to hear any more of your filthy escapades. You show not one ounce of contrition. Now," said the priest ponderously, "as an appropriate penance you will say twenty Hail Marys, read Psalm fifty one, a meditation on the Lord's suffering, then for half an hour consider the terrible power of the flesh over the spirit. Continue with this every night before you go to bed. Reflect upon the purity of the Holy Virgin, then perhaps you might learn something of your own disgusting self. Yes, you've chosen exactly the right word: depravity. At present I've no desire to grant you Absolution. None at all."

"Father, I have made a very, very thorough preparation, like you said we was to. Please let me go on…. Me and Kenny like to get into the pictures and see dirty films, even the x-rated ones, if we can. It means climbing through the window of the Ladies' Toilet. And we always hope to meet up with Polly Townsend, though you have to pay her a shilling. There's a lot more to tell you, Father. Loads and loads. I buy nudie magazines. Naked women on the cover. I know where you can go in town to a dirty bookshop. You can get like disgusting books—"

"Yes, yes, yes. You are a filthy, disgraceful little animal. What else? Get it over with."

Ryan paused in his itinerary. He spoke slowly and quietly. "Well, I hate Nadina Brown, Father. I can't help it."

"Is that right?"

"Yes, Father. I feel kinda sorry for her, but she gets on me tits, sorry, nerves, always following me about."

"Ah, now you see what it is to harbour hatred and anger. Not to forgive. That's very wrong. We all sin, all of us are in the wrong. It's about falling short. And if we don't forgive at once it all gets much worse. Think of our Lord's example on the cross. He immediately forgave the two thieves. And don't forget Peter. He denied he ever knew Our Lord. Now Judas, he did a lot worse. Peter denied our Lord but Judas could have had forgiveness, but he refused. You see, his heart was hardened. He went out and hanged himself.

"Now, what your confession shows me, and I can hardly call it a confession as you seem so pleased with your dreadful behaviour, reeling out that horrible list of filth, is that you are a foul-mouthed, crude, disgusting, dirty-minded little horror. You are, in short, a worthless scrap of humanity. Make sure you wear a suit for your Confirmation, and do something about that undisciplined mop of hair. It looks like a fine crop of wheat disturbed by a storm. I doubt it's seen a comb all year. Now, sin no more. Say the words on the card for me to grant Absolution."

Ryan began, then abruptly stopped. He pressed his mouth to the grille. Aware that this was his last chance, he said, "I do beg your pardon, Father O'Donnell, but as I say I'm too bad to be confirmed and I said at the Catechism I don't believe in nothing – I mean I can't believe in it, the Father, the Son and the Spirit, and that. See, Father, it's for my dad, to please him. Father, I am unworthy to be confirmed. Honest to God, I am terrible bad, sir."

Father O'Donnell slammed his hands against the grille and hissed, "Get out of my sight!"

Ryan, scooping up his papers, scuttled red-faced out of the box.

When it was over and they were on their way home, Foureyes, in the middle clasping each of the other two round their waists and thrusting forward as a rugby scrum, said, "Hey, that Father has a real dirty mind. Know what he asks me? He says: "How many times a week do you play with yourself?"

"Bet you have a job to find it," said Kenny.

Foureyes looked puzzled for a moment, then exclaimed, "My thingy's getting bigger all the time. Honest, it is! But, that's private, ain't it, Rye? He shouldn't ask. It's like going to the lav. He don't go asking me how many times I shite in a week." He looked from one to the other. Both laughed.

Not to be upstaged, Ryan said, "I proper shocked him. Me, I tell him the lot. Pages of it, I tell him. All the dirty goings-on. He was begging me to stop. He says, "Ryan I can't take any more. Please, stop." I give him nightmares, I have. He'll be worn out."

Kenny rolled with laughter. "You damned liar."

Foureyes blinked behind the big glasses, crevices along his forehead, trying to understand.

Ryan was silent. For his plan had failed. He would have to go through with it. Still, once at Southgate though, that would be it.

As if reading his thoughts, Kenny asked, "Think you'll get to Grammar then?" Ryan knew that his friend was equally worried. Just careful not to show it.

"Sure, I will," he answered.

Chapter Twenty Four

She wanted to be the very last so she had swapped with Cyn Peal.

The dim light of early evening revealed the erect figure, shoulders squared, small rapid steps, click-clacking up the aisle, staring the world in the face; unafraid, positive, everything she was not. Nadina imagined her happy confident smile and his smile back. *She'd* get to the Convent alright. He'd give her a strong recommendation. In any case, older sister Margaret was already there and that would tell in her favour.

One day she'd been waiting outside Millie's office. She remembered the conversation between the Head and her deputy. "Well, the main difference between them to my mind, Thelma, is not brains at all. It's posture. You can always tell a lot from posture. Cynthia holds her head high, whereas Nadina! Oh dear, slouching, head bowed, round shouldered, and so unsure of herself!"

"Yes, Headmistress," Miss Ashby had replied, "but as far as spiritual perception and depth is concerned, I feel sure that Nadina is very much more advanced."

For a time, Thelma's words had uplifted her. They were true. She had always known she was ten times more spiritual that little Miss Bossy Boots – that is, until now.

She'd chosen to be last. The last and the very least; the worst penitent in the whole long history of the church to have ever made a confession. A holy place. Holy Innocents', a lovely name degraded, tarnished like the nasty looking stain on the wall by the big west door.

Ahead, in the Confessional, the murmuring of voices. She sighed and looked about her. The lofty ceiling where the angles listened to your whispered prayers, echoing among the rafters. Nothing could ever be hidden from the Holy Virgin, Our Lord and His Holy Angels. An overwhelming sense of despair crushed her, stifling any glimmer of hope. The churning of her stomach never left.. For a time it seemed to subside. But today, worse than ever. Surely the sign of the Lord's deep displeasure.

She was determined it would not – could not, happen. Not after the desecration of a holy place. Surely he'd heard? She'd never given him the severest warning. And she was being fair, she told him. Wanted to give him a last chance. Told him that if he stopped, no one need ever know.

Now, crouched low in the pew, face hidden behind her hands, she looked up. Cynthia Peal would soon be through. Today, this final preparation, she was going to make a special request. She felt her heart miss several beats when she thought of it. He would probably be scandalised by her effrontery, but she believed it could help them both; a cleansing from the pollution of their souls. So afterwards they might begin again as friends in the way he had promised, the way she wanted and dared to believe that it was what he really wanted as well. She'd need all her courage to ask. But after making her confession she would request that they might kneel side by side and that she would listen to him confess.

That last time, she'd screamed and fought him and when it was over, he had gone to the little place carved out of the wall, taken out a little vial of oil and prayed in silence over it. Standing over her he'd whispered, "My sweet little Nadina, I'm so sorry for both of us."

The coolness from the oil on her forehead had soothed and comforted. His words must mean he knew it wasn't only her; that he was sinful too. Despite everything, she felt that they could be close. Not like she and Pat, who fell out so often, but deep down, permanently: friends in the service of the Lord. And what difference does age make when you are friends? What is friendship anyway, but the sharing of problems, ideas and thoughts, like she and Pat in the privacy of her bedroom.

She tried to remember the good times when he'd been so kind to her, listening to her so patiently. There was the time he'd asked her to call him Seamus. But she couldn't. No, she wouldn't do that. That time when he told her he'd take her to Ireland for a holiday. But she'd said no, that wouldn't be right. The others would all be so jealous and be extra horrible to her and besides, she didn't want him to get into trouble because of her. People would get to know about it. That big lout Evett would find out and he would go and tell Pat and it would be all round school and everywhere, even in the town itself. And Father would be in trouble.

Gossip was a horrible thing. People didn't realise it was a sin. Even good Catholics, regular at Mass. A sin that most people never thought of as sin at all.

Could there really be a new beginning? She thought of another scenario. Once she'd started at the Convent School of the Holy Name, she'd be able to drop in to the presbytery on her way home – it wouldn't be far off her route – and she could tell him her troubles and he could tell her his. His loneliness, the many tasks he had, the way he had explained to her how people didn't understand him, his lonely life, the life of a priest, its burdens, responsibilities. Or Saturdays, his rest day, that would be fine if he was too busy during the week.

And Thelma Ashby. Thelma would also be a friend. The little teacher had smiled her lovely smile and nodded when she'd hinted that she'd like to call in on her from time to time in the future, when she was at her new school.

The indistinct murmur of Cynthia's voice trailed on. Nadina sighed. Her head was thumping. Throughout her entire life no one had given her such attention as Father O'Donnell, nor shown her such kindness. She ran her fingers down the mark. No one else had kissed the mark. Ryan? Yes, Ryan, but what a fuss he'd made about it. Lasting all of seven seconds, and then licking it! And that hideous Foureyes!. Two years ago, but still squirming at the memory of that slobbering mouth, grinning up at her, his nostrils full of snot. Ugh! She'd had to pay him. She had scrubbed and scrubbed with a nail brush for days after. A horrible thing, hardly human at all. A little pig, just like Father said.

Her mother never kissed it. Never spoke about it. Ashamed of it, ashamed of her. Daphne, well Daphne, so different with her rosy apple cheeks and her big-mouthed smile. The big legs that she had to keep shaving, but that was nothing to the mark. Mother had given birth to a branded child.

She had listened eagerly when Father told her that the skills of skin grafting were improving. It had begun after the Great

War, he told her, but it still had a long way to go. She'd seen pictures in the newspapers of airmen who'd parachuted from burning aeroplanes, all bandaged up, lying in the hospital. Then the photographs with the bandages taken off. But it didn't look right. The new skin had come up all shiny and different from the rest of the face, as if it had been stuck on. That, of course, is what they did. Took bits of other parts of the body and stitched them on. The new skin didn't blend with the old.

But, yes! Maybe one day! One day that horrible blotch could be removed and the new skin would be exactly the same as her other cheek: pure and clean. Clean! That was it, her face was not only ugly, it was dirty. The mark was a sign of her impurity. To tempt a priest into sin! The thumping of her heart began anew with a fresh flow of tears. Nothing could ever be worse, not even murder. In the stillness, she blurted out aloud, "Oh, help me, Holy Virgin!"

She looked away from the plaster Madonna by the altar and gazed at the central figure. Hands nailed into the wood, splashes of blood-red, arms outstretched, a joyous welcome to all sinners. She understood the teaching that claimed that suffering was an honour, a privilege, where sufferers would be able to identify with their Lord on the cross. But that was undeserved suffering. Her suffering she had brought upon herself. A mortal sin that meant eternal damnation. No wonder when she pleaded with the Virgin for forgiveness over and over and over, there was no peace for her soul. Why should there be? Oh, to know that sweetness of the presence of her Lord that would lift her out of her despair, and make even the blemish bearable.

Suddenly, the sharp sound of footsteps on the stone floor. Hurriedly Nadina dried her tears. How great to be Cynthia. So slim. Such a neat-looking body. Even the freckles were nice, though Cyn didn't like them. Not heavy breasts like hers; no thickening waist line. 'Comfort eating', that's what her mother called her own binging in the middle of the night. She would end up just like her: huge hips, breasts like balloons and the biggest backside ever. She was more than halfway there already.

Cynthia gave her a fleeting smile, picked up her gas mask and her little check-squared jacket in red and green where it lay next to Nadina in the pew.

"That's a lovely coat, Cynthia. Pretty colours. What sort of a mood is Father in, Cyn?"

Cynthia shrugged her shoulders. Nadina guessed it was a stupid question that hardly deserved an answer. She helped the girl on with her coat.

"Same as always. He's a priest. Priests don't have moods." Walking away, Cynthia glanced over her shoulder, added, "Unlike you." The big West Door clanged behind her.

Nadina knelt again. She looked up. On the cross He was looking directly at her, into her very soul. The look He gave Judas at the last Supper; Judas, the betrayer. Father had that wonderful gift of making the Bible characters come to life, just as if they'd stepped out of the pages written all those years ago. Judas hanged himself. Unable to live with himself. Judas went straight to hell.

Palms held upward in supplication she prayed again, "Please, please, O Holy Virgin. O Dearest Mother, may I know Thy Forgiveness. May Thou, O Holy Virgin, pardon my terrible sins and may Father make a full confession alongside me, so that we can put it all behind us and begin in a new way as friends."

A different sound, heavier this time. Arms round her shoulders, squeezing. She looked up. "Now then, my dear little Naddy. Crying again? Why? This is an exciting time, is it not? Preparing for your Confirmation, your time for adult membership of Christ's Holy Church. Surely, this is something you've longed for, is it not?"

He reached in his cassock pocket and brought out a handkerchief. Heaving himself down, catching his breath, he held it out to her.

"You should lose weight," she said. "Me too; I know I should."

He chuckled. The phlegm in his lungs caused him to cough.

"You should stop smoking too." She was going to add another rebuke, smelling the whisky. Stop, she told herself. You're mocking him, the way he mocks you. "I'm sorry," she said.

"No, you're absolutely right, darling. I know. Vile habits. But, come on, let's wipe those lovely eyes. Little girls shouldn't be crying, should they?"

She was about to take the handkerchief from him when he said, "No, let me." He leaned towards her, the tobacco-stained teeth grinning. Gently, he wiped her eyes. "First the left...and now the right. Now, what about a good blow to finish off with, eh? Then you will make your confession."

She nodded, blew her nose, her bottom lip trembling. "I wish to make my confession now, Father."

"Of course, of course. Then you and I, my little darling, are in for a big surprise. Can you guess? Mrs Henderson, at my request, has made another of your favourites – fruit cake! It's simply crowded with dates and currants and sultanas, Nadina. Come all the way from Ireland." His hand swept the veil of hair back. He pressed his cheek against hers. She shivered. His voice dropped to a whisper. "And shall we see if she's left some trifle to tempt us even further? You'd like that too, wouldn't you? And you can bet there'll be sherry in it." The hair dropped back into place. He chortled, rubbing his hands in anticipation.

She stared ahead. "No! Father." She clasped her hands together in her lap. Softer this time, she added, "I've got to get home. Mother wants to take me shopping."

He glanced at his watch. "What, at five o'clock?"

There was silence.

"Ah, these bogus shopping trips. Come on now, nothing to be frightened of. No one's going to hurt you. So, let me hear your confession. I'm hungry." The red face beamed at her; the blue veins winding like river tributaries through his bulbous nose. He was ugly, repulsive. She shuddered. She would go home.

'Tell him, now. Tell him you will not go back with him to the presbytery.'

His head lolled back. He sighed, then chuckled again. "By all the saints, you'd never imagine how tiring it is hearing confessions. And, very, very boring," he added, his big head wobbling, shoulders shaking as he turned towards her again. "You wouldn't believe it, Nadina, dear. The same old sins, week after week, month after month, year after year." He sighed again. His hand moved to her knee, squeezing.

"Stop it!" She seized it with both hands, thrusting it away. "What did Ryan say in his?"

"Oh, my dear child, how could I possibly tell you? It's the seal of the Confessional. I've taught you that, surely you remember?" He began to chuckle, his belly jiggling under the belt of his cassock. "All I *can* tell you is that I've heard some dirty stories in my time, but by all the saints, I reckon your little pal Ryan takes the biscuit."

He was in his silly mood. She'd seen him in his blackest, most terrible moods, times he'd cursed her. And she'd seen him in his best moods: kind, friendly, understanding, listening to all her problems. She'd experienced his preaching mood: direct, business-like, strict, like Miss Millison. But now? This silly, giggly mood. He was always like that before it happened.

She stood up, folded her arms tight to her chest. "Can I ask you something please, Father?"

"Of course, my sweet. Anything you like."

"Will Mrs Henderson be there?"

"Oh, I do hope so. Of course she does have a habit of popping out to the shops, taking a look in on Jack I guess at the same time. Poor Mrs H. But if she does go it won't be for long." There was a silence, then, softly, "You'll be quite safe."

"I believe you want... want to stop." She forced herself to look him in the eye. He met her gaze before looking at the floor.

"I want to make my confession, Father. Then I want..." she bit her lip, took a deep breath. "Father O'Donnell, I want us to begin afresh. Put everything behind us. I'd like you and I to kneel together and... for both of us to confess, because this time it has got to be over, over for good, over for ever. Then I shall be going home. Please thank Mrs Henderson."

He looked up, smiled. "Al-right, have it your way. First things first then. Your confession. I'll get myself prepared for my favourite sinner." He heaved himself out of the pew and stood, breathing heavily, looking down at her with that same mocking smile; paused for a second as if undecided, then took her by surprise. Nadina moved her head away, but not quickly enough. His lips were sticky, wet. He had been drinking again.

He opened the door to the Confessional Box for her, and there she poured it all out. Her fear of being eternally lost. The threat of punishment from God, from the Church, but most of all from the Blessed Virgin and the Lord Jesus for what she had done. Then she blurted out, "I can't stand him, Father."

"Who, child?"

"My father. I know it's wrong and you were right to tell me it's wrong, but I can't talk to him like I talk to you. He never jokes, or if he does, his jokes are so stupid that no one laughs at them, not even Daphne. And only the other day he told me that I would never get to the Convent School of the Holy Name. Please, I must *go there!*"

She stood up, pressed her lips to the grille. In the dim light, there was silence apart from steady breathing and an occasional clearing of his throat. "He told me that I'm going to the Grammar School. He's always telling me. But I'm not, am I? Am I, Father O'Donnell? Please, tell me. Please. I need to know! I need your recommendation."

The silence continued. She sat down breathless, trembling. Love thy father and thy mother the Lord said, but her father was like a stranger. Always had been. They'd always favoured Daphne over her. She covered her face with her hands. "You must listen, Father. You cannot forget the horror of it all. Together. You and me."

Taking a deep breath, Nadina began to speak slowly, quietly. "Since my last Confession..." she broke off, cleared her throat several times, tried again. "Since my last Confession a month ago..." she turned her head towards the grille. "Father, I can't go on! I can't go on!" Her chest was hurting.

She clutched at it, heaving, struggling to breathe. "Oh, God have mercy! Please, I want to be clean. I want to be pure. I've lost my virginity. I... I... don't want... you know... I don't want...." Pausing after each word, her voice dropped to a whisper. Now speaking slowly, so deliberately that he would be absolutely certain to hear, she repeated, "I do not want... I do not want... I do not want..." And then, without any trace of hesitancy, she shouted, "I don't want to have sexual intercourse with you anymore!." Her sobs echoed down the church. Then, because an explanation might be needed, or if she had hurt his feelings, or if she had not made herself completely understood, she continued speaking, her voice gathering speed until the words were tripping over each other, like a runaway train unable to stop. "It's not that I don't want us to be friends, like the way it's been: you telling me of Ireland and your childhood in Dublin and well, you know, all of it. Then I feel you really like me as... well, your friend. You're important. People look up to you. I'm nothing. I am nobody's friend. I want us to go on being friends, Father, so when I get to the Convent School of the Holy Name, I can come and see you, can't I? I know you are lonely. Like me. But not the sex thing. Not that. I hate it. It hurts me." She was sobbing so much she could scarcely breathe.

There was still no response from the other side of the grille.

"Please, Father. You're a priest. You have the power. Please, I need... what I need is Our Dear Lord's love and favour. I need forgiveness. And for pity's sake, I need you to stop it. You did stop... for a bit." Her voice dropped, earnestly she pleaded, "Will we be able to pray together? Confess? Together. Kneel side by side? Like friends, you know? Can we, Father, please? Oh please, I beg you! Then I shall know we've finished with it, once and for all time."

There was the sound of creaking as he shifted in his seat. Father O' Donnell declared the solemn words of Absolution. Her penance was to say the Lord's Prayer slowly and meditate on the words, 'Forgive us our sins as we forgive those who sin against us." Then a psalm of joy, psalm one hundred: *'Oh, be joyful in the Lord.'* His voice hesitant, even nervous, he recited the psalm throughout. *'O go your way into His gates with thanksgiving. Into His courts with praise.'* "Yes, you need to be more joyful, Nadina. Think of the joy of Our Saviour."

She was to meditate upon the words of the fifty-first psalm, a passage where the writer, the great King David, thinks with sorrow about his sin.

As she opened her door of the Confessional box, he side-stepped her. He stared at the floor. "My dear Nadina, as I have said before, I do regret what has happened between us." Then the tone of his voice brightened. "Come into the vestry, will you? When you're ready, dear."

"No, that's not enough!" Dropping her voice, sensing his disapproval, but determined to continue, "Father, I want us to kneel together, side by side asking forgiveness from the Lord together. So we can make a new start."

But he walked away from her.

Back in her pew, thinking carefully through the message of the two psalms, she asked for the grace to be able to love her parents and Daphne. Now leaving her place, she tiptoed towards the statue of the Virgin and knelt there for a full five minutes. Wasn't it too much to expect him, a priest, to kneel next to her? He'd regretted it, that's what he said. Shouldn't she be satisfied with that? But he'd said that before, in the church when he anointed her, after...But this time, he seemed genuinely remorseful, his head bowed low. Were there even tears in his eyes? She had to believe him. And what choice did she really have? Time was passing, the new school year would soon be here, the recommendation should be sent to Mother Clare. The school year she believed started earlier at the Convent.

Rising from her knees, Nadina made her way to the vestry and opened the door. He was standing by the window looking out into the churchyard, smoking. She sat in a chair opposite, stretched out her arms and yawned. "I wish I could be a priest."

He turned to look at her, and smiled. "Ah well, you know, Our Lord only calls men. And you are so obviously a girl, and a very pretty girl." That silly voice again. She was angry. And she didn't bother to hide it.

"I'm not pretty. Only you say that and it's a lie."

"I say it because it *is* true, Nadina."

"Are we going to have tea then? Because I need to go very, very soon."

"My little Naddy is getting a little impatient. Go and sit quietly in the church again, will you? I must go and set up for tomorrow's early Mass, then I'll be ready. Give me five to ten minutes, then make your way to the presbytery."

Nadina returned to her pew to renew her praying. "O holy Virgin, may he give it me," she prayed. "Give it me this very evening." In the stillness she waited, head bowed. Ten minutes later she left the church and walked round to the presbytery. It was still light, early evening. Before the blackout she would go with the letter.

He was there to open the front door to her. He had already changed out of his cassock and was now in an open-necked shirt and the corduroys he wore for gardening.

"I mustn't stay long, Father. Can I ring my parents? I always like to keep on the right side of them, and thanks to you, I'm determined to be different towards them from now on. You've reminded me of Our Lord's demand that we should be dutiful to parents and I've been praying so hard about them. So can I tell them I've been delayed?"

"Of course, Nadina, dear. Best if I do it though, eh?"

Nadina walked ahead down the long corridor and stopped outside the study door. She always felt safer in this room where he worked. And the study was closer to the basement where Mrs Henderson had her domain. He followed behind, then stretched his arm in front of her to open the door. She turned round to face him. "Father, thank you for hearing my Confession. You haven't forgotten your letter of recommendation, have you?" She said it with a smile in case he thought she was above herself. It is what he must have thought when she suggested they kneel side by side to confess together. She shouldn't have suggested it.

Ignoring her he strode over to the desk to phone.

Taking care to avoid the settee, Nadina sat in the armchair by the hearth. She picked up the '*Irish Times*' from a little coffee table. Over the top of the newspaper she watched him light another cigarette while he waited for the exchange to connect him, his head wreathed in blue smoke. Then he was speaking to her father. "Yes, the confessions always take a long time. Wonderful to have such a keen and attentive pupil." He glanced in her direction and smiled. "I'm just going to give her a cuppa and a bite to eat. I'll run her home in the Rover, Arnold. She won't be long. Goodbye." He put the receiver back on its hook and giggled. "Now then, my little Naddy, let me make the nice big pot of tea and yummy, oh yummy, the fruit cake. Oh, Nadina, how delicious!"

"Before you go for the tea, I've got a request to make."

"A request?"

His eyebrows raised, his rheumy eyes twinkled. She thought he had probably been very good looking when he was a young priest. She cleared her throat. It was time to trot it all out again. She wanted him to understand the urgency.

"You know my parents don't want me to go to the Convent School of the Holy Name. It'll be your word against theirs. Southgate is the very *last* school on God's earth I wish to attend. But I know that when you give me your recommendation, so I can take it with me for interview or probably take it to Mother Clare first, they'll never be able to stop me." She raised her voice, "All the applications will be in by now and I'll be too late. It's really worrying me, Father."

He opened his mouth to say something, but she shook her head, held up a hand to stop him. "I know it depends as well on my getting good results in the Scholarship, but I feel sure that will be fine." Her voice gained strength. She thought of Cyn Peal, how *she* would speak. "I want it now, this evening, not tomorrow, not next week, but *now*. You see, Father, I need to be absolutely sure of a place. So, can you swing it for me, please?"

Father O'Donnell raised an eyebrow, "*Swing* it for you? That's a funny expression, Nadina. Now, I am off to get our little feast. Oh, lovely."

She didn't like his tone. He was prevaricating. (a new word for Ryan) And once more that mocking, silly voice. She felt the panic rising in her chest. She mustn't stay. Have her tea, then go. She would be strong. If he didn't write it out now, she would remind him in the morning - and go on reminding him every single day, again and again, until she got it. She would warn him again. Tell him, she'd get hold of the Bishop's address or she'd go to the police. Make it even more definite this time.

He returned humming a hymn tune, placed the tray with the fruit cake, plates, cups and saucers, milk and tea pot on the desk "Gosh, Naddy!" he exclaimed. "This is absolutely perfect, isn't it?"

They sat together at his desk. In between mouthfuls, he talked again about the past. This time it was his love of rugby. He'd played for Dublin, he said. Then for the university. He went on to tell her funny things that had happened in the parishes in Ireland where he'd been. She laughed, spilling crumbs down her dress. Genuinely interested, she asked him about the training he undertook for the priesthood. Gulping down his tea, he was like a little boy, excited, telling her about the life at the seminary.

"We were all together, Nadina, you see, all together, seeking the Lord's blessing. Future priests, you see. It was a great fellowship, erm... camaraderie. A wonderful experience, Nadina. Truly wonderful." He stared down at his plate, fingering the crumbs.

And again she told him of her loneliness. Told him how the other girls laughed at her. "Even Pat, who was my very special friend, she laughed at me. Said I was too religious. And you never did say that, did you? My parents said you did, but I don't believe them. Am I right, Father? I am, aren't I?"

Silently, he poured out two more cups of tea. "Those others in your class. Now, I'm sure they actually feel quite inferior to you, so they put on airs to try and make themselves believe they are your equal or even superior, but I can assure you they are not. You are cleverer by far. And there's a maturity about you—

"Maturity? Matronly, you mean!" She laughed.

"You have a lovely expression, Nadina: calm, peaceful, virginal."

"*Virginal?*" She laughed again, but there was no disguising the bitterness. She jumped up from the desk, pushing the remains of Mrs Henderson's cake away from her. It was time to get the recommendation. "I'm not a virgin anymore though, am I? You know that, don't you, *Father!*"

She watched him sip his tea. Then, looking up at her, a half-smile hovering as he moved quickly to the door, he said, "Sit down, little one."

"No, no! I'm going home. I'll walk. Or I'll get the bus."

His voice was calm, but there was no mistaking his tone. It was his pulpit voice, the voice that bade no dissent. "I said, sit down!" Frightened, she did as she was told. Moved over to the fireplace, sat in the armchair.

"Be with you in a few minutes." He went out of the room. She heard the creak of the stairs. Where was he going?

Losing all patience, she ran for the front door. On the way, stopping at the bottom of the staircase, she looked up and yelled, "Father O' Donnell, I need that recommendation. Are you going to give it me? Look, I can call back tomorrow for it, if it's not convenient now." She waited. One minute passed then two. The only sound was the creaking of his footsteps overhead. "Right, I'm going, Father. I'll call back tomorrow."

Still hesitating, she'd reached up for the latch and was opening it when two hands grabbed her shoulders and spun her round. He was naked, his dressing gown wide open.

With a shout of rage she pushed him back with all her strength, but it was not enough. He tottered, recovered his balance then dragged her into the lounge. While he was closing the door, she slipped from his grasp. He was panting, holding out his arms to her, laughing as if it was a big game. She stood shaking with fear behind the armchair. She dodged under his arms out into the hall, ran for the front door. Again she reached up for the latch, and again he dragged her back. One hand was over her mouth, the other pulling at her clothes. She bit his hand, heard him yell. Then kicked back with her heels as hard as she could against his shins and had the satisfaction of hearing him cry out. Now she ran to the door again, opened it and in sheer terror jumped the three steps to the pavement, an abnormal feat of athleticism for someone so overweight. Sprawled on the paving stones, she picked herself up and ran, not daring to stop.

Twenty minutes later she'd reached the Lairs, a large area of grass, bushes, and woodland; a short cut to Mercia Close. She ran, keeping to the winding, sandy path. A scratch from a thorn bush caused her ankle to bleed, but she hurried on, her nose running, adding to the wetness on her cheeks. She was straining for breath, her chest heaving. Finally, unable to run any more, she dropped to the ground.

Then she laughed. His nakedness had stripped him of all his pretence; all his dignity. Launching his white pimply body at her, that huge ballooning stomach, the little sacks hanging between his legs, his enormous thingy rising out of the grey tangles of his hair. Bile rose into her throat. She shuddered; remembered Ryan's words: "Sure he's just a fella, Naddy. Just them special clothes is all." She had seen more of the priest in those few moments than she'd seen of her own father in her whole life. Once more she laughed, her face pressed into the dirt. Mixed with mucus, hot tears came again with full force, scalding her cheeks. All that talk about himself, his loneliness. He was ridiculous. He was a disgrace, a hypocrite. Stupid to be lonely, anyway. If she ever became a nun, she'd never be lonely. Be far too busy. Too busy teaching people about the true and living God! The God of purity, the Holy Virgin, Christ's Holy Mother. He knew nothing. Impostor, that was the word.

Nadina buried her head in her hands and wept and wept until there were no more tears to shed. Suddenly, her stomach churned. Most of the rich cake and some of her lunch that day was evacuated onto the hard ground. It was some time before she was ready to move

Eventually, she picked herself up and walked on, stumbling through the jungle of bracken and trees until she reached Gregory Avenue. Arriving at last at Mercia Close, she tore up her drive, dashed through the front door, up the stairs and into the sanctuary of her bedroom.

Chapter Twenty Five

Pounding the floor behind the locked door, Nadina tried to ignore the edgy voice of her mother clad in her gaudy pinafore on the landing attacking the enemy with as much rigour and fortitude as her husband exposed black-out defaulters. "Dust, dust, dust! Get out," she exclaimed.

"Are you up yet, Nadina? she called. "Goodness, how many children do you suppose have tea with their parish priest? Offering to run you home, putting himself out. I do think you should have accepted graciously instead of rushing in, all out of breath and stumbling up the stairs, slamming your door, and as usual without a word of explanation or greeting. Shutting your family out, again. That's what you do, all the time, Nadina. Daddy says I'm spoiling you. I should not continue to bring you a cup of tea and biscuit in the morning. I hope you thanked Father. I certainly never had the attention from a priest like Father O'Donnell when I was your young age. I can assure you no priest ever took much notice of me. Oh, dear me, no."

A sudden bang on the door. A fist. Startled, Nadina, now seated at her dressing table in her dressing gown, dropped her hairbrush.

"Nadina? If you're not dressed, you are to get dressed now. We're going into town to shop. Especially to buy your confirmation dress, so we'll need your measurements. You are to have some breakfast before we leave."

"Can't. He wants to see me."

"Again? What on earth for? Nadina, you must come with us. Otherwise you'll have to have Daphne's."

"Alright, I'll wear Daphne's."

"What?"

"I said I'll wear Daphne's." Nadina picked up her hairbrush. She heard her mother's footsteps retreating. She had reached a hundred strokes when the door handle rattled.

"What do you want now, Mother?"

"Well, I've come to thank you, Nadina. Your father is over the moon. That *is* good news, he says. I'll just have to shorten the hem and gather the waist in, that's all. Certainly save a great deal of money, Nadina, in these hard times. Well done, dear."

She heard the astonishment in her mother's voice, the unsteady, heavy footsteps down the stairs, the word 'incredible' repeated over and over.

Sitting before the mirror revealed the rawness of the blemish like an undressed wound. Today more hideous than ever. "Ugly, ugly, ugly," she breathed, and then hurled the hair brush at the wall.

She would force herself. One last chance, she'd give him. His very last. Yes, but suppose he wouldn't? She was closer now than ever before, closer to spilling the beans, showing them just how *wonderful* their 'wonderful' Father O'Donnell was, but she knew they would never believe her. So who, then? Thelma? Thelma had said more than once, many times, "If there is anything, *anything*, Nadina." And Thelma would believe her, she was sure.

She retrieved the hair brush, continued the rhythmic brushing until her arm ached. Two hundred times; the thick wave cascading down like a waterfall. She wanted to look her best, to hide the ugly, freakish thing. She turned the wireless on: ITMA - Tommy Handley and *It's that man again.*' A repeat. Normally it made her laugh. Not today. Nothing could distract the hammering in her head, the trembling of her legs. She sat on the bed, gripping both her knees. She had her excuse she needed: the reading to practise. For the most promising candidate would read from the Scriptures, and after the service, be introduced to His Lordship, Bishop Dennis, photographed with him for the local newspaper, that was always the way.

"So, I imagine that will be you, won't it, Nadina?" Thelma had said with her smudged lipstick smile. "Cyn Peal," the voice had replied inside her head.

Remembering, she stared back at her reflection. In her fury, she spoke quietly, "And if you, you disgusting so-called priest, don't give it me, I will go straight to the police station, you see if I don't, and Thelma will go with me, and everyone will know just how ugly *you are*." With slow, steady strokes she continued to brush the glossy curtain of hair, pausing to admire its shine.

At breakfast she gobbled her cornflakes, deflecting questions with rapid movements of her head, like a spectator at Wimbledon.

"Nadina, I want a straight answer from you. Are you intending to try and get Father O'Donnell to change his mind? Nadina? Daphne will look after you, help you settle in. It's a perfectly good school. Daphne? You will, won't you?"

Daphne nodded, flicking over the pages of '*Picture Goer*.'

"Your sister will show you the ropes, Nadina."

Another nod; and this time a wrinkling of the nose and a tip of a tongue protruding.

"Oh, why do you have to be so difficult about everything? We, your father and I, indeed Daphne as well, care about you, don't you, Daphne? All three us, our little family only want your welfare, Nadina." Her mother took a deep breath. "And so does Father O'Donnell. I've spoken to him again."

Nadina, heart pounding, dropped her spoon. "When?"

"Last night. You came back in one of your raging moods. So, I wanted to be absolutely sure that Father is clear about... well about our wishes. It's for your sake, Nadina!. If he too thinks Southgate would be better for you under the circumstances, then so be it. Father is very experienced in these matters. Will you stop jerking your head like that, please?"

Gathering the empty cereal dishes, Louise turned her attention to the meagre ration of bacon sizzling on the cooker, missing Nadina's scowl. The strident voice wittered on: "We're so glad you'll have Daphne's. That is very generous of you. We're grateful to you for that, aren't we, Arnold? Very considerate of you. Yes, very. Do you know how many clothing coupons that confirmation dress would have used up? And when you think that it would only be worn once – well! Arnold, will you join in the conversation for once, please?"

Chewing on his shredded wheat, lengthy strands hanging from his mouth like teeth gone awry, her father added his smile, broadening to a grin as the loose pieces were swallowed. Turning attention away from the 'Daily Telegraph,' he said, "Seeing you in Daphne's Confirmation dress will certainly bring back happy memories. And if I may be allowed to say so, I think you'll be the star of the whole show. Reading the lesson, I imagine? The best of the bunch. You've shone at that little school. Quite a little star there. Going to see Father, then, are we? Checking up on the correct chapter and verse, that sort of thing. Is that why you're going?"

"Right."

She got up from the table. Her mother turning over the bacon, called out from the cooker, "Don't you want anything else? What's that nasty scratch on your ankle? How did you get it?"

"Just a scratch. Stop fussing, will you? Forget it. Forget everything."

Back in her room, she lay on her bed. Time passed. She heard the back door slam. Daphne off somewhere – tennis probably. Half an hour later she heard the car tyres bumping down the rough drive. The usual Saturday morning shopping trip. She glanced at her watch. Ten o'clock. Do it correctly. No good putting his back up for no good reason with that crabby housekeeper guarding the place like a sentry, like one of those old men from the Home Guard. *Ask politely. Don't raise your voice. Keep calm.*

Nadina tiptoed into the study, took the telephone off its hook, her hand sweaty and trembling. The operator put her through.

Brr-brr-brr-brr. *"Please God, don't let Mrs Henderson answer."*

A gravel voice, unsteady. "Father O'Donnell speaking."

She slammed the receiver back.

'Be strong! Be strong!'

Yet suppose he refuses to see me? Then a note will have to do. An ultimatum. A clear choice: *either, or.* She clenched her fists, held them to her eyes, feeling the tears build up. Her fingers trembling, she tried again.

"Father O'Donnell speaking."

The same slurred speech. This time a note of irritation.

"It's me, Nadina Brown, Father. I need your recommendation. If you... if you... give it me I won't tell on you."

There was silence. Then, "Did you ring before?"

"Yes, and I'll be over in half an hour on my bicycle to collect it... Father."

The silence continued. Heavy breathing, a cough, then a deep sigh. "Nadina, I have no idea what you are talking about."

"Yes, you do! You know you *do!*. Stop pretending. You've known all along." Despite her resolve to be calm, she clutched the receiver, barely able to hold it. She repeated over, '*Calm, calm, calm.*' Then, in a rush, the words spilling out, unthinking, not caring. "And you've been listening to my parents again, haven't you, trying to get you on their side, when you promised me." She drew breath and with a great effort of will to keep her voice level, even adopting a conversational tone, she said, "I'll pass the Scholarship, Father, I've known... well, always known I'll do well at that. I finished the paper before anyone else, the Maths and English. And the interview with Mother Clare. I'm sure I'll be accepted. Just the recommendation... please... give it me and I promise you no one will ever know about... about.... For... forever... always. Please, please." Her voice dropped to a whisper.

If there had been any note of apprehension, it had gone. He said, "I have no intention of recommending you for anything."

Her voice now shrill, spluttering through her tears, her rage giving her strength, "Father O'Donnell, I will go straight to the police! Miss Ashby... she will come with me... yes... and I will write to the Bishop." Then losing all restraint, she yelled, "You'll be finished for good, for ever!"

She heard the click of the phone, then silence.

Fumbling with the receiver, wondering briefly if the operator had listened in – they often did, she'd heard her parents talking about it – Nadina let herself out of the house. He was filthy, he was disgusting. She wheeled her bike out from the garden shed. He should be defrocked. Evil. As evil as Hitler? Maybe. No, worse! Worse! Because he was a priest. He was special. He'd taught them that. Called by God. A holy vocation sanctified by grace. A particular calling. He had desecrated it!

She rode fast, blanking it all out. The tears blew back on to her cheeks in the bluster of a sudden wind. Arriving, she let her bike drop against the railings, rushed up the steps. The door opened at once to her knock. This time there was no welcoming smile.

"So, you've come, have you?"

She pushed past him into the hall. Keeping her voice as level as she could, speaking the words deliberately pausing after each one: "I... will... not... give... you... away." Then faster, afraid she would falter, "That is if you give me your recommendation for the Convent School of the Holy Name." Then almost in a conversational tone, she added, "I'm so sorry I kicked you, bit your hand. It must have hurt you. I'm sorry, Father, but I was scared."

The door stayed open. "Continue," he said.

His calmness unsettled her. She raised her voice. "I need the recommendation. I... I... was frightened, because it hurt. All those other times, it hurt me. Every time, you hurt me. And there's the reading – at the Confirmation. Father, I was hoping... well, that it would be me. Wouldn't it be me? Miss Ashby said she thought it would be me." Her tone was almost apologetic, trailing, then disappearing. She gripped the little hall table for support. He looked down at her with that mocking smile she so hated.

"My dear Nadina, there is no point at all in continuing this inane conversation for I have no intention of giving you anything."

"The Confirmation? I mean I was thinking that I would be the one reading the lesson, be introduced to the Bishop? I don't know what reading it is, so I need to know, so I can practise it in good time."

He laughed then, that tittering laugh, the poking-fun laugh that went up the scale and ended with a sneer. "Oh, did I really? Well, maybe I forgot. But in any case, I've already invited Cynthia Peal."

She flinched as if he'd struck her. She was gripping the table now, suddenly cold, shivering, though the sun was up and the forecast was to be exceptionally warm even for July. "You said you wanted us to be friends. You said I could come with you to Ireland. Didn't you? Have you forgotten that as well? We're both lonely people. We need each other. Yes, you said. You did. Oh, please, Father. I need the recommendation. I must have it. I can't go to Southgate. I hate it. I need t to go to the Convent School of the Holy Name. I deserve it." She was wailing, unable to stop, aware that he was looking down at her, his lip curled.

"I'll tell you what you are. You're an hysterical, ultra-sensitive, highly imaginative child. You skip school, staying away from the instruction I promised you. And what is more I heartily agree with your parents that a spell at the State Grammar School would benefit you far more than the holy huddle of the self- righteous lot at the Convent School."

She gasped, "I can't believe what I'm hearing. After all... all... you've said."

"I have no intention of recommending you, Nadina."

She let go of the table, took a step backward, through the open door, her foot hovering on the top step. "You said to come whenever I liked! You said we would be friends. I have no one. You said..."

The door slammed in her face. Nadina screamed, not caring who heard, "You're disgusting! You're a disgrace to your calling. You've no right to be a priest. I'll get the police on to you. You're a pervert." She hammered on the door with her fists, sobbing, "Oh, please. No, I didn't mean that. Please, oh, oh, oh, please... I'm so sorry. But the Convent School of the Holy Name... I must go there, you see. All I need is a letter, the letter from you. Just a few lines. I will get over it, what we did. My fault too. I admit it. But I, we, will forget it ever happened."

The door stayed shut. Like a tomb. Cold and silent.

On her bike, blinded by tears, Nadina sped homewards. Along the main road a convoy of army vehicles passed her, some of the soldiers in the back of the lorries calling out a greeting. A slight wind now began to stir the leaves in the gutter and she felt the coolness against the mark. Then she said it slowly, fearfully under her breath, no more than a whisper, "God damn you to hell." Then a little louder, one hand on the handle bars, the other crossing herself for protection. "God damn you to hell."

She had cursed a priest.

But there was no lightening, no thunderbolt. She remembered Ryan shouting up at God and how shocked she'd been and now *she* was doing it. She shouted at the top of her voice, the tears choking, her voice carrying into the wind.

"God damn you to hell!"

She'd trusted him, even made allowances for his loneliness, wanting to believe in him, wanting to understand how it must be.

"God damn you to hell." But this time she had no voice left. She whispered the curse through a dry cough.

Father O'Donnell draining a third glass, looked down the list of the names of next year's intake for Class six. Ah, yes, Marianne Jones, the little kid with the calliper. Very bright. Pretty little thing. Good Catholic family: Edwin and Jane. With quickening interest, he lit a cigarette, reached for the whisky bottle.

Chapter Twenty Six

Final Assembly for Class six. Miss Ashby's lot shuffle along the line on plimsoll feet, stomachs churning, mouths dry; convicted prisoners awaiting sentence. White-faced seated on the splintered floor, surrounded by council-green walls crumbling like flaky pastry, they wait for the towering inferno with the huge handbag.

Thelma Ashby had a lump in her throat as she scanned her class, her gaze moving from one to the other: children she had tried so diligently to teach. Apart from the very brightest of the bright: Cynthia Peal, Philip Matthews, Brian 'Bunny' Harris, each looking forward to the future, a glow of happiness on their bright shiny faces, the majority slouched in fearful anticipation. For there was always the possibility, fairly remote for the majority, of ending up at the hell hole of Naughton Road Secondary, where the world-weary Headmaster, Henry Sneard, and his ill-tempered staff, growing increasingly cynical with every passing year, ruled the slowest learners in the county with an iron fist without the consolation of a velvet glove. And there was Nadia, seated apart, head down, staring at the floor, looking so utterly miserable. But for all of them, the clever, the averagely bright, and the distinctly dim, six years of attendance at Holy Innocents' Catholic Elementary had ended and change with a capital C was coming, secret and scary. It meant the closure of their comfort zone. Thelma could see the dawning realisation reflected in their faces and could have wept for them all, especially for Nadina Brown. The usual distressed look more in evidence than ever, but what else could she, her teacher, have done?

.Richard Johnson's future was never in doubt. The disreputable snotty child would join the previous year's Scholarship rejects. "Jobs, not careers for you, and that depends if you're lucky," Millie had proclaimed nastily, sniffing the air as if she detected a bad odour like a gas cloud hovering over the half dozen other cast-offs, bunched together like refugees, the handbag's swing increasing. "And, the kind of jobs you'll get," she'd added, "will be well down the evolutionary scale as far as the need for brains rather than brawn is concerned. Road sweepers, bricklayers, labourers, factory workers and the like." She had ended this warning with a sudden flourish of her right arm, making the sign of the cross, her audience squashed into insignificance like a colony of ants.

Privately, however, as she sipped coffee with her deputy in the seclusion of her office, Miss Millison had admitted to Miss Ashby, that some of the boys from the Naughton Road stable, written off by the Education Authority as hardly worth the cost of a piece of chalk, were now distinguishing themselves on the battlefield. "To be honest with you, Thelma," she'd said, "I don't mind telling you, I am always surprised and extremely proud of their achievements." Thelma forbore to say that she could have told her in the first place.

Now, she looked over the children's heads and located Ryan Brannnighan. Lip curled, the boy was gazing at Johnson, a frown creasing his pallid features.

You poor sap, thought Ryan. Foureyes' cracked lens, carving the eye into two roughly equal parts, glinted in the light of the morning sun that struggled to find a path through the long murky windows. Ryan wrinkled his nose in disgust at the new food deposits that had accumulated on the moth-burgled jersey; a touch of bacon rind here, a few strands of All Bran glued together by milk deposits, a dollop of raspberry jam that Foureyes had failed to lick off. Can't his mam dress him better, he thought, thinking of the crisp, clean, Persil whiteness of his own shirts, neatly laid out for him on his bed, and the tidy piles of underwear sprinkled regularly with moth balls, ready for use in the top drawer of his dresser – covering his accumulating wealth.

He and Kenny had joked in the playground. "Take no notice of old Millie, Rich. She got no idea how high you can rise in government departments."

"How do you mean, Rye?" the boy had asked, busily picking at some freshly deposited cornflakes.

"You're going to get a real good job with the council when you leave Naughton," chortled Kenny, nudging Ryan.

At the sound of 'council,' the divided eye blinked rapidly, the wrinkling of the nose accompanied by a big sniff, the nostrils bubbling green

"See Rich," said Ryan, his arm round the smaller boy's shoulder, "let me explain this to you. Sure, you'll have an important position, see? You just got to make sure there's plenty of bog roll."

"And polish," said Kenny, giggling. "All the seats will need polishing. Yeah, shining so it'll be real nice for your customers an' they can see their faces when they go to crap."

"That's right. And, Rich, you'll be given an enormous broom, spanking new it'll be, to sweep up all the piddle."

Kenny, now anxious to prove that he could be equally witty, added, "Yeah, your own broom, be just for you. Like, personal. Got your name carved on it. Be on a bit of brass, a plaque. There's not many who get their own brooms. You'll be able to sweep up loads of crap up with that, sweep up gallons of it, eh, Rye?"

"Oh, sure, absolutely. You'll get a big shovel an' all to go with it. A broom and a shovel. And if you're in there 'til midnight, it will be overtimes rates, 'cause there's always a lot of business, if you get my meaning." They had giggled uncontrollably as Foureyes, uncertain, a half-smile hovering on his lips, half-believing they were taking the Mick but not absolutely sure.

Now strolling round the playground, Ryan and Kenny had continued advising the future lavatory attendant. "Success depends on quantity. Every night they come in and weigh your pail. I reckon you'll do a great job. You'll be the best shite stirrer in the whole county. What do you think, Kenny?"

"Now, that ain't true," Foureyes interrupted, a grin of dawning comprehension lighting up his face. "They don't weigh your shite, because you pull the chain and it goes down the hole."

Both boys were slightly taken aback at this interruption. "Sure, that happens but only after it's weighed," said Kenny. "Best in the country you'll be. You'll get a gold medal an' go to

Buckingham Palace, I reckon. His Majesty will give you a medal, won't he Rye?"

"Sure, Sir Richard Johnson, Bog Attendant of the year," Ryan intoned. As other pupils began to gather round he and Kenny had walked away. After a moment's hesitation, Foureyes had run after them to join in the laughter.

Remembering, Ryan sniggered and dug Foureyes in the ribs, just as a sudden hush proclaimed the arrival of the top Nazi.

After the song *"There'll always be an England, where there's a country lane..."* patriotic fervour shining on the pale faces of the Empire's children, they chorused the Lord's Prayer three times at their commanding officer's insistence. Now they stood dully, watching a triumphant Miss Millison grinning madly as she waved a large brown envelope in their faces.

"What have we here?" she asked. "I wonder."

Kenny nudged Ryan to whisper, "Come on, you old hag. Put us all out of our misery."

Motionless, the pupils of Class six stared ahead like deaf and dumb mutes. Some sought minor distractions, gazing at the Head's two front teeth beginning their inevitable wobble. Horse-length, yellowing, each year they seemed to gain fresh elasticity. As usual, at the very last minute, a long pink tongue like a lizard's shot out to prod them back into place.

Now, gleefully, as if pleading for attention, Miss Millison held her right hand aloft like a policeman controlling traffic, a white glove donned especially for the occasion. She giggled helplessly, her feet tapping a little dance of happiness as she plunged her hand inside the envelope.

At this point, those elite half dozen, the best and the brightest, were invited to stand. Philip Matthews, looking incredibly smug; Brian Harris and John Ashton, smiling confidently. Behind them, two happy girls: Cynthia Peal, Patricia Smith. And there, several feet distant, Nadina Brown, the long tress of hair, like a curtain covering her misery.

Foureyes wore his usual expression of bewilderment. Ryan, at least fifty per cent Hydeish, whispered in his ear, "Poor wee devil, so you are. You'll know soon enough. Toilet torture, that's what they do first. Put your face into the bowl then pull the chain. Then 'the railings.' Push your head through the gap, so they do. Sometimes they have to call the Fire Brigade. With your large bonce they'll have a job, so maybe you won't get the railings. Instead, they'll bury you alive."

Aware now of Hyde's cruelty and remembering the kindly doctor and anxious to make amends, he put his arm impulsively round his friend's shoulders and squeezed. Then, just as suddenly, mindful that he might be going to the hell hole himself, and just a little scared that Foureyes' dimwittedness might somehow be catching, he pulled his arm away.

Miss Millison started to trill out the results. Ryan's innards were flung about, like on that never-forgotten crossing from Holyhead three years ago. He waited, lips twisting and turning, listening out for the 'Bs,' Listening intently for Shelia Bond's name who came immediately before him on the register. How would he commit suicide? Hanging? He didn't like the idea of a rope digging into your neck, squeezing tighter and tighter and then your tongue hanging out all purple. What about drowning? That might be better. You swam out to sea mile after mile until you could go no further, and the waves came over you and you sank to the bottom. Pretend to fly? Step off a high building? But the mess on the pavement: all skin, bones and blood like tomato ketchup would surely be a terrible sight.

A sharp intake of breath, the roll of his guts like a shipwreck in a storm for it was time. The 'As' had finished. They were taking their places around the walls. Now!

Looks like a tiny bit of Doctor Jekyll coming out here, he thought, feeling a minutia of relief, seeing Millie's ragged eyebrows lift and her eyes widen and glitter, the wobblies pushed back with a quick jerk of a white thumb, voice ringing out pleasurably. "Sheila Bond, a place at Saint Mary's Catholic Grammar." She smirked at the plain girl with the doughy face, the one thick plait hanging down her back like a Chinese. The second ugliest in the school, Ryan thought, with a fleeting glance at Dickerson scratching her spots. Polite and restrained applause followed.

Cracking with emotion Miss Millison's raised her high-pitched whine several decibels. "Listen, everyone. Listen, all of you!"

She raised the white forefinger to the heavens, then pointing directly at a blushing Sheila, articulating each word like a speech therapist, "Sheila has achieved a very strong result: Sixty-seven per-cent. Well, done, my dear." Miss Millison paused, licked the protruding teeth, thumbed them back. The girl's face turned to a deeper shade of sunset red.

"Brannigan!"

Ryan bent double, clutching his stomach, his limbs uncoordinated, changing into the Hunchback of Notre Dame to the amusement of some of the teachers; Groaning, eyelids fluttering like a dying man, gasping for air, then turning his back, unable to face the podium where Millie and the staff looked on wonderingly. After what seemed an age, but in reality barely ten seconds, he turned round, his face scrunched up in agony, head nodding mechanically as if on a spring, preparing himself for sentencing.

Then. Joy!

Open-mouthed with shock, he saw that the long teeth were stretched to their fullest extent. Thrilled, he grinned back, giving a little wave of his hand and a thumbs-up.

"Well, well, what do you know? It must be the luck of the Irish," she said with something between a sneer and a cackle. Someone tittered along his row and received a hard stare by return. Then Thelma Ashby smiled, the warmest smile he'd ever received.

But Millie frowned, a tangle of wires loose like a bloodhound's skin stretching along her forehead, and again the white-gloved finger pointed. "Ryan Brannigan, fifty-three per-cent. Borderline. Exactly my prediction, Irish. Take your place. No, no! Not that far. Go halfway; to the middle of the wall ahead of me. Yes; well away from Sheila. We don't want you near her. She's quite a very different category, so don't get bumptious. Yes, the next wall. Go on, boy, go on, go on; get it right!"

Ryan hunched his shoulders, raised his fists like a boxer who'd lasted fifteen rounds against a much heavier opponent, acknowledging the loud applause from the other pupils. Then, a rolling gait, a sailor on deck in a storm, casual, unconcerned, yet aware that admiring eyes were upon him, especially from the little teacher. His heart pounded in excitement. Southgate! He breathed the name slowly, drinking it in like nectar, luxuriating in the wonderful taste of it. He was safe.

Others of the Southgate contingent would soon be joining him along his stretch of wall. He wasn't bothered especially who it might be, though when she got to the E's and he heard Kenny had scraped a pass at fifty-one per-cent, Ryan applauded loudly, giving him the thumbs up as the lumbering giant of a boy, grinning widely, his big face exceptionally red and sweaty, walking exaggeratedly like Frankenstein - ridiculous in his short trousers - to stand next to him.

At last the results for all thirty-four pupils had been given out. Twenty-three were destined for the Grammar schools, either Catholic or State. Two girls, Cynthia Peal and Nadina Brown, held positions closest to the podium, having achieved the highest marks of everyone present. A hurried whispering between Miss Ashby and the Head then took place, both coming off the stage to speak to Nadina, who shook her head. Three boys standing by them learned that they would be going to Millhurst Catholic High School, their marks well into the mid-eighties. The Head, again glancing anxiously in Nadina's direction, announced proudly that Nadina had scored the very highest score ever known in the county, a total of ninety-three per-cent! Miss Millison, chortling with delight, teeth less secure than ever, to place an arm round the shoulders of the unhappy pupil. She then led her by the hand to the stage to stand next to her. The applause from staff and pupils was the loudest of all.

Away from all the others, the remnants of a ragged and defeated army were herded by one of the teachers to the very furthest wall; six rejects destined for life imprisonment at Naughton Road Secondary. There stood a seventh, three yards distant as if placed in quarantine, who blinked through shattered spectacles at the happy Grammar School successors, grinning at each other with undisguised admiration like members of a victorious soccer side, indifferent to the plight of their less fortunate colleagues along the wall opposite.

"This boy," Miss Millison announced angrily, pointing a shaking finger at Foureyes, "has achieved a result never before known before in the history of every school in the county and not doubt in the whole country. The lowest mark ever recorded: nil per-cent!" In a gesture of contempt, she tore up the envelope, hurling the pieces to the floor. Laughter quickly subsided as the children watched a solitary tear roll down the boy's cheek.

Ryan's Jekyll heart felt soft and spongy. From his exalted position, he moved across, ignoring the Head's shout for him to stay put. Once there he placed a comforting arm round the boy's trembling shoulders. He vowed to himself that he would protect him from the marauding gangs who would soon begin their nightly patrols, searching the streets despite the black-out for the new intake. He would show compassion, be that kindly Doctor Jekyll and Uncle Joe Stalin, England's great new ally. He, Ryan Brannigan, would be there to protect him – well, at least until the new term started. He returned to his place next to Kenny.

"Now!" Miss Millison called out as Miss Ashby took two steps forward to stand beside her. "Now," she repeated, more casually this time, the teeth reappearing and disappearing forced back by finger or thumb. The pupils looked up expectantly. "Now..." her voice became fainter.

Third time lucky, thought Ryan, watching the forked tongue shoot out as the teeth wobbled dangerously and were again negotiated back into place.

"Now, Sunday, this coming Sunday for you, my dear Year six, my top class, this will be the greatest significant event in the whole of your Catholic discipleship. Is that not so?"

For the moment Class six were confused, not knowing if they were to assent vocally or by some form of body language; a nod of the head perhaps, or a smile, or even a clap? But most stared ahead, unblinking, stretched along three walls like lines of washing, frowning in a state of suspended anticipation, while Miss Millison's tongue probed warily for the target area.

"Why am I saying that?"

Philip Matthews' hand shot up. Like a Hitler salute, thought Ryan.

"One boy knows," said Millie. "Yes, of course, it is bound to be Philip Matthews. Come on, then, Philip."

The small letterbox-shaped mouth disappearing then appearing in the creases of wobbling pink flesh, opening and closing, then opened again. He beamed with pleasure, speaking now without further hesitation. "This very Sunday, Miss Millison, is the Confirmation Service. It is at Holy Innocents' Church, commencing at ten o' clock for Class six."

Ryan, vowing to thump the fat pig's head extra hard at break, nudged Kenny in a secret signal.

"Be sure that you are in your places in the church by twenty minutes to ten," the Head announced. "Brannigan, what time did I say?"

"You said twenty to ten, Miss. Heard you good and proper, so I did."

Those children who were destined for greatness, notably Philip Matthews and Cynthia Peal and the two or three others, grinned lavishly at their marvellous headmistress, who leered back with undisguised admiration. Like fiends, the grammar school contingent also grinned. Nadina continued to stare glumly at the floor.

Miss Millison held the silence for a moment longer, glanced at her watch gave one last shove of the two precarious teeth and dismissed Assembly.

Foureyes now weeping openly, both lenses clogged with fear-filled breath like a pea-soup fog on a wintry morning. Ryan crossed the floor once more. "Don't you worry, kiddo," he said, adopting a James Cagney pose and speaking Americanesque. "Don't you worry about a thing, Buddy. Listen, I sure won't let none of them Naughton guys get you, I sure won't. Nor will Kenny, eh Kenny?" he called across the hall, but Kenny was in deep conversation with Peter Steggles. "That's my promise, Baby, and forever. For all time."

Ryan's plan was a cull; once at Southgate, a thorough sweep from the past. Ditch them all: Naddy Brown with the one creepy Jesus eye, June Greengage's crimson lips, newly crayoned daily; Nit-Picker Julie, who he believed was beginning to have a thing for him. He'd even ignore Polly Townsend with her disgusting wart-fingers probing at the pictures. Then there was Miss Ashby, with the too-small brassiere; the long streak of a Headmistress, desperate for the dentist, carrying that handbag like a grenade. Yes, he'd ditch the whole lot of them, everyone. He would go to his new school free of all clutter - and that meant religion, so farewell to the fat Father. Kenny? Yes, Kenny too, in time, with his know-all ways, quoting from the filthy 'News of the World' all the while, and never ever giving up calling him a 'Fenian bastard'.

Now, a wide grin on his tear-streaked face, Foureyes walked beside him, cracked lens winking in the sun, chirping away, the streaks of spilt custard down his front giving an appearance of a canary, his voice louder, more agitated. "Will you, Rye? Will you? You know, protect me like from them lot at Naughton. Rye? Honest, I'm shite scared, Rye. They'll kill me, torture me, like toilet torture, and pushing my head through the railings like you said, and my ears will get stuck, though they don't stick out as much as Kenny's. They'll come looking for me, I know they will." He began to wail, looking up anxiously at his sworn protector.

Any moment I'll hit him, thought Ryan. "'Course, I will. Now shut up, Rich, will you? Sure getting on my tits, you are." He barged him to one side and began to run. The boy called out after him. "Rye, I'm too young... to... die, I am. Wait for me...."

Then Ryan remembered. He'd never really forgotten, it was just old Hyde butting in, interfering. The top word on his list had just slipped a bit, that was all. Remembered the Lord's penetrating gaze boring into the cowardly apostle in the courtyard and Father O'Donnell's shout, 'And the cock crew twice, you will deny me three times. And Peter wept. Oh, how he wept boys and girls.'

So he stopped running; waited for Foureyes.

Into the classroom, he prised off the fingers clinging to his jersey, passed Nadina taking her seat. "Suppose you're going to be with all the other fanatics. That right, yeah?"

She turned to face him. The uncovered eye red and wet, hair wild, tangled and dirty-looking. To Ryan, who always liked to feel nice and clean, apart from overlooking the requirement of a comb, even her dress looked grubby.

"Do you know the meaning of the word deception?" she asked.

"God's sake, girl. What you on about now?"

"Oh, yes, you do." She glanced at Foureyes, "Clear off, Johnson," she said. "I'm talking to this deceiver, you filthy ignoramus."

Ryan gave his admirer a sharp slap round the head from Hyde to help him on his way. The boy slunk away, fresh tears appearing. "Honestly, Naddy, he said, I haven't a clue. Honest. Sure, I haven't."

"Oh, never mind. Doesn't matter. Nothing matters."

Baffled, he turned away. Reaching his desk, he turned round, calling out, "Look, I don't know what the hell you're talking about. But I don't care, I don't. I'm off to Southgate Grammar and I'm forgetting this stinking dump and everyone in it, especially you."

"Look up the noun 'deception' in your dictionary, will you? Or the verb, deceive. You'll find it's all about you, so you should put it to the top of your list."

He sat with his hands over his ears, to shut out Foureyes' whining, now drying his eyes on the sleeve of his jersey blowing his nose and examining the result, "Our last day. I don't want to leave, Rye. I don't want to go Naughton. I want to go with you, Rye." Then, suddenly brightening, "Will you come round my house tomorrow, go and fish for tiddlers. Yeah? Rye, will you?"

Ryan, frowning, made a fist, struck him in the chest, apologising to his alter ego, the ever compassionate Doctor Jekyll, then reached out to pull the unhappy boy to him, giving his thin shoulders a squeeze.

That night, Ryan lifted the big dictionary from its place under the bed with his notebook. He read his favourite words six times, vowing afresh not to forget it. At the very end adding the new word. He was too tired to look it up now. It would do for later. She was a loony, that Naddy Brown and sooner he'd be shot of her the better, same as Rich Johnson, the filthy beggar. He put the dictionary back, turned off the light and pulled the blankets up over his head, but the word kept turning over in his mind, so he turned the light back on and reached down for his dictionary. *'Deception'*, he read, *'the thing that deceives; trick, sham. 'Deceive,' to mislead purposefully.* Like pretending he'd protect Rich when he had no intention of doing so, or hearing Naddy in the playground and them all jeering: 'Leper, Leper, Leper,' and doing nothing. Like his dad pretending to be a solder at the battle of the Somme when he was the IRA. It's all deception. He felt the tears begin. Angrily he brushed them away.

Ryan snapped off the light. He banged his head down on the pillow. Not only me. Everybody's pretending all the time, like the loony religious, like her, thinking herself better than anyone else. God's sake, even Doctor Jekyll plays a trick on you.

Thinks he's good and kind when all the time Mr Hyde is there waiting to take over. And he knew old Hyde was taking over more and more these days.

Chapter Twenty Seven

"The Catholic Church teaches that the Sacrament of Holy Confirmation is of the greatest significance, a milestone along your spiritual journey. It is a responsibility as well as an immense privilege. And, as the name suggests, this great event confirms or strengthens the faith already bestowed by grace at your First Communion."

So saying, Miss Millison returned to her pew next to Miss Ashby. The two had chosen a tactful position a little way down, a few rows behind the parents. Here they would be able to spot any signs of disruptive behaviour. "Watch out for Irish, Thelma," she whispered to Miss Ashby, pleased that both she and her deputy had been granted dispensation by the priests from their own churches in order to support their pupils on this momentous occasion.

And there they all were, the top class, scrubbed and shining, filling the two front pews, boys on the left, girls on the right. Many of the boys wore long trousers for the first time. The girls, resplendent in their white dresses, made last minute adjustments to their veils, their mothers leaning forward, pinning and prodding, whispering advice.

Across the aisle, Richard Johnson's eyes fluttered behind his big glasses, the addition of a new lens giving an appearance of normality, although, despite Father O'Donnell's warning, he still seemed unaware that the occasion merited a suit. The familiar brown jersey contained fresh deposits of food and evidence of mucus on the sleeves where he'd wiped his nose.

Sitting next to him, Ryan felt superior in his best grey suit though the rough wool chafed a bit against his skin. He tried to undo the top button of his shirt. As he did so, he glanced across the aisle. There they were: the mad and the bad: black-eyed beetle Daphne; wobbly Mrs Brown, belly snug up against the back of the pew ahead, and the baddest of the lot, Hyde Brown with the ping-pong ball Adam's Apple shooting up and down, mad eyes swivelling every other minute to stare at him. Ryan yawned loudly: "Your parents here?" he asked Foureyes.

The boy shook his head, "Nah; Dad done a bunk again last week."

Suddenly, the whole congregation rose to their feet as the cross-bearer, acolytes, Father O'Donnell and a half pint-sized bishop, walking rigidly like a tin soldier, passed them. Ryan frowned, yawned again. The news of Mr Johnson's abrupt departures made him thankful that his own parents were always around. Once more he glanced across the aisle, saw that the blancmange was open to the sky. *'Course, like the rest, Naddy'd got her stupid hair pinned up under the veil.'* He shuddered at the sight.

The bishop climbed the pulpit steps. The homily seemed to be all about the Lord's requirement to be as good as gold. "It's easy," the little man said, staring down at them from beneath his mitre like a tea cosy, "once you know how."

Ryan nudged Kenny. Both had the same thought. Might he topple over? For in order to be seen as well as heard, the Bishop leaned over the edge. Ryan was working out the distance. Must be about fifteen to twenty feet. Legs or broken neck or both? Ryan yawned again as the sermon continued.

"It's like this. God is watching over you, just as He's always been, hovering over you in the form of a dove. But now..." the Bishop held up a triumphant finger, "now he's come a little bit closer to you fine boys and girls at this very moment in time. He not only makes you feel good, He gets you to be good."

A dove? A dove is a white bird a bit like a seagull, Ryan supposed. That sweeps down on you, remembering a day out with his family, recalling shifting fast just in time to avoid a stream. He smiled at the memory, beginning to lose consciousness when the preacher emphasised the importance of attending Mass every Sunday and making a confession at least once a month.

The service moved steadily towards its climax. Ryan, rubbing the sleep from his eyes,

reached inside the jacket of his suit and nudged Foureyes. "Where's your bit of paper?" he whispered. The boy shook his head. Ryan tried again, louder this time. "Where's your two names, you dimwit?

Foureyes blinked behind the shining lenses but was silent. A moment later, he mumbled, "Dunno."

Each candidate was required to bring a piece of paper bearing two names: first, the Christian name and underneath that, the name of the saint the pupil had chosen; a saint they most admired. Now, the boys began to form up in pairs; Ryan and Foureyes tagging on at the end.

Standing on the sanctuary step, though by no means tall, Father O'Donnell towered over the minuscule figure next to him, whose mitre just reached his shoulder. The bishop held his staff in his left hand, the other hand poised, ready to be placed on the head of each boy or girl before him, accompanied by the words that would send each one on their spiritual journey: "Confirm, O Lord, this Thy child with Thy heavenly grace." This to be pronounced in Latin, then in English.

The queue shuffled slowly forward. Father O'Donnell looked worried. "Your name, boy? And your saint's name?" Foureyes said nothing. The bishop asked helpfully, "Who is your favourite saint, my boy?" Still no reply. Foureyes blinked up at the two dignitaries, looking from one to the other.

"Is your little friend deaf?" whispered his Lordship to Ryan.

Suddenly, Foureyes blurted out his name in such a loud voice that everyone in the congregation burst out into undignified laughter. "Richard I am. Richard! I've always been Richard. Rich for short." He turned to look at Ryan as if needing verification.

Ryan whispered, "Rich, you chose Peter to be your saint, remember?" There was again a long silence. Then Ryan said, "Peter, he chose. That chief among the apostles, your Holiness, erm... bishop. Peter, the chief of them all."

Foureyes shouted excitedly. "Yes, Peter. That's my saint. Saint Peter." He sniffed loudly, grinning up at the two clerics. Father O'Donnell glared but the bishop winked at Ryan.

Now it was his turn. " I am Ryan and my choice is Judas," he said, holding up his piece of paper with the name of the betrayer scrawled below his own. There was a collective gasp behind him. The bishop raised his eyebrows, puzzled. Ryan felt some explanation was called for. "I know he's no saint but see, I feel sorry for the poor fella, sir. Because nobody likes him, not one little bit, they don't, and he done himself in, so he did, sir, because he was ashamed of what he done, betraying the Lord, like."

Father O'Donnell's glare intensified, but the Bishop appeared to be struggling to keep a straight face. Ryan and Rich then bowed to him, each in turn bending forward to kiss the purple ring on his little finger. Foureyes was curious. He took the bishop's fingers in both hands, examining the ring closely. A little trickle of saliva landed on it, but the Bishop didn't seem to mind, wiping it hurriedly on his purple cassock before giving both boys in turn a gentle touch on the cheek with his fist to send them on their way, declaring that from then on they were soldiers of Christ, ready to fight the good fight of the Faith.

Fergus, from his place a few pews behind, was shocked. Choosing the man the Scriptures named a devil? Yet, when he saw his son bow low to the bishop and kiss his ring in a token of faithful obedience, he felt a surge of pride. For whatever the boy felt now, he would be grateful in the future. The passport to Faith and the passport to Work, for how could you expect a job without the backing of the priest. In the North, of course, it was different. To know a priest in the six counties would bring little benefit. Fergus felt the customary surge of anger.

Outside the church he waited with Marie and Kathie. He glanced at his watch, drawing impatiently on his cigarette. Eventually he spotted Ryan coming towards them, saw him thump the bespectacled small lad on the arm, elbow a fat lad in the stomach, then follow a big one he recognised as Kenny.

Fergus turned to Kathie, who had been joined by Daphne. "Have you any idea what's up with our Ryan? Jaysus, does he not know how to behave in a church? And Judas? For the good Lord's sake, choosing Judas?"

Kathie shrugged her shoulders. "He's an idiot, Daddy. Calling attention to himself as usual. Just wants to be the big shot now he's got to Grammar."

Fergus' thoughts were interrupted by the sight of a girl giggling in the middle of a crowd. At first he didn't recognise her. The veil had gone and so had the thick coat of hair that flowed regally down the right cheek. In its place, a jungle of unkempt, jagged pieces sticking out wildly like a hedgehog's spikes. Had she attacked it with the garden shears? The girl had an arm round the waist of another, whom Kathie said was June Greengage.

"What in the name of the dear good Lord, Holy Mary and all the saints has happened to your sister, Daphne? Tell me, what's going on?"

"No idea, Mr Brannigan," Daphne sighed. "We never know what she's up to. She was always mad. She's gone completely sky high now."

"What in the world's happened to her gentle, pious ways then?" Fergus asked aloud before turning to Marie for a reaction. His wife shook her head looking even more surprised.

Daphne was suddenly serious. "Mr Brannigan, I don't want to say too much, but my poor parents have been really worried about her."

"You mean *even* more than usual?" said Kathie.

"Well, when Mummy saw Naddy's new hair style this morning, my dad's breakfast skidded across the floor. You should have seen it!" Daphne giggled at the recollection. "Two fried eggs and three rashers of bacon. The whole week's ration! Of course, Dad never said anything. He rarely does. Reckon, he's given up on her. Here comes the crazy mixed-up kid."

Nadina sauntered up to them, turning to stare back in the church where the photographer from the local paper was taking shots of the bishop and Father O'Donnell. They watched as Cynthia Peal took her place beside them, her sister Margaret with her proud parents standing by. His eyebrows rising in surprise, Fergus looked at Marie, who again shook her head. Nadina turned back to face them.

Something was wrong, the angry look was new to him and the wild hair was so totally unexpected. Fergus shook his head, utterly bewildered, but for the moment Ryan's behaviour disturbed him more: aimlessly shuffling from one foot to the other, kicking up dust. "Think we've got money for new shoes, the way you're scuffing them?" Fergus growled.

Yet, walking home with his family, he could not get the wee girl out of his mind. There was clearly a problem, but what it was he had no idea.

Ryan too had noticed, but told himself it was nothing to do with him. His mind was elsewhere: Southgate. Baby school was over. And Church too – forever, and that freaky Naddy Brown. Doctor Jekyll was nowhere; Hydeish thoughts filled his mind.

Chapter Twenty Eight

Fergus, sipping whisky at four in the afternoon, a cigarette between his lips and his thoughts meandering as they often did at this time of day with no particular focus or direction, coughed as the nicotine caught, thumped his chest, swallowed the phlegm. "Jaysus," he said.

Ever since the Confirmation, he had been disturbed. It was more of an impression; a disquiet; a sense of foreboding. A week had passed and the memories were strong: her coming to the house, waiting for Ryan with the lemonade and biscuit, meek as a little lamb, kindly, softly spoken, a child whom Marie especially took to. A welcome difference to the others, she'd said, meaning that big lad, that Kenny with the foghorn of a voice, too fond of his own opinions and a bully to the skinny kiddy with the turnip shape of a head and the beer bottle glasses, always seeming to have a cold and those dirty personal habits. Marie had told him to lay off but sure it didn't make a scrap of difference.

He swirled the whisky round the bottom of the glass, stood to stretch his legs. The afternoon, when the sun dipped low behind the trees, a time for the warmness of the liquid gold to strengthen, the best anaesthetic to ease the pain. He rubbed his leg, sighed, his thoughts lingering on Nadina. Seeing her at Mass, reverent, devout, like she had a holy glow around her, bowed so low in the pew you thought she'd disappeared; a lovely wee girl. Two sisters, surely completely the opposite in size and shape and not forgetting manners - well, he'd not much time for the other one: noisy, full of herself, kind of throwing her weight around like the Evett boy. You could tell the stuffed-shirt Browns always favoured that older one. Yes, he'd noticed how the three of them gathered round Father O'Donnell at the door after Mass, chatting, laughing, making their farewells, and her? Nadina hanging back, head down; a lonely, sad child who didn't seem to belong to anyone.

Poor wee girl. To be branded with a ragged splodge of colour on what could have been a pretty face, for the left side had the clearest skin. How many times must she have dreamed that both sides could be the same: pure like the flawless skin of the Madonna statue by the altar?

The way of the Browns was to give Daphne the attention. He'd heard the way the big girl with the black fringe talked at the little one, calling her 'Ugly'. Was he getting like them, Fergus wondered, his lips clamping the cigarette like a vice. God forbid. Did he favour Kathie over Ryan? Marie certainly thought so and told him: "Put her on a pedestal, don't you?"

Yes, one easier to cope with than the other. Again he sighed. Flicking the butt into the coke hod he eased himself back into his chair and replenished the glass. The window rattled and the draught blew through the thinness of his old corduroys reminding him that he must go to the next Jumble Sale. At least Southgate would give him a grant for Ryan's uniform. The state schools look after you.

Lighting another cigarette, Fergus frowned and gulped down his whisky. So unlike herself she'd been there: wild as an alley-cat, shouting and giggling with that other one, the whore's daughter. A child wearing lipstick at the Mass? Surely a proper little slut.

For the good Lord's sake it just doesn't make sense! Like a jigsaw that had lost so many pieces it no longer fitted together. "Crazy mixed-up kid," Daphne had jeered. And even Ryan had shown surprise.

He'd always hoped she would be an influence, set the boy an example, but it looked like the effect on Ryan had been zero. Fergus stiffened, sat upright, the frown deepening. What made her attack her hair like that? Great chunks of her lovely hair gone as if she'd gone mad at it, getting hold of a pair of shears it looked like, and hacking away at it as if in some kind of a rage? But why? And why was the little kiddie, the good Doctor Peal's daughter - the one that looked as if she took a scrubbing brush to her cheeks trotting up to the lectern, sure as pleased as punch with herself? Then the Doc and his missus looking on, beaming away there when the priest led her to the bishop to shake hands with him? So why hadn't it been Nadina? Ninety-three per-cent! Fifth in the whole county! No one like her. And there it was heading the list in the 'Star.' Shifting in his chair, Fergus began to remember. Ryan was always telling good stories, but he wouldn't have made that one up. "Special instruction she's getting, Dad, Miss Ashby tells us." Then another time: "Dad, Naddy Brown tells us she goes round to the priest's house. He gives her big teas, Dad. All the stuff that's rationed, that we don't get a sniff of. Not fair, so it isn't."

Across the Water the priest's house was always strictly private. Being an altar boy, he had seen much of the priest, but there was no way, no way at all that he'd get an invite to the presbytery. Would it be so different in England then? He'd asked Ryan if he knew of others who'd got the invite? And Ryan had said no. For what reason would it be then? This extra teaching - that was it. But why go to the house for it? You always get the teaching of your Catechism in the church. That was the place. Always had been; in the occupied North as well as the South. Why the presbytery?

Fergus, his gaze wandering to the old photographs on the kitchen wall, raised his glass, remembering another time, taking a nip, ready for battle. Forming up, James Connelly leading the troop, the Banner, ready to be hoisted high on the Post Office roof, all of them proud to make a stand, knowing they were hopelessly outnumbered, outgunned, yet sustained by justice, the rightness of their Cause.

He took a mouthful and swallowed. He brushed his eyes, covering them with his hand as the tears threatened to fall, then lifted his head to glance though the window at the shadows racing across a darkening sky. His mind went back to a similar sky a lifetime ago. Back to the village where Thomas Gallagher had ruled the flock.

Suddenly, a coldness cut into him like a knife. By all the saints in heaven, was the good Lord trying to say something to him? The thought stunned him so much that his hands shook. He fumbled inside the cigarette packet with shaking, fingers. For the good Lord's sake, surely it was a hunch, no more than that?

Watching the smoke rings rise, Fergus smoked the Woodbine through in silence then threw the butt into the hod, yawned and stretched. Grabbing his cane he pushed himself out of his chair. The leg was giving him a lot of gyp today. Having to stand so long at the service hadn't done it any good. He looked round the cluttered room. Where was the boy? Massaging always helped the circulation. He could smell the rabbit stew simmering on the cooker. With a sigh he lowered himself carefully back into his chair, bowed his head as if in prayer then shook it and looked up, his eyes narrowed, a deep frown, three or four vertical lines creasing his forehead. No! Something was wrong, something that shouldn't be. Could he not have a little talk with the child? He'd not rush in. That was the mark of a fool, and so often he'd been that fool.

That evening he picked up the telephone, cleared his throat, fingered his collar. Talking to a bigwig like Arnold Brown made him nervous. He couldn't get over the way the man had made those ridiculous accusations, frightening the life out of Ryan, pushing his fist in his face and then trying to put it right with thirty pieces of silver, the Judas. The operator put him through.

"Arnold Brown speaking."

That damned voice. The man never talked natural. Sure he couldn't open his stupid mouth large enough.

"Mr Brown, it's Fergus Brannigan here."

"Ah, yes. How are you?" Not waiting for an answer, he continued. "Interesting service. Louise and I noticed your Ryan helping his little friend out. Very commendable, Brannigan. Of course, as I have always maintained there should be special schools for children like that. He's obviously sub-normal, educationally well beyond the pale, far beyond any teacher's ability to impart anything of value at all I should think. No one in that family seems to have heard of a suit of clothes! The father's a useless moron, a thief by all accounts, in and out of prison. Three years this time. Apparently some shopkeeper tried to stop him raiding the till and got a blow on the back of his head for his trouble. And, my dear Brannigan, what a strange choice for young Ryan to make for a saint? Surely Judas can hardly qualify for canonisation?"

Then, in a sterner voice, "I do think he could have expressed a little gratitude for the monetary gift, don't you Brannigan?"

It was too much. Fergus drew breath, began to count up to ten. Sweat beginning to break out on his forehead. "Can't say I blame him after what you put him through."

"Oh, well, look here, Brannigan, I did hope by now that we'd have put that whole unpleasant business behind us. Personally, I'm somewhat offended that neither of you had the grace to acknowledge our little... erm... compensation. You'll know it was Father O' Donnell's suggestion and I agreed to it, but I must wonder now if it hasn't been a mistake."

Fergus breathed heavily into the mouth piece. The impulse to retaliate could not be resisted. "By all the saints, Mr Brown, I see your Nadina's done a thorough job on her hair, has she not? She get hold of a lawn mower then did she, Mr Brown?" To his surprise the contentious tone softened.

"Yes...well, Brannigan, as a matter of fact I don't mind telling you that Louise and I are extremely upset about it all. It was bad enough when it was all hanging down with the one solitary eye blinking back at you like an owl. Now she's gone to the other extreme. A ghastly, dreadful mess. These youngsters, eh, Brannigan? You never know what they're going to get up to next, do you? Well, you have my sympathy there."

If the plan was to have a chance, Brown's conciliatory tone gave the opportunity. He responded as one father might to another; both perplexed by the strange behaviour of their offspring.

"Aye, you're right there, Mr Brown, sir. Ryan's going through a bad time himself. But, sure, it's all part of growing up, Mr Brown, don't you think so, sir?" He'd not delay longer. It was time to put forward his plan. So keeping to a casual pitch, even adopting the softer tones of the South, he said, "Look, Mr Brown, sir, I've got this idea in my head. By the way before I go on any longer, Mr Brown, Ryan and I accept the gift, you know. And I'm sorry—"

"Yes, yes, al-right. Apology accepted. Go on."

Fergus cleared his throat, now choosing his words with extra care. "You know that your Nadina and my Ryan were really quite a good pair together, one time. Good friends, well I believe so. Well... lately they seem to have fallen out of favour with each other. Your Nadina no longer comes here after school like the old days, nor do you see anything of Ryan. Suppose it's something that all children go through from time to time, Mr Brown, sir."

Fergus paused, took a deep breath. Drawing on his cigarette and leaning heavily on the dresser, he said, "Mr Brown, do you feel that she might like to come round again? Maybe kind of bury the hatchet - isn't that the expression? Now, I'm thinking that my wife and I could have a little tea party. You know, for the both of them. Food is a great way of breaking down barriers, is it not, sir? I feel your Nadina has been an extra good influence on my son, which is how I always think of her, and well, that's the way I always think of her, and I think maybe she's got herself unhappy—"

"What is it you're suggesting?" The voice was harsh, indignant.

Fergus swallowed his embarrassment. Stumbling on like a blind man feeling his way then falling over, he stuttered,. "I'm sorry, sir, I'm not that good with words, but I'd like to see the two of them getting back together, you know?"

There was a lengthy pause, and then, "I'm not too sure about that at all. Unlike you, I don't think either of them is good for the other. To be frank with you, Brannigan, I don't like the influence your son has on my daughter, never mind the other way round. My wife, however, seems to think quite differently and on this matter—"

"I certainly do!"

Fergus held the phone away at the sound of the new voice, loud and irritable.

"It's Louise Brown here. I've been overhearing all that's been said, and, Arnold, whatever *you* may think, I think it's a splendid idea. Your Ryan is a charming little fellow Mr Brannigan, and if he can get through to our Nadina and find out what on earth's the matter with her, I for one will be delighted. Yes, by all means, have a little tea party. Of course, sadly there's no telling how she might react to such an invitation, but we can only ask her, can't we? That is, if we can find her. We never seem to know where she gets to these days.

Maybe round to that Pat something-or-other-a very unhealthy, gawky-looking child I always think. And possibly diseased. I have a strong suspicion that those dreadful spots that litter her skin are infectious. She used to come here quite frequently, but we certainly didn't approve, did we, Arnold? No. She stank to high heaven, and as I told Nadina, that child should learn to wash and treat the spots with iodine. I'm thankful to say we haven't seen her of late. Well, to go back to before all this happened, whatever it is, at least we knew where she was, shutting herself away for hours at a time in her room, secure like the proverbial Fort Knox. For heaven's sake, Mr Brannigan, the locks she demanded, didn't she, Arnold? Two bolts, my husband put on, as well as a mortise, two Yale keys - carrying them all around in her satchel like a jailer." The woman sighed, continued almost without pause. "It's so unnatural. You take Daphne, a little headstrong at times but so different from Nadina. Anyway, since her outlandish display at her Confirmation, so absurdly out of character, the difference is that now, instead of creeping around so you never knew whether she was in or out, shutting herself away in her private prison, she clomps about as if she were wearing Dutch clogs, slamming doors, at all hours playing her wireless so loudly it echoes all round the house." There was a brief pause, "Yes, I can hear it now, even as we speak, Mr Brannigan. No two children could be less alike than she and her sister. It's quite beyond our comprehension, isn't it Arnold? Each one receiving the same care and, affection. Ah well, there you have it. One conforms easily to authority, takes an interest in everything going on all around her, the other.... Well, I mustn't keep on about it. I can feel another migraine coming on. So, to come back to this little tea party, will you wait for a moment? I'll try and get Nadina to the phone."

Fergus heard the receiver clatter as it was put down. He hoped that neither parent would be present while he talked to the child.

"Well, Brannigan?"

"Mr Brown?"

"Yes. As you can gather, my wife takes a different view. And as is the custom, I usually give way on matters concerning our two girls. To be frank, I was never very happy with that tin pot of a school. The Head, a rather imperious creature, seems quite indifferent to our concerns over the behaviour of our younger child, nor it seems does she accept our opinion regarding her future education. My view, and here Louise and I do have common ground, think Nadina's obsession with the Convent School is thoroughly unhealthy. Even Father O'Donnell thinks a spell at the Grammar School would be better, though again, we have not been clear about his views. He seems to change his mind so frequently.. He was thoroughly approving of Nadina developing her religious perceptions. You would think we had a future saint on our hands the way he praised her...Oh, well I needn't concern you with all this. I don't mind telling you, the whole matter is driving me to distraction. I cannot concentrate on my work. Ah, it sounds as though Nadina has agreed to come to the phone. Good day to you, Brannigan."

Fergus gritted his teeth and tried to control his anger. The way Brown lorded it over you, he'd fit in well in the North, like one of the shipyard bosses, siding with the Proddies, hiring and firing, and like the Orange Order men with their bowlers and umbrellas, the nearest they got to a military uniform, making damned sure that if you were Catholic you'd be the fastest out when the lay-offs started and the slowest to be taken on, if you ever were.

Suddenly a voice jolted him out of his abstraction.

"Nadina here."

"Oh, Nadina, hello dear, this is Mr Brannigan," he responded, hoping fervently that the parents had gone. "Are you alone, dear?"

"Yes, just me, Mr Brannigan."

"How are you then, Nadina, dear? You know, I think Ryan's missing you... Oh, yes, well surely a just little bit, you think? He always seems to have got a bit of a mood on him these days and my Kathie says it's got to be because he's got a place at Southgate and it's gone to his head. Now, when it comes to results, I hear you've done so well. Daphne's being saying to Kathie and even Ryan, you know, and he is impressed, Nadina. I seen it in the paper, you heading the list. Fifth in the county, wasn't it? Near full marks, what, ninety two, ninety three out of a hundred, was it now? I was a dunce at school, Nadina. Very near the bottom of the class. Look, Nadina, don't take him too serious, you know. I don't like to see the two of you falling out. Because, well, I feel you got on well together. And I know he behaved bad towards you at times. He's a selfish little beggar. But, look, dear, I'm thinking back now to when you was here after school and thinking you've been such good friends a lot of the time. Do you hear what I'm saying to you, now? True, isn't it?"

No answer.

Drops of perspiration were crowding his brow again; his shirt beginning to stick. It was always the struggle he had with silences when you didn't know what a person was thinking. He tried to keep his voice level. "See, Nadina, what I had in mind was a little get together – you and Ryan. A nice little get together, a little tea party....Are you still there, Nadina?"

"I don't want to see him."

"Well, look here, Nadina. Your daddy made up some pretty bad things against him. It's hard for a young lad to get over something like that. I took him along to Father O'Donnell to try to sort it out. We need now, all of us, don't we, to put the past behind us, we need to try to get over it? You'll know what I mean, sure I know you will."

This time there was an even longer pause. Then, the sound of her crying. "Please, don't upset yourself, Nadina. You're such a nice, well behaved girl, kind, respectful. I've always thought well of you, you know, and it was nice you felt you were able to come round here, though yes he wasn't very nice to you always. I know, he wasn't, was he? But I'm sure he means well, Nadina. I remember the raid – well the one that never was – and he came back with you with your gas masks on, and then there was the time he walked you home through that terrible storm. Nadina, I know he's not always been pleasant to you. Fact is, I am surely ashamed of him you know, the way he speaks about you sometimes and I understand how you feel. But as I say, your daddy let rip at him over... well, of course there was no truth in these accusations. You hear what I'm trying to say, dear. I was no scholar at school. I'm not good with words, Nadina."

"Ryan doesn't want to let bygones be bygones, Mr Brannigan. I've got to go now, please."

Fergus leaned over the table to squash the butt of his cigarette. His voice was racing. He tried to slow it down. "Well, look, Nadina, about forgiveness, it is hard. I know that. The priests talk real easy about it. It falls off their lips like honey, sweet and easy, but I know how hard, how dreadful hard it is."

Again the silence.

"Are you al-right, dear?"

"I know a lot about forgiveness, Mr Brannigan. I know that Our Lord teaches forgiveness and I've always worked hard at it. Father O'Donnell says we should always forgive from the heart and I try. I'm always trying."

How upset she was getting, the words tumbling out of her between her deep sobs. What could he say? "You're a good sweet girl, Nadina. Sure you are and I'm real sorry you've been upset by all this. But listen; can I say something to you in private like?"

"No one's listening. Just you and me, Mr Brannigan. You and me."

"I've no idea why you took the knife to your beautiful hair now. Maybe cutting it all off... well, there must be... you know... a reason? Could it be a penance of some kind? Saint Paul the great apostle, so the good Book tells us, he shaved his head. For him it was like a vow. For you...is it because of some deep sorrow in your heart?"

He drew breath. His lips squeezed together, afraid now to speak at all. For any moment, any moment and it would be too late. Despite his determination to stop, the pace accelerated. "So you tell the good Lord all about it of course. You share your troubles with Him, with the Holy Virgin?" Now, he spoke so deliberately, so slowly, like someone having speech lessons. "This is private between us, Nadina. I think that the Convent School would be good for you. I wish I could get my Ryan to Saint Joseph's."

She was sobbing openly now. Should he go on? Call back another time? Hadn't he said too much? But he couldn't stop. There was something; something so bad; something so wrong. He was sure of it. He couldn't let it go. He changed tack. "At the service, we was expecting you would have the honour of reading from the Holy Word. You deserved that. Oh, Nadina, dear, I can hear you're awful upset. You can tell me, dear. Sure you can, in confidence, like. You can tell me what's bothering you, what made you attack your hair, you know."

There was no answer, just the sound of sobbing and the drawing of breath. Then, finally, "There's nothing to tell."

He was right out of his depth. He'd always admired Eammon, James Connelly, and other leaders the way they sorted out the men's problems, family problems mostly, and of course always fear of the unknown, the fear of dying, of death. Always that. Listening, probing, asking the right questions and always at the right time. He marvelled at the way they did it, wishing he had their skill.

"Nadina, are you still there, dear?"

The silence made him think she had gone, but then, in a very faint voice, "Yes, Mr Brannigan."

He couldn't stop now. It had to all come out. "Likely you've done something wrong and you surely can't forgive yourself. I know what that's about. See, dear, I was in a battle once. I saw my mates killed and I ran away when I should have stayed. When I should have helped. I got this bullet in my thigh, it's lodged deep in and it all seemed like my fault at the time. It was a kind of judgement from the good Lord, I think, me being too scared to stay and help the rest. And I got real angry, you know, with everyone. Marie, she tells me I fly off the handle far too easy. Am I getting you to understand me, Nadina?" He was overwhelmed. In the whole of his life he had never opened up to a living soul in such a way.

"Mr Brannigan, what are you talking about?"

The crying had suddenly stopped, he knew he'd messed up. He had to end it. Give the invitation again and leave it at that. The words tumbled out like an express train. "You and Ryan, you'll be going to separate schools. I hope your mummy and daddy will let you go there. The Convent. That looks like a real wonderful place. I've seen pictures of it in the newspaper. You're only young, but you got a sensible outlook. I'm worried about Ryan for the future. You're a good example to him for the Faith and the way of behaviour. And he's a lazy beggar, you know, Nadina. I should give him a good kick up his backside, actually."

"I've got to go now, Mr Brannigan." Her voice was clipped, angry. Then, with what seemed a tremendous effort, the words jerky and hesitant, she added, "Thank you for speaking to me."

"That's al-right Nadina. It's... it's been really good for me too. I hope you'll accept the invitation to come to tea. And if you feel you'd like to have a little chat sometime. See, I've... well, you know Kathie. I'm a bit on the experience side when it comes to a growing girl—"

The line went dead.

So far so bad, thought Fergus. He put the receiver back on its hook, limped back to his place by the boiler, reached for his cigarettes on the table, his hands shaking, totally unable to know what his next move might be, or whether there would be a next move at all. He picked up his newspaper and sank thankfully into his chair, but he couldn't concentrate, his mind playing with the pieces of the jigsaw, trying to make them fit.

The rumours began, nothing proven, no evidence, just the word of a child, and who can believe a child against the word of a priest? Then suddenly he'd gone. At Mass one Sunday the priest missing; and the next and the next after, then no more. No reason, nothing said. No explanation. Just gone. Months later and they hear their Father Gallagher was at County Cork. Another diocese, another parish. Never did anyone see him again, and no one believed her. And a new priest arrived, still nothing was said. It was as if Gallagher had never been.

And now there were not even rumours, nothing, just his hunch, and what good is a hunch without solid evidence? Fergus gripped his stick, put his feet to the floor and hobbled to the scullery. The floor was wet from her cleaning. Marie was dipping the dishes in the water. He held on to the draining board with his free hand.

"Think we'll be having a raid tonight, Fergus?"

"Could be. Cloud cover, but might be rain." He put his arm around her shoulders, felt them stiffen. "I've been thinking back... thinking of Gallagher."

She stopped still, the dishcloth in her hand, some dishes submerged in the soapy water, the others stacked on the draining board. He remembered the doctor back in Belfast saying, "Water is purifying and cleansing, which is why she loves her baths, Mr Brannigan."

He looked over her shoulder at the murky water. "I've been having these thoughts – about young Nadina Brown. I don't know why, I just don't know why, but I have them. Sure it is that I can't get rid of them."

"Oh, dear God!" She reached out to plunge another dish into the water, her face set.

His cane dropped to the floor. "For the Lord's sake, Marie, I've got to say it! No more than a hunch, no more than that. But for God's sake, at the Holy Confirmation, a complete different Nadina from the piety, so correct, humble. Behaving like a mad thing with the whore's daughter! And something else: would you not be thinking she would have been chosen for the reading? Oh, so maybe she got herself in a temper? No, I don't believe that. Nor does Kathie. Think of it. Father O'Donnell has her at the presbytery? No one else. All alone. Not once. Lots of times. Ryan says he gives her rich food, the best of everything, well the boy wouldn't make that up, would he? I know she's been having this extra teaching, so, well, maybe you know...maybe nothing in it. And I tell myself that, I keep telling myself that. But you never get instruction other than in the church."

He dropped the rest of his cigarette in the water among the dirty crocks. It died with a sizzle. Marie busied herself with uncharacteristic speed, then, "Please forget it," she whispered.

Fergus stumped to the door. Turned to her, grasped his thigh as the pain took hold. "Jaysus, woman! The wee thing cuts all her hair off! You saw her. Dancing away with that little tart, shouting out like some mad thing. Something's gone terrible wrong and I'll not rest until I know."

Marie turned to face him, leaning her back against the sink, her arms folded. "Fergus, haven't we got troubles enough just keeping going over here, making a new life for ourselves?"

He nodded, changed the subject. "He wants to go to Southgate. Not the Boys' Catholic, not Saint Joseph's."

"Well, that'll be the end of it, then. He must be allowed to make up his own mind. You've done the best you could." She turned back to the dishes.

"Listen, Fergus, if you're not happy with this priest, get the bus, go elsewhere."

"I'll ask Kathie to see if Daphne knows anything."

"Keep out of it, please," said Marie, angrily.

"Listen here now, woman, do. When it all happened, wasn't there someone somewhere who would have listened, and it could have stopped. If you were young Nadina, what would you want someone to do? Someone who you knew would believe you, even if no one else would? Surely?

Marie's head was down, staring at the murky water, her voice urgent, "For God's sake, Fergus! God and all the saints in heaven, bless Aunt Mary." Slowly, she signed the cross over her colourful pinafore with the yellow sunflowers. Impatiently brushing away a tear, she whispered, "Aunt Mary was the one, the only one who believed me when no one else would!"

Fergus hobbled back into the kitchen, thumped his chest as the nicotine caught. What should he do? Press on with the invitation, send a little note round, if need be, pick up the phone again? He wouldn't let it rest. He couldn't.

Chapter Twenty Nine

R yan wanted privacy. He decided he had a right to it for he had been told to go to his room. They always sent him there when they wanted to talk about important matters. He cut the notice out of an empty cornflake packet, scrawled three words in red crayon and hung it by string on his door knob. The message was clear: PRIVATE, KEEP OUT.

He lay on his bed that evening, his 1940 *Chums Annual*, last year's Christmas present, open at the first page. The charcoal drawing showed 'Black Death,' a wild black-bearded pirate, carrying a flaming torch. He had mad eyes and a cruel smile. He and his first mate, Crammo, not unlike Quasimodo in shape and disfigurement, brought terror to the crews of merchantmen. Crammo's speciality was to ram their captives' eyes so deep into their sockets that they reappeared out the back of their heads. A natural rather than an acquired talent, due to his giant-sized thumbs. It was an exciting story, but Ryan couldn't concentrate.

Creeping downstairs in his pyjamas he listened at the kitchen door. Not about him at all, but about *her*. As mad as Black Death, she was. Complete freaky. Like the woman at the Fair who'd got no arms and knitted with her toes. He hated people who'd got bits missing or who were loony, like the people from the asylum who roamed the grounds, crying and screaming. Or them without legs and arms home from the war, though he knew he should feel differently. What had happened to compassion? Where was the good doctor?

He crept back upstairs, shut his door, grabbed the gloves and landed a massive punch on the half-mattress, imagining it to be Arnold Brown's stomach. For five minutes non-stop he gave his tormentor a colossal beating. Tiring, he yanked off his gloves, grabbed up a tape measure from his drawer, sat on his bed, and peered down. Surely a bit bigger? Three bits should be growing all the while, he'd decided: biceps, height and willie. He flexed the muscles of his right arm and wound round the tape measure. No change. He stood with his back to the wall behind his bed, made yet another pencil mark to add to all the others over the past month. A fraction of a quarter of an inch. Delighted, he turned his attention once more to his greatest asset. Still no change. Regretfully, he pulled up his pyjama trousers, realised that he had a long way to go before catching up with Kenny, if he ever did. He tossed the tape measure aside and put the gloves back to continue his punishment of Arnold Brown.

It was some time before he heard the hammering on his door. The long-limbed figure stood framed in the doorway, a dead fag, wet at the end, hung from a corner of his mouth.

"Sorry Dad, I didn't hear you."

"By all the saints, son, I've been standing here banging and yelling my head off." Fergus turned away, moved off down the stairs, calling out over his shoulder, "Phone for you."

"Who is it?"

His father gave a casual wave of the hand as he tapped his way down the stairs, Ryan, following. He guessed the identity of the caller. He picked up the receiver from where it lay on the sideboard.

"Yes, Ryan Brannigan here."

"Ryan? It's me, Nadina."

"Who do you say?"

"You sound all out of breath."

"Been boxing, haven't I?"

"Oh, have you? Look, I know you're still in a rage with me."

"You've gone completely loony, so you have. Worse than ever. You embarrassed me at the Confirmation, and me dad and me mam. We was all... I dunno...yeah, amazed, even Foureyes, and he don't notice much, being he's only half a brain, and he thought you'd gone one hundred per-cent loony. Your stupid hair, it looks horrible. You and that Greengage kid went total mad, you did. You was bad enough when you got it all hanging down. It's gone a trillion times worse now. Best if you went complete baldy—"

"Ryan, your father has invited me to come to your house for tea, so we can make up and be friends like we were. How do you feel about that?"

"No thanks!"

Compassion, the block letters at the top of every page. Come in, Doctor Jekyll. She sounded all sad, just the way she was in the classroom, with her red nose and red circles round the one eye like a clown. He remembered when he walked her home and she said she was going to top herself. 'Course, she can't help it, he told himself. Loonies can't. He wanted to say something, thinking Jekyll, but he didn't. After a silence she said, "To be honest with you, Ryan, I don't much care either way, but if you don't want me to come... maybe it'd best if I didn't. My father said it was your dad's idea, and mother is really enthusiastic. So, I don't know. Perhaps you should see it as a kind of peace offering? Putting the past behind us, yes? That's how your dad sees it. Look, I know my father got very angry that you didn't thank him for the money. Talking of peace, were you aware that a dove appeared at Our Lord's baptism and He went from there into the wilderness? The bishop spoke of it if you were listening instead of staring at me. The dove is s symbol of peace. I love that story. So, though I don't really see the point of coming one little bit, I am willing to come. Your dad and mum have always been very kind to me – unlike their son."

He stayed silent.

"So... Ryan? What do you think?"

"God's sake, girl, I dunno, do I? Having to look at you is going to put me off me food, that's all I can say." Ryan had lost patience and old Hyde was back. The compassionate doctor had vanished into thin air like the genie of the lamp.

"You are really polite, aren't you?"

"Naddy, just do what you want."

"You'll be there, will you?"

"Suppose. Me dad will expect me."

"Goodbye, Ryan."

"Goodbye, mad freak."

Hyde is always more powerful than Jekyll – always. He replaced the receiver on its hook. He found Fergus in the larder putting an extra shelf up, the cane propped up against the wall. He asked, "When is it on for, then? This tea time thingamajig?"

His dad turned, the screwdriver in his hand, three screws gripped between his front teeth. Ryan reached up on his toes and held the shelf in position. His dad took the screws from his mouth, one by one. When the shelf was in place, he said, "Look, son, you must have noticed. Something's not right for her to go crazy with her hair like that and like a mad thing at the Confirmation. Totally different. You remember?"

"When's it going to be, Dad?"

"A Saturday would be a good time, I'm thinking. When do *you* think will be a good time?" The effort of putting up the shelf had made him short of breath and he'd already bruised his thumb.

"Don't mind."

"Look, your mam and I think it'd be nice if you and she could be friends. Like old times, you know? And so would Mrs Brown. Seems to have taken a shine to you, son, has Mrs Brown, which is nice for you, isn't it?"

"You said they were both as bad as each other."

"She's taken a shine to you and that's what matters, doesn't it?"

Ryan didn't answer. He was practising his Quasimodo. He pushed his left shoulder as high as he could, stuck his right elbow out at forty five degrees, bent his knees and dragged himself along. Kenny had told him in a rare moment of praise that he was as good as Charles Laughton in the film, 'The Hunchback of Notre Dame.'

Fergus, walking behind, suddenly exploded. "You! Sure you've got the wrong attitude. About time you grew up and learned some manners towards the poor wee girl. And for the good Lord's sake will you stop dragging your feet, now?"

The tea was arranged for the following Saturday evening. Ryan heard his father put on his telephone voice, the one he used to talk to the priest, kind of pretend-posh, and all nervous. He stood next to him, back in Quasimodo pose.

"Hello, Mr Brown. It's Fergus Brannigan here."

He always answers the phone, never Mrs Brown. He imagined Nazi Headquarters at sixteen Mercia Close and Croc-face dressed in the black uniform of the SS, a portrait of Hitler hanging over the fireplace in that swanky study. Him and fatso Louise singing Nazi hymns at Christmas time after they'd finished being good Catholics at Mass.

"Just calling to confirm the time for Nadina's arrival, Mr Brown. Would it be convenient to say five o' clock next Saturday? I think Ryan is real sorry for being unkind to Nadina, you know."

Ryan returned to normal stance, shook his head and mumbled, "No, I'm not."

"Saturday next, five p. m. then? I'll be there to see there's fair play between them, you know?" Fergus gave a forced laugh. "Yes, I agree. You're right there, Mr Brown, sir. We're all sinners on this earth. Yes, all of us needing the grace of the good Lord. You don't need to remind me of that, Mr Brown, sir."

Ryan saw his dad's lips move and guessed he was either swearing or praying. After a moment, Fergus held the phone up and with a half-smile that was more like a grimace, he turned to Ryan and placed the receiver against his ear.

"What a fine priest, Father O'Donnell is, isn't he? He's been such a valid support to my wife and myself and of course to Nadina with this extra tuition he's been giving her. Oh, I've just remembered. Nadina has piano lessons on a Saturday, early evening, though she's dropped them now more or less. Oh, yes, Louise is just reminding me Nadina told her she doesn't want them anymore. There again, another sign of her rebellion. We never had any problems with Daphne, of course, though she's not particularly musical but she's a trier."

His father took the receiver back, said quickly, "Five o'clock, Saturday next then. Goodbye, Mr Brown, sir. No, no. We'll manage. It won't be a swell tea, but it'll be al-right. Good night. Ah no, I don't need the extra. Thanks. Sure we'll manage. Right then, punctually at eight? Well, no later than eight thirty. Fine. Before the black-out. I'll make sure of that. Good night to you."

Fergus slammed the receiver back in place. "That man thinks that we can't provide a decent meal. Get a cigarette for me, will you, son?"

Ryan had sprawled on the sofa by the window, opposite the over-used armchair, only inches off the floor. Fergus watched as he dropped on to the floor, lay for a full half-minute staring up at the ceiling before lurching to his feet. He pulled open the drawer of the sideboard, picked out a pack of ten, lifted the flap so that one cigarette protruded, strolled over to his father.

Fergus took the cigarette. He tried to keep the irritation out of his voice. "Where's the lighter, Ryan?"

A slow shrug of his boxer's shoulders was the response, then into Quasimodo stance. Fergus waved his cigarette and shouted, "Light, son, I need a light, don't I? How am I going to smoke if I haven't got a light?"

Momentarily, Ryan seemed to recover from his nonchalance and return to servile mindset, foraging amidst the jumble on the table.

"Think you're all grown up now since you've got your place at Grammar, eh?" Fifty-three per cent. A bit different from Nadina's, wasn't it? Now, you listen to me will you? You've heard the arrangements. She'll be here next Saturday, five o'clock. So, I'd like you for once in your life to be polite to the girl. And will you stop shrugging your shoulders, dragging your feet, before I thump your head?"

Fergus gritted his teeth. The conversation with the Browns, the anxiety over the arrangements and Ryan's cockiness, becoming more and more apparent by the hour, was unnerving. Above everything, the nagging doubt persisted. Was he being an utter fool? But he remembered great Aunt Mary, who had known Gallagher for many years, recalled the look of horror on the old woman's lined face as she told them that no one had the least idea; no one for one moment suspected. But then a child had spoken and rumour gained pace and spread. And someone must have told one of the high-ups, and then he was gone. Just like that. Moved on. Another diocese, another parish. Where was justice for the victims?

Yet, so what if he did get the poor wee girl to talk? What then? Her parents should know. Steady on you hothead, you go easy, he told himself. Suddenly, the familiar rage tightened his stomach. No wonder Marie had found sex difficult, so painful; turning away from him, making her excuses all the years.

He'd got to try, he must, he couldn't back away. But another thought. Even if she did come clean, told him all, how could Ryan be expected to look up to the Church ever again? He sank back in his chair, the pain shooting up the leg causing him to wince.

Ryan appeared at his elbow, lighter aflame, interrupting his thoughts. Fergus smiled, leaned forward to hold the cigarette to the flame.

"I don't want her here, Dad, not after what she said I done."

"You show her kindness, son, show her compassion, because she's deep unhappy and she'll be coming next Saturday, five o' clock, whether you like it or whether you don't."

Chapter Thirty

He didn't like it, determined not to enjoy it: an outlandish degree of Hyde-ishness had come over him. It was there when he awoke the Saturday morning and was set to last throughout the day. Ryan shuddered at the memory of the mark, like a gunshot wound, open for everyone to see; the zaniness of that hair of hers, spiky like cactus plants, wild and untamed. It was enough for him to see to his own mop after an absence of comb for at least a month.

Now, as five o'clock drew near, he drew back the threadbare curtain to watch her arrive. He didn't wait for her to ring the bell, thrust the door open, covering his eyes with his hands. Peeping through splayed fingers he recoiled, then, frowning, moved forward cautiously to examine her, working his way up from her red sandals until he reached her face. Then, breathing heavily, gasping, clutching his chest, he screwed up his face in shock.

Hovering on the step, Nadina bit her lip trying not to laugh.

Repeatedly closing his eyes then opening, Ryan searched the sky as though they had been visited by some alien from a distant planet. Suddenly, adopting an official tone, he asked, "Got your Identity Card?"

Relief when Fergus, tapping his way down the corridor, appeared with a grin as wide as an alligator's. "Come on in, Nadina! Come on in! It's real good to have you come after all this time, is it not, Ryan?"

Stepping through, she reached into a carrier bag to bring out a round biscuit tin. Ryan now moved into Quasimodo stance. Peering over his skewed shoulder she said, "Mother asked me to bring you this, Mr Brannigan. It's a sponge cake."

"Oh, but she needn't have, you know, Nadina, but thanks, thanks all the same, you know."

"It's powdered egg I'm afraid and there's no sugar, Mr Brannigan."

Fergus elbowed Ryan to one side, stretched out a hand, and repeating his gratitude limped off to the kitchen.

Ryan jerked his head: a signal for her to follow. His feet thumped on the lino. Behind him, forcing a smile, she said, "Ryan, I've brought you a little present. Well, it's from my parents, really."

"In there," he said, yanking open the door to the dining room.

Nervous as she was, her eyes widened in surprise. For on the dining room table, both leaves extended, there were several plates piled so high with sandwiches that they were in danger of dropping off: corned beef; jam; cheese; Marmite; and paste. There were dishes of jellies in pink and green, wobbling invitingly; Swiss rolls; one jam, the other chocolate; jam tarts; a fruit cake; a pink blancmange. Mrs Brannaghan must have been saving coupons for weeks and weeks!

As she gazed at the food, Ryan stretched out a hand over her shoulder to grab two corned beef sandwiches. Unperturbed, from the carrier bag she brought out a small parcel carefully wrapped in newspaper, tied with string. "I'm afraid we've no proper brown paper. My father said it would have to do. He's so mean; said there was a war on, as if we didn't know."

Ryan snatched the parcel, tucking it under his arm. "Not my idea, your coming. I told you that. You decided. Why didn't you cover up your horrible hair, scarf or something, like they do in them Arab places, there's bits sticking out like a damned porcupine. God, I think I'm going to puke."

But despite his abhorrence, it hadn't stopped his appetite, for he grabbed two more sandwiches, jam this time, cramming them in his mouth with the others. "Hate having to look at you. You put me off my food, you do." He stared at her hair then covered his eyes. "Sure, you should have a veil too, cover up your face as well an' all."

Flushing under his scrutiny, she could think of nothing to say. The stick tapping against the skirting-board announced Fergus' return. Ryan swallowed the remains of the sandwiches as his dad carefully placed the sponge cake, now on a plate, in the centre of the table.

Fergus handed his cane to his son, who leaned it against the wall then slumped in a dining chair halfway down the table. "Now, Nadina, dear, where shall we put you? Where would you like to sit?"

"Over there," she pointed to the chair by the door, "if that's al-right Mr Brannigan?"

"Of course dear, wherever you like." Fergus noticed the parcel by Ryan's plate. Smiling hugely, he said, "Now, what have you got there, son? A present, is it now? Open it up and let us all take a look." He placed himself at the head of the table to oversee proceedings and attempt to thaw out the Arctic atmosphere. There was an ache in his jaw through unaccustomed grinning.

Ryan, lips red from raspberry jam, gloomily untied the string and let the wrapping fall to the floor. He held up a wooden pencil case. "Ta," he said.

Fergus looked across at Nadina staring down at her plate. The blemish looked so raw and vivid. He felt a surge of pity. To overcome his nervousness he rubbed his hands in exaggerated pleasure, playing the role of the genial host. "Sure, is it not real nice to have you over, Nadina? Is it not, Ryan? A long time since you was here last and we hope you'll come again. We'd like you to feel you can come anytime the way you used to?" He hesitated, seeing Ryan's sulky look. "And after all that's happened, you know – I mean, between our two families," he added hastily." So now we'll ask the dear Lord to bless our time together."

He bowed his head and instead of saying a Latin grace, he expressed himself informally. "For what the good Lord gives our undeserving bodies, may our souls show in appreciation of Thy eternal favours. Amen."

"Amen," the two children repeated, Ryan, barely audibly, Nadina reverently making the sign of the cross.

Fergus stood, intending to speak, but the words stuck in his throat. He laughed awkwardly, ending with a cough, sat down again with a muttered, "Excuse me." He repeated his appreciation of Nadina's arrival, his voice a little shaky. With an unnaturally wide smile that cut into the corners of his lips, he said, "So now let's eat what the good Lord has provided, or, in other words, what my dear wife has arranged for us." He chuckled then glared at his son, whose hostility was becoming more and more apparent. "Come on, Nadina, there's loads here," his hand swept over the plates, "lots of variety, so many different things to enjoy."

Ryan needed no encouragement. Busy dislodging raspberry jam seeds that had stuck to his teeth with his forefinger, he grabbed a couple more sandwiches, cheese this time.

Fergus, ignoring him, stood to pour the tea. "Nadina dear," he started, his breathing rapid, the words jerky. Tea slopped into the saucer, he had to use both hands to hand her cup to her. He tried again: "Nadina, dear, "I'd like you to know that whatever has happened, you can tell us. Look, what I'm saying to you, Nadina, is that not me, and not Ryan here, is going to breathe a word about it, that is, if you don't wish it. You can talk in the greatest confidence. If you've been through something, like a real hard time of it, well, maybe a terrible time if I'm not greatly mistaken, please trust us. Right, Ryan?"

Ryan, tearing at his sandwich, frowned, "Sure Dad. Anything you say."

Suddenly, Fergus changed tempo. "For God's sake, son, will you offer our guest a sandwich before your greedy hands grab the lot?"

As Ryan handed her the plate with two jam sandwiches remaining, Fergus knew he had spoken out much too soon and cursed himself for his lack of patience. Yet, he bumbled on, not sure where it would lead, staring at his plate, glancing now and again down the table, sure that Ryan had no idea what he was talking about. "He may not show it, Nadina, but whatever else, you've a friend in Ryan here, and deep down he's real sorry for you, aren't you, son?"

Ryan nodded abstractedly, his gaze wandering over the table, hand stretched out to grasp the cake knife. "Suppose you can't help your India, can you, Naddy?" he said with a touch of Doctor Jekyll, levering out a large slice of the Browns' sponge onto his plate.

"But, you know," Fergus said forcefully, "I don't know quite how to put it, Nadina, dear, but I think I have a very good idea what's been going on."

Her response was a slow shaking of her head followed by a deep sigh. "Mr Brannigan, as I said to you on the telephone, I've no idea what you are talking about. No idea at all." Yet the rapid movement of her eyelids, the quivering of her bottom lip showed him otherwise.

Ryan looked at her, then at his father, green jelly wobbling on a tablespoon ready to heap into his dish, his jaw working fast as he consumed the sponge. Fergus frowned at his son, but his mind was elsewhere, recalling a familiar passage from the Scriptures: *'Fools rush in where angels fear to tread.'* He knew he had been that fool, rushing in, not measuring out his words with care. He swallowed a mouthful of tea. Over the rim of his cup he watched, saw that the wide blue eyes were brimming She knew. Surely it was clear that she knew. Suddenly he banged his fist on to the table. The cups rattled in their saucers and the Browns' sponge cake lifted an inch from its plate.

"Ryan, can't you just keep a bit of control over your belly? What in the name of the good Lord do you think you're doing? For God's sake, will you take care of our guest? Go on; offer her a piece of that sponge, before you finish it all.".

Ryan was stirring pink blancmange in with the green in his dish. "Sorry," he said, blinking with shock at the vehemence of his father's tone. His open mouth revealed a mixture of bread, cheese, sponge, corned beef and blancmange. He picked up the plate with the fruit cake, held it towards Nadina.

She shook her head indicating a half eaten sandwich on her plate..

"Nadina," said Fergus in a gentle voice, quietening the anger towards his son, "would you like another cup of tea, dear?" She nodded and handed him her cup. He re-filled it and poured another for Ryan. He gave her the friendliest smile he could summon, changing to a frown as he noticed his son cutting himself a slice of fruit cake, the remains of two half eaten paste sandwiches still on his plate.

This is ridiculous, thought Fergus. Yet he was ninety-nine per-cent sure that his suspicions were correct. Adopting a casual tone and trying to keep his voice even, he said, "Must be an awful nice kind of place there, the Father's house. I've often wondered, you know, I've never had a tour round, I mean. Ryan and me have only seen the study, haven't we, son?"

Ryan burped and waded into another slice of fruit cake. He nodded at Nadina. "It's real posh, Dad, she says, didn't you, Naddy?"

Fergus was heartened that Ryan was at last being pleasant to the girl. Sipping her tea, looking at Ryan, then at him, she said cheerily, "Mind you, Mr Brannigan, I don't especially care for *very* old houses. His study is really nice, though, isn't it? Did you notice all the books? Hundreds of them, they're all round every wall. I asked Father if he'd read them all and he laughed and said not all. He's a very clever priest... I think." She bit into her sandwich. "He reads a very great deal. Not just religion, you know, but other subjects, like politics. He has a considerable knowledge of Irish history. He talks sometimes about Ireland at Catechism, doesn't he, Ryan?"

The boy nodded, once more handing the plate with the fruit cake to her. Fergus, still sipping his tea, was aware that she had hardly eaten anything. For several minutes nobody spoke: the only sound breaking the silence was Ryan smacking his lips as he tackled another slice of the Browns' sponge.

Fergus began to wonder if he shouldn't have told the boy the real reason for the invitation. But he dismissed the thought outright. What would have been the point? What little respect he had left for the Church due to his slightly increased approval of the priest would be gone forever.

What now? Nadina, still silent, picking at the fruit cake that Ryan had cut for her. Realising that he'd come far too fast, nevertheless knew there was now no turning back Fergus had to carry on wherever it led. When they were going into battle, he remembered, De Valera and the others, never clamming up about the dangers, never holding back. They came out with it, telling it how it was. And so, clearing his throat, softening the tone so that it was little more than a whisper, he repeated,

"Nadina, look here dear, you can be absolutely honest with me, and with him there," he jerked his head at Ryan who was now pushing a fourth slice of Mrs Brown's sponge into his mouth. "I think you know what I'm getting at."

The girl shook her head, this time vigorously. "No, I do not, Mr Brannigan. I do not understand what it is you're saying. I thought this was going to be a kind of peace-offering between our two families. That's what my mother told me it was about. She said you wanted Ryan and me to be friends again. What other reason could there possibly be?" Though blinking rapidly to hold back the tears, her eyes glared, her chin thrust forward.

Fergus took a deep breath. There was no point holding back, wrapping up his words in silver paper. Now they came like bullets from a gun. "Look here, Nadina, I know. Oh, dear God, I know. Something terrible wrong happened to you when you went to the priest's house, something done to you!"

Nadina stood up so suddenly that her chair fell to the floor. "Stop it! Stop it! I've no idea what you're talking about. You're wrong and you're scaring me. I'm going home." She threw her serviette down on the table.

Fergus knew when men were lying. When he'd asked for a job in the shipyards, they'd told him with smiles and kind looks that there were no vacancies. But the shuffling of their feet as you stood there waiting told you otherwise, and when you asked them again, they looked away and gave you more of their smiles; aye, sure, wasn't it the smiles of snakes? And if a man continued with his questions, they'd show themselves angry and they'd shout and in the end you'd be told to clear off. They were experts in lying.

Nadina wasn't.

Ryan, gulping his tea, burped again. "Pardon," he said. Then to his father, as he cut himself a large slice of fruit cake, he said, "What are you on about, Dad?"

Fergus now spoke slowly, emphasising each word, "I... think... you...know... Nadina."

"No!"

"What is it, Dad?" Ryan's cup stopped midway, his mouth open, stared at his father. Fergus ignored the interruption, "Tell me, child. Tell me now what happened; things that shouldn't be. Sure, did it not all take place when you went to the presbytery on those Fridays for the extra tuition?"

The girl glared at her host, tears streaking down both cheeks. "No, I do *not* know what you are talking about, Mr Brannigan. Father O'Donnell has been very, very kind to me. I have got parents who... well, they don't care. Don't care at all. They're not interested in me. They won't let me go to the Convent School of the Holy Name, but I *am* going there! I am, Mr Brannigan. I am *not* going to Southgate Grammar, whatever they say. Father O'Donnell will give me his recommendation. I know he will. Daphne, the wonderful Daphne..." She paused and Fergus was shocked at the way her lips drew back into an ugly sneer. "Do you think I'll go to the same school as *her*? Do you, Mr Brannigan? That wonderful sister of mine who can do no wrong? Well... I don't care anymore!"

"Sit down, Nadina! Please dear, will you sit down?"

He saw the spilt tea down the pretty blue party frock and the anger in her eyes. "No, I will stand, thank you. Father O'Donnell, he understands me. He's spent ages listening to me. He prayed over my mark and it is better... getting better. He knows my parents, what they're like. You shouldn't favour one daughter over another. I know that and I don't care what anybody says, Daphne is nothing to write home about. She's... well... she's not nearly as clever as I am. In fact, she's quite dim, actually. I'm going home now."

Nadina hurried out of the room, Fergus stumbling after her as fast as his limp would allow. He reached the front door, which had swung open. She turned and with a bright smile, and in a surprisingly calm voice, said, "Thank you, Mr Brannigan, for my tea. Will you say goodbye to Ryan for me please? Oh, and please thank Mrs Brannigan."

She ran down the path. Fergus followed her, closing the door behind him, called out, "For God's sake tell me, girl. Together, we can go to the police." She slammed the gate, jumped on her bike and without a backward glance was gone.

Fergus hobbled back to the room. Ryan, cutting himself a last slice of the Browns' sponge stared up at him. "She's mad that one, Dad. But what was you on about, that bit about something bad happening?" He stretched and took the lid off the teapot, peered in. "Shall I make a fresh pot of tea for us two then?"

Fergus bowed his head, he held on to each corner of the table, the knuckles showing white. "For heaven's sake," he yelled, "do you not care a fig why that girl is so unhappy? Do you not notice *anything*? Why, why in the name of the good Lord has she gone mad at her hair? Why, why, did she go crazy at the Confirmation like you've never ever seen before? Why did she not be reading the word of the Lord when she come fifth in the whole county? All you was thinking about was your belly and how much food you could pile into it, you damned idiot!"

Ryan jumped up to shield himself crouching behind his chair, ready to dodge the blows, his arms covering his head. "I dunno what you was talking about, Dad," he pleaded. "She's always crying. Never a time when she's not. Girl's a loony. Mad religious, so she is. You ask any of them in the class. You ask her mate, that other freak, that Dickerson."

Remembering his promise to Marie, Fergus pulled up like a car at traffic lights that suddenly changed to red and instead of lashing out with his fists, reached down, grasped Ryan's plate and threw the contents onto the floor.

"Now, get a cloth," he yelled, "and clear it up. And for the good Lord's sake, just get out of my sight!"

Chapter Thirty One

Once Nadina reached the row of dishevelled shops, shuttered and deserted of custom, she jammed on the brakes. Jammed them so hard that the back wheel rose high and she almost went over the handlebars. Her teeth were chattering, an awful coldness swept over her despite the warmth of the evening. She took the headscarf from her basket.

He knew! Mr Brannigan knew. But how?

Obvious! She'd made an unpleasant exhibition - no, stupid - a stupid, stupid, ridiculous exhibition of herself. Grabbing the scissors, tearing at her hair, pulling off huge chunks of it. Then ...dancing in the church with that awful Greengage girl who had a thing for Ryan! She felt a fresh prickle of tears. *'Oh, stop, Nadina, stop it!'*

The Summer holiday would soon be over. Suicide is a mortal sin, but what difference did another one make? She'd had sexual intercourse with a priest and that was far, far worse. Worse than anything; worse even than murder, worse than taking someone's life.

Her guilty secret finally out in the open. The filth of him. Silently she screamed and as silently sobbed. Yet, despite her shame and the horror, she felt an enormous sense of relief. If *he* knew then *she* should know. For five full minutes she waited by the kerb, taking deep breaths, Thelma Ashby's words spinning in her head, *"If there is anything, anything at all, you can tell me."* A swiftly moving stream of pure water seemed to wash over her, moving through her whole body, washing every polluted part, every part of her he had contaminated. She felt in some strange way detached, her mind calmer, clearer. She would live. Justice would be done. She would tell Thelma.

She smiled. Thought of Ryan across the table, his mouth a mess of pink and green, scoffing everything in sight. And there were other memories she would always treasure long after they'd gone their separate ways: that straw-coloured hair dripping down, the rain running into his eyes, their clothes sticking to their skin; him tucking her arm in his. "We're like an old married couple, Naddy," he'd said, then kneeling on the pavement, his lips twisting and turning; thunder louder than the anti-aircraft guns, jagged lightening falling on them and calling out to the Lord to heal her. She laughed aloud.

What now? Her watch showed that it was no more than five past six. She wouldn't, couldn't go home yet. Mother with her never ending questions. *'What's wrong, Nadina? Come on, Nadina, what on earth has happened? We didn't expect you back until at least eight o'clock. Did you enjoy yourself? What did you have to eat? I bet it wasn't nearly as good as the fare Father gives you, was it?'*

Whom did she loathe the most, that horrible O'Donnell or him? Him with his clipped voice and quiet rages; the baby crocodile teeth, owlish glasses and long scaly neck. The way he boasted. It was horrible the way he told them, returning in his immaculate Chief Air Raid Warden's uniform, how he had cautioned people; given them a scare, he said, warning them that if he caught them ever again showing even the slightest chink of light, he'd take them to court.

She would cycle round for a bit, she thought, probably until half past seven, the time he usually left for his rounds, checking up, fault finding, noting names and addresses, bullying them. He must enjoy air-raids: people like us stumbling out of warm beds, putting on dressing gowns, moving to their Anderson shelters in their back gardens, *him* leading the way of course, shining his big torch, being all important.

Reluctantly, she had to admire his efficiency. Everything stacked neatly just like indoors. Tins and tins of Campbell's soups, corned beef, and when they could get them, bacon and eggs, kept fresh on the shelves, changed weekly, despite the rationing. Plates, cups and saucers, cutlery, all set out, handles pointing from right to left, small plates to the front, large plates at the back.

They'd sit on garden chairs, huddled together, hoping and praying the bombs would miss them and kill people elsewhere. She hated it when he was trying to be jolly, cracking his ridiculous jokes, making them sing music hall songs from the last century, or forcing them to play *I-spy*. Only mother, oh, and Daphne, of course – mustn't forget Daphne, must we? – would join in, while she sat quietly reading until that welcome wailing of the All-clear would pierce the gloomy atmosphere. Then they'd all troop inside and stagger back into bed. The searchlights would be switched off; those huge beams that sought out the enemy planes like moths ready to be slain, and the deafening bangs of the big guns on the coast would be silenced, their time of spitting death over until the next raid.

She thought of those who had died recently or who had been horribly wounded: arms and legs blown away, like the woman Ryan told her about. People horribly burnt. She should be thankful shouldn't she? Catholics should be constantly grateful for all blessings, that fiend O'Donnell had taught her that. Yes! All of them bullies: bullied by him, bullied by mother, by Daphne; bullied by the stupid, ignorant lot at Kelliwell Road and bulled by the disgusting priest, O'Donnell.

She pressed her fists to her head. The thoughts, the ideas, the big books he'd pushed on to her, they were too big to take in. She remembered the odd occasions when she'd missed Mass, maybe because she was unwell. There was always the guilt afterwards. And hadn't God given her the horrible blotch on the skin to remind her just how unworthy she was? What was it he'd said? The birthmark would humble her? Redemptive suffering. Even God was a bully. Even Him. Immediately she murmured a prayer of contrition. God would never bully anyone. It was the godless Pharisees who bullied Jesus and had him put on the cross.

"Wrong to hate, Nadina. Honour thy father and thy mother, remember?" And what did he know with his foul breath and disgusting kisses?

"Sure, for God's sake, Naddy, he's only a fella dressed up, and a fat fella at that!"

Yes, you were always right about him, Ryan. An impostor, dressed up like a priest, a pretend-priest, making her believe that he was her friend. A horrible, horrible arch-deceiver.

She got on her bike. Where to? Go and see Thelma Ashby, of course. Tell her. Forest Drive was way over the other side of town. Twelve, fifteen miles. Thelma had a long bus journey.

Two buses. No. She pulled up again. No, because by the time she got back the black-out would have begun. Go tomorrow. Tomorrow in the afternoon, that would be the best time for Thelma was sure to be at her church's Mass in the morning.

Nadina began to cry again, not bothering to hide her tears. Two women passed on their bikes, on their way to the night shift, she thought, summer-flowered dresses, colourful turbans to protect their hair from dangerous machery. One stopped, "Hey, you al-right, kiddo?"

"Yes, thank you. I'm okay." Summoning up the well-rehearsed smile she heard the other say as they rode off, "Lost someone in the bombing I shouldn't wonder." It was on the tip of her tongue to say it: "No, nothing like that. Nothing like that at all." But they had gone on their way.

She glanced at her watch. Six-fifteen. Pedalling aimlessly along the coastal road she thought of the people she liked. The Brannigans for instance. Mr Brannigan, in spite of those horrible teeth and the stench of cheap cigarettes, those Woodbines he smoked and his horrible clothes, he was nice. Than, that strange woman, his wife, Marie, with her wide eager smile, always washing her hands with invisible soap. Thelma Ashby. She was extra nice. Extra kind: probably the one person in the whole world who could never bully anyone. Of course she was strict – had to be, but never a bully. Always fair. Nadina recalled the times the teacher's strong arm had circled her waist; the sloppy lips with the brilliant red lipstick; the way her mouth turned down at the corners and the frown that stretched so deeply all along her brow, asking her over and over, "Nadina, dear, what is wrong? Do please tell me." But she wouldn't; *couldn't*. No, Sunday. If not Sunday, Monday. Definitely, Monday. They'd go to the police together.

Pedalling automatically, not thinking where she was going, Nadina reached the Conway turn. She stopped short. What on earth was she thinking of? He was the last person in the world she wanted to see! She continued. She'd go as far as the barracks on the outskirts of town then go back.

Yes, there were nice people in the world. The girls at the Convent of the Holy Name weren't killjoys, far from it. Not like Daphne, joking about them, making fun of them, shrieking with her horrible laughter with her friends. Not Kathie though. No, Kathie was different, she was respectful.

How she loved to hear the convent girls' laughter. It was different; quieter, purer altogether, not like Daphne and her lot, giggling when one of those lovely girls passed by on her bicycle, making rude comments. Jealousy, of course. That's what it was. Daphne, so coarse! Like those stupid kids at Kelliwell Road who laughed at nothing. Immature and ignorant they were. And that horrible Johnson boy, dribbling all the time, his nostrils always full of snot and never possessing a handkerchief. Nadina shuddered at the memory of the kiss. Fancy being so stupid to pay him! Years ago but never forgotten, his stuff running down her chin. Or that big bully, Evett, doing filthy things with Pat. Sex before marriage was wrong. Come to think of it, she didn't care if she never saw that girl again. Fancy getting all worked up when all she'd told her was basic Catholic teaching; another bully, Pat Dickerson smelling of damp, dirty, unwashed clothes.

Pulling up suddenly, Nadina checked her watch. It was still a long way off half past seven. She carried along towards Clayton-on-Sea. She'd go a few more miles, then turn back.

The early evening sun was not as strong now; the sky tinged more with cloud. Summer was ending. And summer had always been her favourite time of the year. She looked over her shoulder at a little girl playing on the big lawn at the back of the house she was passing. Like I used to do, Nadina thought, remembering listening to the sound the bees made disappearing inside the daffodils and tulips. She'd chase the pretty butterflies, try to catch them in her hands, feeling the fluttering of their wings then letting them fly off to enjoy their freedom. Her mother was nice in those days, bringing bowl after bowl of soapy water for her. Then, with her little clay pipe, she'd see how far the bubbles could fly, clap her hands over them to see them burst. Daphne, of course, hardly ever played anything with her. Hated losing at anything, even if it was only snakes and ladders, make a big fuss and mother would come running and tell her off.

Those long days, when the sun caressed it, warmed it. When she began school, curious classmates poking their fingers in, asking if it hurt. Only when she got to Kelliwell Road did they turn against her. Jeering, poking it, pretending it was catching then running away. Stupid, stupid lot.

Even Ryan was cruel, but he could be kind too. *'Nobody's as bad as me, Ryan, you wouldn't understand.* When she told him she was going to kill herself and if he'd asked her then why, she would have told him – probably. All he did was tell her she was mad, his favourite term, a loony. Ryan could be really, really unkind, horrible. But no, you never bullied me, Ryan, not like the others. And sometimes he would defend her...when that horrid Johnson boy mocked her.

Once again, Nadina checked her watch. Still not time. Six miles, she'd come at least six miles. Another six, and she'd be in Clayton, that run down seaside place, turned into a vast army camp. Best turn round now.

Slowly, she pedalled back, coming past Conway road. Past the the roofs of the houses, the towering roof of the church. And next to it that gaunt ugly house where *he* lived: ugly like him. It was all ugliness. Even the church itself was ugly. Everything was old and disgusting.

What would Mother Clare say at her interview? Maybe her hair wouldn't matter too much. As for Mass, she could always go to the school chapel. They would have Sunday Mass for the boarders. She'd heard that anyone could go How wonderful to have Mass with the nuns!

She pulled up at the corner of Conway Road. Of course, he might not be in. She'd have to get past that witch, Henderson. *'This is Saturday, don't you think Father needs his well-earned rest?'*

He might be out of course, visiting the parishioners or be at the Club, knocking back the pints, surrounded by his admirers. Well, they would soon know: know what a filthy, disgusting, so-called priest they had. What excuse could she give for calling? Didn't matter. *'Quickly! Now, before you change your mind!'*

Nadina pedalled fast, staring ahead, ignoring the thumping of her heart and looking forward to the shock on that big, red, ugly face. She leaned her bike against the stone wall and looked up, high up, to the little bathroom where it all started. How strange that one mistake could have had such consequences, one mistake that led to everything else: a huge, stupid, ridiculous mistake. *'You could have left and gone straight home, then. You could have stopped it, even that very first Friday. But you let it go on and on and on, didn't you Nadina? Why? Because I was frightened, dear Lord, because I wanted his help. Because he was my only friend. Because....*

Moving slowly now, careful not to trip over the uneven paving stones and the familiar weeds choking their way through the gaps, Nadina reached the door, grabbed the knocker with both hands and banged it down as hard as she could.

Mrs Henderson, a frown on her pinched features, eyed her suspiciously. She would have made a good prison warder: glittering black eyes, long nose, arms folded. Face like a smacked bottom! One of her father's rare amusing remarks, gloating after he'd shouted at some poor man about a faint chink showing through his drawing room curtains: *'Oh, you should have seen his face, Louise, he was absolutely terrified; face like a smacked bottom!'*

Nadina burst out, "I've come to see Father O'Donnell. And I want to see him now."

"Have you an appointment? Saturday evening is his sermon preparation time. On top of that, it's his rest day. You seem to have forgotten. I don't like to disturb him. Surely it's not *that* important?"

"It is. It is very important. I want to see him – now...please."

"Oh, very well. Wait there." The housekeeper turned abruptly on her heel. A few minutes later she was back, the face angry, dismissive.

"Father says you can come in. But for five minutes only."

There's always a chill in this old place even in summer. Sunshine never able to penetrate the gloom. A place of darkness. Of sin. Of evil. She followed the sour-faced housekeeper who stopped outside the study door, knocked, then disappeared down the stone steps that led to the basement. Nadina waited.

"Come."

She stood just inside the door and watched the bulky frame heave out of the chair behind the desk. Completely ignoring her, the priest crossed the floor, closed the door then turned back towards her, grinning.

"My little Nadina! Oh, what a surprise!"

She flinched as his thick fingers dug into her shoulders. He stooped to reach her lips. Quickly, she turned her head to one side, then the other. He removed her headscarf. "Oh, my little Naddy, what have you done? What a shocking mess!" He was laughing at her, head back, his shoulders shaking. "Oh, why? Why? Why did you do it? But it's going to grow back, isn't it? You must have been in a very, very naughty mood to attack your hair like that." He grinned, wagging his finger in her face.

That stupid, horrid laugh. How she hated him. How could she ever even have liked him? If she had a knife she'd plunge it into his fat stomach, up to the hilt, like Ryan said he would at Catechism.

His glasses at the end of his nose, O'Donnell stepped back, peered at her, frowning. "My dear Nadina, it is utterly awful." He was laughing so much, his whole body shook. He turned to his desk, quiet now, starting to shuffle papers about.

"Is it there? Have you got it ready?"

Making no reply he moved unsteadily, opened the door to look out. He went over to the sofa in front of the fireplace, sat down. Patting his lap and making kissing noises he held out his arms.

Her words tripped out with a rush like the strong current in a stream. "No. Never... never again. Never. It's over! But I've come to warn you, it is my solemn duty to give you warning. Mr Brannigan. He knows. I don't know how he knows, but he does." She saw the smile vanish. "He tried to get it out of me, tried to get me to tell, but I wouldn't. I didn't tell him. I promise you, I didn't. He made a big tea party to get me to tell on you, but I wouldn't. No, I wouldn't. I wanted to, but I didn't." She gulped, took a deep breath, trying to stop the trembling of her voice, afraid she would cry. "Look, Father O'Donnell, I'll never tell anyone, I promise you that I won't. Not for as long as I live, will I tell. All you have to do is give me the recommendation to post and your secret is safe forever. Where is it? Here?"

One hand grasping the corner of the desk, she turned books and papers over. In her haste some dropped to the floor. She stooped to pick them up. "Where is it? I must have it. I will have it. Must. Must. Must!"

Faster now, she riffled through the correspondence, forms of various kinds, pushing them away, throwing them up in the air, now sweeping them off the desk like so much debris. "Where?" she cried. "My recommendation. Give it here."

From the sofa the priest stared back, his eyes narrowing, lip curling in contempt. "For God's sake, you stupid child, what do you think you're doing?" His speech slurred. A trickle of saliva ran from the side of his mouth. "That uncouth peasant from the peat bogs of the old country and his urchin child, what does he know? Don't you know he's IRA? Think anyone's going to listen to *him*?" His voice changed, the tone mocking, frivolous, patting his lap. "Come on, come on my little Nadina; let's have a little cuddle for old times' sake? And then I'll forget the mess you've made of my desk. Come on, my little Naddy!" He held out his arms, grinned at her, licked his lips as if anticipating a nice meal.

Nadina gazed across the room at him, her voice surprisingly calm. "Give me my recommendation for the Convent School of the Holy Name, or I swear I'll tell." He continued to smile at her. She shouted, "Give me my recommendation!"

He continued to stare, reached in his cassock pocket to bring out his cigarettes.

She pointed her finger, "You confessed, but you still went on with it. You lied to me. You pretended to be my friend, but it was all lies to get your way with me. You are so horrible. Horrible."

He continued to stare at her, the smoke curling up from his cigarette.

All that she'd suffered from *him*, and from her father with his disapproving looks and his coldness, and her stupid, fat mother, and all the time crowing on and on about Daphne,

Daphne, Daphne, Daphne. Her loathing overwhelmed her. "I hate you! I hate all of you!"

With an effort O'Donnell struggled off the sofa, breathing heavily, flicked his half-smoked cigarette into the fireplace, tottered across to her, and despite her struggling, kicking out with her legs and hitting with her fists, he pulled her to him, forced his lips on the birthmark and kissed it again and again, then pressed his lips down upon hers. She was too weak to struggle further. He grabbed both her hands and looked down into her eyes. This time the voice had changed: soft and gentle like the caress of the wind against her cheek.

"Oh my poor dear Nadina, what a big worrier you are. Do you know that before very long you're going to have those big worry lines all the way across your forehead, just like your dear mother? Did you know that?"

She pushed him away, shouting, "Stop it. Stop it. I won't. I won't!"

The priest frowned. He shrugged his shoulders and moved behind his desk, elbowing her out of the way. He stared at the jumble of papers, some still on the floor. Again she began to pick them up.

"Leave them," he said sulkily. "Go home, go on. I'm busy. This is my sermon preparation time and you're interrupting me. Go on. Get out."

She stood with her back to the door, staring at him.

He picked up his reading glasses on the desk, began to shuffle through his papers. "Go on, get out. Go on home to your pretentious, feeble-minded parents, you little slut. You disgust me with your snivelling and your pathetic pretence at virginity. I don't want you here anymore, you absurd little freak."

"Please, Father," she whispered, tears now streaming unchecked. She fell to the floor and knelt before him, held out her arms in supplication. "I need... need... your letter of recommendation."

"That's all you ever wanted, wasn't it? Why you led me on?"

Aghast at what he was saying, she stumbled to her feet, and shrieked. "I did not; did *never* lead you on. You're a liar!"

He held a paper in his hand, glanced down at it. His tone now flat, matter-of-fact, bored even, "Just using me, weren't you, to get into that school? That's all it was. That's all our friendship ever meant to you." Then shouting, "Go! Now! Get out!

He shuffled past her into the hall, grabbed hold of her wrists with one hand, pulled her towards the door, opened it with the other, pushed her backwards. With a cry she stumbled down the steps, just managing to keep her balance. For a moment he stared down at her then slammed the door.

The wireless was playing loudly when Nadina got home. As she crept indoors she could hear it was the Saturday night play from the Home Service. Mother always listened to it. Daphne would be out somewhere, probably with Kathie, and their father would be out in his uniform searching for defaulters.

Ice calm, she crept across the hall, opened the study door, tiptoed across the carpet to the desk, reached for the telephone. She glanced at her watch, seven-thirty. Asked the operator to put her through to one hundred and three Harefield road. "Yes, Mr Brannigan, please."

Chapter Thirty Two

Fergus, afraid to move, silent, waiting until the familiar snore would tell him it was time. Outside, the darkened streets with their familiar sounds: a passing car, the bell from a bicycle, a shout of greeting from someone on his way home from the pub. A full moon chased shadows across the bedroom walls. The chiming of the hour from the Anglican church: he counted ten, held his breath, clenching and unclenching his fists. Give it another five minutes and he would draw his leg up again, cautiously massaging with one hand, then lower it inch by inch. Beside him Marie stirred. He would wait another half hour to be sure.

Wanting to reassure him, noting his disappointment, she'd said, "Sure, the children's quarrels can't be too much our concern, can they? Got to make friends in their own time. And they're all so different. Our Kathie and Ryan, and the big one, that Daphne, a real bully with the wee Nadina – different from them all, that one."

She had begun to giggle then, remembering Ryan, bold as brass, telling the bishop he'd chosen Judas for his saint. Fergus was in no mood to smile. The terrible knowledge was best left untold, like coal deposits deep in the ground; seams not yet ready to be mined. She would know soon enough.

He glanced at his watch on the bedside table, reading the time by moonlight. Saw the hands creeping towards ten-thirty. He'd not wait longer; next to him the sounds of sleep were reassuring. He eased himself on to the floor, the best leg first, the other to follow, padded along the landing to the bathroom, taking care to avoid the loose board at the top of the stairs. Washed and shaved, then tapped his way downstairs. A hasty cup of tea, then away.

He'd oiled the catch in preparation. Taking care like a burglar leaving, he heard the soft click behind him.

Walking was exhausting. Every fifty yards he was forced to stop, leaning up against garden fences, drawing breath. But rage gave him a vitality well beyond his normal capacity, though the red hot needles were like tracer bullets and he wanted to scream as he propelled himself forward along mostly darkened and deserted streets, his strides lengthening, his cane tapping ever faster on the pavement.

At last, the coastal road. "Oh, sweet Jesus, Holy Mary, have mercy," Fergus prayed, wept and struggled for breath, urging himself on. Again and again he called out softly into the darkness, "Oh, Jesus, Holy Mary, have mercy!"

He'd promised himself a cigarette when he reached Conway Road. Once there, leaning back against the hedge for a pillow, Fergus shook his fist at the night sky, cried out loud, "God damn you! You devil! You son of Satan! May you burn in hell!"

Two men passed on bicycles, their lamps shielded with tissue paper to conform to black-out regulations. One called out, "Oi! You watch your language, mate, there could be women about."

He propelled himself to his feet with the help of his cane. Stumbled on, leaned against a lamp post, prayed for strength: "Oh may the blessed names of James Connolly, Patrick Pearse, Michael Collins, Charles Parnell, John Mitchel and Wolf Tone, may they one day be honoured on Earth as assuredly in Heaven. Amen."

He prayed too for the Cause. "God bless our Holy Land. God bless Ireland. May all loyal heroes of the Republic always be honoured, as Thy Holy Name is honoured."

Fergus lit another cigarette, shading the flare of the match in his hands. Under his breath he mouthed an outburst of fresh loathing: 'Union Jacks, the flags of the occupier in the pulpit! A traitor to his Homeland. Using the food he got from across the Water to trap the innocent. And how many more had there been, and how many more would there be?' Fergus fingered his cane; if he'd had his rifle he would shoot the devil's knee caps, the punishment for traitors. First one, then the other.

He pushed forward, a final fifty yards, tossed his butt in the gutter and spat. "You devil Gallagher!"

And now this one; devils the both of them.

Closer now, the big house loomed ahead. He stopped one last time, breathing heavily, sweating though the night was warm. With the aid of a match he glanced at his watch: a few minutes before eleven-fifteen.

Negotiating the uneven path, he limped up the steps and reached for the knocker, hearing the metallic clang echo throughout the house. Silence.

He peered through the letter box listening for the shuffling gait of O'Donnell. He would grab his throat and shake him like a rag doll. Get him to confess his vileness, the evil he'd done to the child.

"Who is it?" An angry tone.

With a crash of keys and slamming of bolts the woman opened the door. She wore a coat and feathered hat. "What do you want at this time of night?"

"You'll know what I want and why, woman. I want the priest. I want O'Donnell."

She stepped backwards. "You just watch your tone. And it's *Father* O'Donnell, may I remind you? And he's gone. Well over two hours past." She peered in the darkness, a torch shining onto the ground. "It's Fergus Brannigan, isn't it?"

"In God's name where, woman?"

The housekeeper sighed theatrically, "Loaded up two suitcases, took a taxi to the station. His mother's ill, so he's going home, he says." She played with the gold band of her wedding ring, twisting it one way, then the other. "For goodness sake he was on the telephone for the good Lord knows how long." She stared over Fergus' shoulder into the blackness.

"How long ago, you say?" Fergus asked.

"An hour or so, two I would think. And I've no idea when he'll be back, or if at all. I asked him when and he just shrugged his shoulders. Well, he can be quite short with you at times, can Father O'Donnell. Probably just a week or two was all I could get out of him in the end. And he's not left any instructions. Not even said goodbye properly." The grumbling tone increasing, "I've got to get back home. I've got a very sick husband. Well, you may know my Jack from the Club? Don't you realise the time?"

Fergus nodded, "I know it's late. I know about Jack. I'm sorry, you know."

"He told me he'd send for his things later. Is he coming back at all? I need to know. I've a right to. These priests are very private people. They tell you little. I'm about to go home. Good night."

She started to close the door when the shrill ring of the telephone startled them both. Fergus leaned against the open door gripping his cane, watched the skinny backside move away. Five minutes and she was back.

"Well, would you credit it? Can you believe it of a sane thinking person? That was the bishop. They're sending a new priest. He's coming for his first Mass in the morning, if you please. No consideration whatsoever. I've got to get his room ready. I'll have to do it now. Father O'Donnell, I asked, is he to return? And do you know what? The bishop just put the phone down on me!"

Fergus could see that she was close to tears.

"Well, that's it," she said. "Five years I've served Father O'Donnell, and two priests before him. When will I get home? This Father Taylor will have to take pot luck, that's all I can say."

As the heavy door began to close, Fergus shouted, "Look, missus, if you hear anything, will you please let me know?" But any response she might have given was lost in the turning of keys and the crashing of bolts.

He stumbled down the steps, nearly losing his balance, righted himself, then pushing himself forward with his cane, increasing his stride every step and ending his journey as he reached the concrete structure of the police station at the far end of Conway road that led into the far reaches of the town.